Advance Praise for *Sea Changes*

"*Sea Changes* is the story of one incident—imagined, but all too believable—in the slow suicide of the English nation. The novel is written with proper sympathy not only for those of the English who wish to preserve England's people and character, but also for desperate Third World seekers-of-a-better-life, who find they have arrived in a country that is fast losing its soul. The villains of the story are the smug status-striving legions who drive the 'diversity' and 'human rights' rackets, and the politicians who pander to them. Derek Turner keeps a steady narrative pace and lets his characters speak for themselves, without authorial editorializing. His story is told with detachment, understanding, and fine attention to detail. An excellent novel."

—**John Derbyshire**
Former Contributing Editor and columnist for *National Review*;
Author of *We Are Doomed*, *Prime Obsession*, *Unknown Quantity*,
and the novel *Seeing Calvin Coolidge in a Dream*

"*Sea Changes* is an often lyrical and well-judged antidote to the PC hustlers who salve their own bad consciences by making normal people feel uncomfortable in their skins—the perfect corrective to a national neurosis."

—**Taki Theodoracopulos**
Author of *Nothing to Declare* and *Princes, Playboys & High-Class Tarts*;
Publisher of *Taki's Magazine* (Takimag.com);
Columnist for *The Spectator*

"A courageous, compassionate and compelling literary treatment of one of the 21st century's most sensitive, important, and rarely-discussed subjects—mass immigration and its often troubling consequences."

—**Sir Richard Body**
Former Conservative MP and author of *England for the English*

"Well-written, meticulously researched and thought-out, *Sea Changes*, Derek Turner's first novel, succeeds mightily in bringing to life the prototypical players in the Western tragedy that is mass migration. The reader becomes intimately *au fait* with the many, oft-unwitting actors in this doomed stand-off: small-town conservative folks vs. progressive city slickers; salt-of-the-earth countrymen against smug, self-satisfied, left-liberals. Ever present are the ruthless traffickers in human misery: both media and smugglers. Like it or not, the dice are loaded. In this epic battle, the scrappy scofflaws and their stakeholders triumph; the locals lose."

—**Ilana Mercer**
Author of *Into the Cannibal's Pot:
Lessons for America from Post-Apartheid South Africa*;
Columnist for World Net Daily and Russia Today

"*Sea Changes* displays the brilliant, biting irony that characterizes Stendhal's best satire. Turner's rendering of today's dominant public rhetoric has the right tone even as it deconstructs it. He is the political novelist we need."

—**Catharine Savage Brosman**
Poetry Editor for *Chronicles: A Magazine of American Culture*;
Author of *Images of War in France: Fiction, Art, Ideology*

"At last! A novel that reflects the world we actually live in. *Sea Changes* shines a bright light on the self-appointed elite who dominate Western governments and media and who, in their self-righteousness, are destroying the free, tolerant, prosperous civilization their ancestors fought long and hard to establish. Casually they hurt the innocent, yet remain convinced of their own moral superiority. The story is gripping. With both humanity and humour, Derek Turner traces the nightmare journey by land, sea, and air of a young man from Iraq to England, where he hopes to start a new life; at the same time he examines the effects of such immigration on the English. While exposing the hypocrisy in "politically correct" assumptions and affected pieties about "racism," he also reveals the genuine, deeply held, if unarticulated, values of the people rooted in the land and its traditions."

—**Jillian Becker**
Author of *The Keep*, the Pushcart Prize story *The Stench*,
Hitler's Children: The Story of the Baader-Meinhof Terrorist Gang,
The PLO: The Rise and Fall of the Palestine Liberation Organization;
Former Director of the Institute for the Study of Terrorism;
Editor-in-chief of the blog The Atheist Conservative.

Radix
Washington Summit Publishers
2012

SEA CHANGES

A Novel

Derek Turner

© 2012 by Derek Turner. All rights reserved.

No part of this publication may be reproduced, distributed, or transmitted in any form or by any means, including photocopying, recording, or other electronic or mechanical methods, or by any information storage and retrieval system, without prior written permission from the publisher, except for brief quotations embodied in critical reviews and certain other non-commercial uses permitted by copyright law. For permission requests, contact the publisher.

Washington Summit Publishers
P. O. Box 1676
Whitefish, MT 59937

email : Info@WashSummit.com
web : www.WashSummit.com

Cataloging-in-Publication Data is on file with the Library of Congress

ISBN: 978-1-59368-002-2
eISBN: 978-1-59368-003-9

Printed in the United States of America
10 9 8 7 6 5 4 3 2 1
First Edition

Table of Contents

Foreword / ix

Figures in a Landscape / 1

Part I

A Long-Deferred Decision / 7

Harvest Day / 29

Songs of Travel / 43

A Bird's Eye View / 57

Companions in Fortune / 67

Vox Metrop / 83

Continental Drift / 105

An Irrelevant Irruption / 125

Number One, Europe / 143

Rude Forefathers / 155

Brothers Beyond Borders / 175

The Sunday Papers / 191

A Journey in the Dark / 213

The Uneasiness of England / 229

Passage to England / 257

Part II

Respite Care / 277

Politic Politics / 291

Awakenings / 313

The Collaborative Spirit / 329

Inquisitions / 347

Today in Parliament / 367

The Uses of Literature / 389

Truth to Power / 405

Part III

Passing Strangers / 425

FOREWORD
By Tito Perdue

The former Soviet Union lies in pieces. Problems in Tibet. Czechs and Slovaks have gone their separate ways. In America, black and white people have not always agreed. (On the other hand, the native people are mostly silent by now.) The four great European empires of 1914 appear to have fallen apart. And where, now pray, are the Araucanian folk who once possessed the land of Chile? Belgium, held together with cords of sand. And meanwhile the historic communities of the European Union are viewing each other through narrowed lids.

Exhilarated by these precedents, and in order, once again, to test a ruined theory, our Western progressives have embarked upon one of the strangest projects ever, namely, to turn a highly heterogeneous (*diverse!*) species into an undifferentiated…something or another. But would they like it if, unhappily, it should ever come to pass?

Psychoses of this sort offer a very rich material for fiction writers of a certain kind. I am speaking, of course, of the sort of writer whom today's publishing industry prefers to ignore, which is to say writers who have eyes to see with and heads holding high-grade brains.

I haven't met, yet, Derek Turner, save by way of his work, and yet he has become my favorite opinionater, antiquary, and second-most-favorite living author. He makes such *clean* prose, and his fiction is perhaps the most fair-minded currently in production. To give one example out of a lot more than just that many, there's an awful journalist in *Sea Changes*, and yet Derek is able to show, quite objectively, just how much more awful he really is. There's an Iraqi youth here, too, bravely carrying out an adventure we wish he hadn't started. And there's the desert, that lean and starving expanse that Derek, one is ready to believe, knows nearly as well as its actual inhabitants. No one could want to set foot there, or be made to encounter some of the personalities our Iraqi boy meets with on his trek to a hoped-for and fuller life.

I don't wish to be too exaggeratedly supportive of Derek merely because he happens to be right. No, there are several other reasons for that, never excluding one of the neatest and most logically ordained plots I've recently seen. This book circles back on itself, leaving the reader just where that person started reading. I should have foreseen what would happen, but it wasn't till the last page that I was able to foresee anything at all.

What a good film this book would make. But don't expect it. He is far too fine a writer, Derek, to be taken up by the businesspersons who have given us our present cultural disgrace.

Tito Perdue is a novelist. His works include Lee, The New Austerities, *and* The Node.

Sea Changes

To Amanda, who gave time

A seachange this, brown eyes saltblue. Seadeath—mildest of all deaths known to man.

—James Joyce, *Ulysses*

Chapter 1
FIGURES IN A LANDSCAPE

East coast of England
Monday, 5th August

All that sighing and significant night, the North Sea had been laying a terrible cargo tenderly along the tide-line. As the stabbing sun raised itself above the rim of the ocean, the revealed brilliant bigness of sand was studded with defeated shapes. But no one was there to notice.

A brown-skinned man lay where the water had reluctantly relinquished him at last, with his face pressed into the fine yellow sand, his inky hair drooping with dampness, his limbs sprawled awkwardly.

A bark-dark teenager lay nearby, his eyes bulging at all that unenjoyed beauty, his refined features petrified in panic, mouth agape as if his life had been in such a hurry to leave that it had forgotten to close the door.

A few feet away sprawled an older man, who looked a bit like the boy, similarly staring straight at the sun without it hurting his eyes, his blue jacket inundated indigo, swollen ankles trying to burst cheap running shoes, a white skull-cap on his head and his thick and curly beard clasping moonstones of moisture.

2   Sea Changes

A young black woman was disposed elegantly 50 feet along—her beauty belied by an equally uncomprehending expression, and a streak of blood that had leached from her nose and was now starting to attract tiny flies. She lay on her left side with one arm aimed appropriately inland, her hands curled in a grab for ground found too late.

The four lay unheeded in the gathering dawn, strewn with many others along miles of strand—lead-heavy leavings which just a few hours before had contained memories and machinations, cynicism and systems, hoards and heirlooms. Pitiable personalia had washed up, too, tangled up with the shells and starfish—suitcases, a comb, toys, a tiny plastic shrine to Vishnu with a blown electrical fitting.

One corpse—until recently almost the only possession of a powerful black man—drifted into a tidal creek and became wedged under an overhanging clump of sea-lavender. Larks nesting among the purple flowers rose and voiced concern, but reassured by its stillness soon returned to feed their avid young despite the glazed gaze from just under the surface.

They would not need to endure those ghastly eyes long, because even before the tide had stopped tumbling the dead man, blennies were nuzzling his face and a crab had stalked inside his slowly rippling shirt. Before 20 more tides, the corpse would be flayed by lips and claws, and magnified by methane—destined to explode slowly and silently in a silver stream of foul bubbles, a blue-brown bundle of bones, hair and flakes of skin rocking with the water, incorporated more each second, purified putrefaction, fibres of food dancing and recombining in cold and dirty eternity.

The sun traversed blithely above these horrors, and all the others which had been waltzed away to be cast up on opposing coasts or drift until devoured. At 5.30—around the time a trawler skipper from Zeebrugge was staring at what had come up in the first nets of the day—a man came over the high dunes with his dog, as he did at this time every day. But today his and everyone's plans would be altered.

Part I

Departure and Arrival

The east stands for lost causes.

—W. G. Sebald, *Rings of Saturn*

Chapter 2
A Long-Deferred Decision

Basra

Ibraham left Basra forever just as the first hard, yellow dates were appearing on the newly green palms. It was always at this time of the year that he most longed to travel, when even in the driest and dirtiest parts of that dry and dirty city some *djinn* entered into men, to make them look up from their work for a moment, and think wistfully of fresh leaves and being young, of the sap rising in everything and moving at will across unbordered spaces.

Whenever Ibrahim looked back over his unsatisfactory life, he would sometimes marvel he had so long delayed departure. He had almost left it too late. But then he had really had very little choice. It was partly a question of destiny—wasn't everything? But it was also a matter of duty—his duty as boy and man, son and brother.

The proximate cause of his procrastination was that during the confusion of the '91 rising against Saddam, Ibrahim's father had, for never identified reasons, been bundled away by never identified men in uniforms. And he had never been bundled back. After several days of wondering and waiting, at 12 his only son had perforce become prop and stay and spokesman for three younger sisters and a mother who had mislaid her wits along with the shock of mislaying her husband. In a city rich only in history, and that history held in low esteem, Ibraham suddenly bore sole responsibility for the Nassouf name and fortune on terrifyingly slender shoulders.

With these salient considerations always central, he resigned what remained of childhood, and found the only work for which he was qualified—labouring on what passed in that tired country for farms, toiling for time beyond computation from pre-dawn until dusk in scrubby sorghum fields just beyond the city limits. He never even tried to total the seconds or the sweat he poured out onto the ungrateful earth, libations to that insatiate deity interrupted once daily by bread, goat's cheese and cigarettes—before more spine-cracking hours as mosquitoes danced in perfervid patterns and his Cradle of Civilization shadow streamed far out in front.

Reeling with exhaustion, he would go home day after day, month after month, Ramadan after Ramadan, to a breeze-block house leaping with life—poor Mother and his sisters, quietly proud that he could just support them with his wage plus profits from gleanings riskily concealed. By the time he'd reached 13, he felt he was decades older than his siblings—a bowed, burned patriarch with a foreshadow of a beard, more like his grandfather than his father, exhausted in the evenings, nodding taciturnly at his mother's babble while an asteroid shower of sisters screamed and scratched and hurt themselves, wiped away sweat or tears, called names, stole from stalls and fondled flea-full cats.

Meaningless days and nights blended, became an era—the same tasks each day, similar things said to the same people in the same sad fields, the same dust-draped bus home past the same statue of Saddam, through kilometres of ochre one-storey squalor, along roads rustling with rubbish scavenged by cats and children. As he delved wirily in the dust, Ibraham would feel the bulk of things weighing him down, bands binding him to the land, a clod-like dullness that made everything ochre. In the evenings, he went early and uncomprehendingly to sleep—but on rare remembered nights he would float high above everything, dreaming of dubious journeys and landfalls in auspicious countries.

He got a job after some years at an oil depot, as laborious but better paid—mowing barely-there lawns, killing rats and scorpions, superstitiously protecting the hoopoes' nest in the date-palm near the gate, sweeping small stones across hectares of baking bitumen, painting vast metal silos in battleship grey, retracing faded signal red warnings, firming up the fencing, cleaning the drains.

He watched the fuel lorries materializing out of the sun-shimmer, and tried to visualize where they were coming from or going to—down first to Umm Qasr, where his father had once taken him to see the huge tankers lolling at anchor kilometres out in the haze waiting to be connected to submarine pipelines, receiving tribute from tugs, moving mammothly into position, departing discreetly in the night, down to the Straits and the oil-esurient world. Basra was, after all, "the city where many paths meet," as the proverb put it, and Ibraham loved this idea of connection to exoticism. Those ships would be visiting America—and London—and—here cartography would betray him.

In the middle of work, he would find himself fantasising about the countries beyond the borders, and he dreamed of one day going to see them, leaving these dirty drab disreputable streets, setting out like Sinbad across the sewage-smelling waters to the fabulous kingdoms.

The outside world was a cool and clean confection condensed from controlled media, pages from which he kept folded up carefully beside his bed, to be pored and puzzled over before he toppled into nightly oblivion.

Those were gorgeous, glacial images—the White House, the President at a baseball game, the Queen at the ballet, red-uniformed cavalry cantering with their horses' breath hanging in the air, Big Ben, football fans, big houses, big cars, and women simultaneously sluttish and sexy.

Sexy—as he passed into puberty, he would goggle at the local girls as they passed, apparently oblivious to the sun-punished youth with the avaricious eyes, but sometimes giggling, certainly about him, the silvery, unreachable melody cutting into his hungry heart. How he wished he had the courage to go up and speak to one of these girls, first as supplicant and then her lord!

And if these local girls, the daughters of manual workers and shopkeepers, were beyond a prospectless labourer wearing clothes too obviously bought at the market stall at the end of the road—how much more remote were the clean, pale-skinned girls he had seen in pictures from the West, whose scandalously undressed state was contradicted by their cool hauteur and the emptiness of their lovely eyes.

Even through the censorship, this outside world seemed open, a place where a man and his family could have what they needed, and everyone lived in houses crammed with unnecessary things. He liked to imagine himself in an interior like the one pictured in the Dubai edition of *Kitchens Today*, which he had once found in the gutter. Almost as interesting as the long-legged blonde with the short skirt were that room's fittings—the brilliancy of chrome, ceramic and marble, the cool curves of the taps, the array of appliances, the warm glow of perfectly-placed lights—not to mention the overflowing fruit basket, piled breads and cakes and racks of bottles. Through the window of that kitchen could be glimpsed an impossibly verdant hillside that he guessed was probably not in Dubai. He wondered how it would feel to be in that room, with that girl—and whether he would dare to touch even the furniture, let alone the girl. He would look at his dusty plimsolls and grimy hands and find them hateful.

Any country which contained lots of rooms like that one was clearly a place of prospects, a place where money was there for the taking for those who worked hard as he worked hard, a country where there was no need to fear the law. It seemed amazingly uncircumscribed, and when he wasn't too tired to think he itched with curiosity.

He sought out foreign news as family and workmates smiled behind his back in kindly contempt. He had not read since he had quit school; now, he borrowed books and newspapers or picked them out of rubbish piles, and read slowly with his finger tracing and his lips sounding out the words. He asked everyone what they knew about England and America—but few could tell him anything new and he guessed shrewdly that much of what they did tell him was inaccurate. But still he liked to have it all told to him again, and in any case the image was as important as the information.

He looked longingly at banked televisions in shop windows. In between Saddam's speeches, documentaries about Israel and Iran, and the soap opera catchphrases ("I cannot believe you said that, Tariq!"), there would sometimes be enticing international exotica—football and concerts; elections and scandals; writers and celebrities, rain and snow and green fields, huge houses and shops crammed with things everyone could afford.

According to the TV announcers, Western women were virtually whores, while their menfolk were hypocrites and oppressors, seeking as in the Bad Old Times to re-extend their pale imperium to snatch the oil wealth from Iraq's children, to arm the Jews to attack the faith, to loot the treasures of Mesopotamia. They were in league with the Iranians, the Kuwaitis, the Kurds or the Israelis—or all of these at once. The West was an unhappy place, racked by riots and crime; the economy was always on the edge. Yet like everyone else in Iraq, Ibraham disbelieved most of what he was told. Baghdad's distortions were counterbalanced by a public perception distorted in the opposite direction—that far from being on the verge of catastrophe, the West was surging in strength, and it was Iraq that was out of touch, in decline. People muttered that Westerners were impossibly wealthy, all had their own houses, cars, holidays, beautiful clothes, rich foods. Even their pet dogs received birthday presents. They had economic security, free elections, free speech, and it didn't matter who your father was, or what tribe or party he belonged to. The most tantalizing stories of all were about newly arrived strangers being given public money and even houses. It couldn't be true, Ibraham told himself—but if it *were*? Could even someone like him possibly stake a claim? And if he could, didn't he owe it not only to himself, but his family?

He had some small savings, hidden under the house's earthen floor in a tin box that had once held DJ Cigarettes. Maybe, just maybe, some day this could help him get out of the shabby Here, to that fabulous There.

But then he would think about his responsibilities, the distance, the language and the logistics, how he would miss things he had thought he hated—and the lovely idea would flit away, like a jewelled bird darting for cover in the undergrowth. But it would stare back at him with glittering eyes.

One significant morning, as Ibraham was painting a wall near the depot gate, a Volkswagen minibus was waved through by the guard. That bristle-chinned, heavy-sweating functionary stood beside Ibraham, staring after the vehicle as it headed towards the administration block. "Americans! I wonder what they're doing here?" he asked rhetorically, and spat before shuffling back to his sweat-smelling booth.

Ibraham loitered for hours until he finally saw the bus return, and then wandered over as if casually toward the gate. As it stopped in front of him where he stood slender and sweaty in orange overalls, the brown-eyed, narrow-nosed embodiment of Middle Eastern manhood, he saw right into the vehicle for several always-remembered seconds.

He registered six fair-skinned foreigners—sleek bodies and physical ease, smiles and untroubled eyes, short-sleeved, crisp, white shirts, ties, and briefcases—and he wanted all those things so sorely that he had to stop himself reaching out to stroke the fortunate vehicle. Instead, his hands closed tightly on the wooden handle of his paintbrush—so tightly that his too long fingernails actually made tiny indentations in the soft wood. Then the van had gone, jolting down towards the harbour, leaving behind a swirl of dust and exhaust—and a sudden sharp focus.

Time rolled on, ignoring Ibraham completely. The army rolled into Kuwait, only to exit abruptly afterwards, which was apparently what Saddam had always intended. The streets took a more jaundiced view. A new word was heard—sanctions. The few foreigners who had been in Basra disappeared or became more discreet, the Waterway was empty, and ever fewer trucks bumped along the deteriorating roads. The shops often had empty shelves, and people had to gather litter or droppings to feed fires. Sometimes army trucks would park at the corner of their streets, and well-nourished soldiers would dole out sacks of flour, drums of oil or vegetables to pushing crowds.

The oil depot closed down, and Ibraham was made redundant. Now he was constrained to kick round on corners while the cigarette box under the floor got lighter—worried tedium occasionally interrupted by foreign jets hurtling over, like falcons flashing from fantastical realms.

Then his sister Ayesha began to cough and it was getting worse, and he could not afford the medicine unless they went without food. He had a solution, but it was one that went against all his inherited morality. But after a night during which he could hear Ayesha coughing incessantly on the other side of the insubstantial wall, he made up his mind as the first of the morning fingered through the window-shades.

The job had been vacant for months because no-one else cared to take it. It was well-paid and the conditions were said to be good—but by taking it he was effectively stepping outside not only the local community, but the moral code they all professed. It was working for the vastly wealthy and therefore hated Tariq Kemali, an Adnanite gang boss who owned one of the Old Town's loveliest private houses—a man doing well out of sanctions, who had foreign visitors and knew ministers socially, and worked all the hours Allah or the Devil sent, while the aircon whirred and the sweat-patches under his pudgy arms grew melon-sized. He controlled almost half of the city's organised crime, and had an informal understanding with his Qahtanite counterpart whereby they kept away from each other's "territory" and only preyed on their own. He was known to be cruel and unscrupulous. If Ibrahim's neighbours had guessed what he was doing, he and his family would have been ostracised. So Ibrahim had to make up a cover story about being a private security guard for even family consumption. They were too young or, in the case of his mother, too indiscreet to be told the truth. They were, after all, women, he told himself.

Hating himself but disguising it like a man, Ibrahim attended at Kemali's house, where over several months, he was instructed in such necessary tasks as driving, using a pistol, searching visitors, padding watchfully alongside his employer when he went out, being menacingly omnipresent while Kemali talked and flashed his chunky jewellery, and how to gather protection money from shopkeepers. Always now cleanly dressed externally, Ibrahim felt inwardly dirty extorting from these men—so bowed-down in their booths, uncomprehending children or too-comprehending wives peering malevolently from behind coloured nylon curtains as Ibraham collected "insurance" from their ostensible overlords. But their loss was his family's salvation.

One awful day, he had to attend as a rival to Kemali was "interviewed," in a lock-up garage regularly used for such private conferences, in a distant suburb where people looked down at the ground or went ostentatiously indoors whenever their BMW rolled up. The man had screamed loudly and for a long time, but the sounds had been muffled by the heat and the street's frightened complicity. He was a Mandæan, and would probably have done the same to them had the circumstances been reversed. But Ibraham was nonetheless appalled by the stretch and creak of the Mandæan's muscles, his shrieks as the chair had been kicked away again and again to leave him hanging by macerated arms from the rusty iron hook in the stained concrete ceiling. Then the blowtorch had been brought… It had not been needed for more than a few seconds, but those seconds had filled the garage with such overweening horror that Ibraham had puked in the corner—for which he was ridiculed by his harder-edged workmates. He told himself often that evening that he would quit. But he had looked into his sisters' faces in the small hours while they slept, and had trooped defeatedly back to work that day and all the days afterwards.

Three more years were thus added to Ibraham's account, with irruptions like his mother's phlegmatically accepted death and interment in the barren city-fringe enclosure. (They could not afford to send her home to her Marsh village—and in fact the village scarcely existed since Saddam had drained the surrounding area to teach them obedience.)

Then there was the time Saddam inspected the buildings built by his cousin's firm to receive imports that were never imported. Ibraham saw Saddam from hundreds of metres away—a stocky, brown-tuniced mannequin taking tank commanders' salutes, while all roofs sprouted snipers and the streets boiled with police.

There was also lust, which he could not assuage honestly because the girls from decent families would have nothing to do with Kemali's men (his secret had leached out). His clumsy attempts at coupling were made down at the docks, where girls who no longer had foreign sailors to service had diversified into new types of client. Ibraham was ashamed of these encounters, and terrified of catching the pox—but there were times when the need became overmastering.

One day there was a bulging envelope with his name and address typed on the front. It was the first letter he had ever received; and when he had read it, he wished the sender hadn't gone to the trouble. But he valued his ears too much to demur, and in any case reflected that it could mean a new start for him—and a means of leaving Kemali's service without incurring his dangerous displeasure. Buoyed up by the thought that he could leverage his patriotic duty into subsequent respectability, he sent his sisters to live with their aunt and shook off civilian life outside No 4 Barracks (Basra District).

The training was cruel, with conscripts sometimes forced to beat each other almost to death—but he had expected no less. The sergeants were of course pigs, but it wasn't personal. Some soldiers had an easier time of it, but that was just the way of things. Someone had slipped someone some money. Ibraham was a capable enough recruit not to get any special attention, for which he was very grateful, and because he knew how to drive, he soon found himself as an army driver, which meant higher pay.

After the training was over, service life contained much boredom—but there was also compensatory camaraderie, whole afternoons when he and his comrades could get away with standing around holding mops, smoking and telling filthy jokes, and evening illicit drinking sessions, when they would share several bottles of arak, and Ibraham would tell them how one day he would go the West and they would all laugh.

There was even some excitement, like the time they were patrolling the mountains along the Iranian border at night and were allowed to fire their AK47s in defiance over their arrogant neighbour's black bulk. At such times, watching the tracer rounds curving through the darkness, Ibraham felt almost proud to be Iraqi. He liked being part of the most powerful and respected group in the country. He swaggered and swore like the others, went home to visit wearing his uniform, and tried to cut a dash with respectable women, who were as terrifying as they were tantalising. It seemed as if he had just become used to instant respect when he was once again a civilian.

But although he was glad to have got national service out of the way, he was back where he had started—except that he had lost two more years. The opportunities of learning new skills he had hoped might be afforded by the army had failed to materialize, or he had failed to take advantage of them. Now here he was again—another healthy but unskilled young man amongst many others in a depressed economy, with women to look after and not enough money coming in. It did not take him long to puzzle out what he needed to do, and two days after leaving the army, he found himself knocking at the door of the Kemali house.

Further tickless years telescoped in the old handsome house, with its jasmine-hung jalousies and narrow parquet corridors, gliding geckoes and murmured conversations heard through half-open doors. Were all lives like this, Ibraham occasionally asked himself, wondering at the complexity of things—millions of feelings merging into a vast nothing, a constant sense of being on the cusp of something that would never come?

Mild sun in the mornings, the smell of mint tea, fat flies tracking across ceilings, a girl's averted eyes, the tang of bad breath, a rumbling gut, an arak-related headache—did such things amount to anything? He seemed always to have been watching his employer's waistline expand and his fingers riffling through the Rolodex.

But now there were two filled DJ Cigarette boxes, and he had started on a third. He would often unearth them at night when everyone was asleep, and play with the notes, smoothing them endlessly and re-folding them, memorizing every detail and character. He wished the nice girls of the neighbourhood knew how much he had. The dock-side liaisons were all very well, but he often felt incredibly lonely for someone to confide in, do some of the drudgery, and give him the children that someone of 22 was expected to have. Over time, and utilizing his work connections, he exchanged the dinars for U.S. dollars, reckoning that even at a disadvantageous exchange rate dollars were likely to hold their value better. And somewhere in his mind was always the notion that dollars would be more helpful when he was finally underway.

Then there was the Great Blow against the Great *Shaitan*, which horrified the world beyond the West Bank. Even Saddam distanced himself from the killers, whom he had expelled from Iraqi territory. Ibraham was amazed that such things could happen in New York, although he felt nothing for victims he had not known and could not comprehend. He wondered sometimes that so many rejected Allah—but knew that there was something indecent, idiotic, about *killing* for him.

The briefly sympathetic mood switched surprisingly soon. Newspapers now said the Americans were threatening to work out their desire for vengeance not on the terrorists but on—of all places—Iraq. They said the Americans had an unaccountable grudge against Saddam, despite the Great Leader's longing for peace and dialogue. The Yankees had already thwarted Iraq's legitimate claims to the corrupt and un-Islamic Kuwait. The bumbling bully Bush—who, they said, was in the pay of the Israelis—was denouncing Saddam (furtive cheers from many Basraites).

Saddam, Father of the Nation, Defender of All Arabs, Inheritor of the Mesopotamian Mantle, was alternately avuncular and defiant. The Americans would rue the day they attacked Iraq, he assured them, bareheaded and brave on a podium, his head thrown back, his sons ranged behind, Ba'athist crown princes heirs-apparent. The Yankees were decadent, and the bodies of their young men would carpet the country if they attempted anything. The people would fight, and they would be fighting for their country, for freedom, for Allah. The Americans had underestimated the power of the united Iraqi people. This would be another Vietnam for them—a Little Big Horn, Suez, Dien Bien Phu, Tsushima or Isandlwana. Bush was a fool, and a dangerous fool. It was the Americans whose unjust and illegal sanctions had denied your children medicines and food. Now they want to destroy our independence and pride. What do they know about civilization? We are the heirs of Babylon. When we were civilizing the world, they were dancing naked in their freezing forests. We want peace, but if it comes down to it, I shall lead you to victory, he swore, as banners bellied, soldiers threw up their caps in joy and passing tanks shook all buildings.

Handsome boys carrying Kalashnikovs were interviewed on TV—"Yes, I am willing to die rather than cede our sacred soil to the invader. *Allah akbar!*"—"Our President has moral right on his side, and moral right must surely prevail. Long live Saddam!" The women were co-opted—from professors to peasants, the womenfolk of Iraq would never give in to imperialist aggression. Iraq's Jews and Christians—strange but sensible blooms—demonstrated in support of the Leader. There were pictures everywhere of Palestinian camps and Israeli airstrikes—French police attacking *Mahgrebi* protestors—a black man who died in police custody in London. There were documentaries on Bush and Blair's secret-society connections and Jewish antecedents. There were visits by outspoken MPs from many countries, specialists in Jews and world conspiracies, arms dealers, technicians, Second-World solidarity-seekers, PR firms, and journalists interested only in the truth, and in blaming American foreign policy. There were patriotic public denunciations, rumours and counter-rumours, straight-talking and diplomacy and photo-opportunities of Saddam in a mosque (the first time in 20 years, went the joke). Sometimes, he was Saladin, or Mehmet II—defending the kernel of civilization against the pallid barbarians. Or he was saintly and misunderstood—a simple family man, at home among his gold taps and blackamoor *torchières*—a reasonable man, puzzled and hurt by American intransigence.

Afghanistan was invaded, the Taliban thrown down—and there was talk of invasion, incursion, insult to our great nation. The ungrateful Kurds (demon-worshipping Yazidis all) were seething, and the Republican Guard rumbled northwards in the night. There were muttered tales of betrayals and secret deals, midnight arrests and sabotage, strangers caught crossing the borders or seen near oil installations and railway bridges or suddenly appearing, asking questions and offering dollars. It was whispered that the Fedayeen Saddam were in the area, and the city's criminals hunkered down for the duration—with the protected protector Kemali one of the few who carried on as if nothing was happening. MPs, press spokesmen, bureaucrats and army officers rose into or fell from view. Iraqi jets screamed defiantly over, the Waterway became busy with mine-layers and patrol boats, anti-tank trenches and air raid shelters were built in Basra's streets. There were curfews and tests of sirens. Dusty troops secured and scoured junctions and jetties, then climbed back aboard lorries to race along to the next strategic point. Trees and buildings were levelled to improve fields of fire, and barbed wire groves grew up by the river. People made stockpiles, and tried to work out what was really being said by the TV announcers or the tinny radios perched on thousands of café counters and workbenches. Cafés were electric, as coffee, cigarettes and high politics imbued the air. Lights burned all night at police headquarters. Half-tracks overflowing with bored soldiers drove ceaselessly up and down the embankment, while small boys watched enviously.

The tension was ratcheted up until it became part of the noise of life. Like everyone, Ibraham sometimes nearly forgot about the prospective Mother of All Battles, while his employer was busier than ever—making and breaking deals, chins wobbling while he laughed, his rings glinting as he riffled his Rolodex, his ear red from the telephone receiver. More long, boring days like so many others in his life, everyone's lives—the menace-mongering become like mosquito noise—coffee, cigarettes and cards contested and conceded across the marble-topped table in the sun-tigered corridor.

He was jolted awake by far explosions. Royal Marines had come ashore at Umm Qasr just as it was getting light—and the army reservists were in full retreat, dropping their weapons in panic, bowling over their NCOs and officers as they fell back towards Basra.

Within minutes, all Al Hayyaniyah was out of doors, and the city was a-thrum with engines revving up and moving out, shouted commands, the snap of boot heels and rifle breeches. Roads were closed and papers checked, barbed-wire augmented and redeployed, sappers turned up in trucks, trains of supplies passed through, and ammunition was opened and issued. Soldiers and police patrolled for saboteurs and deserters— while radio vans broadcast news of American defeats at the hands of the valiant army. The Yankees and English would soon be pushed into the sea—their illegitimate war denounced by the UN and unpopular at home, their troops more interested in Coca-Cola than combat—except for the gangster SAS, who were raping and bayoneting children and women behind the lines. Beware of saboteurs; distrust the stranger; report the stranger. A Free Islamic Legion was on its way, volunteers from all the Muslim nations of the world.

But the crusaders' jets were often overhead, and when they passed even the army winced and sought shelter. Civilians streamed out of the city like an ants' nest broken open—to camp out in the fields and wait for the British or, in the case of Ba'athist loyalists and Ibraham's suddenly unsure employer, to head north towards Baghdad, which they knew or hoped could never fall, or to seek refuge in their home villages— followed by trucks heavy with papers, money, jewellery and the more easily portable museum exhibits, and accompanied by large numbers of minders. Ibraham was never asked if he wanted to go with Kemali, but was summoned cursorily into the outer office by the secretary and given a month's salary in lieu of notice before being pushed out of the house for the final time. Whatever would come later, Basraites were glad to see people like Kemali go—and some evacuees' convoys were jeered and pelted with rocks.

Sinews were strengthened by the arrival of red-booted Republican Guards belonging to the *Al Nida* and *Hammurabi* armoured divisions and commandos from *As Saiqa*, who roared down from the north in warchariots like their historical predecessors—a comparison constantly made. Their hard faces radiated confidence, and their capable hands caressed brand-new Brownings. About half went down upon the fold of Umm Qasr, while the rest took up positions all over Basra—evicting civilians from their houses, turning shops into bastions, dragging camouflage nets over hissing vehicles, smoking as they cursed or laughed, practising their small-arms aim on roaming dogs (and civilians who could give no good account of themselves).

The Red-boots relished a few swaggering days before their comrades who had gone to Umm Qasr reappeared unexpectedly—disorganised, demoralised, disarmed, decimated. They carried panicky stories, disjointed tales of being outflanked, outgunned and outwitted— of swift and responsive British armour, the constant pounding of aircraft (no sign of *our* fliers!) and the unseen but always-sensed SAS. Ammunition, food, water and fuel that had been promised had never arrived, they said. Officers and NCOs had made catastrophic mistakes. The regulars had refused to fight, or had been cut down whenever they attempted to make a stand. Even among the Red-boots, whole platoons had vanished—some killed, more injured, scattered or deserted or gone behind enemy lines, to snipe from foxholes, or creep into camps to cut Coalition throats. The British were right behind them, they said.

And they were right. Within 48 hours, the 7th Armoured Brigade was snapping at their heels, thrusting up from Abdaliyah and Manawi Al Loyim towards Al Basrah. The dismayed garrison found that their tanks were slower and less powerful, their supplies undependable, and almost everything they did was spotted and stopped by planes. The commands from Baghdad, when obtainable, were inconsistent and incoherent, exhortative rather than specific.

Once more in its history, Basra blew up in fire and disaster—watched from kilometres away by the Nassoufs and all their neighbours, camped out near the pockmarked airport. Everything they knew—people they had known—had been cast into the crucible where Iraq was being broken and remade. They were glad to see what was obviously the end of Saddam, but looked constantly citywards, wondering and waiting. They cooked over common fires, scavenged for food and water, and worried about contagion. Some who were old or sick died, hastily bemoaned and buried—the least casualties of the conflict.

The downfall of Baghdad was announced in early April, although Saddam and sons were still at large. As the conflagration was tamped down, Ibrahim and thousands of others filtered back to where their lives had been. They came back sometimes to rubble where there had been houses, cafés, garages and mosques, littered with twisted metal and spotted still with red-booted dead. But many areas had not been damaged at all. The Nassoufs' place was mercifully intact and—a wryly comic touch—Ibrahim's call-up papers were lying outside the locked door.

Tall, blue-eyed liberators with Union Jack flag flashes (or unidentifiable flashes from unknown countries) on their uniform sleeves began to be seen, rolling regally up and down the roads in light Landrovers, handing out food, coffee and medicine from trucks teeming with goods. Some moved amongst the civilians, their new best friends—Kevlar helmets replaced by berets, smiling and doling out chocolate and cigarettes, shaking hands and being photographed with locals. There were weeks, whole months when the troops seemed to be supremely, sensitively in command.

But then the bombs came back—making people look up in panic, followed by sirens and screams and racing engines, sometimes sporadic gunfire, as British soldiers or newly deputised police chased suspects through narrow alleys or shot down roads. The berets were replaced again by helmets, and tanks were seen again on the streets. Districts would be suddenly surrounded, as snatch squads combed confusing complexes and courtyards for elusive insurgents. Shi'ites and Sunnis separated out from each unclean other. Bombs were aimed not just at the occupiers and their police-creatures, but at doctrinal opponents. There were innumerable unrecorded killings in back streets, and doors burst in residential neighbourhoods by masked riflemen—*Mahdi Army* or gangland enforcers, killing for Prophetic lineage, tribal loyalty, private grudge or money.

Every conversation, every transaction was tinged with trepidation. The police were incompetent, or worse. Everyone muttered about the Jameat men, who wore police uniforms but worked for the militias—stealing weapons and money, marking targets, taking over rackets or starting new ones, removing people in police vans for "questioning" rarely to return, their maimed bodies sometimes turning up in ditches or thrown outside the doors of their houses from cars that didn't stop. Echoes of Ibrahim's father—Ibrahim was grateful his mother had not seen all this, but was constantly on edge about his sisters, and worried all the time when he couldn't see them. The British did not know what was going on—or they did not care—or they could not stop it.

Old structures and understandings were gone, in a frenzy of de-Ba'athisation. The hated had been brought low, but some of the low brought a lot higher than they deserved. New bosses were using unwitting foreign soldiers to work out old feuds. Important jobs were given to classless, contextless incomers from Baghdad or Kurdistan or to foreigners—the latter efficient, and laden with gifts for the asking (or taking), but who lacked local knowledge. Tensions were raised by seeing local girls with the foreign troops, girls who suddenly had expensive clothes, or scent, or mobile phones. It was speculated that they must have paid a high price for these items. Iraqis knew they could never compete with this—and this helped fuel the insurgency. The occupiers' promises to bring proper drainage, new houses and new jobs fell drastically short. "Hearts and minds? They can't even give us electricity!" was the gloomy verdict of the Nassoufs' normally easy-going neighbour.

As months became years, even in Basra people started to look back on the Saddam years with something like fondness. Everyone said life had become much worse, that decent men or women couldn't go about their business without the risk of being blown up. It wouldn't have happened under Saddam. He was bad, but we had order. You knew where you stood with Saddam. Now everything was random, vicious. Not even his capture and trial stopped the violence—and he had at least died like a man, more of a soldier than his disguised destroyers. Rumour had it there was civil war in the north and east, with guns and volunteers coming over the borders from Iran. More GIs arrived, and it helped for a time, but what would happen when they pulled out, as America's new (black!) president had promised would happen soon?

As their money dwindled, and he waited in line with thousands of others for food parcels and buckets of warm water from standpipes,

Ibraham constantly revolved his old dream of going to the West. Except that somehow—he wasn't sure when—the dream had become a scheme.

He would do it. He had to do it. There was nothing for him here. There never had been. In fact, there was nothing in Iraq for anybody and would not be for many years, if ever again. He would go, now, while he was still youngish and fit, while he was still uncommitted—to live out his fantasies after so many years of self-sacrifice.

It would be good not only for him, but for all of them. He imagined himself sending huge cheques home, and Ayesha and the others receiving them and blessing his name—kissing the precious paper while their eyes sparkled in well-fed faces.

He had no choice—and he was glad. He felt a tremendous soothing calm washing over him, and all the annoyances and inconveniences of life were softened. He looked at the dirty water in the bucket, the bad food on the cracked plates, the faces of the dirty and shrivelled people and he knew, with a joyous, frightened clutch at his heart, that very soon he would not see them any more.

One spring evening, marvelling at his own temerity, Ibraham met a chain-smoking lorry driver in a café across from the idle cranes by the Roka Channel. The man was to bring a cargo to the capital in a week's time and, for US$100, would be prepared to let Ibraham travel as his truck-mate. And when he got to the capital, he would put him in contact with people who were in the business of getting people into Kurdistan, "or even further." He winked, accepted a $20 deposit, and they toasted the deal in apple tea. It seemed too cheap, too casual, too easy, too quick. In such an amazing and life-altering instant, Ibraham was surprised to feel so detached. He walked slowly and thoughtfully home, through crowds that were already merging into memory.

Chapter 3

HARVEST DAY

Crisby St. Nicholas, Eastshire
Monday, 5th August

Dan was running through the hyper-clear farmyard—panting, perspiring, slightly panic-stricken. It was strangely sunny and still. Although everything looked like it usually did, there was something else there, he knew, close but just beyond his comprehension—a flaw in the fabric of the place.

He was calling anxiously—"Hello? Hello?" But there was no reply—there never was—just continuous loop explosions of pigeons rising in alarm from the roof of the house. The only sounds were the clumsy clapping of their wings, his voice bouncing back from the weathered walls, his breath catching raw, and the ticking of the old clock, oddly loud through several brick thicknesses—the loved longcase with its dial painting of a vanished life—a wide-hatted, long-rifled hunter and a daub of a dog standing an eternity ago in a punt amongst reeds, as faded ducks dashed through subfusc skies.

When at last he came back to the deep-draped bedroom, he was spotted with sweat like in the dream and his heart was pounding passionately out into the stifling gloom.

Dan Gowt was a man more interested in engines than emotions, and this was the only nightmare he had ever had in all his placid decades. But that made its rare recurrences all the more unsettling. At 6:41 on that memorable morning, after a night of jolting awake from fear of falling, when his cheeks were stretched like drumskins and his hands felt too huge—when he should have been up an hour ago—it seemed especially ominous. Dazed and dry, nose blocked and eyes gritty, he looked dully at the light leaching in through the curtains while his body relaxed and his heart slowed to its usual phlegmatic pace.

It was the first day of the harvest, the most important day of the year, and one he normally looked forward to with quiet satisfaction. On these days, he felt an almost metaphysical link to this place, a sense of rightness, of being rewarded at last for all the months of effort. The hired harvester would already be hulking down the narrow marsh roads towards Home Farm, and he needed to get up to take delivery.

He rose considerately; Hatty's breathing told of a night unlike his. He looked down on her for a second and nearly smiled; some of her wrinkles were smoothed away in sleep, and she looked a little like she had looked when he had first seen her at the Young Farmers' back in— well, whenever it had been.

Jackdaws were *chak-chakking* in the chimney, fidgeting in their dust-dry nest, occasionally dislodging a twig to fall *ding* onto the iron lion-and-unicorn fireback inserted in the bedroom fireplace by an ancestor to commemorate the Stuart accession. His diminished descendant stretched clickingly to his full modest height, encased his stocky frame in old clothes, and sluiced his weather-punished face and white-wispy-haloed head with slightly brown water from the old-fashioned bathroom taps with the COLD and HOT the wrong way round. They had never gone onto the mains water, something of which Dan was perversely proud, and relied on the borehole that poked 70 feet or more down into the clay to tap some secretive silty stream. Even through the filter he had installed, there was always a bitty, minerally edge to the water, and the old white bath had a dun hue below the tidemark.

Slow blue eyes with tired whites looked back as he twitched lips and nose away from the vague danger of the razor. Then he clumped down the dark old creaking stairs with their wide oak treads and too-fat newel-posts. He scratched Sammy on his tan-and-white skull, and let the Jack Russell dash outside to defecate. (How ordinary the yard looked, and how foolish the dream.)

Bad beginning though it had been, he could not stop the charm of the day from creeping over him as he released the chickens and felt for eggs in the warm straw. As he went back across the yard, the cracked Delftware bowl brimming with brown-speckled nutrition, he saw with the usual complacent pride that Home Farm was handsome, its irregular bricks and S-shaped iron brick ties soaking in the sun, the sandstone window surrounds scintillating slightly, grey lichen on the wall-mounted sundial with its quaintly cautionary motto—"Quickly Comme, As Quickly Goe." Two collared doves inclined towards each other on the red-tiled roof, important with lazy sexuality.

This side faced east, towards immaculate 19th-century barns and beyond them a white-turquoise hint of the North Sea, a mile away across rabbit-pestered pastures and toad-prowled dunes just too high for him to be able to see the strand from here. It was a vista and a place he knew in every detail, and loved even as he took it utterly for granted.

There was a helicopter over the sea—some RAF exercise. He watched it for a minute, as always admiring the expertise with which it was handled, and wondering what they were doing so early. He always liked seeing the RAF on their exercises—it made him think of the brave men who had flown from here during the war to bomb the continent, many of whom had never returned. It gave him a comforting feeling of continuity and unsleeping vigilance.

Not long before his father had died, the two men had been working out in the fields when some jets cannoned bravely low overhead. His father had stopped what he was doing, and watched them go out of sight. Then he had smiled sadly and said, "Those chaps always make me think of the war, Dan. They were hard times, but they were also good times in a way. We all really felt England was a great country, with Mr. Churchill and the Empire and all. Funny, really!" It had been an uncharacteristically long and political communication from a man who normally confined his opinions to the relative merits of Ford and Massey-Ferguson, or cattle trotting around the ring at Thorpe Gilbert's cattle market, and Dan had always remembered it clearly for that reason.

He was humming a song daughter Clarrie had been listening to, by some coloured girl (shouldn't say "coloured," he corrected himself casually) as he flicked on the radio to hear the usual things. There was that insurance advertisement—must sort that out. He continued to hum tunelessly and thought of weather and yields, as men of his face and name had done in this room at this time of year since—whenever. His senses of history and identity were sincere but always sketchy on dates and detail. Then came the synthesized brass heralding the news headlines and he stood astounded, listening to the village changing forever.

"This is Ray Robinson, with the *Seaside at Seven*. Our region is at the centre of today's international news. News is emerging of a tragic and horrifying discovery on the Eastshire coast. What is being described as 'dozens of dead bodies' have been washed up on a beach at Crisby St. Nicholas. So far, we have few details about the disaster, but we will go straight over to our reporter Simeon Sinclair, live from the scene."

"Good morning, Ray. These are unprecedented and tragic events, in the unlikely setting of this remote community. We are being kept away from the actual scene of the disaster, but a constant stream of paramedics and police officers is heading towards the beach, a few hundred yards away behind those dunes. All access to the beach is forbidden for miles in both directions while a massive search-and-rescue operation gets under way. With me now is local resident Meg Powers. Can you tell us what you have seen this morning, Mrs. Powers?"

A tremulous voice with a strong Eastshire accent crackled on—"There've been police and ambulances going along the lane for about an hour—loads of 'em, with their lights flashing, sort of thing. They woke everyone up. It was Neil Parrish who discovered the dead folk. 'E walks his dog early, you see. They was all foreigners, 'e says—dozens of 'em, dead as doornails."

This amazing exchange was taking place under a mile away. Dan knew Meg, and Neil Parrish's father had been with him at the village school—and the beach had been bounding his horizon for 65 and a quarter years. He rushed back up the stairs he had so despondingly descended and beat on thick-painted old pine doors almost as wide as they were tall.

"Hatty! Clarrie! We're in the news! There's been a shipwreck on the beach!"

"*What?* What's *happened?*"

Four minutes later, they were all in the Landrover—Sammy as usual on Dan's lap in the driver's seat. He had got used to having the dog's small body on his lap while he was driving, awkward though it was, and was always glad of his company—especially on those days expended in ploughing and rolling, or mending a fence in a far field, when he often wouldn't see another person all day.

With him was Hatty, the ever kind and shrewd, the grey of her eyes the same colour as her permed hair, always at home in her clean and practical jumper and slacks, whether baking one of the pies that played such havoc with his waistline or shooing the bad-tempered bull out of the garden. Home Farm was very similar to the farmhouse in which she had been raised several miles away. Like the Gowts, farming was all the Dykeman family had ever known, and when Dan and Hatty had married it was regarded as not only entirely natural but extremely practical.

There, too, was plumper, paler Clarissa, back from uni for summer—fashion-conscious in black jeans and a black and yellow striped jumper. They doted on her obviously and they had always let her have her way—even though Dan was secretly stricken by her utter lack of interest in taking over the farm. He had always cherished, without even realizing it, the romantic fancy that someone of his blood would be farming this place long after he had gone, and that they would pass on something of him to the unguessed generations of the unimaginable England of the far future.

But Clarrie was also now uninterested, apparently, in getting her law degree—or even a boyfriend. All she seemed to think about was dieting, and sending texts, and updating her Facebook account, whatever she needed one of those for. Dan often asked Hatty what was wrong with the bloody girl. Probably, it was a phase, they hoped. The young were strange and getting stranger. *They'd* never had "phases"! He, at least, had never had any. There had always been too much for him to think about—such high expectations of him as the farm's and family's future. These were expectations he believed he had fulfilled, and he lacked understanding of those who just drifted through life. Fecklessness and waste offended some puritanical part of him. If Clarrie had been a boy maybe things would have been different.

But for now he wasn't thinking about these old questions; he was as ghoulishly interested in the local drama as his womenfolk, although he preserved a faux-casual front. As they exited the long drive and came out onto Red Lea Lane, they saw a maelstrom of flashing blue lights and a mass of agitated movement. The helicopter he had noticed earlier was now hanging over Zion Hill, the tallest of the thorn-covered dunes that marched all the way from Fleethaven in the north some 20 miles down to Williamstow—separating level land from a debatable territory of saltmarsh, sand and slimy mud that was over a mile wide at the lowest tides.

There, almost six decades before, Dan had played with his older brother, Pete. Pete had taken a malicious delight in telling him that the mysterious creeks, with their tarantula-like crabs and sucking mud stitched together with birds' prints, were haunted by Jill Greenteeth, a weed-haired hag who came out onto the land at night to feel for food with long pale nails. When Pete had drowned in the Forty Foot Drain, Dan had still been young enough to wonder if Jill had taken him, and even 59 years on he never really liked that stretch of the Drain, where it ran deep and dark between steep and slippery banks and in under the Black Bridge.

Dan had taken on the burden of the farm uncomplainingly when eventually it came, feeling it was not a burden at all—or at least only on some of the bad days between December and February, when winds carrying news of Siberia leapt the dunes and came clamouring around him in the draughty cab of his tractor, bringing water to his eyes and aches to elbows and knees.

There were always regrets of course, about things he thought he could and perhaps should have done and would never do now. But by now he knew that everyone's lives were made up largely of disappointments. And for now there were always things demanding to be done—apart from the seasonal chores and the increasing paperwork, there were things to be maintained and repaired rather than renewed. So decades went and came with the leaves on the willows until his skin grew lined and ambitions became acceptance. But still there were times when the young man inside raised his dark-haired head to peer out in dissatisfaction at the cramped universe his older self had opted to inhabit.

He found a place to park, and they pushed purposefully between dragonfly-hunted hedges, across the old bridge over the New Cut where moorhens sculled among the sedge. The lights and noise had a peaceful, beautiful backdrop like an Antwerp School landscape—distance-blued levels, the dints of dykes, coverts of sycamore, alder and ash, sagging stands of willow, the exclamation marks of poplars, a few old houses, a mill, scattered square church-towers, heat-heavy fields *enceinte* with cereals.

There was a thrilled crowd in the car park, huddled behind police barriers. The beach could not be seen from here because of the dunes, but they could see the winding track between the sandhills, normally a silent pathway arched over by blackthorn, but now hectic with uniformed life.

They were met by near-neighbour Ted Fisher, owner of several thistly fields along Deliverance Lane. Usually laconic to a fault, the last of his line was rubbing hard, dry hands together incessantly. "It's like the war!" he was saying, with grim relish. "Dozens of 'em, they say. Refugees, I shouldn't be surprised; foreigners, any road."

There were several reporters there, mostly from local media—with many more converging on Crisby from across the country. Dan recognized *Seaside at Seven*'s Simeon Sinclair talking earnestly to the body discoverer Neil Parrish. Other reporters were pouncing on police, paramedics, or anyone else who looked as if they could ameliorate the present famine of fact. Most of the local people recoiled instinctively, although a few seemed to have expanded into their rightful spheres, as if they had long expected the world's media to come calling for some reason. The chairman of the parish council had even put on his chain of office. Dan grinned to himself; sometimes young Mark Foster could be as ridiculous as his poor old dad. *Old?* Ha. Mark Foster Senior had been in his class at school.

There were two or three hundred people there, from all over the area—Crisby, Stibthorpe, Skenby-le-Mire, Williamstow, Elmcaster, and even Eastport. Police were ensuring onlookers stayed behind the barriers to leave an exit route for ambulances, their zipped-up cargoes treated with more tenderness now than they had ever been in life, borne in brand-new body bags on soft, clean beds, wafted away by white-uniformed angels under blue brilliants to the sparkling sterility of the County Morgue.

An excited insect hum arose from everywhere—an imbroglio of engines, speculations and statements, coffee and cigarettes, underlaid by a calm and capable conspiracy of paramedics, police, and coastguards. The media soundtrack was all hackneyed horror and clichéd compassionating—close-knit community, dreadful tragedy—but even the most blasé were stunned by the scale of the disaster, and struck by its obvious emerging angle. The dramatic, symbolic possibilities were already awfully apparent.

For the most acutely attuned, this sad stranding was another awful installment in an interminable tale. It was a reprise of too many other disasters—those Moroccans choking to death in the refrigerator truck at Felixstowe, the train-crushed Laotians, or those notorious news agency images from the Mediterranean—disregarded dead on resort beaches, chilled swimmers clinging onto tuna-nets hundreds of miles from any coast, bobbing brothers, pilgrims treading water with diminishing strength, forgotten face-down floaters, whole hopeful boatloads upturned and lost on the way to *El Norte*—the lands of intolerant over-plenty, whose tall grey warships sliced casually through the drifting destitute, captained by cold-eyed men.

It was a parable, a practically self-penning story of seeking and never finding, and a search for new life met by death—a cautionary tale to trouble the conscience of a continent.

Journalists of all styles and viewpoints were now transmitting almost identical stories to the waiting world, surer every second, communicating their concern, their compassion, their commitment. The most alert were starting to hear even more enticing rumours—*bullet wounds*—and they were offering these terrible tidbits diffidently to camera—dreadfully delicious reminders of man's perennial inhumanity.

The world was waking up to woe—"The Bodies on the Beach," already capitalized, categorized, co-opted, described, dissected, and served up on slabs for Europe's edification. The globe's screens were crowded with dignitaries expressing their shock, their determination to get to the bottom of this tragic event, their admiration for the emergency services— and their words were ported planetwide, the chrism of compassion, the Immaculate Conception of the International Community.

Dan, Hatty and Clarrie, adjacent to world-altering events for the first time in their lives, were luxuriating in reflected importance. They stood with buzzing friends and neighbours and a swelling crowd of strangers, shuffling up against the police barriers, unobtrusive yet involved— absorbing the excitement as much as they thought about the victims, then feeling guilty for not caring more. Dan had the odd idea there was some kind of connection between his crops and the gathered people on the beach, but he couldn't put it into words.

His crops... he looked at his watch. The combine must be at Low Field by now. So reluctantly he made excuses and relinquished his front-row place, switching from uncomprehending onlooker to his more customary role as man of agricultural affairs, son of the soil, of the earth earthy, a master of motors, harrows, and seed catalogues. But in that second, as he swivelled in his size-9 boots between the worlds of observation and action, a camera with a vaguely frightening winking red light floated in front, and a pretty blonde was engrossing his eyes. "Are you a local man, sir? Is there any information you can give us about what's happened today?"

With a sinking realization that he was hopelessly out of his depth, Dan shook his reddening head and considered flight—until he saw Hatty looking at him proudly. Well why not—he thought; I'll never be on TV again. So he smiled uncertainly, his face plum-red like the bricks of the older local houses, his voice up an octave on his usual unemphatic tones.

"Yes, I am local—lived here all my life. The name is Gowt, Dan Gowt. G-O-W-T. No-one's allowed down there at the moment, but I've been told that they're all coloureds out there, you know—foreigners. Aliens, sort of thing. Sounds like they were trying to sneak into the country illegally. It's very sad, very sad. Poor people—poor, silly people." He shook his head and tried to clear his throat. He was impaled on the red light.

"*Coloureds? Aliens? Sneak? Silly?* You don't sound very sympathetic!" She hadn't called him "sir."

"Well, I didn't mean silly—more unwise, really—but it's the truth, isn't it? If they were illegal—and why else would they be out there in the middle of the night?—the fact is that they shouldn't have been trying to get into England in the first place. It's a crime, that is. It's just common sense—although it doesn't alter the fact that they died. It must be terrible to come from one of them places, Africa and Cambodia and… and India, where they have all them wars and famines and all."

"But surely that isn't the point, even if they *were* undocumented? The point is surely that people have died in terrible circumstances."

"Well, yes, but they're still breaking the law, aren't they? I mean, *weren't* they? Not that I don't feel sorry for them, sort of thing, but it's not what we're used to around here." Why was she looking at him with what looked like dislike?

But all she said was "Umm, thank you. That will do, Mr.—er, Gowt. You may be on Channel One News later." The red light clicked off, and the crew moved away just as Dan felt he had been getting into his stride. The woman was shaking her head and saying something to her cameraman. Hoping he hadn't made a fool of himself, Dan smiled uncertainly at a reassuringly proud Hatty and edged away through the throng.

Hatty and Clarrie stayed near the TV for much of the day—Clarrie having given up all semblance of studying. Their patience was eventually rewarded—there he was, and in close-up! There they were, too, shifting in the background, crowding subconsciously into the shot. What a pity, they agreed, that he had been wearing that yellow shirt. Hatty rang the neighbours. *They* hadn't made it onto the *national* news.

Dan saw the clip repeated later, sitting in the living room which Hatty had replicated from a "makeover" show. Dan found the show's flamboyant host disturbing, and partly for that reason, and partly out of sheer parsimony, he had always disliked the new scheme, with its bright colours and so-called "art." His beloved clock looked out of place in this out-of-place interior, but it had more right to be in the room than these impertinent furnishings, and it would be there long afterwards.

Someone who looked a little like him loomed up massively, a giant red caricature of a respectable farmer with a grubby yellow shirt and a brick-coloured face, and a too-high, too-fast voice. Normally almost entirely without vanity, Dan had a sick feeling he looked ridiculous— and not just ridiculous.

Somehow, a wrong note had been struck. Maybe he shouldn't have smiled. Should he have said *exactly* what he said? He stood by it, of course, but now it sounded…well, unkind, a bit harsh. He wished they had picked on somebody else. It bothered him more than he could easily account for…

But, there, it was done. It was over. Forget it, he instructed himself—just forget it. And Hatty had said he came across well. Yet it bothered him, like an incipient illness, or the knowledge of a job done badly—like a gate left unlatched and banging.

He went out at last into the stretching shadows, making an effort to think about things he knew and could deal with—the fence to be fixed, the tire to be replaced, the coughing of the smallest cow, the ever-excruciating finances. He relished the peppery smell coming up from the lawn, and watched frantic midges high against the house, churning in the last of the sun. There'd be a decent working moon.

He got into the Landrover, whistling to Sammy. The dog jumped in, and they passed rattlingly along narrow lanes they knew better than most, breaking the bars of westering light that lay across the road and back into shade over and again, sun-shade-sun-shade-sun, making rabbits on the verges dash for refuge while Sammy growled gently and stiffly swished his stump. Swags of mist were clambering out of the ditches and conspiring in old field undulations; and the 14th-century castellated tower of All Saints was beset by rooks.

Seeing the tower, Dan thought, as he usually did, of his mother, below the cow-parsley in the churchyard—one of the last burials before it had been closed like the church. She had loved evenings like this, seeing the sun going down behind the far hills, watching bumble bees bumping in the honeysuckle (she had known all the plants), smiling through the kitchen window at her surviving son riding proudly past in the tractor. He sighed, and drove on to pay his debts to the quick. A few minutes later, with him high in the cab and confidently in control, the giant machine was processing along long rows of rape against an infinite sky.

Chapter 4
SONGS OF TRAVEL

Basra

He was in the passenger seat of a battered truck with a military-issue kit-bag on his knee and an evil-eye bracelet around his wrist—a parting gift from Ayesha. It was just after evening prayers, the engine and his stomach were turning over together, and several thousand scruffy dollars in small denominations were digging into his upper leg. He was acutely conscious of the wad, and felt that it must be conspicuous to the driver sitting smoking a Marlboro, waiting his turn as the truck crept towards the final checkpoint. The remainder of the money he had given to his Aunt Risha to defray the cost of looking after his sisters. Parting from them had been surprisingly affecting, even Risha sniffling, and Ayesha making him promise he would never, ever, ever remove the bracelet. He had even had the mad notion that he should change his mind. But his aunt had steadied and surprised them all by quoting the Koran to show she thought he was doing the right thing—"Allah leaves straying whom He pleases and He guides whom He pleases."

That she could think of such a sentence at such a time made the superstitious part of Ibraham think just maybe this was foreordained.

So he had composed himself, and kissed them all twice, stood up straight and forced a smile before clambering resolutely into the cab of the truck. Now that he was here, and there was no possible turning back, mixed in with the lump of sadness was growing excitement.

A bomb had gone off along the Zubayr road, drawing away many of the police and military that would normally have been patrolling the highway. The policemen on guard at the last checkpoint, watched over by a British armoured car, were tense and tired. No courtesies; just "Papers!" The driver passed them over and yawned as the policeman peered at their faces. Ibraham aimed at impassivity—and he must have succeeded, because the policeman shouted "All right!" and waved for the barrier to be raised. It seemed to Ibraham at that moment that all the red-and-white striped barriers to a wider, better life were lifting in front of him.

As they cleared the zone, Ibraham looked momentarily into the eyes of one of the British monitors, and felt he was staring into his own future. The next time he saw an Englishman, he realised, might be in *London*. He exhaled and gazed forwards into uncharted places. The driver scratched his buttocks and started to sing Ilham's "Baghdad"—

> *I came back to you, a ship returning to its harbour*
>
> *Tired and hiding my wounds under my clothes*
>
> *I went down like a bird heading to its nest*
>
> *The dawn was glowing with minarets and domes…*

Ibraham listened and looked out as long shadows fell away behind them into the exhausted landscape. He was looking not at but through the tired terrain. Exploration fever coursed through him; his stomach felt pleasurably hollow, while his hands clenched and unclenched excitedly, symbolically enfolding new places, touching new things. It was a feeling he had not had since he was a small boy, making his first solo trip down to the olive groves by the river to meet and fight with others sampling life's largeness. Long, happy days—long gone.

There was not much traffic on the highway; it was always quiet now, the driver told him. Once, a U.S. helicopter passed clamorously very low overhead (a pale blob was discernible behind a mounted machine-gun), and from time to time military traffic would flash past towards trouble, or rumble back filled with head-down silent soldiers. Thinking of his own army days, Ibraham had a sudden insight into the foreign troopers' tedious and dangerous existences—watching, patrolling, searching, swearing, sweating, eating, TV, sleeping, shooting or being shot. He comprehended the vast effort of the invasion, and was silent with wonder and compassion.

He smoked and listened to the driver's tales of the road. It would be a long, hot drive in this old banger, and there were at least a dozen checkpoints along the way, and always the possibility of the road being closed if there was trouble. These checkpoints were all alike—helmeted men looking edgily in both directions along the highway and into the black lands behind, raking the gloom with searchlights. The foreigners were trying to introduce economic normality, so were reluctant to interfere with lorries carrying essential items, so when they weren't waved through, the checking was cursory—foreign troops or local police with a flak-jacketed translator, a perfunctory glance at papers, and a look into the back of the truck—a scan with some electronic device, perhaps a couple of dogs put into the back for a moment, then "OK, you can go."

They stopped at a café for tongue-coating sweet coffee and honey cakes, and to urinate among the cicada-heavy scrub. Towns rose up and fell away—untidy clumps of random lights, whose silent, sometimes guarded slip roads they passed without regret. Jolibah, An Nasiriyah ("Ur!"—for a second Ibraham was back beside the metalworker's son in that July-heavy schoolroom with the painting of Saddam above the blackboard), Al Batha, Al Khidr, As Samowah, many others—names from too few geography lessons.

Once, somewhere out there in the huge night, there was a great fire; the Americans at the nearest checkpoint were more than usually brusque, and they never discovered the cause. Shortly afterwards, an American convoy came racing up behind, flashing lights and blowing horns so other traffic had to pull in. "You can't help feeling sorry for the poor bastards," said the driver feelingly, and lit up another cigarette, his face illuminated whenever he inhaled, while Ibraham jolted in and out of stiff-necked sleep.

At Al Hillah there was a premonition of paleness. By Karbala, it was fully light and the road that would become the Hilla Road had become busier—lorries, vans, cars, motorbikes, military. The road ran alongside the railway, and there were freight trains coming up from the coast with plated windows and mounted guns. The capital was exerting itself even in its pounded state, pulling all of the south towards it. The traffic was increasingly bunched, and radios and voices from other vehicles were occasionally heard through wound-down windows. There were tired drivers seen in profile, and big flies buzzing idly into the cab, to be squashed or flicked out again. There were more frequent checkpoints, as cameras swivelled and spread-out snipers stroked sensitive triggers.

In the far distance, black smoke was oiling from east to west. A few minutes later, all traffic came to a hot and hissing halt. The road was closed; somebody was putting up stiff resistance in Arab Jadnor. Drivers got out to gossip, and a few experienced hands even started to set up stalls, from which they would sell food and bottled water.

Ibraham had never been so close to the capital. He wandered around restlessly, watching the sparrows skipping around men's feet, and then joined in with the drivers—listening to their theories and smiling politely at their jokes. He pulled out some dates and pretzels (a rueful thought of home) and sat down to make a slightly squashed and warm breakfast with his co-traveller.

The driver told him the road could be closed for a long time—frustratingly, because the warehouse where he had to drop off his cargo was only ten kilometres away. It was even possible that the road would be closed for some days. There was some local *intifada*—and even when it was finished this area would be stiff with security for an indefinite period. The driver chewed thoughtfully at the pretzels, then seemed to make up his mind.

"To be honest, my young friend, at the best of times, Baghdad is a bit of a dump, and now it's a dangerous dump, too! Why don't you change your plans and skip the capital? If I were you, I would walk it from here. I can give you directions. Go round the city, on the small roads through Khan Azad towards Fallujah. Beyond Fallujah, the border is open towards Jordan or Syria. The Americans aren't too worried about people leaving the country because then you're someone else's problem!"

Ibrahim had had a boyish yearning to see the capital. But now that he had begun at last, he wanted just to keep going, He couldn't wait here for days, and it would clearly be too risky to try and creep through the city perimeter on foot, especially from this direction. In any case, there was no guarantee the driver's contacts would still be there. West of Baghdad, he would be just another refugee, inconspicuous and in control of his own destiny.

So he nodded and paid over the rest of his fee in genuine gratitude. The driver tucked the money away in a dirty shirt pocket, and pulled him over to the western edge of the expressway. An unmetalled track wound away west towards the Jordanian border, 600 kilometres away. "Go along there, straight for about three kilometres, until you get to a crossroads. Straight over again, and keep walking. Follow signs for Al Andalus, then Rahhaliyah. Don't worry; you won't have to walk all the way! Ask everyone about getting to the border. They won't report you—everyone's at it!" He advised Ibraham to stock up on food and water, then his hand circled the horizon expansively. "Good luck, young man—go with God!"

For the second time in 12 hours, Ibraham felt awfully alone—but taking a deep breath, he bought food and water, and set off following his own shadow. When he looked back after about an hour, the road seemed already tiny, "his" truck lost in the long line of still vehicles, Baghdad lost in the thickening heat-haze, above which smoke rose and was dissipated, drifting like him noiselessly into the west.

The country grew disconcertingly silent as Ibraham headed away from the highway, kit-bag over his shoulder, the sun weighing him down. He could feel it even through the New York Yankees baseball cap he had found years ago in the Old Town, and which he felt made him look sophisticated and cosmopolitan. There were hardly any vehicles, except infrequent army trucks, which paid him no attention. There was birdsong and once a small black snake slid neatly into a ditch. The few fields were largely untended, returning to their natural bramble and dust, although occasionally he would see some workers or a tractor on the horizon. The scattered houses were watchfully quiet—closed doors, shops shuttered against the heat as well as the war. Once he heard children laughing, then a woman shouted and the stillness surged back. This was a country on alert, a country shuttered and suspicious. He began to walk more slowly, acutely conscious of the compacted earth, the way its hardness was creeping up his body, and the irreducible immensity of Iraq. The sun pushed down and the earth pushed up.

He was inexpressibly glad when a van stopped. "Where to, brother?" "As far west as you're going!" The man was delivering engine parts to a village east of Fallujah, where there was a ferry across the river. He talked a lot, but didn't ask Ibraham where he was from or heading for—curiosity sometimes seemed to have been one of the war's chief casualties. But Ibraham took advantage while the driver lit a cigarette to tell him that he was heading for Jordan.

"Well, well, well! Half the country's there, it seems! Can't say I blame you, though. I tell you—you need to get right away from Fallujah and Ghraib and then pick up a lift. But there's trouble all the way along that road, with the militias setting up their own checkpoints. But mostly they won't bother civilians who aren't looking for trouble. Cross the river where I set you down (it'll cost you a few dinars), and then follow the river north until you get to the crossroads. There you'll be able to pick up a lift with someone. You'll be fine!"

Then there were huts and an electricity sub-station dropped down together in a greatness of dust and scrub, with just the embanked river to add definition. Ibraham alighted in a sad street, where he made an arrangement with an apathetic-looking man who jerked into excited life at seeing dollar bills. He practically ran down to the jetty, with Ibraham following more slowly, where a dinghy strained gently on its painter.

Ten minutes later, Ibraham was looking wearily along a telephone pole-lined road that threaded along the far bank until it was lost. It was nearly midday, and he had the Mother of All Headaches. So he subsided into the cool shade of an old wall and drank water accompanied by feta and onions. Cicadas were creaking; otherwise, the only sound was the humming of the power lines.

The sun had shifted surprisingly far round when he awoke, puzzled and panicky. A white pick-up was approaching from the direction of Karbala. The incredibly wizened driver seemed simple but his tobacco-tinged grin was sincere, and he would take him to the next village. And that was all he said, as they trundled along to the driver's coughs interspersed with spitting out of the window.

By five, Ibraham was in the back of a Toyota covered with the sediments of several summers, heading for a small town where he might get a bed—perhaps his last night ever in Iraq, he reflected. He was well beyond Fallujah, and the village where he was stopping was not far from Ar Ramadi. The following day, he would need to get around Ramadi, where there was fighting, and then it was a clear road almost all the way.

The day had felt interminable, but he thrilled to think that tomorrow or, at most, in a few days, he would be out of Iraq for the first time in his 32 years of being on the earth. In the meantime he had a tired-looking endless prospect of mud-berried sheep, belled goats prospecting under blasé supervision by boys, small birds hopping, an eagle hovering over a hillock then swooping on something out of sight, scrubby trees, infrequent clusters of single-storey houses, a shut petrol station, a noticeboard with torn pictures of men wanted by the Americans, occasional startlingly modern buildings surrounded by chain-link fences. What a huge country this was! He wished the car was going faster.

It was almost 10:30 when he alighted staggeringly from yet another car, beige with dirt and cramped, a headache flickering on the extremes of his eyesight. He knocked on random doors in the nameless town, hoping to find a bed. But they would not reply—too late, too suspicious—and he felt he couldn't blame them. So he found a slumping stone shed, most of its roof missing and its wooden door pitted with insect holes. He moved loose stones and timbers to check for scorpions, spiders or snakes, and arranged spare clothes to form a makeshift bed. He made himself as comfortable as he could and lay feeling very cold and alone. The shed was very dark, but he could see through a hole in the tiles an impressive array of stars. He hadn't seen such a display since those nights along the Iranian border, and found their hard beauty comforting. He remembered a saying of his mother's—"The same stars look down on us all"—and smiled sadly. Then, driven by an irresistible influence, he prayed for the first time in years.

He had inconsequential and illogical thoughts; he dozed and jerked awake—a door closing somewhere close, an animal moving outside (jackal?), a car passing hurriedly very late—and then the sun was coming unceremoniously through the doorway.

A goatherd and his charges were passing, as boys and goats had passed that way for hundreds of years, as Ibraham emerged unrefreshed. The boy looked curiously at him, and then must have reflected that it was not a good idea to stare too much at strangers in these times, so passed on saying nothing. They were soon absorbed into the blueness.

The aroma of cooking meat reminded Ibraham of Basra in the evening, strap-hanging on the bus from the Old Town. But he had to content himself with fruit and water (at least his kit-bag was getting lighter). Then he started off, dead-tired and dirty, although at least his headache had gone. It was only 5:30—but he had only been walking about five minutes before a battered bus pulled up in response to his waving hand. He got up amongst about 20 labourers heading to a farm south of Ar Ramadi. Ibraham told them where he was going, and there were grunts of understanding and shy smiles. Everyone seemed to know someone who had "gone across." Cigarettes, complaints, anecdotes, advice were exchanged. Even the driver joined in, shouting over his shoulder, grinning at Ibraham in the mirror. He had a brother who had left two months ago. He hadn't heard from him, but no doubt he was in Amman now, doing well. "No doubt!" replied Ibraham stoutly. Soon they were bound in rough solidarity, and a chorus of sincere salutations was left echoingly behind as the bus sped away from him, suddenly solitary on the main road that bypassed the low line of Ar Ramadi. Even from several kilometres away, Ibraham could hear mortar fire. Two American jets ripped overhead, flying from the airbase near Fallujah to strafe insurgent OPs in the city centre. Ibraham was glad he would be approaching no closer.

For a second day he moved painfully slowly across the dust-draped atlas of the Middle East. Hours and hours of parching dust, warm wind from the Empty Quarter, blighted buildings, roads headachy with heat, cars that rose up and departed like mirages, sometimes stopping to take him a few kilometres further. There were old drivers, young drivers, the one with the cigar, the one with the big belly and a broken nose, the one who complained about the Jews and the price of food, the one worried about his son who had got a girl into trouble, the one who put a hand on his knee and was mortified when Ibraham pushed it away—so mortified that he immediately pulled the car into the side and sat looking straight ahead while Ibraham leapt out—the one who sat there silently for sullen kilometres as they bypassed Rutbah, then thanked him for his company.

They passed several *bah'haar* cars—"merchant seamen" carrying illicit petrol towards Jordan—and the burned remains of rocket-attacked convoys. Twice, American armoured cars overtook at top speed. There were no other walkers. The only movement came from a small herd of camels and, once, an eagle or a vulture flying high towards the south. There was violent rain for a short time, whose huge drops made crumping sounds on the roof of the car, and turned potholes briefly into ponds before the sun broke back out to dry them up again and make the road hiss and steam.

That day was a light-headed jumble—cramp, complacency as they clocked up kilometres, nerves, a feeling that he was a prisoner being carried towards a destiny he both feared and desired. But the nearer they got to the border crossing at Al-Karama, there was a strengthening confluence as people were funnelled from every part of Iraq towards this one point. His final lift came from an estate car crammed with five members of a family from Rutbah en route to a cousin in Az Zarqa. Ibraham just managed to squeeze in on the back seat, between the deaf but beaming patriarch and his sniffling 13-year-old great-grandson. They smelled of onions and old clothes. When the hissing vehicle finally joined the tail end of the border queues, three kilometres from the border, Ibraham was extremely glad.

The border post was a huddle of prefabs, buzzing with calm officials and smelling of chemical toilets. A high chain-link fence ran in both directions—impressive-looking, but in fact it only ran about two kilometres in each direction. There was a small stand of trees marking subterranean water, showing why the crossing was here, and not some equally ugly elsewhere. An enormous new Iraqi flag flew proudly over the huddle, and Iraqi soldiers were everywhere—behind a heavy machine gun, watching from roofs or leaning lazily against buildings, walking slowly up and down the lines picking their teeth and chatting, looking morosely at the queue snaking towards Security. There were tanks nearby—Americans overseeing their unreliable allies. Beyond there were large marquees, surmounted by a strange powder-blue flag; Ibraham didn't recognize the United Nations emblem. Loudspeakers on poles made static-suffused announcements, telling those waiting to have their passports and ID cards ready for inspection, listing the items they would not be allowed to bring across the border, and warning of penalties for smuggling contraband. Small boys walked up and down, offering drinks or fruit or cigarettes at wildly inflated prices, and found plenty of customers.

Vehicles were being searched in a special sandbagged bay—scanned first by a robotic device, then felt over painstakingly by white-gloved policemen. The man beside Ibraham glared at these and spat out one experienced word—"Thieves!"—before fading again into the background. Those on foot had been marshalled into a long single file that wound around temporary posts with stretch-tape between. Before they joined the line, they had walked through a metal detector checkpoint, then been searched by frontier police. After that, they were given numbered cards, medical cards and (for some strange reason) pens.

The line went up two steps into a long grey prefab building with an Iraqi crest over the door. They hadn't changed *that*, anyway. Ibraham could see people coming out the far end, where they got onto coaches which then moved away towards the unseen Jordanian terminus. Ibrahim picked out a man in an orange shirt not far from the entrance into the prefab, and kept looking out for him, as the queue shuffled along stickily. At 6:15, Orange-Shirt entered the hut. At 6:35, he emerged on the far side and walked towards the buses. Ibrahim could see that he wouldn't get over tonight—presuming he got across it at all. But he didn't allow himself to consider the latter eventuality.

The crowd seemed to be from all over Iraq, judging by their accents. There had been stories of senior Ba'athists trying to sneak across the border, but the people here just looked tired and hot. There was contradictory chatter—the border would shortly be closed—it was open all night—they were turning more people back these days—they were letting more through—they were shunting people straight through to Syria and Lebanon, and the Syrians were sending people onto Egypt. Syria itself was apparently experiencing security problems. There had been a bomb here 10 days ago—no, two weeks ago—no, it was on the Syrian border. Life is easy in Amman; my cousin's there and he's raking it in. Life is hard in Amman; when your visa expires, you're on your own. Jordanians won't employ us. There were Palestinians and Kurds who had been living on the border since 2003. You'll see their tents when you get through the barrier. "No, you'll smell them!" someone said, and everyone laughed.

The line creaked on as the sun sank over the sought-for Jordan. Floodlights snapped on—then it was announced that the border would be closing in 10 minutes. A groan came up from the crowd, but they had expected it. There was a collective easing, and untensing of the line. Some were already setting up tents or unrolling blankets. Fires were being built; people produced kettles and saucepans, while others queued to use the feculent toilets—or slunk in behind them when they could wait no longer.

Ibraham mucked in with a family from Al Hadithah—a baker and his silent wife, with well-upholstered offspring. Ibraham shared his remaining bread and fruit with them, scavenged sticks and rubbish for the fire they shared, and water from the U.S.-installed standpipe for the common stew and mint tea. They added extra meat and cubes of stock for him, and loaned him a plate. They also let him listen to their radio, which could pick up Baghdad—where, perhaps in the middle of a firestorm, they were broadcasting one of R'Ana's most sentimental hits—

> *How I loved you*
>
> *All the days of my youth*
>
> *But you deceived me*
>
> *And I am alone, and filled with despair.*

The breathy, tremulous words should have seemed banal, out in his here and now of muttering movement, fires and filth, and large moths dancing in the floodlights. Ibraham would scarcely have noticed the song had he heard it in Basra. But here, he felt a starting at the back of his eyes as the overblown lyrics cut into him. They smelt of *home*— the cheap scent of the giggling girls, cooking smells and radios from a thousand breeze-block houses, the scruffy men on the corner forever fixing the same hopeless Volkswagen, murmuring and smoke from the coffee places, the background odour of sewage that rose up cholerically every summer. This might be the last time he would hear this kind of music, the sounds that had surrounded his life. However, it was perhaps appropriate that he should hear such a song here, in the middle of his adventure, at the edge of what he knew, with the starpricked sky above looking like a billion possibilities. Lying looking up at that illimitable expanse, he thought about everything and nothing.

Chapter 5

A Bird's Eye View

West London
Monday, 5th August

Ninety-two minutes after the Gowts left for the beach, 259 miles to the south and lightyears away in tastes and expectations, John Leyden's eyes flicked open. The sun streamed in through tall wood-framed windows—laying lines of heat across the waxed floor, chrome and black-leather retro furniture, last night's bottles, and strewn world music CDs. Maida Vale was moving into Monday.

His vision was a little blurred, and he could still smell cannabis, not as pleasant as it had seemed just a few hours ago, when lazy smoke and incontinent laughter had rolled companionably out of the world-welcoming windows. But it was time to get up for work—and as ever that word gave him a tiny thrill. It was the knowledge of making a difference.

He got briskly out of bed, making Janet groan, and went to sluice away sleep in the shower. When he emerged shaved and shining, Janet was rooting dazedly for clothes—blonde, beautiful, slim, wearing just a T-shirt. The sight interested him. "*Hi!*" She pulled away laughingly and went into the bathroom.

John looked at the closed door. How much longer could this last? They had been together for—what was it, a year? It was a long time, anyway. And so, inevitably, their conversations had become predictable, and somehow constrained. He knew there was something in particular she wanted him to say. But he also knew he would never say it. Marriage—the sheer suburbanality of the idea made him feel wearily superior. *Suburbanality*—he mentally docketed the neologism for future use.

Their relationship had become a bore, at least to him. It had been mostly a sex thing for him—Janet had been the best-looking girl by far at the gallery that night, and he had also enjoyed taking her away from all the other men who had been hovering in her vicinity. Physically, things had always been good, were still good. But in between, there was something lacking in her. Sometimes when he was talking, he could see she wasn't able to follow, as her eyes rolled about restlessly and she seemed to be on some, frankly, less elevated level. Quite often he would tell her about some important political or economic developments, and when he had finished she would come out with something utterly unrelated. It was almost as if she hadn't been listening.

Sometimes he felt sorry for her—sorry that she was unable to intuit things like he could, see things from his radical perspective. She was, of course, fundamentally bourgeois—that was probably why Mummy didn't think her good enough. But then Mummy was *such* a snob. Daddy of course didn't count either way—he was always so remote from mundane concerns that he probably didn't even know John had a girlfriend.

John said "Humpph!" out loud. Girls were always trouble one way or another. But Janet was more trouble than usual, because they lived together. When he got rid of her, he'd revert to his more sensible habit of only going out with girls who had their own flats.

He dressed with understated enjoyment—good cloth against good skin—Mack shirt, Mack chinos, socks from Evremode, Cliveden brogues. He gazed in the mirror and half-grinned. Blue *was* his hue, as Janet had often adoringly observed. He eavesdropped satisfiedly on the comfortable sounds coming through the balcony doors—birds, a bus on the High Road, a girl's heels clicking along the kerb. He went out onto the balcony and watched a trim figure diminish towards the station. He hadn't seen *her* before. He switched on the espresso machine and dropped bread into the retro toaster—enjoying the assembling aromas as he watched blackbirds bickering in the buddleia.

He leafed through a recent *Examiner,* where the sight of his most recent column gave renewed satisfaction. He had read through "Emissions and Omissions: Global Warming and the World's Poor" when it appeared, as he always did read his columns—ostensibly to check for subbing errors, but secretly so those sitting beside him on the Tube would marvel at it and wish they could write like that, or knew people who could write like that. He sometimes felt like saying to these drab denizens, "It's me! I'm sitting beside you!"—although he never gave in to the vulgar temptation.

It was a vain pleasure that had never diminished, although he had been writing for the *Examiner* for seven years and had been published in many equally prestigious publications. He smiled as he thought of the MP who had complained, the letter from the oil company lawyers. But editor Nige had laughed it off, and the e-mails had been uniformly supportive. John always got on average 17 percent more fan-mail than any other *Examiner* writer, and had 2,567 more Facebook friends than his nearest rival. He wondered what all those people who had been so horrible at school made of him *now.* What had they all done, after all? It was only he who had become a household name—at least in the tastefully appointed homes of *Examiner* readers.

He looked absently down onto the garden, mown weekly by assorted east Europeans, with a herbaceous border in which foxes would root and rut. A beer can—even here the late-night fauna were unlovely—was visible beneath the clipped conifers shielding the house from the other large Edwardian villas of the Avenue. Even this area was sometimes slightly urban-edgy—that bit too close to the High Road, along which gold-hampered youths who had never been young strutted or drove after nightfall, their hooded eyes under hooded heads scanning along the cafés, restaurants, and small shops, making others cower as they pimped past. But now the sun lay kindly across the cars, and glossy blackbirds bounced fatly across the gleaming grass.

He sipped the espresso and revelled in that fantastic fleeting feeling of absolute clarity, as if his brain was too capacious and his eyes too large for his head. He flicked the TV remote—an elegant chrome wand, complementing the TV, the whole assemblage by Future Furniture. It looked good in that corner, below the Vonderhausen he had bought as an investment. A very good investment, too! He stopped looking at the large plastic triangle as his eyes were drawn to the TV by the unusually excited and portentous demeanour of the newscasters.

The pretty blonde from Channel 10 was talking excitedly as white text unrolled below—"BREAKING NEWS—Dozens of dead bodies washed up on east coast—Many feared dead in disaster." She was rephrasing what the scrolling words were saying, expressing sparse information in her winning and award-winning way.

She was superseded by shuddering footage shot from a helicopter—a long strand and dunes, with a vast silver plain on the right and multiple blue lights and the outlines of fields to the left—studded with tiny shapes briskly busy or horridly still, draped with tarpaulins and surrounded by barriers. A foreshortened man in a dark uniform was looking up at the chopper, motioning it away. A north-eastern male voice was shouting—

"...scene now, Adelaide. As far as I can see in both directions, there are dead bodies all along the beach. It's a terrible sight. We've counted 22 so far. Others have already been removed. There are police and medical personnel everywhere, and we can just see a Coastguard or Navy vessel out there in the haze. RAF search-and-rescue helicopters are patrolling the sea-area for hundreds of miles. This is now also an international operation, with the Dutch, Belgian, German, and Danish authorities all mobilising aircraft and naval vessels. Trawlers and pleasure craft in the area are also being asked to look out for anything unusual, and of course for any survivors …"

The studio turned to hastily assembled, impressively brisk experts—a specialist in maritime safety, a retired police inspector, and a refugee-rights campaigner. A charged and circuitous conversation commenced.

Janet stood behind John wearing only underwear, while she combed through her light-filled hair. "Those poor people!" But John was too full of the symbolism of the thing to hear, or even register her state of undress. A passionate, powerful column was taking shape, and he needed to get down these words, this passion, now.

He bolted the coffee and, without even his usual "See ya," snatched up keys and laptop and charged out. The front door crumped shut heavily a few seconds later, and Janet looked down to see him vault boyishly over the little white wooden garden gate and walk quickly towards the station. She made a mouè, and went to dry her hair while the TV beamed its awfulness into emptiness.

Tall with thought, John elbowed onto an eastbound between Polish builders and a large Indian family without seeing them. He even stepped on the matriarch's foot, oblivious to her Gujurati glowering—simultaneously thinking about what he would write and enjoying "All Change" on his iPhone, *Recondite Rock*'s Band of the Week. He tapped his foot energetically to jangling guitars and an Old Harrovian's slightly unconvincing Estuarial vocalizing—"I hyte the wye we are todye / Our lives are not our own / We must embryce the coming chynge / We're a million miles from 'ome." The Indian woman looked at him with distaste.

Forty-one minutes later, he burst blinking into the E14 glare, where the morning was bouncing between banked windows, giving him multiple reflections of himself as he walked along Bunyan Street past Wren's St. Adalrics, the Evremode shop, finance houses, the cappuccino kiosk. Finally he entered the *Examiner*'s cool aquamarine offices (nickamed "The Fish Tank"), swiping his card to get through the barrier, oblivious to the smiling Ghanaian guard—up three floors in the mirrored lift (the shirt was just right)—gliding over to his desk. Most in Editorial seemed to be watching the large screen. Ignoring them (although some nodded, because they felt it was good policy to be on the right side of the paper's risingest star) he typed rapidly while his coffee skinned over. He was caught up in the consciousness of his capability, and his responsibility.

He always felt when he was writing that he was sitting in front of a giant picture window, beyond which was spread out a coloured relief map of the whole world. There were clinical central business districts, privet-hedged suburbs and heaving *favelas*, boardrooms, red-upholstered clubs of red-faced men, luckless small people, campaigners and crushers, placards raised then trampled under baton and boot, columns marching forwards and crowds falling back, injustice and inspiration, currents and counter-currents, historical forces sweeping relentlessly over the map and turning everything around.

It was exhilarating to fly this far above the rest, like the chopper over the coast, seeing everything hyper-clearly and through his writing, changing what he saw. Looking down on it all, impossibly distant yet deeply involved, he saw a long white beach under the sun—a beach like a desert—a pleasure ground-cum-frontline—the soft shore of a hard country. *The soft shore of a hard country!* And draped picturesquely across that soft shore was human weed—uprooted by storms, at the mercy of great forces, cast up and forgotten. The newsroom faded out, as fine phrases chiselled something beautiful and strong.

He soon had much more than he needed, so he filleted the copy expertly but with a pang, keeping the phrases of which he was proudest, putting the overmatter into a blank document for future use. It was 11:15. How disgusting cold cappuccino was. He watched that brunette from the Weekend Section as she passed his desk, knowing she knew he was watching and didn't mind. Her rear view reminded him pleasantly of some girl at Oxford.

He found himself thinking more these days of Oxford, no doubt a function of getting older (not that *he* would ever be conventional)—heady half-remembered times of indie gigs with blurred faces seen through speed and sweat, beer and dope and coke—dinner parties in SW districts—*bhajis* in Banglatown where the London brick gave a controlled exoticism—curated exhibitions in white spaces—book launches—Chelsea matches when adrenalin made him forget the incongruity of this communion with chavry—and of course girls—laughing so agreeably, hanging gratifyingly onto his longest words, granting admittance to their flats and friends, their soft mouths and pale thighs.

But Oxford had been much more than these things, which were, after all, the common currency of all his generation. Those things sufficed for most of them, but he at least had picked up a social conscience along with his degree.

Oxford to him had also been the Progressive and Radical Societies, networking that was now standing him in good stead and, most exciting, student union shouting at Christian Democrat MPs, whose anger and fear could almost be tasted, like a tang of blood in the water—no platform, no cuts, no justice, no peace—placards and speeches by *déclassé* allies in cheap clothes, waiting impatiently for *his* turn to make the audience sigh or shout to his formidable vocabulary and mellifluous accent, to make them anguished or angered by his passionate daggers stabbing dead straight at the authorities, The Man, the System, the tainted West. Thinking of the rebel he had been then made him proud. And he still had that same agenda, that urgency—but it was tempered now, he told himself, with incomparably more information, depth, breadth and understanding.

He was hauled back to the present by a horrified murmuring. It was C10 anchorman Mark Clark—famously seen on *Celeb Rehab*, naked and vomiting liberally into a plastic bucket. That all-defences-down and much-watched moment had purged him, and cleared the way for him to re-launch a career that had been in abeyance since his "momentary blip" with the rent boy. The cleansed celebrity was looking out sombrely at the world, as sternly kind as Mount Rushmore:"...even more disturbing. We go now to James Montmorency at Crisby. What more can you tell us, James?"

"Thank you, Mark. Medical personnel have told us that some of the bodies have suffered gunshot wounds. This means that what could otherwise have been simply a terrible accident will probably now become a full-scale murder investigation. There is a more heartening suggestion that at least one man has been found alive. If these stories are confirmed, then unsettling questions will be asked. However dreadful it is even to consider such a possibility—could *local people* have been involved? A horrible thought—but of course so far none of this has been confirmed...."

Thrillingness tore around the Fish Tank and many similar buildings. Unblinking lenses homed in even more narrowly and now also accusingly on the sea-besieged strand and the no-longer-harmless hamlet. John gazed down over the tiny Thames and the cutting–edge towers, and watched a jet descending into City Airport.

Murder! *Racist* murder! Failed states, hunger, fear, poverty, racism, repression, war, gangsters, guns in the night, mouths filled with seawater, hands clawing as they went down, *down*. Hope deferred, hope defeated, the South and East gone West in the North Sea...He turned back to the TV, and listened attentively to a plump, red-faced man wearing an old yellow shirt.

Chapter 6

COMPANIONS IN FORTUNE

Iraqi border

The third day on the road came around with a moaning mass movement, as sleepers muttered, sat up, stretched, scratched and spat. There were long queues for the toilet cubicles, so many relieved themselves elsewhere, evoking protests and threats from more dilatory risers. Everyone looked bleary, except the children, who were playing chase around the still recumbent and the steamed-up vehicles. High laughter leapt upwards, incongruous in such a place of partings.

Brand-new Jordanian and Iraqi flags were raised; soldiers formed up and dispersed. Ibraham watched women gathering happy children and sad belongings, while their defeated-looking men scratched matches against boxes and chewed at food. He became absorbed for several minutes by a pretty girl in a denim shirt and black headdress, tidying herself using a car window as a mirror, and wondered who she was and where she might be from. Her movements were so graceful, so ineffably feminine, that he was ashamed to think how dust-caked and grubby he must look. When she turned around, he looked shamefacedly at the ground.

An *imam* intoned cracklingly over the loudspeakers—and everyone except the foreign soldiers abased themselves in real or convincing humility, south towards Saudi, their thoughts briefly transferred from where their more practical hopes lay. The distorted voice boomed and echoed over the enchanted waste, then tailed away until there was once again just etiolated earth and rock. The line of yesterday started to reform, with pushing, arguments and aggrieved appeals to the police.

More refugees had arrived during the night, and the line behind Ibrahim was already several hundreds strong. Air fuel tankers rumbled in from Jordan; once inside the border, they were joined by US military vehicles, and started off at a stately pace on their journey through the troubled provinces to the embattled city. Ibrahim's line shuffled forwards...

Hours—more hours—interminable, hot, horrible even to Ibrahim, whose life appeared always to have been spent dancing attendance on people and events. He and the Hadithah family, trapped together by politesse and numbered cards, began slowly to loathe each other—although they still nodded politely whenever they caught each others' savage glances. Umbrellas and awnings were raised against the sun; the never shrinking crowd stood and endured with its back to Iraq and the past.

As the sun waxed, the complaints tailed off—even resentment had been seared out. The only thing that evoked vague interest was speculation about whether and when they would be allowed to cross, but even such salient considerations started to lose their savour when considered for the 75th time. Paramedics—mostly foreign—in limp uniforms went along the line offering water, food, logo-covered caps and parasols. Ibrahim looked at them with interest, but also disappointment—they did not look as cool and confident as the Americans at the refinery. But he took what they were giving with genuine appreciation—mineral water, a cheese and pickle sandwich, a chocolate bar—a token of gifts to come. As he nibbled first warily, then with relish, on the sandwich, he felt briefly as if he were already halfway to freedom.

But after a while, he sagged again. His eyes crusted; his lips cracked; his sinuses clogged; and his gut was gurgling in protest at his recent diet. He became conscious of pressure mounting inside, and sometimes this escaped embarrassingly. He visited the toilets more than once—his place in the line kept for him by the Hadithah man, who had passed from sullen to indifferent. An elderly woman in front fell down, and was carried over to a medical tent accompanied by a frantic daughter. Neither returned. Ibraham felt slightly sorry for her, but couldn't help feeling glad that there would be two less to process.

But the line was moving, and at some stage—he did not know what time—he found himself at the bottom of the steps leading into the processing office, in the blissful shade of a small canopy. "In 10 minutes I'll know, in 10 minutes I'll know, in 10 minutes I'll know…" he thought mechanically, grimacing at yet another gut-gripe. After another few minutes, heart pounding and gas grumbling, the guard allowed him to pass in. As he entered, he looked back over his right shoulder and saw for a second an image of Iraq's inglorious end—a ragged line of baseball caps and *dishdashas* extending endlessly back into scorching haze, the woman behind catching his eye, sourly impelling him onwards.

Below squeaking ceiling fans and fluorescent lights, sweltering clerks sat interviewing even hotter applicants across a trestle table adorned with little Iraqi flags. Several policemen were loafing against the "Wanted" postered walls, feigning interest in every arrival. Telephones rang and hidden people talked behind partitions. A camera panned wearily over the room. Coffee, sweat and feet—mostly sweat.

"Here!" said a sweat-beaded, semi-shaven official, as he pointed to Ibraham, then the newly-vacated chair across from him. The chair's previous occupant, an elderly man with thick glasses, was heading creakily towards the Jordanian-side exit. "Here!"—more sharply. "Number card, ID card, and medical certificate!"

Ibraham passed them over nervously, with five $10 bills secreted between the ID card and medical certificate, as he had been advised was the usual arrangement. The impassive clerk tossed the numbered card in a tray, from where it would be collected for some other supplicant, leafed through the passport, made notes on the form, and tapped something into his computer. He spoke without looking at Ibraham. "Why do you wish to enter Jordan?"

"To see family, *hajji*—my sisters are there!" Ibraham spoke too quickly, but the clerk just rubbed his nose.

"Where will you be staying?"

"My sisters are in the Al-Azzawai hostel in Az Zarqa; I will stay somewhere close to them. Obviously, I do not yet have an address."

"How much money have you to support yourself?"

"Five hundred dollars."

He tried not to think about the other money in his pocket, superstitiously concerned that the clerk might sense its presence. "You know this visa will only last you 30 days? After that, you become illegal, a non-person, so far as Amman is concerned. If you wish to retain your Iraqi healthcare and pension rights, you will then have to come back. If you head onto another country, you will lose these rights."

"I know, *hajji*," replied Ibraham agreeably. The clerk went "Hmm..." typed in some more information, and picked something out from between his teeth—leaning back in his chair until the plastic belt on his slacks threatened to burst open. Then he yawned and nodded. "OK. Give this to the man at Jordanian immigration. Go with God. Next!"

He returned the ID card and medical certificate, from which the $50 had been abstracted by hands defter than they had looked.

That was it. Four minutes, $50, and some perspiration, and Ibraham had quit the country of his birth, and his parents' birth, and their parents' birth—the only place he and his family had ever known. Within one more minute, he was on a bus and it was already trundling through the debatable zone, looking at the nearing red-white-black-and-green-bannered Jordanian border post over drooping brunet heads. After passing a huddle of tents surrounded by nominal fencing—some Kurds had been stuck here in legal limbo for a year—in another three minutes, he was sitting in another prefab at the Mahat'ta, facing another clerk, this one below a picture of a well-fed and pleased-looking king.

There were the same questions as on the Iraqi side—plus whether he had any military equipment, meat or fish products, agricultural produce, historical artifacts, drugs, prescription medicines or political literature, and whether he had ever been involved with any of some 40 groups, of whom Ibraham had only ever heard of Al Qaeda and the Ba'athists. He answered no to all these with a clear conscience. A policeman went through his kit bag quickly but thoroughly. Then there was just the "administration fee" of $30, upon receipt of which the clerk sighed, and stamped permission for one Ibraham Nassouf, Iraqi national, by profession gardener, to enter the Hashemi Kingdom of Jordan for a period not exceeding 30 days, purpose of visit to see family members already resident. "Welcome to Jordan! Next!" Was there a sneer? Ibraham didn't care, but just stepped down into abroad.

The unbending road to Az Zarqa and further—much further—lay at his sandal-tips. Now he had *really* done it! Muttering a prayer—this was becoming a habit—he went towards a group of sun-beaten buildings, with wilting boards advertising food, money-changing, cigarettes, shoe repairs, and buses. There were dozens of the recently-arrived, milling confusedly around this excuse for a town, looking in windows at under-par, overpriced goods, clutching Jordanian newspapers, watching the giant television in the concourse, or queuing at the information kiosk.

It looked like Iraq, yet everything was subtly different—street signs, car registrations, brand names, the colours of doors. There was a wider variety of things for sale. Even the people carried themselves differently. Ibraham looked down at his shiny green shirt, khaki jeans and dust-crusted plimsolls, and felt appallingly provincial. He changed $100 at a kiosk, paying the extortionate fee without demur, then rushed into the toilets and relieved himself just in time down a malodorous hole in the ground surrounded by soaked newspapers. My first shit in a foreign country, he thought, and grinned at the absurd thought.

He bought coffee and food and wandered to where new buses waited under a concrete canopy coated with dove droppings. One was just about to leave—so he paid and took the last seat beside a strained-looking boy of about 13. The doors hissed shut and the driver pulled out after a laughing exchange with one of his mates. Then he turned up Radio Amman (similar music to Radio Basra, but too loud and with bad reception) and nudged out onto the highway, which was already busy with refugees' cars. The super-amplified static bursts made everyone start and mutter, but no-one felt they wanted to complain. They were tired and relieved to be away from trouble, and after all this was not their country.

The scenery was monotonous—level desert, stone outcroppings, rare clumps of trees, birds of prey very high. But to Ibraham it looked thrillingly new. With every second he was getting further from Basra than any Nassouf had ever been—and closer to Europe. The road was good and the bus ran down the horizon effortlessly, flashing past petrol stations and apparently purposeless settlements. Ibraham wondered what his sisters were doing, as he struck out on his and their behalf into this huge and hopeful world. Memories flashed past like the wayside settlements—but they seemed unimportant at the moment, and he dismissed them quickly. It was too soon for introspection.

At length, he dozed—although he kept jerking awake, with a stiff neck and knees sore with being bent, panicky about missing Az Zarqa. The bus purred powerfully towards the streaming sun, the driver black against the refulgence. Most passengers were dozing. They had experienced hard days and nights on the road—and those days and nights were the culmination of months and years of insecurity. Now, really safe for the first time in years, long-coiled springs were de-tensing. It was delightful to let go of care for a while.

A few hours later, the desert had been superseded by industrial units, lamp posts, pavements and frenetic motorcycles. There were car-horns, trucks and factories, bicycles and beggars. "Az Zarqa! Az Zarqa!" bawled the driver, and the bus buzzed alive. Ibrahim felt small and tremulous as he looked at the thronging streets. In a few minutes he would once again have to move under his own steam, and make decisions.

Then he was standing dazed clutching his kitbag, as people pushed irritably past. Only a few had alighted, and they seemed to know where they were going. He stopped one—a final face from home. "Please, *hajji*—I am new here. Can you recommend a good hostel—not expensive?"

The man began to give directions to a good clean place he had heard of out on the Al Mafraq road. But Ibrahim's brain felt befuddled, and the phrases were curiously meaningless. He had never heard of Al Mafraq, and didn't know which direction it was in—so all the details about what shops and mosques he would pass, and how many intersections, meant nothing. He felt he could never make sense of such a complicated city. He shook his head as if that would help him clear it. It was an effort even to put a sentence together. "Thank you, sir. I'm sorry, but can you also tell me where I might find people who can take me north—to Europe?"

The man looked at him with closer attention, and whistled slightly. "Europe, eh? I admire your pluck, young man. But it's a very long way, and very risky. Are you sure you're doing the right thing? There's work right here. I work in a factory, and it's always crying out for new workers. They aren't too fussed about papers either. I'm legal myself, but there are lots who aren't—some from my own village. The boss took them on because I recommended them. Maybe I could get you a job there. Where are you from? What is your trade?"

How could Ibrahim convey to this well-meaning man without seeming disrespectful that he had not come all this way to work in a *factory*—that there were great things in store for him in England? He shook his head smilingly. "You're very kind, but I really do want to get to England. I'm from Basra, by the way."

"I thought I recognized your accent! We're from An Nasiriyah, so we're almost neighbours! Well, well, well! That makes it different. Maybe you're right about trying to get to Europe. There you can get a lawyer, good house, your health taken care of. People have rights. If I was a young man, I'd give it a go myself. But you can see…"— waving his hand at a bored woman and bored teenage girl nearby—"…anyway, I'd get aboard a train heading north. They go from here all the way into Turkey, maybe further. If you can get into a freight car when no-one's looking, and keep quiet, no-one would discover you. The government here is quite happy for us to just keep going on through. You wouldn't have to pay anyone. And if you find a load of fruit to hide in, you can even eat the cargo! The train station's just over there, and you can get into the marshalling yard easily. But if I were you, I'd rest here for the night. Tomorrow, buy a few things for the journey, and then sneak onto the train. Easy! In fact…" He turned and had a speedy consultation with his wife. Then she nodded, and half-smiled at Ibrahim.

"So that's settled! You can come and stay in our apartment tonight. I have told my wife that you are from Basra, and in need of hospitality. Tomorrow, I'll show you where you need to go." Ibrahim could not believe his good fortune, and kept saying so until the man stilled the torrent with a good-natured wave.

He was Bilal Gharab, and his wife and daughter were both called Sumira. He was very garrulous—talking about Basra, the war and the exciting day American bombs had fallen near his village, killing only a few goats. He told the anecdote more than once. He had been a mechanic, but his present job in engineering offered him a much higher salary. They had been in Jordan since 2003, and were legalized. They had just been back to Nasiriyah to see family, and bring them washing powder, soap, and other things difficult to obtain in Iraq. A lot of his anecdotes were lost or garbled among the surrounding noise and rush, and Ibrahim was guiltily glad. They sounded tedious and besides he didn't want to think of home.

They lived in a modern apartment. The main room contained a divan, a table, two new chairs, a talismanic carving, a good old rug (a family heirloom, he was told proudly) and a vast television. From the third-floor windows, there was a huge and hideous view. Zarqa was a town that looked better at night, Gharab admitted cheerfully. His wife came in with meze, cous-cous and grilled lamb skewered with onions and peppers. It was delicious, and Ibrahim's stomach was ready for it now. He sensed appraising, surreptitious glances from the younger Sumira, which made him feel he wouldn't mind staying longer. Yet they also had the paradoxical effect of making him feel manlier, and more adventurous. He gave them a much embroidered account of his adventures, delightfully conscious of her attention, and after they had all gone early to bed, he lay awake for ages.

Amplified muezzins were booming between buildings, the rising sun unkindly revealing their cracked cement seediness. Ibrahim woke wondering where he was, and when he realized felt reluctant to get out of bed, both because it was comfortable and because he knew that the act of getting up would inaugurate another day of nervous effort. But he knew what he had to do, and he was ready when Gharab looked cheerfully in around the door. "Ah, so you're up, sleepy head! Good. But hurry, hurry—it's almost time to go!"

He let in a noise of traffic and the allurement of coffee. There was just time for some, perfectly sweet and grainy, and bread with honey (he was deflated not to see the younger Sumira), before the two men were out in the still chill street. As they walked, Gharab explained where Ibraham could stock up on food and water. There was time, just, for rushed thanks, then his benefactor left him standing on a swarming street corner—feeling if anything even lonelier than when he had alighted from the bus.

He bought food and water, and then all roads converged on the train station, built in 1860 by a French architect in an already outdated neo-classical style, which looked extraordinarily inappropriate amongst all the simpler vernacular buildings which crowded up to its once aristocratic eaves. Ibraham walked around behind it as he had been directed, and parallel to the line beyond the main terminal until he saw the sidings, with trains being shunted and a sound of hammering. There were trains close to the fence—and that fence was just a rusty few strands with wide gaps between. The street was empty, the facing wall windowless. It was the work of a few seconds to scramble through and get behind a train and out of view. He tried a few doors—all locked!—and was starting to feel very conspicuous, when the fifth door he tried rolled back silently, revealing serried crates of dates. Perfect!

He threw in his kitbag, jumped in and tugged the door back into place—just in time, for two overalled men turned the corner a few seconds later, and walked along talking a couple of metres from where he crouched amongst a smell of new wood and distant fruit, covering his mouth so they wouldn't hear his breathing. Now, he would just have to wait, and hope that the train was going north.

He shifted uncomfortably on the hard planked floor for a long time, and listened to other trains arriving and leaving, cars on the road, occasional shouts and a burst of laughter, and something scratching around at the far end. A rat? He'd root it out when the train set off. It must have been around three hours later that he was aware of a gentle jolt as a manoeuvering engine nuzzled the first of the long linked file of freight cars. There was a coupling clank, more chatting railwaymen passing close—then with a long scraping squeal, the engine started to strain out of the station.

At last he could move and make noise. Through gaps in the wooden upright planks of the sides, he watched grim suburbs falling away. Then the train was ejected into the desert, picking up speed as it pointed towards Syria. Once over the border, it would not stop until it reached Damascus, and after that Turkey. The dates were intended for Europeans in five star hotels. He could not have picked a better train.

After about 30 minutes, the train slowed down until it was moving at walking pace. Then it stopped, for a long time. Men's voices, speaking Arabic in an unfamiliar accent. Syrians? He peered through the slats. A group of border police were crunching along the trackside gravel with a guard. As they came to each car, the guard would throw open the doors and the police would look in cursorily, tick a clipboard, close the doors and pass a thin cable through the handles, securing it with a little lead bonding seal.

Ibraham crouched into a breathless ball while they looked into his carriage. Squinting under the pallet, he could see a policeman's head for a second, then someone said something, and the door was slammed shut. There was a scratching sound as the cable and seal were applied, a hawking sound and a copious-sounding spit, then receding scrunching footfalls. Ten minutes later, with a creak and a jerk, the train was off again, and Ibraham was in his third country in 48 hours—a double refugee, doubly illegal, doubly delighted and frightened. He would have been more frightened if he had known about the violent demonstrations in Damascus and other cities.

Glimpsed through the slats, between flicking telephone poles, the landscape looked like Iraq—level, thirsty, still except far-off birds or rare people with mules, defeated-looking villages, concrete sub-stations. It soon became boring, and he began to nod—so he nearly fell over when a crate down the far end was shoved aside, and a young man emerged, blinking and scruffy.

"I saw you climbing aboard in Zarqa. But I kept quiet until we had got over the border. Are you from Iraq?"

They eyed each other warily, but Ibrahim was secretly pleased to have company.

"Where to?"

"Turkey."

"Me, too."

"Where are you really going?"

"England."

"Me, too. I've got a cousin in Manchester."

Ibrahim had heard of Manchester, but it conveyed only one thing. "David Beckham!" They laughed at the cliché.

He was Maged el-Jannah from Najaf. His father and mother had been killed by a bomb. His soldier brother had disappeared, and was probably dead. He had been in the army, too, but had simply gone home and hidden his rifle when the Americans got to Najaf. Maged had no ties, but he did have a few thousand dollars obtained by selling some things that he had "found." Ibraham respected the vagueness. Who was not hiding some secret? He wasn't going to start telling people about working for Kemali.

Maged was talking. "I'd be a fool to stay. This mess could go on for years. I've heard anyone can get into England, and the chances of being expelled are very small. I've even heard—get this!—that they'll give you a house to live in, and help with your food costs, and pay you if you aren't working. And there are free schools and hospitals. And if you feel like working, you can get rich! And then what about those girls?"

He talked about women and lots of other things with an apparent expertise that made Ibraham sick with envy. As the train clattered towards Damascus, they talked and dozed until eventually the train swung and squealed into Damascus, resuming their places of concealment while the train was stationary in the marshalling yard. Beyond the station perimeter were ugly tower blocks, with laundry sagging from balconies. Over the background rumble of traffic and what sounded a little like shooting, someone was playing Choubi Choubi very loudly, followed by a song by local girl Abeer Foda, who was also popular in Iraq. "We won't be hearing much of *her* in England." Ibraham observed thoughtfully. Neither spoke again until the train started to pull through the northern suburbs.

Rattle and squeak, rattle and squeak, rattle and squeak, and a soothing sleepy rhythm, while the wide desert became farmland. They ran out of things to talk about, so played guessing games. They broke into a crate of dates and killed a stowaway tarantula, taking care that the broken-in side could not be seen from the doors. The day ended and they were enveloped in fragrant dusk occasionally relieved by the filtered flickering lights of unknown towns. There was an icy draught from the crack between the doors. The floor was hard and unyielding, and Ibraham got a bad splinter in his hand.

At about 11 o'clock, the train again slowed. The border! Their adventure could end here, with discovery and deportation—*or* they could get across the last barrier before Europe. They checked their possessions were concealed. They stood up and sat down again. They could see nothing except occasional lights, or the headlights of cars passing nearby. Then they flinched in a glare of striped halogen as they crawled into a floodlit zone. Finally, the train shuddered to a halt and the engine was turned off. For the first time in 24 hours the carriage was motionless. There was a brief outburst of voices and footsteps, then all was quiet. The border was closed, and they would have several more hours yet in suspended animation.

They looked tensely towards each other in the obscurity, occasionally exchanging whispers—the sibilance almost as loud in that quiet as normal speech. But the only sounds that came from outside were cicadas and the buzzing of lights. Outside, a CCTV camera described ceaseless circles but all it showed the bored guard in the control centre a kilometre away was a pair of jackals, snuffling slyly just on the edge of vision. He tapped his feet to Damascus Radio and wandered in and out of wakefulness. There was trouble in the capital again, and the tanks had gone in hard, but out here it was pleasantly quiet. The refugees always headed for the road-crossings.

The cold became intense, and the travellers sat back-to-back for warmth, wrapped in all their blankets and draughts blocked off as much as possible with kitbags. But the draughts came from every direction, and they could not stop shivering. Ibraham would have given a great deal for a hot drink. Yet he was still sufficiently filled with the sense of adventure to try to cheer up his companion by saying, "I bet in a few years' time we'll be looking back on this little episode and wishing we were back here, having this great adventure!" Maged snorted and swore under his breath.

It was a bleary-eyed relief when the day shift came on with a blast of engines, cheery voices, the slamming of doors, cheap cologne, and cigarettes. Powerful trucks started up close by, as vehicles that had not made it across last night rolled towards the barrier-booths. Voices were heard without warning just a couple of metres away, and brisk hands rattled the doors—"Yes, this one's fine!"—then the voices were gone again, to be heard again one carriage down, two carriages down and gone away, while they swallowed their hearts back down and smiled in relief. The train engine shuddered into rheumy life.

They were the unknowing beneficiaries of the ending of a decade of distrust, as the Syrians distanced themselves from their Kurdish protégés and an Ankara frustrated by Europe sought new strategic partners. The train nudged forward. Peeking through the gaps, they could see official buildings, a long line of trucks, two high flagpoles, one with the pan-Arabist emblem of Syria, the other red with a white crescent moon and star. Two uniformed men were standing close by; Ibraham could see hawk badges on their green, peaked caps. He wondered what kind of men they were, and what Syria was like. He suddenly realized that he had been all the way through a country without touching its soil, and the thought disturbed him. It didn't feel like travel. Then the train was picking up speed, and the flags were receding as they passed unnoticed out of the Arab world.

Chapter 7
Vox Metrop

Aldgate, London
Tuesday, 6th August

As so often happened, John's article summed up a sensibility.

> The world woke yesterday to a tragic reminder of the evil of exclusion. Although it is still uncertain exactly what happened to the 37 men, women and children (and one surviving man) whose bodies were washed up on the Eastshire coast, what is clear is that they would still be alive if this government did not pander so cynically to the grubby agenda of the tabloid press and the organized racism of National Union. As too often before, xenophobia and ignorance have triumphed over generosity and humanity.
>
> There are disturbing suggestions that some victims reached the shore alive—only to be murdered as they lay helpless. This is a new kind of viciousness, based on the lowest of emotions—hatred

and fear of 'The Other', an inhuman unwillingness to let those who have nothing share in our wealth and privilege—emotions that are exploited by editors and politicians to sell products or get the racist vote. They should be ashamed, for what they have done out of greed and ambition—and we should be ashamed, for tolerating such sickening abuses in the 21st century.

This is part of a planetwide pattern of *Poujadiste* prejudice. How many more lives must be lost before we see action against the xenophobes? We must educate, enlighten and enlist those who have still not come to terms with shifting realities. The world is changing. The world is on the move. The world is coming here. Its advent is culturally desirable and economically essential. It is also inevitable—and should be embraced, not excluded. Those who cannot modernise are the enemy.

One fat farmer interviewed on TV even smirked, and called the tragic ones 'aliens', and said they weren't 'what we're used to around here'. But his world is dying—ours is being born. A challenging but exciting new reality is being born—emerging from a thousand planes, scrambling out of the backs of trucks, exploding out of the holds of ships, downloaded from the Internet, broadcast through the media, springing to life in the installations of a thousand people's artists. We are all outsiders now.

We must come to terms with change. We must send uncompromising signals that we will no longer tolerate the intolerable. The police must not only solve this terrible crime, but act against broadcasters and editors who have exacerbated the climate of hatred. Freedom of speech—which we cherish—does not mean a licence to be offensive.

Legislators and campaigners need to start urgent debates not just about people smuggling, but also the limits of hate-speech, and whether a modern nation-state really needs immigration controls at all. Apart from being historically and intellectually incoherent—who are 'indigenous Britons'?—immigration controls give comfort to those who target the most vulnerable in our society.

His conclusion was destined to be cited globally:

> Let this cataclysmic event be a wake-up call to our politicians, broadcasters, artists, teachers, civil servants, and to Britain as a whole—a wake-up call that proclaims to the world that this really *is* a country of tolerance and fair play. Let the Crisby Catastrophe go down in history as a turning point, marking the time when racism was finally washed up. We must speak with one voice—NO to the politics of fear, YES to the politics of freedom.

He was thrilled to see his name emblazoned right across the top of the front page—above and larger than that of Jan Hradcany, a former priest who had been part of the anti-Soviet underground. That'll drive the old hangover *mad*, John thought exultantly. Who gives a shit about all that ancient history, those polysyllabic sentences and abstruse concepts? *This*—he smacked the paper, causing some sitting near him on the Tube to look at him curiously for a second before remembering their manners—*this* is what counts. *These* are the battle-lines of the now-and-future wars. He was pleased with the phrase and wrote down "the battle-lines of the now-and-future wars" with his fountain pen in the little leather notebook he used to differentiate himself from the clones.

Approbatory e-mails awaited him in the office. "So BRAVE! Keep fighting the good fight!"—"As always—controversial but incontrovertible. Well done"—"Totally rad!"—"*La lotta continua!*" The best came from a Cabinet minister: "Congratulations on a courageous piece of writing, with which I agree wholeheartedly. Rest assured at least some of us in government feel the same way."

There were a few pseudonymonymous messages he liked less: "Your'e article is politicl correctness gone mad"—"This is OUR country—England 4 the english"—"if u love them so much why don't u live their?" He deleted these messages with a faint cleansing feeling—as if he had cleared a blocked drain. If only the repellent "writers" could be disposed of so handily.

There was also a message asking if he would appear on that evening's *The Capital Today*. 24/7 Media was one of the broadcasters he disliked. It had recently screened a play by a playwright who had been assaulted in Johannesburg and who had extrapolated from the particular to the general in an incandescent diary entry. John and many others couldn't believe that they had simply shown the play and *never once* alluded to the man's obnoxious views. They had also done a *Puck of Pook's Hill* adaptation for their children's channel, without even mentioning Kipling's unacceptable racial stereotyping. So his first reaction was to refuse. Yet *TCT* had an audience of millions. It could be a rare opportunity to use the medium against the Establishment. After all, he reasoned, why should views like his be excluded because they were controversial? And not that it mattered, but the fee would come in handy—he had his eye on that Mzoso neon installation, for the dark corner beside the bay window. Mzoso always retained his value. So he e-mailed an acceptance before checking other messages—Mummy, Janet, Charlotte, Mummy again. He didn't feel like speaking to his mother at the moment—more moaning about her operation, probably. He wasn't in the mood for Janet either. It would be more whinging—"When will you be home? Not late again, I hope!" It was so typical of her to think only of her own needs. But Charlotte…he hadn't seen her for *weeks*. Excitement tingled through him.

Later, he was in a new Audi, gliding along unexpectedly rainy streets, sitting unstuffily beside the driver as that operative stop-started along Fleet Street, heading for the *TCT* studio at MediaHub/e1. The traffic was even worse than usual, and hunched people pushed along puddled pavements, or picked their way across the road towards Cannon Street and fuggy trains out along dirty yellow viaducts to south London or ruined Kent. The *Nightly News* vendors alone stoically endured—pulling limp copies out from under golf umbrellas for the rare customers who stopped long enough for the sake of instantly soggy sports news.

Privates, the gay-soldier musical Janet wanted to see, was on at the Grand; but he had vetoed going to the theatre with her ever again, after the Ibsen when she had decided to feel sick and had pushed past everyone practically *running*. Everyone had glared. She had ruined the play for everyone. It was sadly typical of her. If only she would *try* sometimes! She really would have to go, but he quailed at the thought of the scene she would make. He wished he had never allowed her to move in—but then he hadn't wanted to hurt her feelings. Next time, he'd put his needs first. But the driver was speaking. "What programme are you on tonight?"

"*The Capital Today.*"

"Oh, yeh, Imogen Williams's programme. I never see it. I'm always working when it goes out. She's a bit of all right though!"

The driver leered conspiratorially, and John gave back a tight smile. He never quite felt fully at ease with the kind of people who made sexist comments. But it was his duty, in a way, to engage with this kind of person, however difficult. The driver went on, "Terrible business up in Eastshire."

"That's what we'll be talking about tonight. I feel very strongly that this government's really to blame."

"Oh? Why's that?"

"Well, if there weren't immigration controls, there wouldn't be any need for people to come in illegally, would there?"

"Err, well...I suppose not"—A guilty sideways look of rain-strained eyes—"But don't you need immigration controls? You know—terrorists, drug-smugglers...and you can't have too many people coming in. The traffic's bad enough as it is!"

John exhaled loudly, and the driver winced. This was *it*, thought John—this was the Great Enemy in person (if you could call such an insensate lump a person)—the great ignorant idle lump that re-elected governments year after year, decade after decade, or sometimes even voted National Union—the caucus that perpetuated injustice and exclusion, kept the tabloids in business, ate in burger places, and watched movies about car-chases.

The issues were so obvious—but not to these people, so secure in their smug inertia. How could someone like this, with his limited education, comprehend such abstractions as economic necessity, cultural enrichment or international obligations? How could someone like him see that migration was just one facet of an overarching problem—poverty and environmental degradation and Third World debt and racism and shameful histories and resource wars—all thrown up, tumbled together on a deathly silent beach?

This driver—all the country's drivers—never thought for themselves, but relied on talk radio and tabloids for their facts and opinions. His family and friends would be just like him—as were too many millions of others. John felt sorry for them—so uninformed, exploited, afraid of change.

But then he remembered for whom pity should be reserved and began to feel faintly contaminated by the man's proximity—so close physically, so remote intellectually. Duty or not, it just didn't seem worth the effort to explain to this fat-armed man with his bad barbering, faint hint of sweat, and too-small nylon shirt, so he said merely. "It's a long story. Watch tonight's programme…oh, you can't!"

"No."

The rest of the journey was stiffly silent except for the sluicing of the wipers and the rumbling swish and leaping-up iron walls of buses. The shower tailed off and there was a stripe of sky and a sudden stab of sun on glistening Portland and phalanxes of windows—MediaHub/e1, the vast "Communication Cosmos" inserted sensitively into a redundant church, urban-edgily surrounded by thronging Bengali suburbs. The driver pulled up beneath a canopy. "This is it, mate." John muttered, "OK, *mate!*" and got out, slamming the door to draw a line under the unsavoury memory of the journey.

A skinny, purple-haired woman was waiting inside. John's eyes flicked over her analytically. Bad hair. Flat chest. Eyes too close. Lesbian? "Mr Leyden? Oh—*Dr.* Leyden. Sorry—no-one mentioned that to me! Anyway, hello. I'm Lesley."

He followed her along a brightly carpeted windowless corridor with photos of previous guests who had appeared on the award-winning show, and into the Green Room. John abstracted a glass of dry white wine from the smiling steward, and went over to the other contributors. He knew them, or most of them, so cut through Lesley's introductions with an airy wave.

There was Richard Simpson, Workers' Party MP for the former mining constituency of Newtown, who was nicknamed "Spitson" because he sprayed as he spoke—short, chubby, red-faced, thick-lipped, white-haired, Estuary, wearing a repulsive light green suit which looked as if it had been made for a slenderer man around 1974. He was old-WP, out of sympathy with the reformists' coalition government with the Fair Play Alliance—ex-binman, ex-shop steward, non-conformist millenarian Methodist turned militant millenarian atheist, always angry veteran of the Anti-Fascist Front and anti-capitalist rallies.

Any remote possibility of rapprochement with the government, as well as his acceptability to the WP Left, had been lessened recently after an employee in his constituency office had denounced him as a sexist and racist who joked about saris and curry. The case had gone to a tribunal—covered relishingly by the right-wing press. He had been exonerated, but it had cost him. To add to his problems, the National Unionists were making electoral inroads in Newtown. There was also controversy about an expenses claim for a topiary hammer-and-sickle at his country home, which seemed rather less of a good postmodern joke now than it had at the time.

Both because he was genuinely concerned, but also because he was determined to recapture lost moral territory, he had spoken out that morning on the airwaves and asked if the Home Secretary would condemn the racist killings in Eastshire, which were a totally sick'ning tragedy and a travesty of yooman rights—and whether he would also condemn recent attempts by certain Opposition politicians to exploit racial sentiment for political purposes. CD Leader Doug McKerras had agreed with his otherwise opponent that the deaths in Eastshire were a very great tragedy, and that exploiting race for political purposes was part of a planetwide pattern of *Poujadiste* prejudice.

John saw people like Simpson as a kind of necessary evil, a rough auxiliary against reaction, and shivered with inward repulsion as he noted that Simpson's polyester lapels were stippled with ancient saliva. But he had read John's column and had even noticed that the Opposition Leader had picked up on John's phrase about *Poujadiste* prejudice. John couldn't help being pleased—but he stood beyond splutter range.

There was a second MP, Evan Dafydd of the Fair Play Alliance—an earnest barrister, fluent in Welsh, blond, brachycephalic, immaculate if inexpensive clothes, irreproachable private life, fervent believer in international law and clean drains. He was the Coalition spokesperson on Transgendered Ethnic Minorities, and as rotating chair of the Fair Play for Islam Forum, he had recently been commissioned by a major publisher to translate the Koran into Welsh. Dafydd was a notorious bore, but a bore who was likely soon to be a cabinet minister. He was the kind of reader John wanted, so he smiled politely and assumed his listening face.

Then there was the required Opposition representative, Sir Stanley Symons, who had returned gratefully to the backbenches after the last CD government had fallen, leaving his department roughly the same for his three year incumbency as Minister. He had no ambitions left now, but he had also forgotten the knack of working—so he let his legal practice slide as he languished on the Opposition benches, his sneering, unhandsome features reinforcing the popular impression of the Opposition as a misanthropic, anachronistic rearguard out of sympathy with the times. He was a burly man with huge ears and a mottled wattle, which moved faintly horribly when he talked—which he did a great deal.

But as John had always acknowledged, whatever else you might say about the CDs, at least they knew about clothes. Symons' pinstripe was well-chosen, the stripes sufficiently slender and the right distance apart. Yet he had Executive Scalp. The jacket's shoulders were scurfy, the thickest drifts immediately below his amazing earlobes, which were so long they almost touched his shirt collar. Westminster wits called him "Dumbo"—partly because of these attributes, but also because of the paucity of his contributions to debates in the House.

But he had a lot on his mind that evening. He had been given a hint that he was in line for a peerage and was wondering if this would make any difference to his new secretary's delightfully haughty demeanour. A lot of ladies would do a lot if they thought they might become Ladies. This was all he could think of as he was pumping John's hand without any idea whose hand it was. "Delighted, delighted," he boomed absently, releasing surprisingly noxious breath that made John blink.

Then came the more agreeably regular features of Dylan Ekinutu-Jones, of the Forum for Racial and Ethnic Equality (FREE). He was the 29-year-old son of an English mother and an absentee Nigerian businessman, a graduate in politics, quick-thinking, quick-talking, working as a WP researcher and anxious to become an MP.

He was also discreetly homosexual—his father would have *killed* him if he had known—and more than anything else, Dylan had always wanted to do what his father would have wanted. As a boy, he had even had a superstitious notion that if he did the right thing, somehow his father might even come home to Edmonton Crescent. It was partly to overcompensate for this embarrassing erotic orientation that he had learned to emphasize his blackness. It was a more acceptable badge of difference—and he soon discovered he got instant respect. He had just become a Cohesion Affairs adviser to the police—youthful misdemeanours notwithstanding. In fact, he had been told by a police inspector that these had actually helped him to get the position, because they had given him special insight into the alienation of youth in an exclusionary society.

His eyes widened when he met John, who was one of his favourite writers—but he found himself unexpectedly stuck for words. He stood there listening to John's commonplaces with a rapt smile and approbatory nods. John thought Dylan likeable and clearly intelligent, and said to him pleasantly, "You know, this is the sort of human contact racists miss out on." He turned away to say something else, and didn't notice that Dylan wasn't pleased by the remark.

The only panelist John didn't recognize was Carole Hassan of the Muslim Alliance, the daughter of a devoutly Catholic roadworker who had exchanged Mayo for Leeds in 1965. Much to her parents' perturbation, she had converted to Islam upon a just-in-time marriage to a local newsagent who had tumbled her in his stock-room amongst boxes of out-of-date chocolate and unsold copies of *Big Boobs*. Her father had never reconciled himself to the idea; he vaguely felt it was even worse than if she had become a Protestant. To please her new husband and his contemptuous extended family, she swiftly became a stricter Muslim than they had ever dreamed of being. But it had not sufficed to save the marriage. Husband and wife now lived a continent apart, he in Lahore, she and their daughter in West Dinsdale, where she worked hard as an equality adviser to the town council, salving her guilt about not being a full-time mother by opining on global Islam. She was so busy with this that she scarcely left the house outside work hours. Her pale and doughy face (too much sitting and starchy food) peered out through the black tube of a *hijab* at a world she couldn't comprehend but could occasionally influence.

She nodded unsmilingly at John, and ignored his proffered hand; John pulled it back with a flash of self-anger. He should have known better. She didn't approve of the *Examiner* anyway, with all its profanities. Besides, the intellectual effort of that day had already been considerable. She had left home early to speak at an European seminar, "Muslim and Marginalized—Life in a Northern Town," at a hotel in Kensington—its Regency icecream elegance in notable contrast to her new-build. John found himself slightly intimidated by her moon-faced physiognomy, looking out defensively from its sable cocoon. It seemed to him perverse that anyone would wish to set themselves apart from society—and that anyone could seriously believe all that shit about "The Prophet." But he also felt a kind of curious envy. She was both a relic from a securer world, and an emblem of the future. He turned back to the others, while Carole stood slightly apart, envious of their male masonry, their articulacy and command.

Symons excused himself fruitily in answer to the demands of his prostate, and while he was gone, Simpson jumped in joyously. "You know why 'e's 'ere, don't you? That racist researcher used to work for 'im!"

He was alluding to a recent incident in which a CD employee had used her work e-mail to send what were coyly described as "offensive e-mails" to someone who had forwarded them to a blog used by National Unionist sympathizers. Disowned immediately by Doug McKerras, briefed against by shadowy "senior colleagues" and quizzed by the police, she had apologized and stressed her commitment to Christian Democrat Core Value 1, which all employees were supposed to carry on their person at all times—"We seek an equitable society, in which diversity is balanced with duty." But it was much too little, and she had always been too late; the following day she had dematerialized from political life. A relieved Doug McKerras told the Commons—"Our rapid response to this crisis has shown that we will not tolerate offensive sentiments. Such sentiments are wrong in themselves and divisive in their effects. We are committed to rooting out racism within society. Insult one, you insult all"—and the Prime Minister had thanked him for his responsible approach to richness. The Fair Play leader had reminded the House that they must not be complacent—and all but one of the 650 MPs had hear-heared and waved their papers at the united statesmen.

The sole dissenter was the newly elected MP from National Union, a chubby dipsomaniac who had been elected in a West Midlands seat against all the odds, and now formed a one-man caucus that met with itself in inconvenient corners of the bars, while other MPs laughed and chatted ostentatiously across and (morally far) above him.

"And Symons?" asked Dafydd, secure on this subject, and all others.

"Stan's all righ.' Wish I could say the same for all CDs! The rycist communi'y is part of their core vote. If thye didn't 'ave the CDs to vote for, they'd vote NU."

John cut in, also totally secure on the subject. "But such views shouldn't be tolerated from *anyone*. If the CDs want to be treated with respect, they need to get rid of their dinosaurs. Then they can vote to ban NU without worrying about losing some of their supporters."

Dafydd was worried. "I'd like to ban NU as much as you, but it's difficult with the human-rights laws. Even they have rights—some of them claim they're human!"

Comfortable laughs from everyone but Carole. Like her, John was thinking about Simpson's tribunal; he had been critical of Simpson himself. Even well-meaning people were often tainted.

Lesley shepherded them towards a door, and they were suddenly pierced by lights, with a multihued blur of faces fidgeting beyond the glare. Imogen Williams came to say hello, while a technician adjusted the microphone on her classic blue suit.

The celebrated anchorwoman looked tired up close, her mascara caked and crinkled around once arresting eyes. The arc-lights glinted on the metal slide restraining slightly less metallic hair. She had been born in Glasgow, but had been trying to live it down ever since—so successfully that most presumed she was from the Home Counties. This perceived "poshness" made her relationship with Scum, notorious "polysexual" singer of Atrocities Against Civilians, all the more intriguing to the tabloids.

"Are you all happy? Good, good. You know the format? OK, ya. Obviously tonight's about the Bodies on the Beach. I'll ask you for your reactions. You will have the chance to make one answer—about a minute each. Then there will be a short series of video reports. Then it's a general Q&A. After about 30 minutes, all of you make a closing statement. It should all be finished by about 8, and we can all get home to see it when it's broadcast! OK? Great!"

She had already turned away, her "Great!" hanging parentless in the nervous air. Then somehow they were all seated and wired around a round formica table with an outline of London edged by tiny red bulbs, waxing as the lights above were dimmed. The stage lights went up to tinny trumpets.

"Good evening and welcome to *The Capital Today*. I'm Imogen Williams. Tonight"—the vast screen behind was filled by an aerial shot of the sad strand—"BODIES ON THE BEACH—Murder and racism on a quiet coast—the high water mark of hate."

The trumpets faded, and all eyes swivelled towards Imogen, pretty and petite, clever and committed, in front of the screen. Squaring her shoulders and daring the camera to move with her impassioned gaze, she began:

"The east coast is a place of donkey rides and kiss-me-quick hats. But this week, it became a much, much darker place. At least 37 men, women, and children, apparently asylum-seekers, have lost their lives seeking to enter Britain.

"As if this was not terrible enough, it now seems likely that several of these unfortunate people got ashore alive, only to be murdered in cold blood. It is almost impossible to believe it, but these castaways—desperate, in need of urgent medical attention, and full of human dignity—may have found death at the hands of local people.

"Only one man knows the answer, and tonight he is fighting for his life in hospital. Tonight, as a massive man hunt continues across the North Sea, *The Capital Today* investigates what it is like to be an asylum-seeker in Fortress Europe, with three true stories. We will also examine the shocking and violent reality of rural racism. And finally, we will debate what this means for our immigration system. How can we prevent further terrible tragedies? How can we turn hate into *hope*?"

She turned to Camera 3.

"Preliminary investigations suggest that the victims were asylum-seekers from many countries. At some time on Tuesday night, the refugees, including women and children, had been thrown overboard from a ship by human traffickers. The police speculate that the people-smugglers dumped their passengers in a hurry—perhaps fearing boarding by customs or coastguard officials. But the story becomes even more horrific. Three of the dead bodies, and the surviving man, were found to bear gunshot wounds. Police are working on the hypothesis that these unfortunate people reached the shore alive, but were then attacked by local racists. To discuss this shocking event and what it means, and decide what needs to be done, we have assembled a distinguished panel of experts."

Simpson's harsh tones were ameliorated by his altruism.

"Thank you, Imogen. This, lydies and gen'lemen, is a terrible business, a disgryce to a so-called civilized country. It must—repeat, must—myke us tike radical haction. The cancer of racism must be torn out of our society. I 'ave my differences with the gov'nment, as yoo will know, but on this we hagree—we need to find a wye of improving our himmigration laws so that such tragedies cannot recur hagain. Racism must be heradicated. We need a compre'ensive, broad-bysed agreement to reform our hantiquated immigration laws, and clamp down on people-smuggling. But we need more than that—we need a total chynge in attitudes, so that the most vulnerable in our society are protected now and forever."

Enthusiastic applause—then it was Sir Stanley, the light accentuating his port-wine physiognomy and visible pinkly through those extraordinary ears:

"Richard is absolutely right. All of us in the mainstream parties condemn unreservedly the traffickers and those implicated in this terrible, terrible crime against humanity. It is vitally important that we stand together to defeat these common enemies. We need to use the utmost sanction of the law against all who are responsible. We need and want immigration, but it is important to aim for a truly colour-blind, meritocratic society—with an aspirational but appropriate immigration policy."

There was noticeably less applause at the cooler sentiment—although there was always less applause at anything any Christian Democrat ever said. Evan Dafydd was pleased to be next, his attractive accent lent force by appropriate gestures. From an extended generational string of chapel-goers, expressiveness came naturally to him—as had his school nickname, "Dafydd Yadda Yadda." His blondness was enhaloed by the lights. Parallel hands, safe hands, palms facing in, fingers pointing towards the audience, to explain and encapsulate everything.

"Good evening, ladies and gentlemen. No-one condemns this horrible crime more than my party. We have always supported the relaxation"—hands opened outwards and upwards, embracing freedom—"of our immigration laws, both for economic reasons and because we know how much society benefits from diversity. We have also always supported tighter control of guns, and of legislating against race-hatred. We believe in *embracing* the world, not excluding it."

His hands were boxing in the grave but manageable problem. Then they reached out in acceptance and supplication. "I hope that these events can bring forth a common response from all actors and stakeholders, and become a driver for change. Events like this underline our common humanity—and reinforce the need for radical action—for all our sakes."

Redoubled applause and then it was Dylan, nervous but quietly insistent, looking into the camera while plucking at the desk:

"The innocent people who died on Tuesday were trying to make better lives for themselves—away from violence and upheaval, torn away from their own cultures and peoples. It is sadly ironic that they should have met such terrible deaths so close to what they must have seen as a Promised Land. Maybe some of them were hoping to join friends and family here. When I hear about events like this, I always ask myself what if one of these dead people had been *my* father? I feel ashamed of my country (and it is MY country) for two reasons—firstly, that our country can harbour thugs who could harm refugees—but equally importantly that this government has made it so difficult to immigrate that desperate people have to go to such lengths to get into the country. I hope we can work together to eradicate the evil people-smuggling racket, and to combat domestic racism—and turn Fortress Europe into FREE EUROPE!"

Then it was Carole's turn. From out of her cocoon came a flat West Riding voice, which many members of the audience guiltily thought inconsistent with her garb.

"As a representative of the British Muslim community, I am thinking of my brothers and sisters aboard that ship—how they came looking for safety, but found only death. It's key we find those who are responsible. Tonight, there will be feelings of unease among the Muslim community. This is potentially dangerous, as British Muslims are already alienated by institutional racism, social exclusion, deprivation, and this government's foreign policy. This government needs to reassure the Muslim community by clamping down not just on traffickers in human misery, but racists at home."

Her concentration on Islam made some in the audience uneasy. A turbaned man in the front row looked at the ground and did not applaud.

Then it was John's turn. Clearing his throat, looking commandingly into the camera, the epitome of coolness and compassion, he delivered the words he had been rehearsing all afternoon:

"I believe that there are times in history when issues suddenly become very clear—and society is galvanized into radical reform. This is one of those times. The dead bodies on that beach are the harbingers of a kind of revolution—a revolution against a system that doesn't care, and against a tiny minority who are both cruel and stupid. For too long, the Establishment has gone along with xenophobia and racism—and has silenced radical voices who speak up for humanity. It's time for this to stop. It's time to reform not just our laws, but our whole country and way of life. It's time to MAKE BRITAIN BETTER!"

As he uttered the last sentence he rapped the desk on every word to add emphasis. The applause exceeded even that given to Simpson—who, for a millisecond, was caught on camera looking annoyed. Then all faces smoothed and opened, as the huge screen filled up with an enormous face. A young Rwandan woman was speaking, and in her soft, subtitled voice, there was a universe of suffering.

Afterwards, excited questions and engaged opinions bubbled up. Varied accents and educational levels—rapid-fire and nervy, stately and sure, shrewd or naive—a warm bath of worry, and wanting to help. There was a generous pity for all who had died—as *they* might have died, if *they* had been on that ship. Why had it happened? Who was responsible? *Who* could do something like that to fellow humans? What should be done? Could there be more cooperation between governments— NGOs—international bodies? Couldn't our government do more to improve conditions in the countries from which the immigrants came? Could more be done to educate the public?

The panellists and audience testified together to their outrage. It was a release for people who too rarely felt they were part of something bigger. Tonight's debate 'ad demonstrated, Simpson opined, how far we had come as a nytion. It was time, Dylan believed, to make racism socially unacceptable. Reality had hit the nation in its pasty white face.

(Some pasty faces seemed less certain for a few seconds, but they knew it wasn't *their* fault, *they* could transcend, were transcending.) The lessons of the past were too obvious to need to be explicated (although they were). We must not forget. Never again. Not in *my* name.

There was a certitude and connectivity in the studio—a feeling that whatever else everyone might disagree about, this was a common cause—a trust derived from human rights, or God, or a blend of both. The audience, recently strangers, had formed a conspiracy against evil. It was a meeting of brave individual minds. The format loosened and flowed, becoming a conversation between friends. Smiles were instinctively thought inappropriate—but there were approving murmurs, sympathetic groans, outbursts of applause, fingertips joined politely below attentive chins. Members of the distinguished panel agreed with their distinguished opponents, all friends for tonight, and all paid tribute to all the actors and drivers for change—and of course the bravery and nobility of all the featured immigrants, whose *sans-papiers* experiences brought angry tears to some eyes. Even Imogen seemed affected by the little wise imp-face of Jacob, as he loomed up on the large screen, telling what his 7-year-old eyes had seen, and how he had felt when the Italian policeman had found him, cold and hungry, alone on the big, clean train.

The only slight wrinkle was when a man from Romford called Daniel Williams raised a stubby-fingered, hard-palmed hand, and said in an accent as carking as a crow: "I feel sorry for the people that died and all, but illegal immigrants 'ave always tiken risks. All I'm saying is that this ain't our fault. And we do need himmigration controls. We 'aven't had no controls for years!"

There were intakes of breath, shocked looks, shaking heads. How could such attitudes be among us, as out of place as a Neanderthal lumbering down Oxford Street? Those who sat near the questioner leaned away—not wishing to be thought his friends, or to be lending even tacit support. Young Asians with goatee beards stirred angrily, while everyone muttered and glared. Imogen Williams honed straight in, Torquemada in Armani—"That seems a very harsh way of looking at this tragedy. Surely no law is worth the death of human beings, even if they are undocumented. These are people dying just because they haven't got some pathetic piece of paper, for God's sake!"

One of the Asians spoke with a Caribbeanized accent. "It's OK 'im talking like tha'. 'e's never been a refugee, 'e's never had to flee no oppression, 'e's never had no racist atti'udes against 'im. People like 'im 'ave to move wiv the times. Know wot I'm sayin?'" Emphatic "Yehs!" and cheers.

A young black man interposed, "We ain't got no reason to trus' the police. It's OK for 'im, but black peepol don't trus' them."

A young black woman, her brow furrowed by distaste, chimed in. "I can't *believe* people can still think in this way. Someone of my background means little or nothing to him. I suppose he's a *Sentinel* reader. Besides, we're all immigrants from *somewhere*. Come on—join the human race!" Prolonged whoops, clapping and foot-stamping.

An elderly white woman, a charity worker filled with certitude (and two gins and tonic), told him to cheers and claps—"I feel *sorry* for you, young man. You are *so* closed to the world!" Whoops and cheers, satisfied laughter, feet banging. The boom microphone swung back towards Daniel Williams, and he tried again. "All I'm sying is tha' a country's got to have controls, hannit? You can't just let everyone come, can ya?"

"Who let *you* come tonight—the zooman?" shouted a triumphant West Indian voice suddenly, and everyone laughed. Williams was mired in turpitude, beneath contempt, dismissed, lost; they were deaf not only to his argument, but his existence. He shrank back into the bright background, crushed, beneath consideration. The dissonance dissipated, and ironically made the atmosphere seem even pleasanter because now here was a short, balding, badly dressed, badly spoken, fidgeting foe of the people—out of tune with his times, an appropriate figurehead for indefensible views.

The incident was smoothed over, the hour was up, and Imogen Williams was holding Camera 1 with her come-on eyes. "I'm afraid that is all we have time for this week. But we have had an in-depth discussion of all the issues raised by the tragic events. I would like to say thank you to our distinguished panel members—to our well-informed studio audience—and, of course, to you at home, for watching. See you next time on *TCT*!"

As the theme blared out, audience members were already gathering their raincoats and searching for bags. Danny Williams pulled on his anorak, and shuffled along with the others. A few looked pityingly at him as he went into the E1 evening—and as he walked away, one woman plucked his sleeve, looked around and muttered fiercely, "Well said! *I* agree with you anyway!" Then she hastened away without looking back, and he never even saw her face. The rain had stopped, although fat drops were plopping from the gutters, and a fiercely orange sun was jabbing through lifting cloud. The foe of the people clumped homewards past breeze-bothered puddles reflecting lurid sky and trembling pediments.

Chapter 8
CONTINENTAL DRIFT

Turkey

The train turned north, and the cold carriage became warm and sticky. The rhythm was no longer soothing, but nauseating. Ibraham became homesick for stillness, and felt an almost irresistible urge to jump out of the train—just to feel earth again. Turkey seemed a very large country; he wished he'd learned more at school. Maged had a slightly better geographical grasp, and the names of some of the places seemed to mean something to him—but that may have made it even worse for him, because he was impatient to notch up the next landmark.

The line climbed through wayside vignettes of vineyards, pistachio plantations and tobacco fields. They passed through Gaziantep without stopping—outline of a fortress, chimneys and the smell of soap. The line levelled, and they appraised good-looking farmland with the eyes of men who still knew about land. By 10 o'clock, they were in dramatic-looking mountains with olives and oranges, low trees and lakes. Ibraham longed for an orange. He was still feeling queasy, and wished there was a breeze. The two men were starting to annoy each other—fidgeting, standing up and sitting down, sometimes nearly falling when the train lurched around a bend. Maged was whistling through his teeth; Ibraham had always hated that kind of whistling.

The train wheezed gratefully into Konya main station, as the outside temperature hovered around 30 degrees, and Maged's digital watch told 3:15. The cargo was destined for tomorrow morning's market. They concealed themselves and their bags, empty bottles and food debris, and listened apprehensively to the rising hubbub that had replaced the engine's sound—Tannoy announcements, officious voices, the whirr of a forklift. It was plain that the carriages were being opened and emptied. But all they could do was sit tight.

Their turn! A snap and a click, and a sinewy arm threw open the doors and fixed them back. A cannonball-round, mustachioed head appeared and vanished. There was an electric motor, and the tines of a forklift appeared in the doorway looking like the tusks of a robot elephant. They slid in neatly under one of the pallets, and the driver hoisted and retreated with practiced ease. The travellers nodded to each other, tiptoed to the door and peeked out. Except for the forklift trundling towards a double-doored warehouse several hundred metres away, there was no-one nearby. They jumped out and away. Ibraham staggered and almost fell as they landed on the ground, his legs weak after the enforced idleness, and unaccustomed to the stability of the surface. Maged gave him a steadying arm, and by the time the forklift came back, they had slipped through a providentially empty office—there was a cup of coffee steaming on the desk, and they could hear someone laughing—and shot through a door into a shadowy cul-de-sac crammed with cars. Just a few hundred metres away, they could see a busy road, with a troupe of schoolgirls walking in single file behind their teacher, patriotically smart in brown blouses and red skirts. They looked at the girls longingly, then grinned at each other in complicity.

They felt increasingly conspicuous as they walked towards the junction. It all looked so clean and prosperous by the standards of home. Disorientation was deepened by the sight of advertising billboards in unfamiliar characters. These underlined how far they were away from home, and how difficult it might be to make themselves understood. It was a relief to see poorer-looking buildings, like the ones they were used to—and to see that the people looked not unlike themselves. They wandered on observantly, anxious not to attract any attention. They had been told that the Turkish police would not be well-disposed, and that if they claimed asylum in Turkey they would almost certainly find themselves on the next train back to Syria. Even if they tried to claim asylum in Turkey, it would take years, and they would be held in camps while their cases were being processed. There were bad stories about those camps.

Eager to show Brussels that it was capable of controlling Europe's potentially vastly lengthened borders with failed states, some years ago Ankara had ordered police to turn around illegal immigrants and put them straight back over the border, and raid poor districts in search of overstayers. Detention camps were starved of cash to make them less attractive and a blind eye was turned to beatings by police or warders. Ankara was then perplexed to be criticized by the EU for human rights abuses—and an exasperated minister had said in a cabinet meeting "Well, if they love them so much, they can have them!"

After this, there had been a culture of non-enforcement or even facilitation of entry into Europe, while ebullient delegates signed international agreements on migration and security. There was a quiet forwarding-on of problems to refugee charities in Istanbul, especially Kurdish ones. It was also known officially-unofficially that other refugees made it to small coves on the coast, from where fishing smacks would sail at night for the Greek islands. In one celebrated instance, a local police chief had been taking a proportion of the passage-fees from boats manned by his cousins. This was regarded as unsubtle, and he was very publicly reduced to the ranks. Sometimes, refugee boats would be lost to weather, or picked up by the Greek navy. This was all the better, as they were no longer Turkey's problem. The raids on immigrant areas continued, but now those picked up were as likely to be sent west as east.

Ibraham had always assumed he would be traveling via Istanbul, but after much debate he and Maged had decided they would get a boat to the Greek islands. The Greco-Turkish border was apparently heavily guarded, and neither country would be overjoyed to see them. They had a much better chance among all those islands. The Greek navy couldn't be everywhere.

But first they needed to make themselves look less conspicuous. They felt everyone must notice their stained and crumpled clothes. Eventually, they happened upon a small clothes shop, a narrow, long establishment loud with pop music and lined with clothes in cheap fabrics—traditional styles juxtaposed with T-shirts bearing band and football logos, or almost English-language slogans like "Sexy Beast Contained." The clothes looked marvellously sophisticated to the travellers, and they laughed as they read the slogans and recognized the footballers. They selected a variety of things in dumb show with the help of one of the proprietor's sons, while that notable watched suspiciously from behind the cash desk. He guessed what these unkempt foreigners were, with their unease and their kitbags. That was none of his business, but he knew the sort of tricks they might try.

They had selected slacks and shirts, and Ibrahim asked how much it would cost in dollars, by holding up a bill and looking quizzical. The owner wrote down a figure on a pad and passed it across. He was favourably impressed when Ibrahim paid the grossly inflated price without demurring. He smiled and asked loudly in Turkish, then fractured English. "Are you from Iraq? IRAQ?" There seemed little point in trying to deny it, so they nodded.

"You go to Europe? EUROPE?" They nodded again, relaxing slightly. The owner spoke to his son, who left the shop. "No, no, friends" smiled the Turk, who knew that if he did call the police they would not be grateful to be lumbered with the migrants, and he might have to give back the money he had just taken from them. "We are friends—friends. One who speak Arabic come now—SPEAK ARABIC!" He put his hand near to his mouth and opened and closed the joined fingers in a crude pantomime of speech.

An awkward silence descended while the three stared at each other, until the son came back a few minutes later with an elderly man. The newcomer's Arabic was halting, but through him they were able haltingly to tell their stories and their plans to the shop owner, his son and his daughters, the latter peeking appraisingly from behind the curtain.

"Ah," said the clothes shop man, "England! I have a cousin in Birmingham. Well, a cousin a few times removed. He's been there 10 years. It's easy to get in—and once you're in…heh, heh. Here, have some tea! TEA!" There was a scurry behind the curtain, and a clinking of glasses.

"I've seen a few of you lads passing through. Now, have you thought about where you're going to go from here, eh? Antalya's the way to go. Up at the border, the Greeks are watchful, and they put people back across the river and smash up their boats. They're none too gentle, I hear. But Antalya is very big, busy—lots of tourists, police very busy, so they won't notice a couple of quick lads like you. Plenty of fishermen looking for readies. The Greeks don't watch down there too closely, because most boats go from further north. You can get to Rodos, maybe one of the smaller islands. When you get there, go into a police station and tell them you're Kurdish refugees—they won't know the difference. They've got to give you a place to put your head down, and food. Then they'll transfer you to the mainland, and with a bit of luck you'll be allowed out while your case is examined. And if you don't want to wait around for that—eh, eh?" He spread his hands, smiling hugely.

"I wish I was a younger man; I'd come with you!" he added archly to tease his unbothered wife, who had come in with the tea, then winked at his guests. He was enjoying his role of arranger and life-changer.

"OK, so the next thing is how you two get down there. There's a big fruit market here almost every day, and there are trucks going down to Antalya and lots of other places. I bet if you went there tomorrow morning there might be an open lorry, or one with the refrigeration not too low, or you could even sit in the cab if you find a friendly driver. There are plenty; you'll find someone."

In the meantime, they would need a bed for the night, and the shopman's cousin Mehmet—who, helpfully, spoke some Arabic—lived near the market. He'd see them right, and wouldn't charge them much. It's best you lads stay out of sight. The police might be looking for you by now.

Soon, considerably poorer, but wearing new clothes and with the powdery taste of apple tea in their mouths, Ibraham and Maged set off under the guidance of the shopman's son. Ten minutes later, after paying him off with a large tip—he had declined the smaller first offer contemptuously—they were in a modern apartment overlooking a concrete shopping mall and a narrow street with a mosque at one end, sipping yet more tea to the sound and smell of buses funnelled up to their window, trying to tell their new contact Mehmet—whose Arabic was minimal—about the war while he stared through thick glasses and disconcertingly wiped nose-pickings on the side of his chair. Then mercifully he went back to work and peaceful if dull hours ensued, with Maged watching television uncomprehendingly while Ibraham dozed on a too short sofa, flicked through an incomprehensible newspaper or stared at a print of Old Stamboul. The city seen from the apartment was a medley of brown and grey roofs with forests of TV aerials, moisture-stained walls, laundry, sounds of car horns, people shouting, smells of exhaust, drains, and cooking. Ibraham reflected ruefully that the bit of the world he had seen so far wasn't much to write home about.

Mehmet came at about 6:30 with food, and news that he had found a lorry driver going to Antalya next day, who was willing to take them for $50 each. What was more, for another $100, he would introduce them to someone who had a boat and experience of transporting unusual cargoes. Ibraham and Maged looked at each other with satisfaction.

They were chattering excitedly in the bright early morning, as they sat up front with the burly 50-year old driver. Nazim was dour, but it did not matter. They were young and they were, after all, driving in a powerful German truck through a new and wide world—zigzagging along tortuous roads down towards Antalya, at the westernmost end of a fertile coastal strip sheltered from the winds by mountains whose crests were studded with Achaean, Ionian, Byzantine, Seljuk and Crusader fragments. Seeing the successive generations of slumped walls, Ibrahim felt the whole district was ringing with remembered arrivals and departures.

The driver knew a few words of Arabic, and had been on the Iraqi border with the army, so they managed stilted conversation. He eventually conveyed that he knew a man who had a boat (rowing gestures) who might give them passage. He had done it before. Two other Iraqis, last year—and a Chinaman (they guessed that was what he meant by his epicanthic mimicry). It was risky though, as the Franks were always on the lookout (hand shading his eyes, peering in all directions), and it would cost them quite a bit (finger tips rubbed together). How much? Shrug. One hundred dollars? Two hundred? Three? He shrugged again and lit a Marlboro, and then they were in the outskirts in the late morning, heading down a sharp incline as the Mediterranean became the horizon. It was the first time Ibrahim and Maged had seen the Mediterranean, but what interested them most was the Old Harbour—empty now, but that would be filled by mid-afternoon when the fishermen returned.

For now, once Nazim had dropped off his cargo, a café beckoned for the three—coffee, raki, dominoes and watching Galatasaray play Izmir. Nazim was a partisan of Izmir, and the café was full of *confrères*—who roared and banged the tables to see the local boys beat the Istanbul side three-one. Nazim never offered to pay for anything, and the others didn't want to offend by asking. He might just dump them here, or he could even hand them over to the police. They still needed him, and besides he had insisted on prepayment—so they tried to view his enormous meal and drinks as an investment.

They got to the docks around 3. The harbour was nearly full now, with more craft nosing between the moles and piers. Everywhere juddered with engines. Streams of cooling water gushed into the basin, crates of shimmering things were craned out of holds and sent skidding across quays; there were particoloured cats and audacious rats, chandlers, men with hosepipes, food and cigarette vendors, a few sightseers and even, just beyond the dock gates, a few girls who had found a distasteful way to assert their independence. Plastic bottles, papers and dead fish bobbed amongst oddly beautiful diesel slicks.

The driver brought them to a burly, weathered, and practical-looking man with a thick square moustache, wearing a blue shirt and bleached jeans, standing smoking on the foredeck of *Fatima* A54. The *Fatima* was a 40-foot trawler originally built for anchovy-catching, but whose catches had been consistently decreasing, despite using the smallest mesh and least legal nets her skipper could find. The deck and sides were stained with rust, and there was pitted corrosion in parts of the superstructure. The boat's painted name and registration number were obscured (Ibraham correctly guessed deliberately) by rust, salt, and piscatorial slime. Yet the scruffy hull and superstructure concealed a well-maintained engine and a crew skilled, daring, and united because they were all cousins. The radar and radio aerials were new-looking against the stumpy, streaked mast. There were also two rifles hidden behind the bridge bulkhead. Having fulfilled his part of the bargain, Nazim wished them luck and walked away, slightly unsteadily.

The skipper was Salim Burnu, the son, grandson and great-grandson of other fishermen from this coast, who had some time ago decided to augment anchovies with more lucrative cargoes. He had had some success. He looked shrewdly over Ibraham and Maged, and picked a fleck of tobacco off his lower lip. He could speak only very basic Arabic, but he could make himself understood by speaking very loudly and very slowly, and resorting occasionally to mime. By now he had considerable experience of such transactions.

"One thousand five hundred dollars for you, same for him. To Rodos. Five hundred now each. Two thousand when you get there. No money back if we fail because of Greek navy." His voice was hoarse from tobacco, and there was a faint yellow stain on his moustache.

"Fifteen hundred each? Impossible! How far is it?"

"Two hundred kilometre here, 200 back. Dangerous coast. Coast guards everywhere. I get ten years if I'm caught…"—his hands clasped imaginary bars in front of his face—"…a big fine, and lose my boat. You won't find a better deal in Antalya. Nazim told you I'm reliable. Get to Greece, and you get anywhere in Europe. I leave tonight at nine. There will be others, but I can take you two. Take it or leave it. You need to go more than I need to take you." He spat over the side as a coda.

"We have to think about this," Ibraham insisted, more as a negotiating tool than because he thought there was an alternative. Salim shrugged, and turned ostentatiously away to attend to some minor problem, while Ibraham and Maged walked up and down on the quay discussing their situation. Between them, they had only $6,000, and Maged had other concerns.

"I don't like his looks, and I don't trust him. How do we know he's not just going to turn around after a few hours, saying it's too dangerous? How do we know he won't dump us on some Turkish beach and tell us it's Greece? They could rob and kill us once we're out at sea. I've heard about that happening!"

But it always came back to what else they could do. They didn't speak Turkish. They were 400 km from Istanbul, and didn't know how to get there. They would have to pay to get there anyway. And even if they did get to Istanbul, it was further again to the border, and there they would be faced with a well-guarded zone with tough police on both sides. They could go to another port, but that meant more delay, they would be in the same position when they got there, and such journeys increased the chances of their being picked up by the police.

So they went trailing, slightly shamefacedly, back to the *Fatima* and the unsurprised Salim. They didn't mind haggling, and the language barrier made it a faster process than it might otherwise have been.

Within five minutes, they had settled that they would both be put ashore in Rodos for a total of two thousand, six hundred dollars—half upon setting off, the rest just before they were landed. They agreed to be at the dock by eight, Salim spat on his hand and they shook, then excused himself with a seemingly sincere salutation. It seemed all right. But back ashore, Maged purchased a sturdy-looking knife from a kitchen supplies shop. "You can never tell!" he said grimly.

They got coffee and kebabs and sat in the Stadt Park, enjoying the sea-zephyr. They felt they were getting looks from a policeman, so wandered off to another park with a plaque to a fez-wearing man, where sparrows flapped in a cigarette butt-filled fountain. Then they wandered back into the main streets and looked curiously at the tourists, wondering if any were English. They found the tourists often disappointing—fat, pasty or sunburned, wearing clothes that looked, they felt, like things homosexuals or prostitutes would wear. They mingled with the crowds, passing judgment or admiring—thinking always that soon they would be among millions of such people, in the home of the "pale barbarians." Maged remembered those broadcasts, and they laughed inordinately.

By eight, they were on the *Fatima*, each poorer by $1,300. One of the crew members—they all looked alike—signalled to them to get below. So they clambered down a slimy ladder into a stinking hold, from which all they could see was sky and a segment of oxide-stained wheelhouse.

There were 10 others, six of them Egyptians who had been creeping slowly north along the Levantine coast in similar vessels for the last six weeks. The other men were Sudanese, and had only a few words of Arabic. They had been travelling for months—they couldn't say how long exactly. The 12 stood looking at each other in unimpressed incomprehension. From the bilges arose a complex compound of fish, sewage, and diesel, and Ibraham bit back vomit. Some of the Egyptians were pleased to have new people to talk to—there seemed to be tension with the Sudanese—and conversation became almost animated, until a crew member ordered them to keep quiet.

After an hour, the engine chugged into activity, and crew members pulled a tarpaulin over the opening. It was Ibraham's first time aboard a ship. His stomach had not quite got back to normal, and his nausea increased as the tarpaulin locked in the hold's distinct bouquet. He tried to breathe through his mouth, but he could still smell it. There was shouting, the sound of the mooring rope hitting the water, the thump as the loop hit the side, and then the boat slid sideways. He managed to keep himself under control until the vessel cleared the breakwater and a long, slow, swell coming up all the miles from Egypt started to slop against the side. His balance fell away, his stomach turned upside down, and he just had time to turn his head into a corner before the stench of vomit was added to the atmosphere. The Egyptians seemed to think it was very amusing—and he looked at them with dull dislike as he cooled his forehead against the sweatily frigid metal.

But soon the tarpaulin was drawn beautifully back, the released smell of vomit eliciting coarse laughter from the deckhands. They shouted "OK!" and beckoned the migrants up onto the deck. The minute Ibraham's head emerged, he felt much better.

The coast was receding gorgeously astern, a heaped up and stupendous bulk, its greens and browns now merging into wistful blue. The lights of Antalya extended much further than Ibraham would have thought, and there were other settlements' lights springing into life over to the west, in the narrow plain along the Gulf, which had already lost the sun behind its fringing mountains. Further south, a lighthouse was sending finding, feeling fingers over the calm water. To the east, the land was much further away and still sprinkled by sunlight, but there were lights shining out ever more strongly. Here and there, although not close, were the masthead lights, starboard lights and cabin lights of other trawlers, all heading in the same direction—out into international waters, in roughly the area where straight lines drawn south from Gelidonya Burnu and west from Cape Arnauti would intersect. Even through his seasickness, Ibrahim was startled by the beauty and by the timeless, efficient movements of the sailors, carrying out their incomprehensible tasks before such a backdrop of splendour. He had heard that some men felt sea-longing, and now he knew why.

Salim knew that if he went the most direct route to Rodos, hugging the coast, he would be spotted by the Greek coastguards—and that the best chances lay in giving a wide berth to Megiste. They had been very vigilant down there ever since those Africans had been found out in the middle of nowhere, clinging to the tuna net. That was where stupid old Sayed Bafra had gone wrong. He should have left them, and now he was sitting in some filthy Greek jail, and would have no livelihood to come back to.

Once out in the deep water, the *Fatima* would then be able to slide slowly westwards, as if drift-netting, and hopefully get to within 20 miles of Rodos by darkness tomorrow—ready for a quick dash into a quiet beach Salim knew in the darkest hours of the day after tomorrow. The moon was in its smallest quarter, and the forecast for tomorrow night was for cloud. He walked up and down in the little wheelhouse, taciturn, edgy. He did not need to consult charts, although he did occasionally look at the old GPS with the white numbers that clicked round, and listened to the shipping forecast. He grunted with satisfaction to see a mass of cumulus forming far off to the west.

The little boat chugged stolidly as the night hunched massively around. The travellers started to drop asleep where they lay on the deck, huddled on coiled-up ropes, wearing all the clothes they had with them. A cool wind soughed across the deck, yet no-one fancied sleeping in the hold amongst the dead fish and bilgewater. Their fitful movements and murmuring were lost in the thrum of the engines. Maged soon joined their number, but Ibraham simply could not relax. Perhaps it was the motion, or simply because he thought one of them should stay alert; he tossed and turned and couldn't help wondering where he'd be this time next week, next month, next year, 20 years from now, 30 years from now. He smiled at the swarming stars.

He dozed and woke, dozed and woke—and became preternaturally awake when the engines stopped, and the stilled trawler began to rock longer and more slowly, caught in the swell. He could hear individual drops plop-plopping in the hold, and wavelets slapping crisp and short against the drum-like emptiness. An engine problem? No, it was too peaceful; Salim walked by yawning, off to his bunk. It was just the trawler heaving-to for the night, having arrived at its abstract location where the lines intersected on the chart. To avoid going too far out of their way, and to save diesel, in good weather the skipper would often just switch off the engines, and let the ship ride for the night, with a deckhand on watch.

Ibraham could see this responsible person now, smoking on the fo'c's'le, his face periodically illuminated by tiny inhalations. Ibraham watched a finished cigarette describe an incandescent curve into pale blue nothingness, then snap out. The sky was sugary with stars, many more than he had ever seen at Basra, with its angry orange streetlights. As he watched, tiny pieces of them started to rush past the earth—and for a few marvellous minutes, the cold vista was dotted with points of vanishing brilliance, as the meteor shower finally flamed and flickered out impossibly far above. He lay astounded, and with a feeling of private privilege, as if this stellar *son et lumière* had been put on specially for him.

He couldn't have felt more awake, and anyway nature was making impertinent demands. So he went over to the bulwark, delicate-stepping among the snorers. Undoing his trousers, he grabbed a tight hold of two stanchions, and aimed his meagre buttocks out over the black water, just in time. The sound of the excrement slapping into the sea was surprisingly loud, but no-one reacted—except the deckhand, who turned in surprise then looked away repelled. Ibraham adjusted his dress, and wandered off to join him, feeling a need to communicate with the only other man in the world who was seeing all *this*, now, here. He nodded and received a wary one in return.

The Turk's face was wide and pale, with narrow eyes and a thick nose, and his head was set squarely on a strong and stumpy body. Faces like his had looked out over these waters since their 7th-century ancestors had thundered down from the mountains to raid the fat Greek cities of the Hellenized coast. He was humming some monotonous melody—a tune that to Ibraham seemed to be suffused with a hint of the movement of the sea and horizons that would never be reached. Ibraham gazed out with him over the blue and grey immensity. Looking back at the wheelhouse, Ibraham could see the green glow of the navigation light and, several metres above, the disembodied white riding light. He did not like to look at this; it yawed and pitched too much, as small waterline movements were translated through the superstructure and up the full height of the mast. Very far away, he could just make out two similar lights, indicating where another trawler was riding out the dark hours. He wondered if there were refugees aboard that one too. Other than these, there were no other lights anywhere.

He had never felt more isolated, or realized just how large the world was. There, here, he was in a tiny boat filled with men he didn't know, in the middle of an incomprehensible ocean, suspended in a rust-bucket above black depths filled with creatures from dreams. He and the *Fatima* were out of place; deeply daring, deeply vulnerable. He was bobbing between lives, and between continents, even between elements. The enormity of it suddenly struck home, and his mind sought instinctively for small comforts—images of his parents laughing one *Eid*, and home with the sound of prayers rising from the blue-and-white-tiled Mehmet mosque. What would his mother and father have said, if they had been able to see him now, here? He couldn't or wouldn't guess. The past was too close; he did not wish to unman himself.

His creeping melancholy was interrupted by something wonderful. A black bump broke the water, and sank again—but it left a greenly glimmering trace. Then there was another translucent trail, and another, a rounded shining snout and another one, as the porpoises curveted and dodged dissolvingly around the prow. He and the half-smiling sailor watched them in silence for about 15 minutes, before they sank and were lost. Ibraham peered out hopefully for another hour, but they never returned. Once, however, a tiny lump of opal fire came out of the blue and dashed horizontally for a few seconds before being extinguished. Some kind of fish. What blind panic, Ibraham wondered, had possessed the little animal down in that impenetrable waste—what looming menace from the shifting shadows had forced the little fish to fly out of its element, as Ibraham had flown out of his?

After an unreckonable time, he had a mundane thought—but maybe it wasn't so mundane. There was something about all this limitless space and beauty—something about being young and rejecting constraints—that led him finally to make a decision he had been deferring.

He pulled out his personal papers, squinted for a second at the little picture on his ID card, taken years ago in that studio in the centre of Basra. Looking at the picture, he could still smell the photographer's garlicky breath, which had permeated the stuffy little studio.

He had been told it might prove counter-productive to have papers if he wanted to claim refugee status. He still did not think of himself as a refugee—it seemed too contemptible a status. He was really a risk-taker, an opportunist, a man in a man's world. But according to everyone, being a refugee was the likeliest tactic to succeed. So now, still with a faint sense of shame, he took a last look at the way he had been—then skimmed his papers over the side, committing himself ineluctably. The deckhand noticed what he had done, and looked at him with a faint interest. Ibraham pulled his knees up to his chin and relished the decisiveness of his action.

He kept staring out at the rolling night until he felt suddenly stricken by cold. He rolled himself back into the warmest possible bundle, but with the deck insinuating even through all his clothes and blankets it was impossible to get comfortable. He was still grappling with the difficulty of reconciling soft bodies with metal surfaces when the morning sun rose full into his grainy eyes.

That nighttime of delight and discomfort was followed by a slow, sly day. The *Fatima* would creep west a few kilometres, then stop its engines again. The captain hoisted the 'towing nets' diamonds, then actually put out the nets—inching forward to give the semblance of really fishing. There was no other vessel in sight—but perhaps they were being plotted on long-distance radar. But there was no sign, and each time they turned they were a little further westward, a little closer.

Ibraham was excited that afternoon to spot a silver fish of around 30 centimetres spring out of the water, and skim along for about 50 frantic metres. He recognized it for what it was—the cousin of the dasher in the darkness, the fish which had leapt between worlds for a marvellous moment. He pointed it out to Maged, and they began a competition to see who could see the next one. But their eyes soon wearied of the dancing, winking lights and swirls and things that seemed to be but weren't.

There was little else to watch. A young turtle floated by not far away, strands of seaweed streaming behind, and a shoal of attendant fish. Two crew members were over the side in bosuns' chairs, doing something to the anchor. The migrants sat slumped long-sufferingly, or exchanged infrequent inapposite remarks. Even Ibraham, half in love with the sea since last night, started to believe they had always been there, doing nothing out in the middle of a huge nothing. It was an effort to think about either past or future. Memories and dreams alike seemed empty of immediacy. He sank into superheated apathy, sipping water and nibbling food he didn't need.

There was a brief alarm when a small plane was heard, and Salim made them duck into the hold. But the plane passed at least two kilometres away, and did not come back. Jet airliners passed occasionally thousands of metres overhead, bringing pasty Europeans to wallow in chemical-blue pools by concrete towers or gape dutifully at Ephesus. Later, two more trawlers were seen on the horizon, and Salim sent his passengers back down again into the fishy abyss until they had gone. The day and the *Fatima* held their breath, and their places in space.

By eight, they were as far west as Salim would venture until darkness. There were only another few miles of international waters, and he was not happy about a slowly-approaching craft he had detected on radar, but could not yet see. He chugged a little eastwards, watching the other vessel's movements all the while. He only started to relax when he saw the other craft change direction. Probably just a yacht after all! Soon, it had vanished. But the incident had made him nervous, and the *Fatima* altered course towards the south-west, and picked up speed. He would head for Kallea instead. There was a quiet beach he had never used before. The boat's new purposefulness was detected by the migrants, who were both cheered and nervous.

Salim need not have worried. After a relatively cordial Greco-Turkish summit on Cyprus, Athens had decided to bring about a new dawn in Aegean relations. Greece and Turkey were after all modern nations, the politicians declared, with a common aim of regional peace and prosperity. The minefields along the land border, into which some previous would-be migrants had been mischievously directed by their prepaid conductors, were to be made safe—while the (highly expensive) naval patrols would be scaled down to signify the new trust.

The historic signatures, the handshakes and shoulder-slappings, the multiple photographs with the beaming Swedish intermediary in front of crossed flags had all resulted in some essential routine maintenance work being carried out on the gleaming patrol vessel *Mithridiates*, and its crew being given that Saturday night at liberty. Politics and logistics were conspiring to overlook the tiny ampoule creeping across the resounding waters.

The day thinned and reddened; the sea was smooth and shining, except where the *Fatima* scraped stripes of wake. The floating republic of sweat and diesel and fish had the darkening universe to herself. The clouds descended as had been expected, and Salim smiled. This time there was no relieving pool of light at the masthead, no green and red radiance below the wheelhouse, and no cigarettes were permitted on deck. The nets were dragged in, almost empty except for weed, jellyfish and a few uncommercial fish which were thrown back in. The decks were cleared for action, and the migrants told to get their effects piled up ready on the port beam.

By now, the *Fatima* was well inside Greek waters. There was still no sign that they had been detected—just the lights of some small town against a hill, sensed rather than seen. Then even this suggestion of civilization vanished to starboard, as Salim turned the *Fatima*'s nose towards the south, and were eventually lost behind a great bulk of blackness (by day, goat-wandered hillsides of heather and bent olives, divided up by scorpion-stalked walls). The radar screen showed an approximation of the ragged shapes of the archipelago, but there was nothing moving anywhere on the black and orange disc. It was 1:45.

They were close in now—three kilometres to go. Salim throttled right back on the engines and sent two of the crew down to the migrants. It was time for the rest of his money. He did not want to linger at the dropping off point. The crew members were brusque, and the migrants knew they needed to be silent, so they paid up without demur. The money was taken to the wheelhouse, and Ibrahim could just see Salim's head and shoulders as he bent over the heap of cash.

After a few minutes, his head jerked up and the engine picked up speed, the *Fatima* now heading determinedly for a sable promontory with creamy bubbles around its base. The boat rocked with the extra speed, and the backed-up effects of the water pushing and plucking at the rocks. "Two minutes!" Salim breathed, and one of the crew went midships, holding up two fingers silently in each of the eager faces. Maged looked at Ibrahim and grinned; Ibrahim looked back, but could not summon a smile. This was too terrible. His hands tightened on his kitbag, and on the gunwale—the only fixed point in a rocking, rolling cosmos.

The cliff leapt up, there was the sound of water sucking on rocks, 12 hearts felt as if they were going to explode, then someone breathed "Now!" A hard hand banged Ibrahim's shoulder, and he was somehow over the side with his kitbag, half-jumping, half-falling into startlingly cold water, others splashing and spluttering behind him, the squared shape of a long, low building suddenly showing where a second ago there had been just indeterminate indigo. The water was only waist-deep and the seabed pebbly, and within 30 seconds Ibrahim was ashore, and the others were there with him. The moment was too sweet, and he felt like crying. He turned around in time to see the *Fatima* heading back out of the cove, a crewman pushing off from rocks with a long boathook, racing to get back to neutral waters. With luck, the boat would be back in Antalya—Asia (home, Ibrahim thought)—in 15 hours. As Salim backed the *Fatima* skillfully out into deeper waters, the off-duty captain of the *Mithridiates* was in a bar, talking about his ship to impress a blonde from Leicester.

Chapter 9
An Irrelevant Irruption

City of London
Tuesday, 6th August—Thursday, 8th August

Albert Norman was the veteran columnist of the *Sentinel*, an old and perversely old-fashioned newspaper with a large circulation and modest intellectual pretensions. He was 70, obese, almost completely bald, and his breath smelt of vegetables when it didn't smell of brandy—and he had only got the job because his father had been the foreign editor.

All the old *Sentinel* people had gone, with their rose-gardened Edwardian villas and double-barrelled names—all except for him, left behind by the retreating tide like some magnificent wreckage. Almost everyone he knew had been replaced by revolving-door journalists who ebbed and flowed rather too easily to and from other papers, and by editors whose priority was to maximize reader numbers by increasing the celebrity count and accepting advertisements for sex-chat lines.

Albert was an artifact from a robuster past, when the paper had been sued by Lloyd George, lauded the General Strike volunteers and Mussolini's employment policies, denounced the creation of the National Health Service, supported Enoch then Maggie, opposed the Bilderbergers, and called the EU "a continuation of the Third Reich by other means."

Those stances had been sloughed off one by one, and the memories of them almost erased, as ever-changing management teams sought to broaden the paper's appeal. Where there had been informative if partisan news items, conspiracy theories, City reports, and "Palace & Personalities" snippets, now there were horoscopes, health tips, pictures of footballers in Tudorbethan new-builds, and Channel 11's cheeky chick Jasmine's underwear (or the piquant information that she had not been wearing any). The hard elements of the paper had been subsumed within lifestyle and lasciviousness—and the formula had been lucrative for the paper's present owner, a Russian oligarch who collected media outlets in the vain hope of improving his atrocious public image and eventually collecting what he called "a Sir-hood."

Yet squatting there still like a toad, ugly but reassuring, on the bottom right-hand corner of the Views on the News page was still to be found, twice a week, a redoubt of the *Sentinel* as it had been—Albert's "Broadside" column, the column's name evoking the tactics as well as the attitudes of another time. Embarrassed editors had sought to pension him off, or tried moving his column around within the paper—but the discomfiting fact was that it was the most popular single item amongst readers. Every innovation was greeted with protests from loyalists, with a deluge of letters starting off along the lines of "I have been one of your readers man and boy…" and finishing with a variation of "What will the end of it be?" In the maelstrom of change, the paper's many small-c conservative readers found Albert's continuing acerbic presence a sign that all was not yet lost. Such fierce reactions had always frightened the managers, and so editor after editor had deferred making that particular decision until he had taken his golden handshake and left, to make equally forgettable impressions on other papers.

Albert's articles were the favorite subject of readers' letters—almost all supportive, many intemperate, some mad. Albert relished the maddest ones, and kept "the crème de la crap" in what he called his Special Vintage File for when he felt despondent. "Let's SVF this one!" he would say to his shared secretary, Sally, and it would be added to the musty, bulging file. Occasionally, the great man would even condescend to reply to some of the letters, and took malicious joy in writing superficially polite but subtly rude letters to those who had written to warn him of conspiratorial networks, or the advent of a prophet. He often plagiarized Disraeli's letter to a nuisance correspondent—"Thank you for your letter. I shall lose no time in reading it." Some of the correspondents had been writing to him for 20 years, never realizing that their heartfelt communications were read out in the office to explosions of mirth. Happily, these same readers also purchased a satisfying number of items from the paper's advertisers.

Once Albert had had a sort of agenda, if a purely negative one of saying that *this* and *this* and *this* were heaped-up ordure, from which nothing positive could ensue, even if you left the heaps where they were for a million years. And once every 10 years or so, usually after a longer than usual lunch, he had even allowed himself to believe that he was having an inverse impact, in the sense that everything he endorsed was certain to fail. So reliable had this rule been that a few years ago he had experimented by publicly endorsing a peculiarly repulsive Workers' Party MP—only for that MP to rise to the rank of Prime Minister, the position he still retained at the head of the "Big Tent of All the Talents." After this disaster, Albert had desisted; it was clearly a fey power he had, only to be wielded by adepts.

So Albert had persisted on the pages and on the payroll, while smaller journalists and a multitude of initiatives swirled around him, hulking massively, cynically in the poky little office on the fourth floor that he shared with the Obits editor ("the Dead End" everyone called it inevitably—even the jokes were venerable in this Rorke's Drift of Reaction).

That office, which Albert visited only twice a week and then only for a few hours, contained two filing cabinets which had lost their keys, two sad-looking computers with finger-greased screens on coffee-stained tables, the requisite number of swivel chairs (Albert's bowed by his great weight, even when he wasn't in it, with foam protruding from the permanently indented PVC cushion—and crunchy with crumbs), and drifts of letters that would never be answered. There was a view from the solitary (and always rain-stained) window into a dank space made up of glass-sided buildings or Portland-faced 1920s blocks with bad guttering, air-conditioning tanks, and dead pigeons. The telephone rarely rang, and it was used mostly by the secretary from Accounts, whose handsomer but less private office was a few doors up. The walls bore a noticeboard with infrequently refreshed company notices, a map of Europe from the 1980s, and some newspaper clippings stuck up with tape.

These clippings reflected Albert's sardonic humour—such as an exposé of the wildly popular African socialist, who when he wasn't enjoying films of his opponents being tortured had been secreting the money earned by his country's cooperatives in his personal account at Geneva (plus a separate item, showing said African socialist being embraced by a damp-eyed *Examiner* journalist, none other than John Leyden's present editor). There was also a story about an idealistic American who had worked in Rio's slums, only to be raped and killed by a man she had been trying to help—and one about an ecologist killed by a shark of the species he had been campaigning to save from extinction.

Another subsection was headed "The Broken Record Award" and contained copied extracts of the most hackneyed political prose he could unearth, and from time to time, he made columnar announcements as to which opinion-former had received this most prestigious "award." But he had discontinued the practice after the number of contenders had grown unmanageable.

Albert had always liked the idea of self-satisfaction coming to a sticky end. He called the clippings the Wall of Sanctimony, and treated it jokingly as if it were a religious site—like the Western Wall his ancestors had regarded reverentially, and which he remembered seeing as a boy, bewildered by the Homburged men, nodding and muttering beneath punishing sun. He invented rituals for whenever new items were added to the Wall; Sally, designated the "Vestal Virgin (Revisited)," would advance reverentially and place the carefully clipped news item in its final position, while he stood on one leg and recited the first verse of *The Ancient Mariner*. He had an idea that this kept worse nonsenses at bay.

His columns were waspish, bilious, dismissive, sneering, reactionary, and proudly Philistine—although in his (extremely) private life, he was a dedicated oenophile, a connoisseur of the Antwerp School, and had an informed love of the songs of Purcell, some of which could bring him to tears in the Kensington home he shared with a Ghanaian art-dealer called Anthony, whom he always called his "close male friend." He occasionally wondered how his readers would react if they had known about his domestic arrangements, but he never worried. He was as happy in his skin as someone of his personality type could ever be, and the contrast between his image and his reality was simply funny. He didn't need the readers, and he didn't even need the income; it was just force of habit now, plus a residual enjoyment of the protests that he was sometimes still capable of provoking. Once, dozens of people had chained themselves to the railings outside the *Sentinel* offices, in protest at a column in which he had called for the return of birching for children. He treasured the memory of one placard—"Albert Norman wants to beat your little lad."

Albert held the record for being the most-complained about journalist in the British media, having been assailed over many years as snobbish, elitist, heartless, homophobic, sexist and racist. It was a record in which he took considerable pride. In certain circles, his name was a byword for all that was least appealing about Britain, while in wider but less frequently heard circles, he was a lodestar of aggrieved commonsense—or, as Albert called it, "raresense."

He was often unsure whether he really believed the things he was writing, or just liked being the centre of attention. He relished the memory of the time he had sued the *Examiner* for calling him a racist (against the wishes of the *Sentinel*'s then-owner, who hadn't wanted to create unpleasantness at the Reform Club)—and had come exultingly out of the court, waving the relevant issue of the *Examiner* over his head. The large cheque that paper had been compelled to give him in settlement had done little to improve the relationship. Even now, the *Examiner* would snipe constantly at him and pore over his articles, hoping one day he would "go too far."

Amongst the items on the walls of his office were several *Examiner* articles referring to him. His favourite headline was "Race row as 'wildly offensive' journalist is warned on Roma." This was a reference to a late Thursday-afternoon lucubration about "tinker benefit-junkies," which had led to another demonstration outside the *Sentinel*'s office, and the delivery of a floppy parcel of excrement—which the alert Albert had thrown unopened out of the window onto the roof below, where it presumably still lay amongst the pigeons and puddles, outside the Accounts Department's never-opened windows.

It was therefore entirely predictable that when the Beach Bodies were found that the *Examiner* would take one position and Albert, whatever was most directly opposite. John Leyden was a regular butt of Albert's witticisms. Albert had often said that John had never had a real feeling in his life. "Listen to this fucking shite," he shouted through the open door to Sally, who smiled tolerantly while he read out the article with his usual scornful energy. Albert would probably have been surprised to know that John had at least one real feeling—a deep hatred for him that he masked behind a semblance of amused insouciance. John loathed being laughed at, especially by Albert Norman, whom no-one could ever quite ignore.

John always first opened the *Sentinel* at the Broadside page to see what the old dinosaur was saying this time. The column was contemptible, of course, but he always read it with a certain fascination. There was a strange near-grandeur about this man who was so curmudgeonly—so consistently on the wrong side of history and so proud of the fact. John almost envied Albert's adamantine perversity; it had a strange kind of style. A pity such energy wasn't used for better ends! Often there were also little snippets of useful information in the Broadside pieces, which John and a surprising number of other journalists filed away for future use—often without even realizing they were plagiarizing the country's most reviled writer.

So it was with a sense almost of predestination that Albert settled down to write a response. If he could finish by 12 he would be able to claim his corner seat in the Prussian Queen. Another *Sentinel* tradition he maintained was that of drinking a few pints of bitter at lunchtime, each one chased by a single malt. He used to joke that he was contractually required to support anything named after European royalty, of whom there should be a lot more. With a scratch and a belch, and a slurp of an already cooling coffee (another coffee ring to add to the sticky, brown, overlaid Olympics logos on his desk), he wrote,

Beach Bodies—A Pity But It's Not *Our* Fault.

He admired this for several seconds, then went on, breathing heavily:

> No-one can blame anyone for trying to get to Britain. Even under the present government, Britain is still the best country in the world. You'd be mad not to want to live here rather than in some Third World hellhole. But when people come here illegally, creeping into our coastline under cover of night, they know they are taking risks.

> The Bodies on the Beach, in their pathetic array, were plain unlucky—expendable pawns in a great criminal game of cat-and-mouse that spans the whole world, but who too often end up here in Britain, the world's rubbish dump. Had they been luckier, they would have just waded ashore, and disappeared into Britain's shadowy underworld, criminals amongst hundreds of thousands of other criminals.
>
> While no-one would defend the crimes of the traffickers, this is a problem created in Whitehall and perpetuated by Whitehall and the Quisling press. Britain's immigration system isn't a system at all, but a shambles. So-called 'Fortress Europe' is really a Bungalow, and the key is under the mat.

He continued for another 482 words—better immigration controls, a clampdown on "refugee racketeers and professional whiners," deportation of illegal immigrants, the repeal of race relations legislation—strong if formulaic. He attacked the mainstream parties, the police and immigration authorities, and the "grossly irresponsible *Examiner* 'newspaper,'" and finished with a mixed-metaphor crescendo—

> We need to take the bull by the horns and stop Britain from becoming a Labradoodle Nation.

That would do. The Queen was calling imperiously. He put it onto a disk (he had chosen not to master e-mail), the disk, into a manila envelope marked "Views," and waddled over to put it into the tray. He waddled on into the lift, declaiming over his shoulder to Sally (as always) the only part of *Ulysses* he could remember—"We will sternly refuse to partake of strong waters, will we not? Yes, we will not. By no matter of means."

Sentinel loyalists were not the only ones pleased to see Albert's column. There was an awkward slot on the *Examiner*'s page 3 that needed something exciting, and Albert's mention of the *Examiner* made it personal. Their headline ran across three columns:

Race row as *Sentinel* calls Beach Bodies 'criminals' and Britain a 'labradoodle nation'—Campaigners say 'offensive' journalist must be fired.

There was a large picture with the caption: "Dylan Ekinutu-Jones says *Sentinel* must sack 'insensitive' columnist." There was a quote from the new era institute, a think-tank with fashionable lower-case initials: "This is a disturbing article reminiscent of the worst invective of racist and populist movements on the continent. It is unacceptable and many people find it offensive."

The article ended with a bland threat, "A spokesman for the police said that they treated incidents of racial abuse 'extremely seriously,' but that they had not yet received a formal complaint about the article. No-one at the *Sentinel* was available for comment."

Sitting up in bed in W8 the following morning, drinking bitter black coffee, Albert couldn't believe his luck. His only regret was that he hadn't beefed up the article a bit more. "Here we go again!" he called out to Anthony, and wiggled his gouty toes in delight, as the phone started to ring.

The first call was from the Views editor. "What'll we do? The old man's livid!" He had not been in the job long and had come straight from the Cornwall local press, so found Albert's reiterated "Don't worry!" less than wholly reassuring. Then he rang off, and the legal editor came on the line, annoyed at having his holiday in Mauritius interrupted by urgent phone calls from London, to confirm that the police had received a complaint and would be launching an investigation. "Fuck 'em!" Albert suggested, and the man, who had been through this before, half-laughed and went back to his beach. There were calls from amused friends, and Sally, who told him that the office phones were alive (pro-him). Then it was the Views editor again; he suggested that it might be wise to backtrack a bit, and had even come up with a form of words. There had been a lot of complaints, he told Albert. "Orchestrated! Ignore them!" Albert replied, and refused even to listen to the approved form of words. "Keep saying 'No comment,' and they'll soon get bored," he advised. Later, the calls slowed, then stopped. "There, you see," he said to Anthony—"it's just a matter of keeping your head."

But the next day, the race row had migrated and mushroomed—from the *Daily Digest & Register* inexorably downwards through the *Chronicle* and *City News* all the way to *Tits & Bums*. Dylan's still-aggrieved countenance obtruded itself into the faces of both CEOs and the unemployable. Albert lounged about in his dressing gown, reading them all with quiet enjoyment. He liked this feeling of being under siege by a world for which he felt nothing but contempt. Anything *They* hated was *ipso facto* good. Well, he didn't really believe that, but it pleased him to pretend that he did.

The phone rang a lot that day, and after a while Albert felt perhaps he ought to answer it. It was the Views editor yet again, wondering where the fuck he had been and what the fuck did he mean by it, and the office is a fucking madhouse, and the old man keeps ringing to ask what's fucking going on. Albert let him get it all off his chest, while he absentmindedly filled in some clues on the cryptic crossword—("Chiromancy consonant with devotional author"—PSALMIST). He soon sensed that his calmness was not having the desired soothing effect on the Views editor, who refused—rather rudely, Albert said—to give any help at all with the awkward clue that stretched right down the middle of the puzzle. "Capital adornments for ecologist in trouble." The call closed with the other man telling him the "old man" wanted a word with him personally at 3, and that he must be there to receive the call. "You will be there, won't you?" "Fear not, sirrah, I'll be here." That was it, and how appropriate—WIGS ON THE GREEN! Overall, it looked like being a good day—maybe even a very good one.

The "old man" came on the line punctually at 3—the *Sentinel*'s editor, whom Albert had only seen once, and never actually spoken to. The "old man" was actually 32 years Albert's junior. He had worked mostly on regional titles and had never had a furore like this before. Jangled nerves made his delivery faster than he would have liked.

"Hello, er, Albert—this is Dougie. Although we've never met, I feel I know you through your columns. I am very much aware that you're one of our institutions, whereas I have only been here about five minutes."

A slight chuckle. A crafty touch, thought Albert—man to man, cards allegedly on the table, plain speaking that wasn't plain, friendliness that wasn't friendly, an attempt to enlist sympathy for-the-predicament-I'm-in-you-must-understand. It could have been a powerful approach, if Albert had had that kind of personality. His respect for the lad rose slightly.

"The thing is, Albert, your column today—well-written though it was—is making some waves."

"Lovely pun!"

"What? Oh, yes…Ha, ha. Seriously, um, Albert, the Board and I have been fielding calls and complaints about you all day. And the switchboard and e-mail bulletin boards have been red-hot. There have been some calling in support, but many others who feel very strongly that you are being insensitive and—I'm sorry to say it, but I'm just passing on feedback—racist. And I have to say that reading over the column, while I understand what you wanted to say…one can see why it could, aah, leave that impression—even on someone like me, who's on your side!"

"Ha!" thought Albert.

"I wonder if you realise how significant this event really is, and how emotional people—*very* many people—feel about this. The thing is that I think you may not have taken this into account when you were writing."

There was silence. "Albert?"

"Yes, I'm here. I'm sorry Dougie, but I just don't think it was racist. "Insensitive," "offensive," maybe, whatever they mean—but then that's what I do. As for the people who say they're offended, frankly who gives a flying fuck about them? They're wankers, one and all—and not our readers anyway. Dylan fucking Egregious-Bore, some stupid bitch from some stupid group, and those terminal tossers at the *Examiner*—that's all it is. The same old same olds. This thing will die in a day or two."

The connection hummed with tension. This time, it was Dougie's turn to be silent for several seconds. There was a harder edge to his voice. Albert felt almost sorry for him, and started to doodle a small woodland scene on the pad. The pad was covered in tiny landscapes, some quite well-drawn.

"Again, Albert, I don't think you quite understand the situation. This isn't a normal article we're talking about. This story has struck a nerve in everyone. You must have seen that. All these articles, TV reports, Parliament recalled…this is a very, very sensitive subject, and this story's going to run and run. The Board and I are coming under pressure from readers, shareholders, commercial partners…"

(Here it comes. Advertisers.)

"And the police have said they've received complaints, and want a criminal investigation. I'll tell you frankly, Albert, this has come at a very difficult time for us, with the forthcoming restructuring. The last thing we need right now is to have the police hovering over us when we're making our arguments. I am not denying you your freedom of expression, but I think you need to clarify what exactly you were trying to say. We'll make space on tomorrow's Views. That should do it. I know it's a bore, but it's the right thing to do."

"Look, Dougie—I'd like to co-operate, I really would, but I don't feel I've done anything for which I should apologise. If you think the column was bad, you should have seen the first draft!"

"Albert, you're making this very difficult—*very* difficult. You don't appreciate the pressure I'm starting to face—pressure which can only get worse. I've been defending you all day today…"—Albert smiled wolfishly—"…but this isn't just going to go away, whatever you think. I'm not asking for an apology, I'm asking you just to *explain* what you meant—you know, put it in context. An old hand like you could have the piece done in about 10 minutes, and then I'm happy and you've covered your back, and everything's fine."

"Not for me, Dougie—not for me. I stand by what I said, and I have no need to apologise—because dress it up however you like, that is what this would be, a snivelling apology. The people who hate us have always hated us, and always will. We have to ignore them. They're *nebbish*, dolts, idiots. If the rest of the world goes mad, then it's all the more important that *we* stand firm. That's what our readers want—a bit of outspokenness, a little scepticism, a bit of salt in the sugar-bowl of modern life."

"You still don't get it, Albert. I have told you that I have come under unprecedented pressure. To give you an example, Fonesco—who are, as you know, one of our biggest advertisers—are talking about pulling their ads; it seems they are being put under pressure by their shareholders and customers to dissociate from us until we distance ourselves from your views. Need I remind you that a newspaper depends on advertising revenue? Fonesco and others pay your salary—and mine. I can't tell them to get lost."

"We can't let ourselves be blackmailed by some stinking mobile phone company. They're whores; that's all they are. They need us at least as much as we need their shitty advertisements. Wait and see—even if they pull their next batch of ads, they'll be back for the batch after that."

This was true, and Dougie knew it (although Albert had only guessed). For some reason, the ads in the *Sentinel* were far more lucrative for the phone company than those in other papers. That year, Fonesco had put all its advertising budget into the *Sentinel*, and had not regretted its decision—until today, when they had received complaints about the advertisements from two incandescent-sounding customers. They were reluctant to alienate the emerging ethnic-minority male key demographic, but their calls to their advertising agent and that agent's calls to the rep at the *Sentinel* were bluster. They had no real intention of pulling the advertisements, unless the pressure became serious. But they did want a quiet life. Dougie tried again.

"You're making a mistake, Albert. And you're making this *very* difficult. I have certain responsibilities to the board, the shareholders, our readers, and to society. It would be irresponsible of me not to listen to what our readers say…"

"Our readers, eh? I wonder how many of them have complained. I hear the phones have been ringing and ringing, and that almost all of the calls are in support."

Dougie somehow projected a frown down the line. "I don't know where you heard that from."

"I can't reveal my sources!" Albert tried to lighten the tone to calm his caller, who sounded like he was reading from a script. (In fact, Dougie had made copious notes in advance. His secretary would smile contemptuously later, when she saw them still up on his screen.)

"Look, Albert—I didn't want to put it this way, but at the end of the day, I am your editor, and you are my employee. If it was the other way round, you could say what you want, but I have the good of this paper to consider. And I feel that from the paper's point of view, we need to distance ourselves from the kind of sentiments you expressed in your column. Speaking frankly, I have to say that I don't feel they really belong in this paper in this day and age."

"What you're saying is that *I* don't belong at the *Sentinel*. Isn't that right?"

Dougie had never had to go through such a conversation before, with a man so much more experienced, and who was, furthermore, not only the paper's chief (maybe only) asset, but a vinegary national institution. Life at the *Mitham Messenger* had been so much easier, with even redundancies carried out by e-mail. He now had a handsome top-floor office, with St Paul's in the distance and a building full of respectful servants all instantly summonable (or dismissable) by button or phone, but he felt like a boy who has wandered into someone else's company. Droplets of discomfort studded the spotty white back beneath his beautifully made shirt. He was not ready for this confrontation—not yet.

And although the Board had not exactly been pleased about the possibility of a police investigation, its members had been more relaxed than he had implied. "It's just Albert. It's his way. I don't think we need to do anything about this just at the moment, do we gentlemen?" the chairman had said with a twinkling smile, just before they all broke for their monthly lunch at La Belle Cuisine. And Dougie had acquiesced with superficial good grace, while the board members whom he had cultivated before the meeting (and who had told Dougie he had a point) smiled back loyally at the chairman. He was not prepared for this confrontation—not yet.

"Of course I'm not saying that, Albert. Please don't misunderstand me. You're an institution, and we wouldn't wish to lose you. I think we've both lost our tempers a little bit, haven't we? I've made it absolutely clear that I'm just trying to find a way forward for us all. At the end of the day, we're on the same side!"

"Dougie, we've been here before, and we'll be here again. This will all be forgotten in a couple of days. Wait and see. By next week, this will all be ancient history."

By the time they finished speaking to each other a few minutes later, one might have thought they were on reasonably friendly terms. But when they had hung up, both men sat looking for a moment at their phones. This was the most serious warning Albert had ever had, and for a contemptible moment, he even wondered if he should tone down the next column.

But he pushed aside the unworthy thought, and went to make some coffee, humming *Wondrous Machine*. Now *that* was a song! It was so perfect it put all of his work into its proper context. When it came down to it, he was a hack writer for one of England's worst newspapers, while Purcell was a copper-bottomed transecendent genius.

> *To thee the Warbling Lute,*
>
> *Tho' us'd to Conquest,*
>
> *Must be forc'd to yield:*
>
> *With thee unable to dispute.*

"With thee unable to dispute," indeed, oh poor dead Henry P.—coughing your lungs up once and for all at 36, while Albert went on and on and on. But which of them would always be remembered?

Meanwhile, a much less composed Dougie was drumming on his desk, while the tightness in his face eased and the sweat below the fine cotton of his shirt dried cold and uncomfortable. Then he picked up the phone again, and rang the Advertising Department. This wasn't over. This wasn't over at all.

Chapter 10

NUMBER ONE, EUROPE

Kallea, Greece

It was just after two in the morning, and they were in *Europe*. Ibraham moved dazedly up the track leading away from the beach slightly in advance of all the others, past an ugly concrete building in which electricity hummed. Apart from this and the waves, everything was silent, expectant—but the travellers conversed only in whispers. They could see the outline of a mountain against the stars, the lights of a small town and the scattered speckles of homesteads.

There was a faint breeze from the far coast, as they trudged towards the inevitable encounter with the Europeans—the dreaded authorities. One of the few things all 12 had in common was atrocious experience of governments, and despite all the stories that had enticed them to come to this beach at this point in history, they shared a dull dread that Western governments could not be as kindly as they had been led to believe.

They came to Number One, Europe, a one-storey bungalow dalmatianed with ink-black geraniums, with a low wall between it and the single track road. Inside, a dog barked, experimentally then more certainly, the deep and slow sounds of a large animal, and for some the sound aroused unpleasant memories. They hurried past with their heads down, and by the time the householder had got up to see what was troubling her dog, the travellers were several hundred metres away, absorbed into olive and brown obscurity—phantoms flitting by beyond anyone's notice and beneath contempt. They instinctively silenced themselves and walked as quietly as possible whenever they passed any of the isolated houses, although many of them looked as if they were uninhabited. It wasn't a very impressive approach to the fabled continent.

After about two hours, gilt started to feel along the horizon, and the streetlights they were approaching burned paler. There were birds moving in the scrub, and the tocsin of a cockerel came bravely over the fields. The road was lined with citrus and cherry trees, although the fruit was only just forming. With the daylight, they started to talk rather than whisper, and one began to hum a popular Egyptian pop song—a catchy melody, and they all soon picked it up. There was no point in hiding now, and even if there had been, the daylight revealed a coverless country, with no roads apart from the one they were on, and no settlements other than the nameless town.

They came eventually to edge-of-town uncertainty—an industrial unit, lock-up garages, a building site with holes where drains and lamp posts would be placed, scrappy fields doomed to development, fly-tipped rubbish, broken glass. It was a very disappointing-looking place. A car came along the road from the town. The male driver gaped at the unexpected vision, especially the Egyptian defecating in what would be the front garden of an expensive holiday home. The car went past them and turned, then darted back through them back as if to rouse the town.

By the time the procession had flopped down in the town square, wilting from their walking efforts, a policeman was waiting, unusually conscious of the pistol at his hip, talking to a scandalized elderly woman. A minibus of tourists came down the road from the capital, and they stared at the group as their vehicle passed through the square—doughy German faces, disapprobating the sight and hating their disapprobation.

A police bus came at last and the travellers were shunted aboard. The driver glared at them all and opened all of the windows ostentatiously, as if conscious of a particularly unpleasant smell, before turning on his radio very loud. He then proceeded at a faster than strictly necessary speed, as if ensuring his passengers felt every bump and pothole. A trickle of foreboding passed through them all. Ibraham noticed Maged hiding the kitchen-knife he had bought in Antalya down the side of one of the seats; he saw Ibraham looking and grinned weakly.

The soon-reached capital was rather like the worse parts of Basra, except that there were churches instead of minarets and strange advertisements, including one showing a nearly-naked woman. Maged nudged Ibraham and pointed, and they ogled the image until they turned a corner. The town was cleaner than Basra, and the shop windows were crowded with merchandise. But it was clearly no paradise, and disquiet ran through Ibraham. Had he come all that way for *this*?

Men were rolling up security shutters and cars were nosing dispiritedly along the narrow streets. Some locals noticed the foreign faces staring out of the side-windows of the van, and one wiry, bearded man spat into the gutter as he caught Ibraham's gaze.

Messages had passed to Athens—to be greeted with groans by civil servants just coming into the office. The Athens evening editions would lead with the story and a young centre-right politician would begin to build a prestigious, pointless career with the speech he commenced at 3:15 p.m., while the world's stop-press editors wondered where they could slot in the little snippet from Greece. Meanwhile, Salim singing lascivious songs in the wheelhouse and the cousins chiming in on the refrains, the *Fatima* was heading home through fresh and brilliant waters.

On the *Fatima*, time had seemed contingent but now the refugees were being docketed and processed by the massed forces of the Dodecanese Prefecture and Athens and, far beyond in the unimaginable North, high offices overlooking classical Belgian parks studded with statues. Ankara signalled that it had, of course, known nothing but took its security obligations seriously, and was investing millions of lira in this sector. Greater integration of procedures, Ankara said, was needed in this most sensitive of areas. All around the Western world, refugee campaigners and charity workers were registering the existence of the Kallea 12.

Kallea Town's prison had been designed for rare dynamite fishermen and drunken tourists, so the new arrivals overflowed into the lobby of the police station, where they drank coffee under the unimpressed purview of the desk officer. He didn't speak Arabic and none of them spoke Greek, and no-one appeared to have retained their passports or other documentation. The two sides looked at each other uneasily. A doctor came and treated a cut on the arm of one of the Sudanese, covering it with a large sticking plaster, a beige rectangular island in the ebon ocean of his epidermis. Other police came and looked, shook their heads, muttered or made jokes to the desk officer, and went away again. The overused latrine began to advertise its presence. Sandwiches were brought—some of pork luncheon meat, had the men known, or cared—and disappeared rapidly. There was a noise of traffic through louvred windows. The chief's peevish voice could be heard occasionally, somewhere in the warren of rooms behind the front desk. Flies strolled high up in the once-cream corners. Warm. Stuffy. Ibraham nodded, jerked awake, nodded.

A brisk-looking civilian came after a few hours, accompanied by an interpreter, and there commenced a question-and-answer session with the men, during which they lied lustily and he pretended politely to believe some parts of their stories. By 11, he had e-mailed Athens that the arrivals, nationalities debatable, were all claiming asylum, and recommended that they be transferred to Lavrion—much to the relief of the police. Hitherto, Kallea had escaped the attentions of people-smugglers, and the sooner this ominous vanguard was off island, the better. It was terrible for the refugees, they agreed quickly, but Kallea was too small to deal with it. They didn't want to be the Greek Lampedusa. They hadn't got the infrastructure or the resources, and they'd be better off amongst their own people in Athens.

The plane would not arrive until the following morning, so the police were left with the headache of finding accommodation for the night. Afternoon-long negotiations ensued, because local hotels, sports and village halls all seemed unusually full, and the policeman who did the ringing around told the owners in confidence that he couldn't blame them.

Eventually, the men were offered accommodation in a nearby church. The priest, a voluble PASOK supporter, secretly hated the prospect of having the men in his immaculate church with its famous Byzantine mosaics—and he resented the fact that it had been the perma-stubbled police chief, a notorious unbeliever as well as a New Democracy supporter, who had pointed out with a sneer that it was after all his Christian duty.

Hating himself for his reluctance, he came personally to throw back the rarely used double doors, and help the migrants set up camp-beds. The church hadn't seen such activity for years. He removed the silver Venetian crucifix, communion plate and candlesticks from the altar, and a valuable 17th-century icon from the sanctuary. "They might get in the way," he explained to the supervising policeman, "and, beside, I don't want to offend these fine fellows." The policeman curled his lip cynically. Ibraham noticed what the priest was doing, and felt slightly insulted—but he didn't much like the look of those Sudanese either.

It was his first time in a church. It was a simple, limed, intensely cold building, off-white except for some fresco fragments—half a face of a green-eyed, golden-haired saint or king; a tiny basilica cradled in his surviving hand— with round-vaulted plain walls and small high windows. Disturbed dust tumbled through sunbeams. The church smelt of damp and disuse, rather than the stale socks he associated with his own theological tradition.

A reporter from the *Kallea News* turned up, much to the annoyance of the police chief who had often been criticized by the paper. He refused permission to speak to the men, but the priest readily gave permission for photographs to be taken of himself with his "guests." He expounded at length on the church's relief efforts, explaining, "this should not be seen as a problem but as Providence," and said that there was an urgent need for the church to respond to the demands of the modern world, "for in a way we are all on a journey towards sanctuary." The reporter and photographer went away happily; it was their biggest story in years.

Ibraham hated the attention, and was glad when eventually there was just a single bored policeman on the far side of the church, with his chair tilted against the wall. The interpreter had announced that food would be brought at 8 a.m., and they would leave by 9. The travellers talked for ages, wondering what would happen when they got to Lavrion, but however fascinating these conjectures, one by one sleep overthrew them and the conversation faltered and failed. Ibraham lay awake for a while longer, looking up at the high white vault, or over at the policeman, who was cleaning his nails with his keys in a puddle of lamplight. He was thinking about girls again, and longed to masturbate. But this was a holy place; it would be disrespectful. He had forgotten about prayers, and in respect for the place tried to make up for the omission—simple circular murmurings, murmurings, m-u-r-m-u-r-i-n-g-s....

There had been a bomb by the side of the road, and everyone was running, shouting, and there was blood...

To wake with a start and a grunt in this place soughing with snores, with even the clean-nailed policeman succumbing, was an almost overwhelming relief. Ibraham looked towards the dimly-discerned ceiling through deeply grateful eyes.

An icy draught; brisk sandals clicking along flagstones; clanking and clinking; coffee. The clean-nailed policeman joked with two women carrying scrambled eggs, bread, grapes, bananas and coffee pots. Ibraham's eyes flicked wide to see full sunlight outside the open doors, and Maged sitting up while he let off a tremendous fart. Ibraham said, "I cannot believe you said that, Tariq!"—and they laughed uproariously.

After making a hasty meal, they were turned out onto the steps in front, at the foot of which an old bus was waiting. In the centre of the square was a statue of a man with a drawn sword, a noted 15th-century defender of the island—a bulwark of The True Faith betrayed by a postern-gate traitor, crucified by jeering Turks just outside the looted town, his head delivered to the Sublime Porte before being kicked into the Bosphorus. The statue had been erected just after Greek independence, a reborn nation's tribute to heroic inadequacy.

They traversed a white and terracotta blandness of buildings before their bus was waved through the airport barrier. The men were taken to a special waiting room where their baggage was searched (although not their bodies) and their names were compared against the unreliable master list.

A military transport waited on the apron, green-and-black dazzle-patterned except for a blue-and-white roundel on each wing and blue-and-white stripes on the tail, which had flown in that morning from Kalamata. They were bundled up the rear ramp into the plane's cool echoing belly, where a sour dispatcher pushed them brusquely onto benches along each side and attached them to the safety harness. His face made it plain that their safety was the least important thing in the world so far as he was concerned. When they were all secured, he pressed a large yellow button and the big door at the back rose hydraulically. Ibraham said to Maged that it was their last sight of the first of Europe, and was pleased with his wit.

It was the first time any had been in a plane. After Maged had scorned him for seasickness, Ibraham was maliciously pleased to see that Maged now looked very tense. He felt quite relaxed himself, but nevertheless prayed privately as the great machine lifted up its skirts, took a deep breath and began to gather speed. Some of them looked at each other, trying to smile, and others had their eyes screwed shut as the plane scrambled into the air. The rattling stopped, ears filled and popped as the machine banked northwest.

Far below, sometimes glimpsed through the few windows in the fuselage whenever the plane banked, was an antique geography of crinkled, haunted islands scattered across a silver sheet of sea. It was very cold—most only had thin clothes—and the noise made it impossible to talk, while one of the Egyptians was puking eggs and coffee onto the deck. The dispatcher looked on in even deeper gloom, and moved his elegantly booted foot away from the thin stream.

After about an hour, they started their long descent, and bumped in minor air pockets—a sensation Ibraham quite enjoyed, especially when he noticed how frightened Maged was. Nor did he mind the jolt and backward-racing engines when the machine touched down—but he clapped in genuine gratitude with all the others, gratitude for the human skill and divine protection. The engines powered down and the airman pressed the yellow button to admit a growing segment of Greece. He had said nothing during the whole journey. They were shunted roughly aboard a tarpaulined truck, and two helmeted soldiers with rifles and double-headed eagle badges on their arms jumped up behind, slammed the tailgate and closed the flaps.

It was more than two hours drive to the asylum centre at Lavrion—with diesel exhaust pouring up through the broken wooden floor of the truck into the almost airtight interior. Ibrahim's cockiness at escaping air-sickness was knocked by the nausea and headaches that washed over them, including the soldiers, as the fumes insinuated themselves into everything and seemed to coat them in dirty grit. Their buttocks became sore from the uncushioned benches, and they were horribly thirsty. And they couldn't even look at the scenery. But in the end they arrived somehow at a prefab office, where they were lined up in front of a long table behind which sat a tired-looking policeman, a beautifully-dressed woman with bunched, bleached hair and a huge pile of papers, and a plump and ill-looking interpreter. The latter explained that they were now in the official refugee centre, where they would stay until their status became clear. Their human rights would be guaranteed by a lawyer, Miss Karatakis. The well-dressed woman spoke through the interpreter.

"Welcome to Greece. My name is Joanna Karatakis, and I am a human rights lawyer. I know you have been through difficulty and danger to get this far, and I am determined to safeguard your fundamental human rights. Conditions here are not pleasant. There is overcrowding, and you will not be able to earn any money. You will be here for several months, maybe more—with no guarantee that your applications for asylum will be successful. But please be assured that you have not been forgotten about, even if it seems to be taking a long time. Many of you, maybe all of you, *will* get your pink cards, and the right to stay in Europe. If you need to see me or one of my co-workers, tell a security guard; they are obliged to contact my office. Consultations with me or my colleagues are confidential. Together, we can make your stay tolerable—and ensure that you retain your human dignity."

The interpreter then translated the same questions and answers for each applicant—name, nationality, place of birth, date of birth, profession or occupation, reason for coming to Greece, were they claiming asylum, were they aware that unjustified claims for asylum were a criminal offence, did they have a criminal record, did they know anyone in Greece, did they have any communicable diseases, were they on medication, had they ever been a member of this or that group.

The lawyer interjected sharply several times, and twice the policeman altered something he had just written. While this was going on, the travellers looked at her with keen surmise. Ibrahim admired her lovely clothes and her clean hands, and her green eyes, like those of the fresco in the church. After a while, he realised she was aware of the migrants' scrutiny—and enjoying it. He found her combination of coolness and approachability exciting.

The procedure did not take long; some were telling the truth and the rest had learned their stories well. Ibrahim's carefully considered story—Marsh Arab activism, wanted by Saddam's police and still by Saddam loyalists, father and mother executed, sisters to support—was more compelling than some, and he was sure Miss Karatakis had looked at him with extra interest. She then quit the room, walking, Ibrahim was certain, deliberately provocatively. Ibrahim wasn't quite sure what human rights were, but he felt glad he had them.

Chapter 11
Rude Forefathers

Crisby St. Nicholas
Wednesday, 7th August—Thursday, 8th August

The ambulances had gone and the police presence was lower-key, although parts of the beach were still off-limits. Crisby looked almost the same as usual—but the global village was far from ready to let it return to normal. Crisby held secrets, which needed urgently to be unearthed.

The leftish *Weekly Meteor* led the charge, reminding readers that farmers kept guns "…in their own homes and these are easily accessible—such accessibility affords a terrible temptation to the socially excluded. The government must act NOW to close this lethal loophole."

The *Bugle* outdid their rival by commissioning Dr John St. Germains—the "Shrink to the Stars" more famous than many of his clients—to write one of his celebrated Psychopathological Profiles on the theme. Such an article was not only appropriate, but also expedient, the editor calculating that a strong stance on this might influence an ongoing police investigation into a recent editorial on Muslims.

"Psychopathological Profile 25: The Rustic Racist" was illustrated by a reworked image from *Straw Dogs*, showing a tweedy, blood-spattered man cradling a shotgun. On his lapel was a badge with a robin emblem like that used by National Union—except that the bird had been subtly amended to make it reminiscent of a German eagle. Across his veiny, empurpled forehead was "HATE!" in a font that resembled dripping blood.

St. Germains began with a reference to his childhood reading matter:

> Sherlock Holmes: 'It is my belief, Watson, founded upon my experience, that the lowest and vilest alleys of London do not present a more dreadful record of sin than does the smiling and beautiful countryside'. Dr Watson: 'What a horrible thought, Holmes!'

> It is a horrible thought indeed—and especially when passing in a train, like Holmes and Watson, through England's pleasaunce on a perfect English summer's afternoon. But Holmes, as always, was right. Human nature is human nature whether it is encountered among streets or in fields and whether its owner is wearing training shoes or green wellies, driving a Jaguar or a tractor. The tragedy in Eastshire has thrown up the dreadful spectre of rural racism—a festering slurry-pit of prejudice all the uglier for being found in 'smiling and beautiful' surroundings.

> The countryside is loved for its conservative values and sense of identity. But what when these go too far? What if, in the loneliness of some isolated farmhouse, in some bleak and windswept fen, alienation has been building up in the hearts of some who are not well-educated, or who have been unsuccessful? We academic psychologists call it Selkirk Syndrome, after the real-life castaway Alexander Selkirk, who became the model for *Robinson Crusoe*.

Many isolated farmers are almost as literally insular as Alexander Selkirk. In the 19th century, Fenland poet John Clare wrote of how cottagers "talk of 'Lunnun' as a foreign land" and how they "view new knowledge with suspicious eyes". In some parts of the country, things haven't changed. The distance between ignorance and abhorrence is short. It would in fact be surprising if some people had *not* made that last logical step.

Just last year, only 43 miles from Crisby, Selkirk Syndrome sufferer Jake Jiggins shot his ex-wife and her lover, then himself, in a quiet tree-lined road. He had been trying to get financial assistance and had even written to the agriculture minister, but he received no help. He was a withdrawn and inarticulate man, who spent most of his days working by himself, with hardly anyone to talk to for days at a time. His family had always been in farming, literally stuck in the mud, and Jiggins only left the country once in his whole life. He drank and was cautioned by the police after allegedly hitting his wife. Then the police forgot about him, even renewing his shotgun licence a mere two *years* before he killed his wife and her lover.

Country people are literally marginalized, and many feel that this government is against them. They are only too susceptible to scapegoating—in an ironical over-identification with the society which has let them down. And what more visible target than members of visible minorities, whom they have been conditioned by the media to view as criminals? Those of us lucky enough to live in cosmopolitan areas have the opportunity of seeing how the media distort reality—but those in rural areas do not have such opportunities of exposing the countless negative portrayals of visible minorities.

Someone as disillusioned and unstable could also easily become influenced by xenophobic extremism. In Jiggins' constituency last year, the extreme-right National Union obtained 15.1% of the vote in a by-election. The late Christian Democrat MP for the area, Sir Barnaby Figgs, was a chairman of the ultra-Right True Christian Democracy. Our hypothetical Selkirk Syndrome sufferer could well have been exposed to retrograde or racist opinions from a very early age—and had them fertilized in the incubator of isolation. These could all too easily lead to a bumper crop of horror.

On a late night program, a professor of social anthropology placed manicured fingertips together and sighed that many ordinary people felt disenfranchised and powerless, and that therefore it was "...theoretically possible that some individual could have overreacted in this way—if a gun is to hand, who can tell what might happen? A moment of madness, which could lead to a terrible event..."

At about that time, on a very different program, Imogen Williams's boyfriend, Scum, the vicar's son who fronted Atrocities Against Civilians, declared his hand: "Some fuckin' peasant has shot those fuckers!"

These dark hints soon filtered down to a convinceable Crisby. Even those who had always lived in the area and knew everyone now found themselves eyeing neighbours appraisingly—especially those they didn't like. Some were uneasily aware of their own suppressed feelings, and this encouraged them to search for external sources of impurity. Obviously the idea that anyone from Crisby was guilty of such a terrible thing was ridiculous—*but*...there was always that *but* fluttering bat-like over all conversations. It was rumoured that the Eastshire Police was reopening old files under the supervision of specially trained officers from London. Sightseers stared at the locals, and wondered which of them were hiding a terrible secret.

Dan had been a *Bugle* man for almost 40 years, like his father had been—usually just the home news, football and weather (except for an ashamed look at his horoscope, when Hatty wasn't watching). But he had the odd idea that "The Rustic Racist" in some oblique way applied to him. He thought a lot about his ill-starred TV appearance, and couldn't stop thinking that he had crossed some invisible boundary.

Commentators agreed that Eastshire was impoverished, deprived, and small-c conservative. There had never been a Workers' Party MP anywhere in Eastshire; the area may as well have been *Deliverance* country—a whiter-than-white, milk-and-water, roast-beef-and-two-veg, semolina-bland, uncultured, overcooked, unchallenging, ripe-for-spicing-up sort of a place. What did the locals *really* think of immigrants? What did they think of modernity? What primeval pulses resounded yet amongst those reeds—what secrets lay drowned in those stagnant swamps and aptly-named drains?

John felt he knew only too well what was up there to be discovered, but as he said to Janet, he was after all a journalist, and couldn't judge until he had seen the ground for himself. He got permission to file a "Dispatch from the Political Frontline" for Sunday's paper.

There had been a slip two years ago when he had got a bit caught up in the adrenalin of a story and filed a bumptious Dispatch from the anti-G8 riots without actually leaving the hotel bar. Nige had eventually accepted that John had been true to the spirit of the riots, but John knew he had been very lucky and couldn't pull a stunt like that again.

After all, what would he do if he were demoted, even sacked? Writing was his life, and he had so much of such importance to impart. The prospect of having that outlet and audience taken away was so appalling that he had more than once actually dreamed about it, waking Janet with his worried mutterings. The first time, she had woken him so he could escape from whatever was haunting his dream, which he had appreciated, But when he had told her what it had been about, unfortunately she had laughed "Is *that* all?" He traced his disenchantment with her from that night. A really good Frontline, maybe even an *award-winning* Frontline was surely possible. Then he could lay that particular ghost (and do some good for society).

He had already tried a tactic that had paid off before, and phoned Dan Gowt's number. The man himself had answered, and John had switched smoothly into a Cockney tone, introducing himself as Ben Jenkins from London.

"I wanted to tell you that I agree wiv yer one 'undred-and-ten percent, mate. It's about time we told these niggers where to go. And not just the niggers—but the Pakis, the Chinks, the lot. They come over 'ere, and they're on the take. Take the money from us and use it to support their kind. I was glad to see you on the telly, telling it like it is. It's about time we showed these people where they get off, dontcha fink?"

"Well, I…"

"Meantersay, they come 'ere, with their families, and go to the top of the 'ousing queue and they get all the benefits on God's earth. They have jobs set aside and they're all involved in crime and drugs and guns—all kindsa fings. We need to keep them out of the country! Am I right or am I *right*?"

"Look, Mr Jenkins…"

"It's p'litical correctness gone mad, that's what it is. The whole country's gone mad. And what does the government do? Nothing! *Nada!* Well, it's about time *someone* did something about it. Don't you agree?"

"Mr Jenkins, *please*. I've got nothing against coloured people—nothing at all. I have to say I don't like your tone. It is wrong to be rude and disrespectful; after all, they can't help being who they are. Now, I must go, so good night!"

John replaced the receiver, smiling ruefully. It was always worth a try with the likes of Dan Gowt.

Now his BMW coupé was pulling smoothly up the A1 on an afternoon of sun and showers. It was a great feeling to be riding out of the city to accept the challenge—almost medieval, but not in an insensitive way. The car was handling very well, tugging like an eager warhorse, and the sense of surging power beneath him was truly joyous.

He was to rendezvous with Giles the photographer at Crisby. Their relationship was a blend of professional respect and private dislike—yet they had worked together with great success, each relying on the other's ability always to see "importance in the seemingly insignificant." That phrase had formed part of the citation when they had jointly received the Hopkins Award. Their exposé of racism at a northern university had led to the early retirement of no fewer than three formerly "distinguished" dons, the rise to public notice of a promising young Students' Union activist (none other than Dylan Ekinutu-Jones), and the eventual adoption of a magnificently detailed Code of Best Anti-Racist Practice. It had been, as the citation said, a "truly antiseptic analysis of the rotting cadaver of so-called 'Western learning.'"

The *Examiner* had already used one of Giles' photos—tastefully muted sky, sea and shore bleeding for ever beyond the page's margins, drawing the eye into limitlessness—only to be brought up brutally by a solitary shoe on the edge of the picture, a sand-flecked plimsoll with a tiny piece of seaweed draped over the toe. The shoe had been lost by a tourist the previous summer, but the appropriateness of the image transcended the "truth" of the circumstances.

With the showers tailing off, John swished past St. Erkenbrand and east along progressively emptier roads. He had never visited Eastshire before—he couldn't think of a single news story connected with the place—and looked around for local colour he could use. Even to his fault-finding gaze, everywhere looked guileless and some of it, even attractive. There was a market town of gold cockerel-tipped spires and centuries-smoothed sandstone (even a grammar school—*quelle surprise!*). He turned onto smaller roads, where he had to drive slowly because of tractors and pick-up trucks laden with bales of hay and Jack Russell Terriers.

Low hills—slanting acres of linseed, rape, borage and wheat—squat, embattled church towers—Old Post Offices, Old Forges, Old Coach Houses—lichened walls—cast-iron railings—red cattle, black-faced sheep, and stands of trees—pheasants crossing a field—a hare racing for a few seconds parallel with the road—everything rich and solid, like a cliché of the countryside.

John hadn't been in a place like this for years. It reminded him of the Devon of his boyhood. ("Christ," he marvelled—"I'm *really* becoming nostalgic!") Some of these houses looked like Daddy's rectory with their handmade bricks, Regency railings and ornate iron lanterns, their outbuildings with pleasingly peeling paintwork. One day, when his work was done, he might live in a house like these.

Janet chose that personal moment to ring. She was *always* interrupting his me-time. He had warned her about that, so he let it go through to answerphone to teach her a lesson. She sounded very distant, and a bus was rattling past in her background. "John, will you pick up, please? I want to talk to you…Well, obviously you're busy, or you haven't switched on your phone again. Hope you're having a lovely time, you lucky thing. I'm not; in fact, I'm having a *terrible* day. Anyway, speak soon. Love you!"

His calm crept back as he entered a wide territory of green-brown sandstone churches and brick barns, rookeries and signposts down B-roads to quaintly named places—Castle Grisby, St. Anselm, Little Monkton, St. Nicholas-le-Marsh. He relished these, and the soothing steady 75mph on straight, empty roads—the gleaming sun in his mirror, and his car's foreshortened shadow preceding him—jangling guitar and arthouse lyrics from the CD. Tonight, a country pub—tomorrow, the chance to sniff out wrong—and the day after, to change things…it was like being 19 again. The land revealed itself, and he out-sang the CD as he headed for the coast and critical acclaim.

As the daylight was failing, he switched off with relief behind a rambling early 19th-century former coaching inn in Thorpe Gilbert.

The rear elevation of the Perseverance Hotel was a mess, with bins and crates of bottles, a smell of damp brick, cat and human urine. But it was the only hotel in town, and it had charm, with its odd angles, low, wide doors, and lamps on windowsills behind rippling original glass. He came into a bar buzzing with talk and a smell of cooking from the Carvery. Carvery! He smiled at the word. Fondue sets, Blue Nun, *Abigail's Party*. A large, clumsy girl whose blouse was not quite long enough to tuck neatly into her acrylic skirt showed him to his outdated but clean room.

The room overlooked a market square ringed with butchers (the only independent butcher near him in London was that disgusting *halal* place—Janet ordered all their food on-line), a grocer, estate agents, and an obviously unused black door, which he later discovered belonged to the Diocesan Surveyors and Court of Common Pleas. There was an independent department store, Addleways (pure Dickens!), which listed the monarchs it had seen out. There were old shop fronts with bow windows and dentilation, and Victorian street lights, converted from gas but still giving off a mild glow one half of him found appealing. "Trollopean" came to mind, even though he had never read any Trollope. Amazing that places like this still existed!

After a meal from a menu that veered between bland and trying too hard, and was in any case overcooked, he walked into a pub called the King's Head and ordered a pint of "Howden beers—the glass that cheers" ("charmingly kitsch!" he noted). The barman was pleasant in a perfunctory way, and his eyes kept wandering away to look at TV footballers. After learning that it was fairly quiet tonight and that Bosnia-Herzegovina were leading by one goal, John asked him about the tragedy.

It was terrible, the man agreed absently. He couldn't remember anything like this. There had been shed-loads of people into the area—even some coloureds (he did not notice John's pupils dilating). "And we don't see many of *those* up here!" Then he went to serve another customer and John examined the notices pinned up in the main entrance—a Demolition Derby, line-dancing, beetle drives, WI meetings, caravans for sale, and someone selling Jack Russells ("good workers—reddy now"). He smiled at the spelling mistakes. They were just the sort of ads he would have expected.

He strolled back to the Perseverance along winding Gates, following medieval desire lines past leaded windows, pargetted plasterwork (dates and initials of proud 17th-century craftsmen, flowers and birds unknown to taxonomists), redundant red-brick warehouses and old archways, and stuccoed houses with fanlights, box hedges, and sundials. One house, larger than the rest, had a naïve but imposing pair of limestone lions which had been clawing the air atop the gateposts for the last 431 years. A large ginger cat lay curled up on the windowsill of what looked like a private library—complacent symbol of the shire.

The crocketed spire of St. Blaise's could be seen from all parts of the town. Seen from directly beneath, the spire seemed to sway slightly. Moisture and midges arose from the damp grass in the churchyard, and the deep-cut path between the banked-up dead was lined with grave slabs—crude cherubim and tools-of-trades, inscriptions ranging from the perfunctory—"A. M. 1818"—to the dramatic—"Hurried into his Redeemer's presence, By the Hand of a Murderer." John read some of them and shivered involuntarily. He pulled up his shirt collar to baffle a hitherto unnoticed draught and strode away to the warmth and light.

By 8:30 a.m., after declining the "Full English Breakfast" with a fastidious shake of his head, John was charging across a part-ravaged plain—too few trees, huge fields, caravan sites, wind turbines. But the open window was admitting the cleanest air he had inhaled for years, and he was out-singing the CD. He sometimes wished he'd learned the guitar. What it must *feel* like to be up on the stage with everyone cheering!

He slid into Crisby past the Old Tollbar, now a second home, and pulled up outside the Crisby Arms, a Victorian monstrosity with black-painted pine fascia boards and encaustic tiles, some of which were missing. Giles was there, self-consciously shabby as always, carrying two cameras. "Hi" constituted most of their stock of small-talk, but then there were plenty of professional angles to arrange.

There wasn't much to Crisby, they decided—the pub, the redundant church, a tiny school, a Tudorbethan village hall built in 1919 in memory of a squire's son, a few caravans and bungalows and a few nicer houses, all defaced by plastic windows. Two lines of dunes protected the settlement from the sea. To the north, west and south, there were rapeseed-heavy or just-harvested fields divided by dykes and dotted with farmhouses, and in the distance, gentle blue slopes, where the land had made a half-hearted effort to rise above mean sea-level. John could see St. Blaise's spire at Thorpe Gilbert, an elegant exclamation-mark far away across the flatness. Small red cattle moved unhurriedly across a field, noiseless except for a faint *champ* as they tore the thick grass.

They wandered towards the beach, efficiently absorbing local colour—honeysuckle-hung hedges, yellow wheat, a cock pheasant stalking across stubble, an old brick farmhouse at the end of a winding track. It all seemed very peaceful and bland. But there was prejudice here, John sensed; there was *always* prejudice—hooded eyes looking out from huddled houses.

They crested the sand-dunes and John found himself taken aback by the ionized emptiness. The light was almost too strong, the expanse, too untrammelled. The sun on the sand actually hurt his eyes, and the landmark-less miles were profoundly disorienting. The dead must have looked tiny and insignificant in this vast context.

And if this place was unsettling now, what must it be like in the months when winds rolled straight from the east to jostle the low coast like an angry mob, casting stinging sand and making the beach alter its topography, throwing dunes up and back down again, strewing snow amongst the thorns, sending washed-up plastic bottles skittering, gulls tumbling and crying in raucous protest? This was not exactly the soft shore John had envisioned.

He could see now how somewhere like this could harbour resentment—because the locals would always be subliminally aware that they were only there on sufferance—that any wind or winter could swallow them as it had swallowed other ports and places along this same coast. It was an impermanent shore, the eroding edge of a contracting country—it was a frontier as much as it was a rearguard.

The sea had frequently carried unwelcome visitors to these isolated communities at the end of long lonely roads…raiders, invaders, press gangs, dead slimy creatures. There was a lichen-covered concrete pillbox a few hundred yards away. What would it have been like to have been on sentry go there in 1940? That was the real nature of Crisby and this coast—watchfulness and suspicion. It was a skeleton coast—a zone of transience and death. He found a place to sit and look, while his eyes got used to the hard brilliance, and soon he pulled out his laptop and began to write. Giles took a photo of him as he worked, then wandered off to find his own angles.

They left after 10 minutes and went into the village shop, making the door-mounted bell jangle. Christ, thought John, it was a *fabulous* shop, with a great 1950s vibe—firelighters, candles, biscuits, a post-office counter. Against such an unselfconscious background, it was surreal to see racks of newspapers with headlines about the disaster in this very place. The peroxided woman behind the counter stopped talking to the only customer. "Can I help you?"

"Hello. I hope so. My name is John Leyden, this is Giles…err, and we're from the *Examiner* newspaper. We're doing a piece about the tragedy. It's an opinion piece, so we're interested in finding out about local feelings. We hoped you might answer a few questions."

"Well, I don't think I will have anything very useful to tell you. I don't take any interest in politics."

"Nor do *I*," interjected the other woman, with a fragrant shudder.

"I'm *more* interested in the views of non-political people. Besides, in your important position, you must hear what all the locals are saying. How has the tragedy affected the village?"

"Everyone was very shocked of course. Nothing like this has ever happened before, although Tim—he's our local historian—did say that there was a big shipwreck here in the war, and there were bodies washed up on the beach at that time. But obviously *I* wouldn't remember that—and anyway that was a bit different, wasn't it?"

"How do you mean, different?" She was slightly on edge. Was he imagining it?

"Well, you know, in a war you expect that sort of thing. And those were Germans—not *real* foreigners. I really don't know. You should go and ask Tim; he'd give you chapter and verse."

The other woman struck in. "It was terrible. We'll all be talking about this for a long time to come. Maybe the village will be in the history books now."

"I think it probably will! Tell me—is Dan Gowt one of your customers?"

"Dan Gowt? Yes! He comes in from time to time. Lovely man, nice family; Hatty—that's his wife—and their daughter come in, too. They're—you know—respectable. My husband's in the Rotary with him, and I go to the WI with Hatty."

"Well, maybe you didn't hear what he said on television about the dead people. You wouldn't defend that!"

He watched her discomfiture detachedly, hiding a smile. Giles admired his technique.

"I—I wouldn't say I defended it—but as I said, I have no interest in politics. We don't need to. I don't remember what he said. All I know is that he goes to church, looks after his family—never in trouble. You know, respectable. But if you want to ask him what he said, you'd better go and see him yourself. He lives just up the road—Home Farm, you can't miss it. Down Sea Lane, left up the Hill, right at the bend, and there you are—it's the big old house at the end of the track."

They strolled down Sea Lane and turned up the Hill, an almost unnoticeable incline up to the local eminence of 14 feet above sea level, dotted with immaculate fields of wheat and hummocky fields of

Friesians. At the top of the Hill, there was a Hilderesque vista and a red wooden postbox on which was painted "GOWT—HOME FARM" in white. It was the old farmhouse they had noticed earlier. Neither would have been very interested in the Bronze Age barrow of Wainman's Bump, the dyke dug by the Romans, the moat that had protected the castle that had been where the farm now stood. It was too familiar to notice.

Hatty darted a furtive look from an upstairs window. She guessed they were reporters, and ducked back in mild panic. But John had noticed, and waved whilst wearing his nicest smile. She had little choice really but to come down and open the door, and listen to their introductions—and 60 seconds after that to invite the insinuating visitors into the house. Suddenly they were in her living room, drinking awful coffee. John commented on what a fine old house it was, and how well the wallpaper suited the room. It had only cost £8.99 a roll, Hatty informed him—glad to find someone at last who took an interest in her beautification efforts. Doesn't look it, John said, looking amazed—it just shows what you can do if you have good taste.

"We're here to do an opinion piece about how all of this fuss has affected the village. I hope you don't mind if I ask a few questions."

"Of course, although I can't promise I have anything interesting to say. Politics isn't my strong point! We're all as shocked as can be. I mean that sort of thing doesn't happen every day. We'll be talking about this for *years* to come!"

"It does seem to be a very quiet kind of place. And I suppose you don't see many strangers, or perhaps I should say foreigners."

"Well, it's true we don't see too many outsiders. There's the caravan park, of course, but they're no trouble. It's the right kind of caravan park, thankfully. Some of the caravanners at Williamstow are not so nice. I know I shouldn't say it, but a lot of them are, you know, Romanies—and you know what *they're* like."

"Really? What kind of things do they get up to?"

"Oh—littering, stealing, getting drunk in the middle of the day, don't you know. I saw one just the other day, in Thorpe Gilbert—sprawled out under the market cross. A lot of them are on benefits."

Clarrie had been lured from her studies by the sound of unfamiliar voices, and walked into the room at that moment. "Oh! I'm sorry!"

"Hello, dear. Don't worry—these are two gentlemen from the—the—I'm sorry…the *Examiner*. Mr Leyden and Mr…They've come to talk about the disaster. This is my daughter Clarissa."

John stood up, and introduced himself and Giles. Clarrie was perfectly shaggable, he thought, as he smiled straight into her reddening face. She wished she spoke the way he did. She had never liked her flat Eastshire accent, and had made a conscious effort to rid herself of it since going to university—something which annoyed her father greatly.

"What do *you* make of it all?" John asked Clarrie's breasts.

"Oh, hee hee, I don't know really! I'm just here for the holidays. I'm a student at Milton—studying psychology. None of us have been down to the beach since the disaster, so I don't know what we can tell you, really. But obviously it's terrible."

"Terrible. But it looks like your father—your husband, Mrs Gowt—has views on this subject. We saw him on the television. He's obviously a man of strong convictions."

"Well, I suppose so, although he doesn't take much interest in politics normally. I think he was taken a little by surprise!"

"I wish he hadn't said what he said, Dad's not really like that, you know."

"Like what?" asked John blandly.

"You know, intolerant, bigoted, a bit of a racist. He's not like that really. It's just a generational thing."

Giles sighed in admiration as John replied casually.

"Well, anyone can make a mistake. I wouldn't worry about it. And there are a lot of immigrants in the country, which does cause tension. Sometimes I wonder where it might all end."

"Well, that's right, Mr Leyden. Did you know there are Muslims living in Thorpe Gilbert? We're always saying that they'll want to build a mosque next!"

"Oh *mum*! You can't talk that way these days!" Clarrie looked at John and rolled her eyes in generational complicity, but she was smiling too.

"Well, you know what I mean, dear. They *are* different, and that's all there is to it. I like that Mr Ali down in Thorpe—and his wife is lovely, too. And such a lovely little coloured girl they have, with those big brown eyes! Everyone around here feels the same, Mr Leyden—live and let live, but still they're different."

"Oh *mum*!" Giles was so unobtrusive, and John such a good listener (and so well-mannered and good-looking) that they were laughing together like friends when Dan let himself in at the back door half an hour afterwards. His head full of work, he was annoyed to see strangers sitting there on *his* sofa, especially as he knew they must be reporters, which reminded him of things he had been trying to forget. He also resented their expensive clothes, their clean shoes, their accents. To think Clarrie wanted to be like these...these...*boys*!

John's heart was thudding at the arrival of this retrograde with his big hands, with the disadvantage of being on his territory, his ugly carpet, below his heirloom longcase clock (the only nice furniture in the room, Joh thought), crammed with his instant coffee and custard creams. But he shook Dan's hand so firmly and was so polite that Dan started to thaw. "You see, I'm not used to the media!" he demurred.

Surprisingly soon he did get used to them—specifically the idea of holding forth to these gratifyingly attentive gentlemen in the comfort and safety of home, where he had a natural moral advantage. Being here in his place gave him the confidence to express his opinions fully and forcibly. Soon, he had told John and Giles that these had been tragic events, an awful situation for the people in those countries with their awful governments, our government was awful, too, there are an awful lot of immigrants in Britain, they are very different, everyone in the village feels the same way, it will lead to violence some day, you mark my words.

By the time John and Giles had left for London, and the Gowts sat down to eat, Dan was in excellent humour. Really, he told Hatty as they watched television later, he didn't know what he had been worrying about. Such nice young men, Hatty added—not at *all* what you'd expect. Clarrie was upstairs, trying to settle down to work, mortified to find herself thinking of the interested blue of John's eyes.

Chapter 12

BROTHERS BEYOND BORDERS

Lavrion, Greece

Ibraham was on his bunk, staring through the wall. Europe's Promised Continent charms had palled after 100 days spent largely in this tiny, three bedded room with a malodorous Moroccan on one side and on the other a Chinese man whose snoring frequently kept the other two angrily awake for hours. Once, they had jumped on him in the middle of the night and thrown him onto the floor in frustration—which alleviated the problem for that night but had made the atmosphere in the room very tense.

There was nothing on the stared-at wall except a few unidentifiable stains and scratched graffiti in a medley of languages—and nothing in the room except the beds, and a formica wardrobe with a few miserable effects that even Lavrion inmates ("clients," Miss Karatakis called them) would not bother to pilfer. Like everyone else, Ibraham always kept his dollars on his person (in his case, wrapped tightly and secured by a rubber band around his right foot, inside his sock) and had made a pairing arrangement with Maged that when one of them was in the showers the other would take care of the other's possessions. The almost completely ineffective ceiling fan squeaked maddeningly as it tried to make headway against the morbidity of the atmosphere. It was air that had been breathed too often.

He and Maged had drifted apart, partly because they were in different rooms and partly because there was nothing for them to talk about. Yet they had once been comrades of the road, united in adversity, and that counted for something. Seen from today's tedious perspective, their trip on the train and the afternoon at liberty in Antalya seemed almost as far off as memories of youth, unrecapturable times of high adventure and hope. The routine of this drab place, with its appallingly rude staff, got to everyone in the end, with inmates wandering dispiritedly between their rooms, the latrines, the dining hall, the television room and the shadeless yard—the only place they could get untinned air and see anything beyond the centre. But even that was just the backs of industrial buildings behind a high chain-link fence with warders always watching.

The days were unvarying—unrefreshed rising after stifling nights, queuing for meals (*halal*, thanks to Miss Karatakis), buying sweets or soap from the trolley with a dwindling supply of tokens, goggling at television, lolling on benches or bunks. The only excitement was occasioned by football in the yard, when it was not too hot, thefts, quarrels, and a nasty fight between three Kurds and a man from Fallujah, after which the latter's right eye was left hanging repulsively on a string of muscle. The injured man was taken to hospital, and never came back to the centre. The Kurds stayed for another few days—a glowering gang that always sat at the same table—then one day their table was filled with Egyptians. The Kurds didn't return either.

There was a Sudanese named Mandoor, with deep scars on his cheeks—small, vicious-looking, with slightly crossed eyes that bulged in different directions. He rarely spoke, just stared disconcertingly at people who, if they were wise, moved away quietly. Even the other Sudanese avoided him. One who had complained about him to the warders had ended up in the infirmary with his legs broken. Mandoor's scars were gang marks, it was muttered—while others said a bomb had gone off in his face. Whenever he came in to a room, people would fall silent or leave, until he had gone again on one of his ceaseless padding patrols, during which he would search others' rooms for valuables.

He took an interest in Ibraham—perhaps because Ibraham kept to himself, or perhaps simply to find out if he had anything worth stealing. Whatever the reason, he made Ibraham terribly afraid.

One afternoon, they came face to face in the corridor. Ibraham tried to move meekly past but Mandoor blocked his way, leaning one arm menacingly on the wall. "My friend, you avoid me, huh?"

His voice was oddly high-pitched, his Arabic filled with dialect words—which made him all the more menacing.

"I'm not avoiding you."

"I get the feeling you don't like me. Now why?"

"I've told you—I'm not avoiding you. Now, if you don't mind, Mandoor…"

"Actually, I do. What's in your pockets—or maybe it's in your shoes?"

"Nothing—look, I don't want trouble…"

"It's no trouble, my friend—just give me what you've got in your pockets and your shoes and then you can go about your business."

"I don't have anything. Now, please…"

"So you're calling me a thief? Is that right—a *thief?*"

He was smiling, but his whole body was tensing and he was clutching something inside his shirt. Ibraham forced a smile.

"I didn't say that."

"Oh but you did. I'll give you one more chance…"

Two Egyptians came around the corner and almost bumped into the two men. Ibraham tried to break away and follow them, and Mandoor pirouetted and leapt a few inches into the air while pulling a sharpened spike of metal from inside his shirt. It looked like it had been made from one of the bedsteads. He shouted "Give me your fucking money!" as he raised the weapon to slice downwards into Ibraham's shoulder. But Ibraham had turned in reflex, making the jab go wide and Mandoor lose his balance, upon which Ibraham grabbed his knife hand. They fell in a wriggling heap onto the tiles, Mandoor on the bottom struggling mightily, trying simultaneously to stab, kick, shout and bite. Ibraham could see the dagger point coming closer, and the crooked eyes of his adversary popping wider and wider with the effort, while his teeth and tongue actually snapped at Ibraham's throat. He stank of sweat and fried food, and Ibraham found himself fixated by a greasy boil on his neck. Larger though Ibraham was, he could not long withstand the other's crazed commitment, and was anticipating the slicing pain of the dagger when at last the Egyptians piled in, and one of them kicked the dagger out of Mandoor's hand while another worked out everyone's hatred by booting him hard and repeatedly in the crotch, which made his eyes bulge at even stranger angles. Then, unexpectedly quickly, Mandoor gave up moving, except when his body was impelled by the violence of his assailants.

When at last they wearied of kicking him and were standing panting and looking down in faint surprise at what they had wrought, Mandoor lay face down on the tiles, his curled, bloody body racked by weeping and oaths. Ibraham and the Egyptians looked at each other, all sweating and their clothes disarrayed, and they laughed and high-fived to see their enemy's utter downfall. It was the only time during his sojourn in the centre that Ibraham felt uncomplicatedly happy.

Mandoor was taken away the following day, never to return—and then the tedium of Lavrion reasserted itself. Ibraham learned to hate it in a way he had never hated anywhere else. He hated its smells— disinfectant, toilets, boiling vegetables and dirty clothes. He hated the food. He hated the sticky scum on the never-wiped tables. He hated the blaring television and radio, all the other residents (except Maged), the warders. He hated being incarcerated. He hated the tensions that surged in the dingy corridors and common-rooms. He was disgusted by the Sudanese boy who offered fellatio for tokens. Even the sunlight was filtered and defiled through finger-smeared windows, behind which listless men smoked or played dominoes.

The image of Miss Karatakis revolved repeatedly and lubriciously. She was the only exciting thing connected with this whole awful place. But she was *awfully* exciting. Furthermore, she had seemed interested in him. He nearly hit Maged once when the other man had made a passing jocular remark about her—and wondered afterwards about the strength of his reaction.

Without knowing exactly what he was doing, or what he would say when he got there, he made an appointment to see her—and spent the following 10 days thinking of nothing else, and looking at himself in the mirror in the washroom, as he smoothed his moustache and beard, snipped straggling bits of hair and flexed his biceps.

When the panted-for appointment came around at last, he found her sitting at her crowded desk, talking to the local interpreter—an elderly quarter-Arab whose grandfather had deserted from a cargo ship in Piraeus during the 1920s. She was even lovelier than he had remembered, although a severer critic might have animadverted on the unconvincing hue of her hair, or discerned faint dark hairs under her thickly-layered foundation below her nostrils. But to Ibraham at that moment she looked like all of Europe. He inhaled deeply as if he wanted to ingest her through his nostrils, and she gave him a quizzical but amused look. Again, he sensed she relished such attention.

She motioned away the interpreter to the other side of the room and asked Ibraham to sit down on the chair across the desk from her. Sitting there, he couldn't see her ankles, but he could still see the swell of her upper body and his stomach hollowed out in hopeful pleasure. And she was so close—with only about 18 inches separating his clammy hands and ravening appetites from her satiny skin. She smiled widely, and he was both her slave and would-be subjugator. This was a *woman*...and what a mother she would make! He could envision how their children would look—the girls would all have her complexion and her eyes, and they would one day play havoc with men's hearts as their mother was doing now with his. *She* was surely the most beautiful thing he had ever been so close to.

She also made him feel like they were alone, even though everything had to be relayed through the interpreter. She had clearly read his file. She sympathized obviously sincerely. She asked about his background, and his early life. He told her about his escape from Iraq, and the *Fatima*, while she listened and made notes. He stared at her large earrings, the rhythmic swell of her breasts beneath her tight jacket, the soft green of her eyes, and envied her chair and even the keyboard of her computer. And she was looking at him in a very particular way, too! He couldn't credit his good fortune, and it was all he could do to stop himself leaping out of his seat and reaching for her. But the thought of doing so was almost as good as the act itself would soon be. *This* was why he had come West!

She explained the difficulties as he half-listened as he pictured all kinds of graphic scenes. He didn't really mind what she was saying, if she would only keep talking. Every syllable that rolled forth from that luscious mouth was a velvet cord binding them more tightly together.

The government didn't like refugees, she was saying, and had been criticized by the United Nations. It could take months for his case to come to court and he might easily fail, and get deported. There were racists out there who had no sense of justice, or humanity. Even the police were racists, who would try and have him sent back to Turkey. But there were always appeals against unjust decisions. She and others would always be fighting for people like him. There were fine people out there, too—idealistic students and activists who would go to any lengths to protect fundamental human rights. *Any lengths*—and that would some day include fighting the pigs, and the bankers. If he ever found himself without friends in Athens, he could go to any university and ask for the anarchists; the police would not be able to follow. This last piece of information did strike home through the sensual reverie; it made him realise, for the first time, that Europe really was a completely different continent. Such jejune insolence would never have been permitted at home. He toyed with the idea for a moment, but it soon drifted away, carried out to sea with every other care except for the leitmotif of TOUCHING her. He breathed deeply, trying to ingest her essence whole.

His half-hour was up. He had said almost nothing all that time, and she hadn't even asked him why he had come. She had all too clearly enjoyed talking to *him*—explaining things to him. She surely would not have taken such trouble with anyone else. Incredible though it was, this angel had chosen him out of all the other men in that place, in the world, to be her husband! It was only the presence of the interpreter that kept him from confessing his lasting love, and her from modestly reciprocating. He was drowning in the fine beading of moisture along her top lip…

They stood up together as the rencontre ended. Still with her beckoning smile, she held out her hand for him to shake, wonderfully West-like. His went out to meet hers...the interpreter was looking away, bored... their hands connected and charged, and without knowing what he was doing, out of his mind with desire, he clasped both her hands in his and pushed his face into hers as he had seen the film stars do...

...and then his seraph had become a shrew, and his left cheek was stinging, and that lately lovely mouth was SCREAMING in outrage and the words were tumbling out ugly and meaningless in all languages...SEXIST, HARASSMENT, DISGRACE, FUCKING CHAUVINIST, PIG, SWINE, HOW DARE HE, HUMAN RIGHTS...

He rocked in shock and shame as the interpreter tore him from her, and didn't resist as he was bundled out of the office, feeling he had been banished forever from Paradise...

A few weeks later, on an even more turbid than usual afternoon, the air conditioning failed and the temperature built up until even the wary bluebottles seemed too hot to fly—even to escape from the rolled-up Arabic newspapers that were flown in every week. Ibraham had never imagined that Europe could get so hot.

The fat, brusque Guard 114 lumbered through the common areas, with a more than usually unhelpful expression. One television channel showed a goalless football match from the Greek League; the other a rolling news programme—a large bomb in Baghdad, forest fires in Corinth. On a yellow and orange schematic of the Balkans, swirling coloured lines represented high pressure and more coming, with a stylized sun to drive home the message of heat followed by heat. Bored and irritable men of 21 nationalities and two denominations of Islam sat fanning themselves.

And then a Syrian accused a Lebanese of cheating at dominoes—an unjust allegation angrily denied, but unfortunately augmented with an animadversion on the Syrian's antecedents. A blur, and the Lebanese had blood waterfalling from his nose—shouts, and the lounge was full of fists, feet and chairs. 114 rushed in and blew his whistle—but someone punched him in the stomach, and he toppled onto the carpet tiles, where feet worked out months of insult on his face. A window smashed, and someone was screaming. Someone threw a chair at the television, which exploded in a satisfying blue glass flash.

The big female guard with the dyed hair came with a male colleague, only to be driven back out again by a suddenly unified mob. They retreated through the doors with the reinforced glass panels, but were followed by men whose original quarrel had been forgotten in their grudge against The Power. Ibrahim, standing irresolute at the back, saw the woman's never lovely nose dissolve as she was pushed into the door with the weight of four men behind—their hands groping up her skirt even as they ruined her face. More windows went in, and alarms were going off outside. Shouting men raced through halls that were suddenly theirs, and everyone was running and shouting, throwing fire extinguishers through windows, pushing into offices and overturning filing cabinets and dashing everything off desks onto the floor. Some men were rooting through drawers and shouting in joy as they pocketed pens and calculators, batteries and coins. Wallcharts were being ripped down, and phones and computers from their sockets. Flames suddenly erupted from a wastepaper basket, and men ululated in ecstasy. Then everyone had gone with the onrush and left the room at a run—with the exception of a vastly fat Burundian, who was looking greedily up the female warder's skirt—and Ibrahim, who had been struck by a fantastic idea.

Into his mind had flashed a picture—a certain segment of sagging fence, an alleyway beyond. Even as the female guard sat up, felt for where her face had been and tried to pull down her dress over chunky legs, Ibrahim snatched the bunch of keys from her belt. The Burundian didn't even register Ibrahim's theft of the keys; when Ibrahim last saw him, he was reaching for the prostrate woman with his huge hands for quite another reason. Ibrahim heard her scream and then the fire door shut off the sound.

He hared down stuffy, empty corridors. The sirens and shouts and things breaking were barely audible at all. He was heading for the yard, and the flawed fence that he had noticed without noticing that he had noticed it. He was thinking as he ran that this would be the last time he would see this corridor. He rushed into his room, with its strewn clothes and piled ashtray, dived under his metal bunk for his kitbag, pulled it out in one smooth movement and ransacked the chest of drawers where his laundered clothes were kept, throwing armful after armful into the bag. Then he took some of the Chinese man's spare socks and underwear; they were about the same size. It was only about 60 seconds before he was heading off again along still deserted corridors.

Thirty seconds later, he arrived at the glass-panelled doors that led into the yard, and peered out nervously into the yard. *Empty!* His quick fingers flicked through the bunch of keys, he found the one he wanted and flung back the door.

The unstirring air was somehow hopeful as he charged the hundred metres towards the fence. O beloved of Allah—there it was, still sagging, and the alleyway beyond, baking silently, and all the guards had rushed inside. Behind, the ruckus rose to a new height. He threw his bag over into the alley, went back ten metres and ran at the fence, and up. He caught the drooping top strands—they held! A sharp strain in his upper body and his leg was seeking purchase on the bowing wire— found! And then the other leg was over, and he was on the other side, almost falling as he failed to free his foot quite quickly enough, looking back momentarily at the buildings where he had languished so long.

Then he registered the other man, also running towards the fence—also tossing a bag high up and over, also taking a running jump and scrambling over the protesting wire. It was a man Ibraham had seen around, but never spoken to—he thought from Morocco. They looked at each other for a second, and grinned; outlaws thrown together, resourceful brothers beyond borders. Without needing to say anything, they picked up their bags and dashed along the alleyway. At the corner where it joined the road, they held back for a second while they looked rapidly in both directions. A police car, its lights flashing! They ducked back in time, and the car rushed past towards the main gates in the next road.

Ibraham and the Moroccan looked around once more, half-smiled and nodded to each other, and walked rapidly in opposite directions, never to see each other again. Ibraham had the strangest feeling that they might have been friends, if they had spoken to each other, and occasionally wondered afterwards what had become of him.

But for now, his priority was to get away from Lavrion. It was 90 km to Athens. He hoped the riot would go on for a lot longer, and the police would be too busy to notice one or two strays. He mustn't draw attention to himself. He forced himself to slow down and look casual. He hoped that his face and clothes weren't too dirty, and that nobody would notice that he looked foreign.

He was worrying too much. The presence of the centre meant that the nearest streets formed a mini-ghetto, with specialist shops and several informal mosques. Now, all he needed to do was to try and find some fellow Basraites—which might not be that easy, because he knew that the Iraqis in Greece were predominantly northerners, and Sunnis. He walked as casually as he could past dirty looking shops and dirtier cafes.

At last, he saw a grocery shop where the window contained a small colour photograph—a small sob in his heart—Old Basra, with Roka behind. A bald, middle-aged man with tiny eyes was sitting behind the cash desk in the otherwise empty shop. "*Salaam.*"

"*Salaam.* Can you help me? I'm from Hayyaniyah, and I want to get to Athens."

The man looked at him non-committally. "Police trouble?"

"I've run away from the centre. I want to get to England."

"So *that's* what the sirens are all about? Well, well, well. One moment."

He went to the door, and looked along the street, then came back winking and smiling conspiratorially. Ibrahim didn't like the look in his eyes. They were piggy eyes, weighing him up and somehow conveying scorn.

"You can't stay here. The police will come. You must get away, and the sooner the safer. Have you money?"

Ibrahim had over two thousand dollars in his shoe. "Some" he admitted warily. The other man threw up his hands.

"OK, OK—don't tell me. I don't want to know! I just thought if you could offer money for a lift to Athens—or, better, Piraeus. My neighbour Naseem has a car. He's from Basra too, so he would stretch a point. It's 85 kms, and he might get prison if he's caught. You'd have to cover his petrol, and his time, and then something for his trouble. He'd do it for 200 US."

"*Two hundred!*"

"Well, there it is, my friend—and don't forget you've got to make up your mind quickly. This road will be crawling with police soon. And if they take you back there, it's solitary confinement for you, my lad. And then your chances of living here legally are practically zero. Two hundred—take it or leave it. The money would also purchase my discretion, which otherwise I could not absolutely guarantee."

He grinned nastily and wandered off to rearrange some bad-looking fruit in the window. Ibraham made the only possible decision. "OK! Can we go and see him now?"

"Let's see the money first, my friend!"

Ibraham pulled the wad out of his shoe, and extracted some very creased and slightly smelly notes, which he held in the air in front of the shopkeeper's enthralled eyes. "Wait here," he said, and went out.

He was gone about five minutes—during which Ibraham felt sick, half-expecting at any moment to hear police sirens, and to see their cars screeching round the corner. The radio behind the desk played Arabic-sounding music, and Ibraham remembered the last time he had heard such music—on the train passing through Damascus. There it had sounded normal, and sad; here, it sounded tinny and incredibly incongruous. Then the man came back, with a grimly satisfied air.

"OK, it's all fixed. You can meet him in five minutes on that corner, and he'll take you to Piraeus. His name is Naseem. Two hundred for him, fifty for me." He extended his hand, palm uppermost.

"You didn't say you would expect a fee."

"Well, that's just the way it is. Think what that $50 buys you. You wouldn't want the police to know where you've gone or with whom, would you?"

Ibraham remembered how it had felt to crush Mandoor's face, and his fists balled…then he took a deep breath and handed the money to the extortionist. "Sensible, very sensible. Now go and wait on the corner, friend. He has a blue Ford. Go with God!"

Ibraham slipped out of the shop, banging the door behind him. He had almost expected Naseem not to be there, but there was an old blue Ford waiting, a fat man smoking behind the wheel. "Naseem?" The man opened the passenger door silently. As soon as Ibraham had got in, he said "Money?" Ibraham showed him the dollars, and asked "Piraeus?" Naseem nodded, and pulled out towards the Athens road.

He drove without talking for over an hour. The ugly little town dropped away unregretted, and they were on the open road, with clouds closing over. It was wonderful to be moving again. Ibraham hummed a tune he had heard on Greek television and drummed his fingers, as they passed from town to industrial park, fields, villages, fields, industrial park, onto wide roads lined with new houses that gradually got older and more crowded. They were in the suburbs of Athens, and still Naseem had said nothing. Ibraham stared out at the virtually identical houses, with their cream walls and olive trees, and had a fleeting fantasy that he was back in Basra. Big drops of warm rain began to smack onto the insect-spattered windscreen. The air outside boiled with static. At last, so startlingly that Ibraham jerked, Naseem spoke.

"I will leave you in downtown Piraeus. It is a big port—lots of international traffic. You can get on a boat to Italy; there are men who'll look the other way for a few thousand Euros. Or you can just look round for yourself—find your own lorry. Lots of stuff goes north and west from here—fruit—meat—shoes—clothes—oil. There is also a cafe there where you can find men who will get you onto a truck for the north. I will show you."

He fell back into taciturnity. Ibraham muttered "OK" and didn't know what else to say. Naseem's reminder of the obstacles still to be overcome made him feel tired and small. After everything, still to be a fugitive—creeping into countries, a continent still to cross like a thief.

There was thunder, and sheet lightning which illuminated a hideous vista—football stadium, crowded dual carriageways criss-crossing, graffiti-covered factories and grubby apartment blocks. Naseem turned onto another dual carriageway, then down a slip road which led to a non-place of bars and cafes, lorry parks, fenced fields of unregistered imported cars and offices for unsuccessful companies with world-straddling names. He pulled over outside a freight forwarders—a peeling sign over a brown warehouse, with broken windows and guard dogs apparently roaming at nights. Ibraham wondered why they bothered guarding such a place. The rain was still heavy, although the storm was passing—making the air seem slightly sweeter. Naseem pointed to a squalid café. "There—ask for Abdul Aziz. Now…"

He held out his hand for the money. He checked it and shoved it into his slacks pocket, then sat looking straight ahead. Ibraham grabbed his kitbag and ran through the faltering rain towards the café—appallingly alone in a bad neighborhood in an unfriendly country, wanted by the police and at the mercy of strangers.

Chapter 13
THE SUNDAY PAPERS

London
Sunday, 11 August

The dead had made landfall in more than one way. They had been the People's People, opined a columnist hitherto best known for having been punched by an actor he had tried to interview outside a night club at 3 a.m. He added that those who could not feel for the People's People were not People. Another journalist fought back real tears as her cameraman homed in on a salt-soaked teddy rolling slowly on the edge of the sea—for which she would deservedly win that year's Excite! Social Conscience Prize (formerly the Thanatos Pesticides Shield).

For John and a few important others, that week brought contradictory emotions—horror, guilt, moral certainty, satisfaction at being proved right and a sense that great affairs had somehow been set in train. To them, the recumbent ones were a standing reproach, a symbol of all that should be altered. They were exhibits in the case against everything that was wrong. They were polychromatic pilgrims, MLKs for the

XBox generation, Chés for today, drowned James Deans, rebels and martyrs, dead in the name of love, saintly for being silent, idealized for being unmet. They were enzymes of change. They represented a billion whorls of life passing and repassing south to north, east to west, First to Second to Third, poor to rich, fresh to stale, surging to senescent. People just like you and me (morally better than you and me)—fleeing war, famine, poverty, disease, and smothering tradition, shuffling towards our setting sun, coughing, crying, sighing and dying *en route*, to be trampled by illimitable followers with no possessions except authenticity, and always ill children held in always stick-like arms. They were dry scarecrows waiting to be woken into life—an army coming in peace, hoping for crumbs from the groaning tables of those whose cars they would wash, whose children they would nanny and care homes they would staff. They were bringing colour and vitality—enlightenment and folk-wisdom—welfare state salvation and low wages. Our world was dying. The tide had turned, and sea-longing was filling everyone with a desire to see the wide-open countries of the North. The world's *They* were on their way.

But there were some who could not comprehend, and who would do *anything* to preserve their privilege. Standing athwart history was a perverse coalition—business*men*, bankers, landowners, the military, white-bread holidaymakers who strolled blithely along beaches ignoring the imploring, populist politicians, pudgy provincials. These had thrown up bristling barricades against the future—fear and forms, police and procedures, guns and indirect discrimination, meeting tears with tear gas.

Others tried to understand, but they were imprisoned by age and class. John put his own parents in this category. As a means of overcompensating for his unhappiness at school, at home John had always sneered at the platitudes of his father—what he would later term the "blanditudes"—even rolling his eyes and yawning ostentatiously in the front pew while his father held forth from the Jacobean pulpit at

St Botolph's, peering down like the mildest of deities onto dwindling polyestered congregants before leading them in new hymns they neither knew nor cared for. Looking back now, John could see that Daddy had always been moral but muddled, too Anglican-enmeshed and middle-of-the road to live up to the family's heretical heritage.

Leydens had lived in their part of Devon since at least the 15th century, and over centuries which they had helped to make turbulent had combined Protestant fundamentalism with political radicalism—"an hereditary taint of democratic revolutionism," as a 19th-century Tory had written in the *Quarterly Review*. Some Leydens had hazarded their lives for their beliefs; two brothers had actually been martyred under Queen Mary, and their neglected monument still stood in the nearby market town. But none had ever recanted. Atheist though he was, John was proud of his ancestors' determined dangerousness, and saw himself as following in their tradition. It was, in fact, the only tradition he valued. Like them, *he* wasn't afraid to take unpopular stances despite considerable personal sacrifice.

He now took a slightly kinder view of his father's Biblical commentaries, which had been well-meaning and informed by post-structuralism—but they were still *Biblical*, written in a wisteria-clad rectory beside a 14th-century church down the far end of an oak-embowered Neolithic trackway. Where was the risk or relevance in *that*? Like all his generation and class, Daddy had no idea what it was like to feel the sting of social exclusion. He was still festering away there in Devon, although now in Leyden Hall (he had retired from the Church), still writing letters to the *Times*, some of which were published, on matters ranging from moral decline and welfare cuts to the fine spiritual example set by Dr. Martin Luther King.

His safe stolidity was complemented by Mummy's cushion-making and easy listening. Her sole concept of caring was to send off conscience-salving large cheques to various charities. John had never made the mistake of simply sending money to charities. What was needed was revolutionary reform rather than palliative care. Everything was linked; all boats must rise at the same time. His parents had never engaged in such deep analysis, or attempted to view the world's wrongs as different aspects of a universal problem. He had often tried to explain this to them, but it had been a waste of time.

He had left all this behind as soon as he could, and by the time he had finished Oxford, he felt had effectively resigned from his compromised class and joined The Conspiracy of *Us*—the alert, liberal, open, noble, generous, cultured, committed and courageous—just a few who saw the big picture, and brave enough to say what must be said. He had never looked back, except in faint anger.

He rarely saw his parents now, but spoke to his mother quite often—mostly in relation to financial matters. But now she would also moan about their health and ask when he was coming down to see them. He found her crude moral blackmail quite amusing—as was the way they tried to exert financial control through his yearly allowance. They had even bought him his flat in a flagrant attempt to buy his favour. But he was too independent-minded to be fooled like that—and anyway weren't there more important things to do, for the world's sake? John was supremely aware that his was A Good Work, and he hummed as his hands flew facilely across the laptop keyboard.

Dylan Ekinutu-Jones was in his Africana/retro furnished flat overlooking where the Hackney Marshes had once been, half-listening to a play called *The Undocumented*. The *Examiner*'s "Culture Czar" had recommended it—"a coruscating, compassionate, sassy, streetwise, earthy and enlightened *bildungsroman* following the lives of six *sans*

papiers as they take a rollercoaster roadtrip through Europe's underbelly. A ballsy fable for our times."

But he found the thing unconvincing—it had been written by a minor Scottish aristocrat who pretended he was a working-class Glaswegian—and his mind strayed restlessly to the real-life drama up at the impossibly sequestered-sounding Crisby St. Nicholas.

Like John, Dylan also saw the dead as symbols, but he also felt an illogical empathy with the dead. It was a reaction based on an misplaced sense of consanguinity. He thought they-could-have-been-me-or-my-dad. It was—the odd expression came suddenly—a *blood-pact*. The dead had been like him, he felt—unwanted, unappreciated, unloved. They had lost the battle against prejudice and persecution, against the hypocritical, hated, embraced, envied West; it was the same battle he had always fought, was fighting, would always fight until, like them, he fell storming the bastion. He read the details over and over, and hot tears started to his eyes. It was all so *unfair*.

The House had been recalled to discuss the crisis and all week Members displaced their displeasure at being recalled from holiday by vying with each other to apostrophize History in the most hyperbolical terms.

From Parliament on cross-party wings flew a statement condemning "the inhumane trade in people's misery" and "the racism that blights lives and shames us all." Richard Simpson's energetic contribution at the first debate was wonderfully representative: "Mr Speaker, 'onourable members, this is not a time for sadness but for *anger*. ANGER! We need haction to make sure such fings never 'appen agine. We need a full hinvestigation, and we need it *NOW!*"

He sat down to huzzas and frantic waving of papers. The House rushed and resounded like trees in a gale. The place smelled passion and decisiveness, and it rose to their heads like the Members' claret. The PM had parried with appropriate expressions, but looking at the surging House, he was conscious that he had failed to gauge the mood as well as Simpson. "Look at that shit Spitson," he thought. "He's loving every second."

On Friday night, maroon-blazered Jim Moore, "Pinner's Perry Como," troubadour to lower-middle-class women and gay connoisseurs of kitsch, had halted his sell-out West End show to announce a moment's silence "for all the world's unwanted." Many members of his audience, prone anyway to lachrymosity, found emotion welling up as the gilt cherub-decorated theatre subsided into fidgety quietude—still except for thousands of thronging ghosts, the imminent unrequited future asking "*Why?*"

Afterwards, when he sat at the baby grand to strum the first chords and hum the first lines of "A Babe is Born"—when the lights played on his well-styled hair and well-made shirt, and seemed to be making his eyes mist—all dams began to break, and the hall was awash with uterine upset, streaming faces flickeringly lit by several thousand provided safety lighters.

"It was truly the 'Best of' Jim Moore," one columnist wrote feelingly, "a spine-tingling moment when one felt that good old-fashioned compassion can still move mountains. Moore is a man of bounding sincerity, with almost too much heart than is good for him."

"Moore does Moore" was the *Meteor*'s view. "Big-hearted Jim moved his audience to TEARS last night as he sang to raise money for the Bodies on the Beach. Fans SOBBED in the plush New Parnassus Theatre in

London's West End as the millionaire singer brought the house down by singing "A Babe is Born" to a CAPACITY crowd. Then the crowd dug deep to raise NEARLY £80K for refugees. Goodonyer!"

Also on Friday evening, in a huge converted warehouse on the edge of London, Atrocities Against Civilians, notorious for deaf-making volumes, depressive lyrics, drugs and the "polysexualism" of vocalist Scum (of which Imogen Williams had had recent disappointing experience), had halted halfway through their anthem "Dead God" and said that they would only play the rest if the audience stumped up £70,000 "for those poor fuckers on the beach who only wanted a better life for themselves and their kids. Nowo'imean?"

The cheering and stomping audience—white collar workers dressed mostly in black—did know what he meant and delved for their credit cards while the drums kept up an insistent pounding and Scum alternately harangued them and snorted cocaine from the top of an amplifier: "Come on you tossers! We wanna see your fuckin' money! No money, no music!" The audience groaned and swayed as they paid. For almost half an hour, harassed venue staff passed through the crowd collecting card details and cash, while Atrocities' drummer beat his kit with unrelenting amphetamine-induced energy. Then suddenly, the drums crashed back into familiar pulsations, the guitars growled, the giant torchières flared, and "Dead God" restarted in all its manic might, Scum filling the stage with flailing arms and filthy mouth, like some angular Anti-Christ.

At the end, after the band had departed the stage with a final flurry of scatology and sweat, and the audience was thinking about nannies to be relieved of their charges, the huge screen behind the stage displayed "£81,045 and counting..." A tired untidy cheer came up from the exiting fans, faltering as they sniffed the cool night air coming through the opened doors.

The crowds outside St Peter's bent their heads as the Pope entreated *Urbis et orbis* to pray for all lost souls—cut adrift by war and injustice, and beset by perils—for we are all travellers on life's dangerous pilgrimage—indifference should never be a sentiment for human beings. The words of the tiny, fragile figure boomed around the vast square below the stern gaze of outsize stone saints, and far beyond to pierce Catholic hearts from Coimbra to Cuzco.

Although nominally Catholic, Dylan was less impressed, and commented in his blog, "His white Holiness and his so-white Curia are part of the problem, not the solution. His exhortation wasn't translated into a single Asian or African language. What message does that send out? The Vatican is as out of touch on racism as it is on "family values." They're all at See on this burning issue. Rome needs a new and more representative Establishment."

Meanwhile in Eastshire, there was a special service from Williamstow Minster. Sensitively-selected schoolchildren trilled a song that had sprung into existence that very week. "A Land That's Free to Make Us Proud" had been written in just a few minutes by a Pentecostalist on the day the bodies were found, and fortunately overheard by a radio producer who happened to have been passing the church in West London. It had been recorded in a rush and played repeatedly since, a classic-in-the-making:

> *We're sending out a message to all people,*
>
> *From mosque and dome to synagogue and steeple.*
>
> *We're sending out a message to the world –*
>
> *The flag of Jesus' love has been unfurled.*

Now it's time to send our love out to the stars,
And raise our voices clear and high and loud –
It's time to shout our passion near and far
And build a land that's free to make us proud!

The words rose moistly into the Norman arches and nave, capering around the grotesque capitals that had looked down for eight centuries on bored Catholics, then bored Anglicans. The radio programme *The Rite Stuff* broadcast the service live into the homes of thousands of ladies with shelves of self-help books and wall calendars showing kittens sleeping in flower pots. The winsome sound washed over kindly ladies roasting beef and Yorkshire puddings, or looking out from PVC conservatories over immaculate gardens studded with resin statuettes.

Crisby went one even better with an unprecedented ecumenical event, as Jimmy the Team Vicar held a joint service on an unseasonably damp afternoon, with representatives of the Methodists, Baptists, Primitive Baptists, Unitarians, and the Catholics. There were local councillors, representatives of the emergency services, the Scouts, Guides, Women's Institute, village hall and playing-field committees, the local papers, and almost all of the villagers, including the Gowts. The local MP Roger Swithin had turned up and was standing over near the Coast Channel cameras, looking very pious—although everyone had heard that he generally did not trouble the local churches with his presence on Sundays, being too busy with constituency business in the shape of the married woman who chaired the district council. There were also several black and Asian people—the first Dan had ever seen on the beach. He reproached himself for noting the fact.

There were also five strangers who called themselves the Icthys Brethren. They wore thin robes with stylized fish emblems and their bare feet were linked at the ankles by real chains. They bore hand-lettered signs— "Pilgrimage Against Prejudice" and "Walking the World to Wake the

World." Dan noticed that one of them was shivering helplessly, and his eyes had a disconcerting distant glitter, as if contemplating the shores of Jordan. Dan liked religion well enough—it did him good to go to church once in a while, and in any case, it was expected of you. He also found something reassuring about seeing old churches—but he could never understand the sort of impulse that could make people wander the country looking—he felt guilty thinking it—ridiculous. He wondered how his useful week's work—all the crops in, and good ones, to fill people's bellies—would weight against those of these fish-men.

Behind the Brethren stood Crisby's school—33 fidgety children, resentful and embarrassed, especially the boys, all carrying pink balloons with heart designs and little tied-on teddy bears.

There were two guitarists, a flautist, a keyboardist with his own little amplifier, two cornet players seconded from the local Salvation Army and two tambourinists. They led the congregation through "For Those in Peril on the Sea"—a strong performance, sincerely sung—then "Psalm for the Poor," written originally for schools but quickly withdrawn for being too specifically Christian. The calypso chorus went:

> *This is a psalm for the poor,*
>
> *A song for all the world –*
>
> *It's time to open the doors*
>
> *And let the sun shine through –*
>
> *The su-uu-u-un shine through.*

The sun wasn't shining through today, as light, large rain began to splash soundlessly on the sand. "Just as well the harvest is in and stowed," Dan mused. The playing and singing were ragged, but the clerics struggled gamely, tapping their feet in time as rain splattered sand onto their shoes and the hems of their cassocks. Dan wondered what it must be like to drown. He shuddered and tried to concentrate on the lyric. But it wasn't as good as that other song—the one he'd heard so much on the radio, something about "A Land That's Free."

The clerics each spoke shortly, the funereal assemblage sheltered under gaily-striped golf umbrellas. Their denominational differences were suspended, subsumed within the greater story of a giant wave of misery, rushing through the hot countries to cast up its destitute victims on the bad conscience of the North. We were all Peoples of the Book, which was a comfort wasn't it, and their grieving relatives must find it helpful at this difficult time to know that the whole world is bound up with them in sorrow. Prayers went out to them all, from us all. The Icthys Brethren were walking the world to wake the world, and would welcome your sponsorship.

And so to the climax—a mass release of balloons, to represent those souls now ascending to A Better Place. All watched in mild interest as the balloons and their tiny ursine hitchhikers ascended against the drizzle and were taken by a breeze to be pushed out over the sea. Then there were Amens on behalf of the international community, and a scuttling for cars. Hatty and Clarrie joined in the scuttle, but Dan waited behind for a moment, standing still looking over the scuffed-up strand—at the dark clouds passing slowly, the scudding balloons and the cratered sand. "Poor bastards!" he said out loud. He turned and walked slowly after the others.

The *Examiner on Sunday* featured a hastily commissioned poem called "Leaving the Craft," by Emanuele le Sage, the first female Antiguan Poet Laureate:

> Is it time, then,
>
> To leave the craft?
>
> To step into the coldness and the rain?
>
> Isn't it time, friends,
>
> To calm the seas
>
> Of change that rush and rise, to conquer pain?
>
> There are no strangers, we are all strangers,
>
> Each to other –
>
> Each other's brother,
>
> Each other's mother.

Below was a cartoon of a man with a crewcut and buck teeth, brandishing a pitchfork to halt a mass of undifferentiated but obviously "non-white" faces. Five pages were taken up by John's "Frontline—Where *Dad's Army* meets *Mein Kampf*—the racism that shames the shires," which that cultural critic read proudly as he strap-hung towards Tate Modern. His enjoyment was only slightly marred by a boisterous gang of young black men, one of whom (John was sure) had been staring at his MX phone with LAN, WAN, i-info, FreeRoam™, and lightweight NASA-patented alloy with racing green enamel trim. He pushed the handset into his pocket and buried his head in the paper to avoid perilous eye contact.

> In Thorpe Gilbert, it is still possible to believe in England. The town evokes Trollope, a million chocolate boxes, with its small shops, handsome old buildings and quaint streets, all dominated by the huge spire of St. Blaise's church which has stood at the centre of civic life since the late 1400s. The streets are bustling and cheerful, and there is a palpable sense of belonging and of community. It is a nostalgic dream of a town for those who live

there and for visitors, who find in places like Thorpe Gilbert echoes of the England they long for. It is cosy, comforting, neat, structured, reassuring—and racist.

Because it doesn't take too much digging beneath the 'heritage' to uncover a very different town—a town of suspicion and endemic insularity that on occasion can manifest itself in bigotry and violence. In the Middle Ages, Eastshire was a stronghold of the resistance against the Reformation, and illiterate peasants marched on London to preserve superstition and privilege. In 1788, the non-conformist preacher "Glory" Gibbons gave a sermon outside the doors of the church that caused a riot, during which a prominent local Catholic was badly beaten, and his private chapel burned.

Today, the area's ultra-conservatism and fear of 'The Other' is subtler, masked by hypocrisy, but it is still present, a cesspool churning below the smooth surface. This is a town one of whose weekly newspapers, the *Thorpe Gilbert Intelligencer*, just a few years ago described a crime suspect as being 'of African appearance'.

I meet Rizal Shah, chair of the Rural Racism Task Force, which last year opened an office in the town, and issued the landmark report by Saffron di Montezuma and Ben Klein, *Why Should There Always be an England?—Change and Continuity in the Counties*. A quietly spoken, tired-looking man who came from Kashmir in 1960, Rizal has had long experience in this field (pun intended).

He told us 'There are specifically rural forms of racism, based on ignorance. To add to this massive problem, there is also an institutional denial of the BME experience in rural areas. There is a widespread perception that where there are not many people from ethnic communities, there is no need for anti-racist education or multidisciplinary multiculturalism. We are starved of resources. We need a more positive approach to diversity in order to facilitate community cohesion. That is why we are working in conjunction with trades unions, the local education authority, the police, and other key players to formulate a strategy for change that can prepare the county for the challenges of our interdependent world. We highlight the inevitability and desirability of change—a change we can direct and drive forwards'.

Wise words, but if you want a more graphic example of rustic racism, ask Amir Khan. Amir came to Thorpe Gilbert 35 years ago with his family. They opened a restaurant on Cattlegate—a bastion of good food in a town of fish 'n' chips. Amir remembers the Saturday night in 1987 when terror came to town. 'It was 3:15, and we were all asleep. Then we heard the windows being smashed downstairs, and the next thing we knew, there were people shouting and laughing, and the smell of smoke. I rushed downstairs, to find all the windows smashed, and the curtains on fire, but the men had gone. I called the police, and put out the fire by tearing down the curtains and throwing them into the street. My wife was screaming, and the babies, too. It was terrifying. And the police never caught the men who had made this racist attack. I will never forgive them.'

Amir's face fills with pain, the pain of a decent man who cannot comprehend the injustice of the world. His wife looks on in silent solidarity, as he goes on, 'When we came here, it was like a dream—clean lovely country, lovely people, we were happy. But since that night, we have always worried, wondered. Since that night we have known what lies behind the friendly and smiling faces.'

I nod sympathetically. What else can I do? How can I explain to someone like Amir that this is a town where outsiders can never become insiders—that his family's terrible experiences are connected to the religious riots of the past, to the radar installations on the hill above the town, erected to guard against Russian missiles that never came, to the cultural conflation of 'blood and belonging', and pastorality and permanence created by 'heritage' tea-towels and the forces of conservatism? I leave the family's cramped terraced house feeling that nothing can ever compensate Amir for the faith he lost that night.

But if Thorpe Gilbert is hopelessly provincial, what about Crisby St. Nicholas, the tiny village catapulted to infamy this week? In comparison with Crisby, Thorpe Gilbert is a vibrant, cosmopolitan metropolis.

Ten miles from Thorpe, along roads that gradually become tracks, turning its back to the land and to life, surrounded by walls of trees and staring seawards with suspicion, there it is—a handful of houses and a church dropped down on the edge of England. It is a place which has shunned modernity. It is a place which has always been suspicious of strangers, of governments (it was a hotbed of smuggling in the 18th century), enlightened influences of all kinds. TV programmes and newspapers may as well come from another planet, and are seen as irrelevant in relation to the activities of the Women's Institute, of the church hall committee, and the farrowing of prize sows.

It is a place where people stop talking when they see you, and openly refer to everyone from outside the village as 'foreigners'. It is a place where unregenerate racists are regarded as upstanding members of the community because they belong to the Rotary Club. It is a place where the mere fact of someone being 'not from around these parts' means they are up to no good. A *vox pop* in the village shop, the briefest conversation with any of the locals, reveals an abyss of ignorance, an inability to empathise. There is a 'combine culture' of casual chauvinism.

Crisby, like many other places in this septic isle, is a cultural desert, without theatres, concert halls, art galleries, nor even a good restaurant—just demolition derbies, caravans, bungalows, acres of cabbages, takeaways, and a pub where the beer comes from metal kegs. The nearest they get to public art are misspelled notices advertising Sharon's line-dancing lessons.

Giles had supplied a picture of a morbidly obese, tracksuited couple waddling past a bingo hall.

And if Crisby is a cul-de-sac, local farmer Dan Gowt lives up a cul-de-sac within a cul-de-sac—a highly appropriate location for his old family farm where he lives with his wife and daughter.

Mrs Gowt admits that her CD-voting husband 'can be a bit peppery at times', but insisted that they were churchgoers who had often given money to Third World charities—a remark which merely demonstrated how village viewpoints are shaped by media stereotypes deriving ultimately from colonial era racism. Their psychology student daughter Clarrie, 22, is refreshingly independent-minded, admitting that her father was 'a bit of a racist'—a view reinforced by neighbour Charlie Davies, who told us that he often argued with Mr Gowt, and that he was 'very intolerant, always complaining about something'.

Dan Gowt was brusque, but it was not long before we realized that his notorious interview had not been an aberration. Is there too much immigration, we asked. 'Yes!' came the chilling reply. Should the undocumented be repatriated? 'Yes' he barked vehemently. This vitriol just a few hundred metres from the calamitous strand. It was a performance of stunning insensitivity—all the more surreal for being experienced in a sunny English room filled with 1980s décor mistakes, with the sound of birds coming in through the window, and the scent of roses hanging in the air. We came away, depressed and defiled.

He concluded eventually.

Crisby is by no means unique. All across these islands, there are similar places, living in the past, fearing the future, basking in complacency and furtive fascism. These villages are emblematic of the way all of England used to be, class-ridden, hanging monkeys as Frenchmen, and now venting their spleen against desperate refugees. One can feel strangely sorry for country people whose horizons extend no further than the edge of their territory. In a way, they, too, are victims of education cuts.

It is comforting to think that they are increasingly unrepresentative, and the department store that brags of seeing out seven monarchs may soon see out the old England, as we pass into a new phase of our shared story. Dan Gowt said in his notorious television interview that refugees were 'not what we're used to around here'. Well, he had better start getting used to them. Because 'they' are 'us'—whoever 'we' are. The deaths may not have been in vain, if they have shed light on England's shame. From beyond the grave, the dead can teach us about tolerance, transcendence, and truth.

The rain had stopped, and Home Farm looked washed and lovely in the late afternoon. Tired after a week of late nights and early risings, Dan and Hatty were settling down to watch *Detective Inspector Davies* when the phone rang. Hatty went to answer, and Dan yawned whilst looking out at a thrush bounding perkily across the soaked lawn. He would long remember that moment of peace.

"Dan, it's someone for you from *The Messenger* newspaper. What do *they* want?"

"Oh no—haven't we had enough of these people. Tell them I'm out."

"I can't—I've already told them I'll get you. You have to speak to him now. He sounds very nice. It mightn't take too long."

Groaning, Dan went into the hallway. It was a southern voice, of the kind he always called "stuck-up."

"Mr Gowt, my name is Nick Vittorio from *The Messenger* in London. I'm sorry to bother you on a Sunday. But I wanted to ask for your reaction to the article in today's *Examiner*."

"Goodness, I'd forgotten all about that. It's been such a busy week."

"Ah, so you haven't seen it. That's a bit awkward. I have a copy here. I can read some of it to you—only a small bit mentions you, but what there is is—well—rather negative."

Dan groaned. "Oh, well, if you don't mind. Mr.—Mr.—I'm sorry."

"Vittorio. I'm afraid it won't be pleasant to hear it."

Dan's heart was thumping, and it was difficult to take in the meaning of the words. "Mr. Gowt? Mr. Gowt?"

"Err, yes, um, sorry. I'm amazed. He's misrepresented us something awful!"

"I'm afraid it does look bad. But how are you going to respond? You can let him say these things, or you can put your side."

"I'll need to think about this before I give you a reply, and I'd like to read the full thing."

"I understand. May I call you back later then?"

"Yes, yes, Mr.—er. Goodbye."

A little later, he and Hatty were looking at the paper in considerable consternation. Hatty had one hand on his shoulder, the other on her open mouth. Her eyes were puzzled and wide. "This is *terrible*! What are we going to do?" Dan was very grateful for the "we," and he twined his arm around her still-slender waist.

"I don't know, Hat. I don't know. I'll ask the other chap when he calls back."

Hatty was foreseeing conversations stopping as she approached, people she knew turning away, expressing sympathy while secretly recoiling.

"Wouldn't it be best just to ignore this? No-one around here reads this paper."

"But they *can't* talk about me like this, Hat. It's just not *right*. Other people will have seen it. Charlie Davies will have a copy, for one. He's mentioned in it. You can imagine what *he'll* make of it! No, I've *got* to set the record straight."

"But Dan, you can't take on a *London* newspaper!"

"Oh can't I? They'll see they've messed with the wrong man. Sorry, Hat, my mind's made up. A mistake's been made all right, but not by me. I tell you, they've taken on the wrong man! You wait and see, I'll get an apology from them. They may think they're big stuff, down there in London, with their lawyers and all, but they've overstepped the mark and they are going to back down before I do!"

Hatty had rarely him look so angry, and she knew how stubborn he could be. So she shook her head resignedly and retreated to *Detective Inspector Davies*—although she hardly took in anything of the plot. Her husband talked more and more agitatedly to *The Messenger*, and when eventually he put it down it started to ring again.

After he'd finished on the phone, about two hours later, Dan spent almost three hours writing a heartfelt letter to the *Examiner*, with his tongue poking through pursed lips, his tired eyes 1970s NHS-spectacled, his neck stiff, and his wrist aching with the strain of using his father's gold fountain-pen, which he had unearthed eventually from the old bureau stuffed with bits of machines and old animal medicine. He felt instinctively that his customary biro wasn't a serious enough tool.

When he had done, he felt proud of his production—which contained what he considered the right mixture of dignified sorrow and pointed outrage at liberties taken. It would surely strike home with anyone with any sense of decency. The letter would never be published, but by Tuesday he would have other things to worry about.

Chapter 14
A Journey in the Dark

Piraeus, Greece

The place was one of shadows and shouting. The curtains were closed and the lights were off. When Ibraham's eyes became accustomed to it, he was surprised to find it almost empty, except for two Arab men at one chipped formica table, and a third behind the counter. They were all watching a football game on a vast screen; the shouting was coming from the fans on the field.

"*Salaam.* I wish to speak to Abdul Aziz."

The counterhand looked over involuntarily at the table, then asked surlily, "Why do you wish to speak to Abdul Aziz?"

"It is a business matter."

"What business matter?" It was a new voice, authoritative, from a burly, older man at the table. His companion watched narrowly.

"Are you Abdul Aziz?"

"Who are you and what do you want?"

"It is a private matter."

"Speak it out; I am Abdul Aziz."

"I am from Basra, and I wish to go to England. I have been told you can help me."

"That is illegal. Naturally, I know there are people who arrange such things. But it is illegal and therefore expensive. Where in Basra are you from? Who is your father?"

"Hayyaniyah. My father is dead. He disappeared. He was against Saddam."

Aziz picked his teeth with a toothpick thoughtfully. "What is your name? How did you get here?"

Ibrahim told his name, and about his journey. He omitted only Lavrion, not wishing to alarm Aziz with the prospect of a police manhunt. Even without this, grudging respect dawned in Aziz's eyes. He signed to Ibrahim to sit down. "You seem honest. You must understand that we need to be cautious. The Greeks don't like us. They think we're like Turks—what they don't know is that we're a whole lot worse!"

Ibrahim smiled politely.

"I think I can help you—mostly by putting you in touch with others. Do you have money?"

"Not much left now."

"That is a pity. The people I will introduce you to are not like us; they are hard people, greedy, not really followers of The Prophet, praise His Name. They are Albanians, and they are involved in many things. I do not like doing business with such people, but we do not have the contacts they do. If anyone can get you to England, they can. Come back here just before evening prayers."

The rain had stopped when Ibrahim left, feeling easier but wondering how he could while away four hours in that place. He bought a kebab and a bottle of Coke, which he consumed as he walked. If he stayed in one place he might attract attention. He wondered if the police had discovered that he was missing.

Those were heart-sinking streets. Sometimes the asphalt had worn away to reveal old cobbles and rail tracks. There were waste patches and building sites where scabby cats yowled—flat-fronted old warehouses with tiny barred windows—prostitutes in doorways—roadworkers, office workers and naval recruits in white uniforms—walls of political and rock-band posters and graffiti from the previous weekend's anti-austerity riots—closed-up churches—cranes that hadn't been used since the 1970s—shining offices waiting for their first tenants, who were not expected soon —a torrent of trucks that sent up waves of brown water from new puddles—Green Line suburban trains. There were *halal* and non-*halal* butchers and bakers, with windows of too-pale carcasses and fly-buzzed bread. He could see the funnels of ships above rooftops—and then once, briefly beautiful between two houses, the suddenly sunlit sweep of the harbour known to the ancients and even to Vikings, who had scratched runes on the stone lions that had once guarded the gateways before being looted to Venice. Ferries were crossing and re-crossing in the sparkle, and there was a rumour of graceful grey from the naval dockyards at Zea (where the *Mithridiates* had been built). Further away, there was a tantalizing hint of the magical Europe he had hoped to disover—tumbling rocky headlands with large villas and beyond again to blue islands.

He was back at the now closed café at the appointed time, where he was met by Aziz. They walked for several streets speaking very little, then through a dusty blue doorway and up a long flight of uncarpeted stairs. An era ago in 1867, this had been a newly-rich merchant's prestigious new house, with secure storage in the cellar and trace elements of neo-classical splendours in the cornicing. There were original mahogany doors disguised under layers of white paint gone grey and greasy with unnumbered fingermarks. Now, it had been sub-divided, sub-let, subsumed. Legal and illegal transients shared the rambling, crumbling building with drug addicts, single mothers, and a former dockworker who secretly, despairingly, voted for whatever was the furthest right party on the ballot.

One of the rooms, once a dining room whose acanthus frieze survived, now divided its degraded hours between television room for an extended Iraqi family and a Shia mosque. The blue nylon carpet was stained and worn, a statically-charged highway for slippered feet by day, a rich hunting ground for brown beetles after dark, themselves hunted by mice which teemed behind the coming-away skirting. Tall uncurtained windows looked over damp-streaked walls, blown guttering and overflowing dustbins—and through the tall windows a grand vista over the promontory, backdrop to two-and-a-half millennia of Athenian navigation.

The room filled with a plethora of accents as men arrived for prayers, and laved their hands and feet in plastic basins. The women and girls worshipped in the smaller room downstairs. There were jeans and T-shirts, robes and hybrids of these modes, from Iraq, Saudi, Kuwait, Egypt, Yemen and yet more places. Ibrahim was intrigued to see paler complexions—the first white Muslims he had seen. Aziz whispered, "There you are! Now, those whites are the Albanians! Those are the fellows who can help you. They've got many friends, and don't mind what they do. People, drugs, drink, guns...whatever they can get. Between us, they're scum, but you need them!"

Ibraham wondered how these "scum" told each other apart. They were wearing new-looking European clothes, and took little notice of their Arab co-religionists. One took a call on an expensive-looking mobile. But one also had prayer beads, and when the *imam* went to the head of the room, near the inked-on *mihrab*, the Illyrians knelt with the rest, bowing and sitting up apparently as assiduously as the rest.

Afterwards, most of the worshippers filtered away, but Aziz went over to a short, slim, black-haired, crater-cheeked Albanian of about 50, wearing jeans, sports jacket and a big-collared black shirt and white tie. This was Lekë Kruja, a former sergeant in the Kosovo Liberation Army and a prominent member of a clan from Veliki Trnovac. He was a legal refugee, augmenting his benefits income transporting diverse cargoes across Europe without asking questions of the transporters. He looked at Ibraham searchingly while Aziz explained, and even at a distance Ibraham felt abashed. Aziz came back took him aside.

"They can get you to the coast in a truck leaving tomorrow, then they will put you on a boat to England. The journey would cost you $1,700, and take four days. That includes the boat. You would bring your own food and water. It will be uncomfortable, but it might be the quickest and easiest way. It's also cheaper than I had thought. But he must know now."

England in a week! But it would mean all his money gone. And the Albanians had eyes like scorpions. "What do you suggest, Mr Aziz? If I pay this, I will have no money left. And I don't like the look of these people."

Aziz looked over his shoulder. "These people are filth. But they know what they're doing. And they keep their promises because it's good business. The police can't break them, because they've got family all over Europe—Kosovo, Serbia, Italy, Germany. They call it *kanun*—family honour—and *besa*—secrecy. No-one will screw with these guys. It's a lot of money, sure, but whatever way it will cost you a lot. And this will be the quickest way. Take my advice, and be on that truck—and in a week's time you'll be drinking *chai* with the Queen of England!"

So Ibrahim handed over $100 as a deposit, with another $100 to be paid when boarding the lorry, the rest to be given up in Rotterdam. Kruja nodded, barked instructions to Aziz, then clumped away down the uncarpeted stairs. The hard sound made Ibrahim remember he had nowhere to stay that night, no money, and the streets were damp. But Aziz seemed to have taken a liking to him.

"Where are you staying, my friend?"

"Nowhere. Can you suggest a very cheap place?"

"I've got a room you can use!"

"But I have no money!"

"Forget it; call it Basra *kanun!*"

Ibrahim was intensely moved. He had not expected such disinterested helpfulness on the journey. He felt bound to be honest.

"You are very kind. But I must tell you something. I escaped from Lavrion. There was a riot—and I saw a chance to get away. So the police may be looking for me even now. I do not wish to place you in trouble or danger."

Aziz laughed and slapped him on the back. "No trouble! You are not the first young man I have met who does not want the police to know where he is. Those police are racists and infidels. Who cares about them and their filthy laws? No, my friend, I offered you hospitality and hospitality you shall have. The police—ha!—the police can look after themselves!" He snapped his fingers scornfully, took Ibrahim by the arm and propelled him down the noisy stairs and onto the clamorous road.

He lived in a new house with his wife and ten-year-old son, who had joined him in Athens last year as part of a family reunification scheme. They shared lamb *pilaf* and apricot while Ibraham told of his journey. By contrast, Aziz was obviously reluctant to talk about how he had got out of Iraq, and it would have been impertinent to persist. Ibraham wondered what he was hiding, or trying to forget. There were secrets there.

But whatever had happened in Mr. Aziz's life, whether it was sorrow or shame, their kind hospitality over the ensuing 24 hours made him even more anxious not to implicate them in his troubles. He was therefore relieved, but also genuinely sorry, the following evening to make his *adieux* and accompany Aziz to the metro stop.

Ibraham had never been on a metro before, but he did not have much time to relish the experience, for the rendezvous was just a ten-minute hurtle away. They alighted on an almost deserted road of old factories, alongside a fence behind which waited dozens of lorries in a floodlit enclosure. A few hundred yards away across the road, a shape stood smoking. Aziz grunted "That must be our man," and led the way.

"You'll be travelling in one of these lorries, Ibraham" he explained. "It will not be very comfortable, but it should be reliable. Anyway, it'll only be for a few days—and you will have company. They didn't lay on this little trip just for you, you know!"

"I know, Mr Aziz—I'm sure I'll be fine." But he wasn't at all sure.

The waiting man was Kruja. As they approached, he looked at his watch and along the street. "So you are here. Good."

"*Salaam*; here is the young man."

"We must go now—but first I must search you."

"Search me—for what?"

"Recording machines, cameras, weapons."

Ibraham stood while Kruja frisked him professionally and searched through his bag. Then he walked away, clearly expecting Ibraham to follow. Ibraham turned to Aziz.

"Thank you, sir, for your kindness. I will send you a letter from Great Britain. Goodbye."

"Ha ha, best not to do that, eh? But goodbye, and go with God!"

The Albanian was already 20 metres away, stomping towards a gateway in the fence, and Ibraham had to run to catch him. He was amazed to see Kruja simply walk past the security guard in the kiosk, who never even looked up from his newspaper as Kruja and Ibraham stooped under the red-and-white barrier. The guard was a poor man, and the small bundle of Euros he found in the desk every month came in useful.

They walked through the lorry park without meeting anyone, although the Albanian looked around constantly. They stopped beside a large, new refrigerator lorry bearing the logo of an Athenian meat processor. Kruja looked around one last time, then unlocked one of the back doors. A blast of cold air rushed out. Ibraham looked at him in suspicion and surprise. The Albanian said in execrable Arabic: "Is OK. Warm inside. Secret compartment."

He clambered up and Ibraham followed warily. There were rows of cow carcasses hanging from hooks. The interior was divided into compartments, with doors between each one. The Albanian flicked on a light, and walked between the carcasses to the end of the first compartment, where he opened a door, lit another light and went through, leaving the door ajar. Tensed for some trick, Ibraham came slowly in the Albanian's wake into the second compartment, past more dead cattle—and the bodies of pigs. He shuddered superstitiously.

Kruja fidded at the bulkhead at the end of the compartment—and somehow revealed a small, secret door. Ibraham saw now that the second compartment was shorter than the first, and a secret area had been created by placing an insulated false wall partway along. The door had been painstakingly cut and disguised. A dim blue light crept out, and the Albanian beckoned.

The secret compartment would have been surprisingly spacious, if it hadn't been for the 11 people sitting against the bulkhead, packs beside them, some with bedding already unrolled. The space was lit by two battery-powered lanterns. There was a smell of chemical toilet, mixed with the smell of feet and sweat. Bottles of water were stacked alongside the toilets, and there was a small air conditioner linked to hidden ventilation pipes. It was an impressive operation.

He took a deep breath and made to enter, but Kruja held out his hand and said "One hundred dollars." He examined the proffered bills with a magnifying glass. "OK," he said, and withdrew his arm so that Ibraham could enter. "We go one hour. Stay quiet."

Ibraham sidled in smiling nervously, and found a space in a corner, uncomfortable against a right angle of the bulkhead. He unrolled his blankets and tried to make a tiny zone for himself. He was already feeling claustrophobic, and could not help touching those on either side. The large black man seemed mercifully to be asleep. The Arab on the other side glared, ostentatiously rubbing his leg. "Sorry! OK!" said Ibraham in Arabic and smiled placatingly. The man sat back with a martyred look and shut his eyes, pulling a black PVC jacket around his delicate torso.

As Ibraham's eyes acclimatized, he could make out more detail. Opposite Ibraham, there was an Indian couple with a very young baby, the man's feet almost touching his. There were two more Arabic-looking men. There were five Africans, one of them a good-looking girl, and four young Chinese men. Some had huge rucksacks; others just a plastic bag. It was much too crowded. It was sickening and stifling. He was thinking about changing his mind just as Kruja came back and said in Arabic and again in English:

"We go ten minutes. Close doors now. Open doors soon. Plenty air and water. No cigarettes. No talking when not moving."

Then he and another man closed the secret door with a horribly conclusive *crump*. The bright light and coolness from the frozen compartment were sealed out, and Ibrahim had a spasm of panic, which he beat down angrily, surprised at this unsuspected phobia. Childish! Contemptible! He plugged his ears so as not to hear the squeaks of screws being driven home. Then there was the muffled roar of a blowtorch as the Albanians welded the seal. The noise stopped, and the men could be heard dragging heavy objects along the floor, and securing them against the bulkhead. Those in the compartment listened with fascination. Ibrahim couldn't stop thinking of tombs, until somewhere within him he found reserves of endurance and faced down the *djinn* of small spaces.

He tried to make conversation with the Arab men, but the exchange languished. The Africans talked in a language Ibrahim didn't recognise, while the Chinese were introspective. The baby cried, and its mother seemed unable to stop the noise. The lorry's back doors were heard and felt being banged shut. The engine started; the lorry lumbered through the raised barrier, waved through by the guard, and swung north.

Almost lightless except for blued lantern-light which made everyone look like corpses, barely tolerable hours elapsed. Time lost all meaning in that unchanging light, with those unchanging faces, with the carbon dioxide building up slowly in all the breathed-on corners. It was a confused and miserable recurring ordeal of creaking and rattling, dozing and waking, stillborn conversations, whisperings, headaches, morsels of food and water, smells of what slopped over the side of the toilet, plus vomit from the child, which was in a state of low-intensity misery. The mother made unavailing noises, while the father stared hopelessly, ashamed of what he had brought upon his family. The mother would try and breast-feed her child—at first turning away in an attempt at modesty, but eventually openly. Yet the baby kept crying, and the mother's face was streaked with dirt and tears.

Kruja and the driver took turns handling the rig, to the accompaniment of ribald talk, cigarettes, and whatever rock music they could find on the radio. Cities, counties and countries rose up and fell down before the German wheels, as the machine powered tirelessly across southeastern Europe—the drivers now piercing darkness, now squinting into a brilliant sun that hurt tired and grainy eyes, now climbing through high passes, now cruising on the flat. The sites of important events were seen but ignored, passed by incuriously in the monotony of adding one junction number to the previous one.

Every few hours, whoever was driving would stop the lorry to relieve himself or get food. Each time, the hidden passengers would look up in hope—only to subside into stuffy apathy as the engine started up again.

Unknown by the cargo, the truck swopped Greece for Bulgaria, where they were waved through at the border, before stopping for the night at a motel near Sandanski. The tired Albanians went for a long meal and some beers. They were distantly related, and had served in the same KLA brigade. They had both been present on a certain sunlit afternoon in a small glade near Novi Sad, with the rest of their brigade—that memorable day when they had paid back the Serbs. They laughed and reminisced, while their clients sweltered purgatorily and tried to sleep.

They were glad beyond measure when sometime, some day, the engine juddered into life again. But that day, too, was destined be a choking, cramped non-event, while the hung-over drivers rumbled through western Bulgaria, the outskirts of Sofia, then across the Danube and the Romanian frontier into the Wallachian plains. The plan was to stop for a short rest at Turnu-Severin, then sleep near Lugoj, where they would check on the "merchandise."

In the compartment, the smell and atmosphere were becoming intolerable. Even the most robust of the passengers were by now dizzy with bad air. There was increasing concern about the child, which was clearly suffering from diarrhoea, maybe dysentery. The mother was always smoothing the boy's hair, babbling soothingly in his perfect ear, trying to interest her miserable husband, apologising in fractured English to everyone else. Everyone had headaches, was nauseous with carbon dioxide, boredom and frustration. Ibraham found himself hoping the baby wouldn't wake up from one of its rare dozes—then felt ashamed for thinking that. Poor little mite!

When at last a yawning Kruja parked outside the Lugoj motel, there was delight as the passengers heard boxes being moved away from the bulkhead, and then the oxyacetylene torch. Ibraham had never enjoyed a noise so much. The peering-in Albanians looked like ugly angels.

Everyone got painfully to their feet and poured out, anxious for *air*. Kruja warned them to stay quiet and close to the truck, and out of sight of the road. The last to emerge were the family, and the man went over to the Albanians. They were in the darkest corner of a carpark, alongside a wide and brightly-lit road with a constant stream of trucks. There was a sad cicada-creaking hedge of low oak between them and the road, with drifts of litter along the bottom. Several hundred metres away were long, low buildings—motel, petrol station, shops, industrial units. They could have been anywhere.

Ibraham felt dazed and stupid, overwhelmed by poisonous air and this night-time continent of unfriendly metropolises separated by impossible distances, with big-engined trucks hurtling perpetually between. He shook his head; after all, he was young and resilient, and had already survived a lot, and there was coffee and cake bought by their conductors with their passengers' money (naturally, they overcharged grossly).

There was good news, too — the Indian couple with the baby had decided to leave and take their chances with the Romanians. The Albanians were angry, saying that this would increase the risk of discovery for everyone else. The argument had gone back and forth, but the Albanians were eventually defeated by the insistence of the mother and the rest of the travellers. The father finally gave them half of the agreed fee, and promised that they would conceal themselves until midday, by which time the lorry should be over the border.

They all slept in the compartment, with the refrigeration off and the back doors open. Someone had considerately poured away the contents of the brimming toilet under the hedge, to join a new stratum of bottles, used nappies and food wrappers. There was a suddenly sympathetic attitude towards the child, and the mother smiled for the first time.

The compartment door was closed at 5 a.m., sealing in a clearer and quieter compartment. The family had been left behind, and reminded to stay out of sight until midday. As the lorry powered away, Kruja looked in the mirror and cursed; he could see the three by the side of the highway, darkly incongruous. But it would be hours before a police car arrived to check a report of "blacks" on the hard shoulder, by which time the lorry was Hungary's problem.

The truck thrust aside the kilometres with ease—Timisoara, Arad, the Hungarian frontier. Here, the vehicle underwent a spot check by the Ministry of Agriculture. Unknown to the hidden, an official in a white coat climbed into the back, looked yawningly into the second compartment, signed some papers and went away.

The secret cargo saw nothing of the countries they were traversing, and the men who could see them weren't interested. The truck followed old invasion routes past slighted castles, dark towns, great houses-become-hotels—and all the traffickers noticed was junctions and filling stations.

The Great Plain gave way to Pest, and they crossed the Chain Bridge beside the lambent Parliament, tourists looking dreamily down from the Fisherman's Bastion as the vehicle dared the Danube. Buda gave way to steeper roads and ivory Esztergom—then the increasingly crowded carriageway skirted frontiers before diving across Austria into Slovakia. Western Europe could almost be smelt, and the Albanians told risqué jokes over Turkish cigarettes. They were well over halfway, and the roads from here were wide and fast. They pounded on and on, the driver twice nodding then jerking awake as the truck veered across the white lines. When they stopped for the night, they were only 40 kilometres short of Vienna—in a lay-by located, had they been interested, just where a Turkish army had encamped in 1683, fearful of the Lion of Lechistan.

Inside, the atmosphere was so much more pleasant now that the Africans started a sing-song, led by the big man from Equatorial Guinea. No-one else knew the tunes, but they listened admiringly as his rich voice sang traditional songs of love, battle, and exile remembered from his far-off village among great trees, along a wide river. His girl sang a song, too, accomanying herself by drumming on a plastic box, and everyone smiled and cheered. The man in the PVC jacket contributed a tender Algerian love song in a pure if nasal tenor, and the Chinese men combined in a vulgar catch only they could comprehend. Ibrahim shook his head shyly when invited to sing.

The truck was barrelling along *Autobahnen* in strong sunshine. Regensburg, Nürnberg, Würzburg, Offenbach, Bad Godesberg—heavy rain, rushing spray, dry again—Köln—astounding spires seen from the ring road—Aachen. There were thunderstorms over Limburg, then the industrial estates of Eindhoven, City of Light set in a Realm of Radiance. These lights were reflected in black *grachten* running straight and silent. Bosch's s'Hertogengebosch, over Maas, along its north bank, north round Dordrecht and they were in Rotterdam's atrocious suburbs. The lorry slowed as the traffic thickened, the driver watching for a sliproad as Kruja spoke on the phone. (In Timisoara, an Indian family sat slumped while a police inspector wondered how he could get rid of them.)

The sliproad was taken, and the passengers became conscious of slower speed and the different sound of the road. "We must be almost there!" Ibraham looked into the faces of his fellow-passengers, and wished he had made some effort to get to know them. An anonymous African caught his eye and grinned as the engine powered down for the last time.

It was 3:20 a.m. The Albanians smiled wearily at each other, climbed into the back and worked at the wall while those inside fidgeted unbearably. Soon the buffeted, blinking merchandise was listening thrilled to the sound of gulls, and taking deep draughts of a shivery, briny breeze.

Chapter 15
THE UNEASINESS OF ENGLAND

Crisby St. Nicholas
Tuesday, 13 August—Sunday, 18 August

The kitchen table was awash with newspapers, and there were more on the floor—and Dan was in most of them. He sat shocked beside a grimly silent Hatty, nibbling at his nails while he read about someone who looked, talked, and even thought a little like him.

He turned to the *Messenger* for comfort only to find, "A bitter war of words has broken out between the *Examiner* and Dan Gowt, the farmer at the centre of allegations of racism after the bodies were found on his local beach. Speaking to the *Messenger*, Mr. Gowt commented, 'This is political correctness gone mad.' But he refused to apologise for his extreme views: 'Those people took the risk, and I don't see why we are being blamed.' The *Examiner*'s John Leyden responded, 'The world is changing, and Mr. Gowt should wake up and smell the Fair Trade Coffee.' There was much more. Dan counted up the total number of his words—87—as opposed to 334 for the other side. So that was what that bastard had meant when he'd signed off with the cheery words, "Don't worry—we'll see readers are left in no doubt about you!"

He thrust it testily from him, and turned next to the *Register*—his mother had always read the *Register*—but it had an even worse headline—"Beach 'bigot' behaved like Ranjit suspects." This was an allusion to an Indian student kicked to death five years previously by a white gang, which had become a *cause celèbre* in a Northern town. According to the article, in his TV interview, Dan had "sounded weirdly like something said by murderer Ebenezer Lampard...There was a feeling that Gowt's words were similar to Lampard's horrendous outburst"—although the journalist added, somewhat grudgingly, that Dan had no criminal record. (Miles away, Albert, reading in his bath like some gross caricature of a triton, inhaled sympathetically at the unactionable inference.)

Dan went on doggedly, as all the papers started to blend into one. He had spent a fortune buying all these, and that was almost as annoying as what they contained. *The Clarion* stuck out, because they had gone to a lot of trouble, with "Auntie-Semitic—Bigot's Fascist Links," co-written by no fewer than five people. There were large photographs of Mussolini, Mosley, Dan (a very recent picture, taken long range, him sitting on his tractor looking, he thought, remarkably unintelligent), and a mannish woman with a snub nose and marcelled hair, in an unflattering black blouse. Great-Aunt Elsie!

Dan had never met her, as she had died in 1942, nor had he known she had once belonged to the British Union of Fascists. All he could remember of her was his mother once saying, "Poor Elsie was always a bit, you know, in the head." This had not been because of her politics, which Dan didn't think had ever been mentioned—but because she belonged to a splinter of the Primitive Baptists, whose members had believed the world would end on New Year's Day 1960. "Lucky Elsie died when she did; she would never be disappointed!" his mother had once said, with her gentle half-smile, looking out at rain sliding slantways into the long-ago garden.

> When Dan Gowt said that the tragic Bodies on the Beach were 'silly' and 'coloured', the nation was outraged. Now, thanks to a special *Clarion* investigation, we can reveal EXCLUSIVELY that his family has a history of virulent racism. Elsie Edmundson, Dan Gowt's great-aunt, was a leading light in the Wilburtham branch of the racist and anti-Semitic British Union of Fascists in the 1930s, the private army built up by Sir Oswald Mosley in homage to Hitler's stormtroopers. Our investigation team has unearthed a picture from 1937, showing Mrs. Edmundson at a Nuremberg-style rally held in Piddle Hole.

The article went on to the "Wilburtham Reign of Terror," when a synagogue had had its windows smashed, and Elsie's "living down her secret shame" by enlisting in the Nursing Corps. The editorial chimed in:

> There will always be racists; it is just the targets that change. It is time for the government to banish blackshirt attitudes to the recycling bin of history!

Dan had always been dubious about the strict accuracy of newspapers, but had believed in the good faith of most journalists. He couldn't fathom why a respectable paper like the *Clarion* would go to such lengths to insult a woman who could not defend herself—who had obviously said some damn-fool things, but had nevertheless been a decent human being. Did such things count for nothing these days? His mind sought for hers in pity and empathy.

He perused all the comment and letters pages—pathetically grateful to writers who did not mention him, or were less unkind than they might have been. But the collective sentiment was terribly clear: inappropriate, out of step, offensive, has no place. Mercifully unguessed at, there were also blogs and comments, where he was damned as an intellectual cow turd, a pig-ignorant, venomous, sickening, unacceptable, inegalitarian, old school, colonialist, toffee-nosed, and privileged white male. There were threats to report him to the police and the Equality Commission—and one anonymous commenter posted a message on the *Bugle* website (quickly deleted), saying, "the fucking fascist had better watch his fucking racist back."

It had been Ben Klein who had "come up with the goods on the bigot Gowt," as he exulted on his blog—thanks to a remarkable archive and a pertinacity which bordered on the psychological.

He was the founder and sole proprietor of the National Anti-Fascist Foundation. Despite its fame, NAFF amounted to little more than 31 filing cabinets, crammed with clippings, photos, pamphlets, leaflets, books, court papers, posters, stickers, recordings, and ephemera all about the political Right, indexed using an eccentric but reliable mental filing system. Many documents had never found places in the cabinets, but teetered on tables, chairs, and windowsills, with Post-it notes protruding to show where subjects began and ended. The small NW11 house, with its barred windows and CCTV, contained more bile, crankiness, and obsessiveness than even Albert Norman's office, and it was added to daily.

Ben remembered names, faces, defects, indiscretions, embarrassing incidents, financial finagling, linkages, and long extracts from newspapers, books, and court reports. Thanks to donations from jumpy private donors, trades unions, government and EU grants, he had been able to give up his accountancy job to dedicate all his time to unearthing racism.

Since then, he had come up with the goods on all kinds of people, from Nazi Satanist bikers to CD MPs, and all intermediate stages of intolerance, and was much relied on by journalists who needed to fill a "far Right" slot and knew he could supply a near-instantaneous thumbnail of a public figure with a past to hide or a hooligan with nothing to hope for. Over the decades, he had helped lots of journalists—except, of course, for the perverse Albert Norman. Ben could never decide what made *him* tick. Self-hatred? Anxiety status? It was curious that someone so clever didn't realise that however hard he tried to assimilate, he would never be accepted.

He had tried to point this out to Albert once, when they had fortuitously met at a dinner party years before (their only meeting—their circles did not often overlap), but Albert had merely laughed and steered the conversation in other directions. Ben couldn't understand the other man's lack of critical faculty, or his obsession with all that boring classical music—music written, after all, for tyrants and absolute monarchs, and used to distract the masses from social questions. Besides, who was Albert Norman anyway—but a perverse (and perverted) dinosaur, refusing to let go of a dying world? Yet a part of him envied Albert's arcane knowledge—Ben's father had apparently sung both synagogue and *klezmer* with skill and verve, and would probably have wanted his only descendant to take an interest in such things.

But Ben was fervently loyal to his father's shade in more important ways. His office was in fact a sort of shrine—a way to touch the lost past of the man he had never had the chance to meet, an educated and kindly man gunned down in the main street of a Byelorussian *shletl* by *Einsatzgruppen* one sunny spring morning in '43—just after he had secreted his pregnant wife in a storm-cellar, where she had lain unguessed at for a day before re-emerging into a horridness of smouldering houses and strewn neighbours, as larks rose and rang beyond the greasy smoke and the smell of incendiarized epidermis.

Mother—and Ben, born two months afterwards—had squeaked through the ensuing years, thanks to the forbearance of a *Wehrmacht* commander sickened by the SS, and feeding herself and her baby by working as caretaker of a vast wooden onion-domed church on an island in a lake in an immensity of grass and great bustards. When the Soviets rolled back over the area, there was no more room for monks so the church closed and she drifted west, alone except for little Benny. She told her son about his father, the life they had led, and the eternal vileness of Germans and Russians. No-one else ever knew what privations and humiliations she had suffered (she was a proud woman). Afterwards, they had come, somehow, to Finland, Sweden, and, ultimately, London, where she had almost immediately expired, worn out but secure in the knowledge that little Benny was safe.

He was safe, indeed, but un-Jewished, coming into contact with Marx soon after he left school. Decades later, he would realize that Marxism had not worked, but he blamed this on the Russians rather than the ideology. And anyway, its shortcomings paled into irrelevance when compared with the alternative—contradiction-carrying capitalism with its opiates of flags and faith, Germany reascendant, Mosley marching again in London, guarded by his "right" to "free speech." Ben would sometimes go with comrades to throw stones at Mosley's men—those were almost sexually ecstatic interludes of fists and flick-knives, kicking Cockneys and Teddy Boys in the balls, ripping down their posters and bearing away their banners as trophies. Some of the Union Movement's faded fustian still resided in filing cabinet drawers, and occasionally he would come across these souvenirs by chance—and he would touch them and remember how and when they were won.

This still dangerous Europe was reinforced by an America raised on rancid foundations—a country he had always refused to visit on principle, nauseated by its imperialism, inequality, and space programs run by ex-Nazis, while the grandsons of slaves lived in shotgun shacks—that place where Jim Crow met Salem met Madison Avenue.

The further Ben moved from faith, the heavier his burden of guilt—his feeling he had betrayed his parents by not being able to believe what they had believed in and died for—to share fully in that extirpated culture. It was to assuage this feeling that he had finally decided to dedicate his life to ensure *IT* could never happen again.

He was unmarried (unsure about his proclivities, he had decided never to bother), bald but with a thin, curly reddish-grey beard, experienced blue eyes peering acutely from a thin face on top of a thin body of just five feet four inches. His fingers were always working out, always riffling tirelessly through papers, snipping, folding, following text as he leaned close over it, breathing through his mouth like Albert Norman did, reading things in a barely audible mutter as the traffic poured past outside, sometimes saying out clearly to the empty room "Hah!" or "Well, well…" or "Gotcha!"

He sat alone but connected, feeling for and finding fascism almost everywhere as governments arose and fell, and the Jewish delis in the nearby Parade became Kurdish kebab places. Sometimes he found it, and twice his worst fears had been confirmed when skinheads smashed the windows of the house and daubed hateful slogans on the front wall. Ever since, his house had been wired into a private security firm's emergency circuit, and occasionally the local police would visit to check that everything was all right.

He would have rejected the suggestion angrily, but the peculiar truth was that he had brooded so much on his enemies that he had become dependent on them, even a little *like* them—conspiratorial, defensive, angry at the hand he had been dealt by Fate. The always small numbers of his friends dwindled as the numbers of his contacts grew. His chunky leather-bound address book held an unusual combination of names, from East End enforcers and *agents provocateur* to academics, MPs, peers, police, media organizations, corporations, and overseas governments. Hidden beneath these often-conjured names, there lay, like an erased ghetto cemetery, other names—the Tippexed-out details of friends dropped and deceased. Sometimes in the relative silence of the smallest hours, lying in his grey and grubby bed in his mould-spotted bedroom, watching headlights pass across the ceiling, he would remember with a sweet pain some of these friends, and places seen years ago. But in the practical daytime he would block them out again—loved but lost like autumn leaves, necessary sacrifices to historic justice.

The filing cabinets around the walls were not just furniture, but fortifications, and sometimes even a little like people. He even had a nickname for each one, like "'30s Stuff" or "Big Grey 'n' Black." They were his secret resource, his reason to wake every morning and get "on the blower," as he called it East End-like. He spent whole days and weeks scarcely leaving his office in what had once been an elegant Edwardian sitting room, except to root in some less-used cabinet in one of the chill other rooms.

There were no personal pictures on the walls—just wall-planners, charts and maps, photos of him with celebrities—including the PM, taken just a few weeks ago at that big dinner when they had such an enjoyable conversation. He had a lot of time for the present PM. Then there was a shot of Ben in a TV studio, when he had blushed to be called "Britain's bravest campaigner" (that phrase was emblazoned across his business cards), and newspaper clippings of his successes in forcing enquiries, purging organizations, having meetings cancelled, winning legal actions, once ever having an ancient Cistercian exposed as a former *Ustasha* militiaman, and drummed out of the monastery where he had been since 1946, hypocritically building up a reputation for sanctity and good works. "YES!!!" was scrawled in large red letters across a copy of the man's obituary.

Ben was now clipping out the bits from today's papers to add to his files, while his darting eyes were already analyzing the next paper. It was perhaps premature to list this pig-ignorant farmer as another success, but wait and see! He clipped and felt clean and whole, while the traffic poured past day and night.

Dan picked up the phone warily, to be greeted by a man with a strong local accent. "Mr. Gowt? My name is James Lyle. I'm chairman of the local branch of National Union."

"Yes?"

"I just wanted to say that we all agree with you, and we all thought you have been very brave in standing up to this political correctness. Well done! It takes courage to stand up to PC tyranny."

Dan had seen NU's coarse-looking, apparently always shouting leader on TV, usually surrounded by angry crowds. He was uncomfortably aware that the party was very extreme, and he had never voted for them or knowingly spoken to any of their members. He wondered why any would live in Eastshire, where there was no race problem. Or—aha!—maybe that was why.

"We'd like to invite you to a meeting next Saturday in Eastport. We hope you might be prepared to give a short talk about your experiences, and the wider issues. You're quite a celebrity! We'd love to hear what you have to say."

"Thank you, Mr. Lyle. Now, it is kind of you, but the answer is no. I have no interest or involvement in politics, and I am happy to keep it that way."

"I do understand your wish to keep away from politics, Mr. Gowt. But you have already become involved in a way. I bet there's a lot more you'd like to say!"

"The answer is still no. I'm not a political animal, and have got caught up in this more or less by mistake. Frankly, the sooner all this dies down the better."

"Well, Mr. Gowt, it's a great shame. People like us have to stick together. At least, that's the way I see it. But if you're sure I can't persuade you…"

"No thanks. As I say, I want all this to die away, so that I can get back to just being a farmer again—and we can have some peace."

"I think we'd all like that, Mr. Gowt—I've got two daughters myself—5 and 7. I sometimes wonder what kind of country they'll grow up in…"

Dan saw he was being soft-soaped. "Please, stop trying to get me to change my mind. I've already told you that my mind's made up, so I must decline your offer. Now if that's all…"

"That's all, Mr Gowt—that's all. It's a shame though."

"Goodnight, Mr Lyle; thanks for the call."

"Goodnight. If you change your mind…"

"Thank you!" Dan put down the phone, feeling for the first time in two weeks that he'd made a sensible decision.

But he had not escaped quite so easily. The following afternoon, he was rolling Fifty Acre Field when he saw a rather too clean 4x4 crunching hesitantly along the cinder track—the *private* cinder track. His face set grimly, and he stopped the engine. There had better be a good reason for this intrusion. He didn't recognise the hard-faced driver or the man holding the camera—but he had seen the blond, stocky, besuited man somewhere. With a rather too-wide smile, the stranger came walking towards him—across the bit he'd just finished! The man with the camera came after, looking down, he at least conscious of spoiling the pattern. The hard-faced man leaned on the car in the pleasant warmth—although he was always looking around. Then Dan recognized the blond man, and he felt a surge of anger.

"This is a private road—and I've just rolled that bit!"

"Oh, is it? I'm terribly sorry; we didn't know. And I'm sorry if we've messed up your field." The man's voice was pleasing in an unclassifiably midmarket sort of way, as he looked up at Dan, shading his eyes.

"Mr. Gowt, I presume? My name is James Fulford. I'm the chairman of National Union. This is our local organiser James Lyle; I think you spoke to him on the phone."

"Yes, I did, and I know why you are here. I've already explained that I have no interest in politics or in getting involved with your party, or anyone else's."

"But Mr. Gowt, if I can just explain…we have a real problem in this country caused by immigration. It's going to cause…"

Dan put up his hands. "Look, I've made up my mind. I don't wish to get involved."

"But it will affect you like everyone else, and someone with your high media profile is ideally placed…"

"Look, I've told you. My mind's made up. Now if you'll please leave my property…You can turn around over there and go down to the bottom of the track, then turn right. That'll bring you back into the village. Now goodbye to you, and I don't want to see you again on my property."

He slammed the door of the cab and drove off—leaving a humiliated Fulford receding slowly in the rearview mirror, James Lyle privately smirking that his leader's boasting about being able to persuade Dan had come unstuck. He opened the car door for his flushed leader, biting back a smile, before the car descended the track again. A man from the *Midland Mercury* was parked near the junction taking a phone call, as the 4 x 4 went past. Looking in, he got a split-second but unmistakable sight of Fulford glowering in the back seat. "Aah!" he exhaled pleasurably, and his eyes travelled up the track the car had come along, where a tractor could be seen glinting in the distance.

And so it was that a small local paper had its first ever national scoop, and a young reporter, his break at the big time, with his story that the NU leader had been having secret talks with Beach Bigot Dan Gowt.

But Dan was only one aspect of a story pushing out in all directions. As John Leyden said memorably on a radio show, "Only a sociopath could not feel guilty. We all must unpack our prejudice knapsack, here on the too-White Cliffs."

Channel One was compelled reluctantly to quash the rumour that no less a luminary than Adenya Ukingo, the Eminent Pilot of All Africa, might visit the scene. The Eminent Pilot's motto, "For every villager, a voice—For every person, a cooking pot," had once been satirized by a relatively fresh-faced Albert Norman (he had never been fully fresh-faced) as "For every *kraal* a Kalashnikov—for every person, poverty." At that time, Ukingo was still the Pancho Villa of his part of Africa, a crossborder revolutionist whose followers' devotion to the cause resulted in regrettable excesses. But he had renounced the armed struggle in the 1990s in favour of Local Love—and now LL groups were everywhere, from North Korea to Greenwich Village. A visit from him, it was felt, would be the perfect antidote to Local Hate. But the great man was attending a Slavery Reparations Palaver in Ozangwe (formerly New

Croydon) and then was due to give an eagerly anticipated presentation to the UN; he wouldn't have the time to grace the scene. By way of compensation, his office issued a Special Ukingo Communication deploring the loss of "hopeseekers, hopegivers, teachers, and reachers."

But there was some heartening news. A UN emergency extra session on Euronativism was to be held by the Global Justice Agora, and a distinguished Indonesian scholar would be sent to the UK to examine its record on racism, asylum, racial profiling, police brutality against minorities, and employment opportunities.

At the press briefing, Dr. Mansoor Tiakara said in excellent English, "The recent events on the British coast make me feel deeply apprehensive about the position of the undocumented and underprivileged within the United Kingdom and in Europe. Social and racial justice must progress hand-in-hand. My first visit to your beautiful country will be a milestone in many ways." The British minister responded that Mansoor's visit was brave and long overdue (a gracious nod from the gallant scholar), and he would meet with every assistance from actors, stakeholders, and facilitators. She was confident that British attitudes towards managed migration were consistent with traditional British values of tolerance, fair play, and global guidelines, and she thanked him in advance. Dr Tiekera looked politely sceptical.

A TV comedian morphed photos of Dan into blacked-up pictures showing him as "Dantor Gopinder" and "Dan G'tondo." Inspired by this, advertising agencies rang around their biggest clients and hastily booked a series of TV and press advertisements under the rubric "Marketing to Mend the World." The advertisements were familiar pieces of copy, in which all the white protagonists had been morphed into non-whites. A car advertisement which had featured a smiling white family with the caption, "It's time to rev up your life," now showed an Asian family and the caption, "It's time to run down racism." A well-known blonde who featured in an ad for shampoo was reworked to give her a torrent of curly black hair, which gave "It's the shade that matters" new layers of meaning. Another famous model wrote a "healing blog" to "redress the karmic imbalance."

The prestigious New York weekly *These Days* published a Special Dispatch—"UKKK—Land of Hate and Morons." The front cover bore a shaven-headed, lantern-jawed man wearing oversized boots, a Union Jack vest and a bowler hat, with a drooling bulldog on a chain. The copiously illustrated 6,000-word essay explained that U.K., Inc. had run out of moral capital. It was time Britain "put a period after prejudice." The Brits may have played a role in abolishing slavery, but it had been patronizing to have presumed that African-Americans would not have freed themselves. This sorry legacy continued—"There are few brown or black faces to be seen on London's catwalks. Those who want to see the public face of fashion here truly reflect diversity may have to wait some time. Yet racial discrimination is perhaps hardly surprising in a country where conservatism and classism are rife. The national anthem, "God Save the Queen," makes Britain's embattled liberals wince with embarrassment, with its calls for the Brits to 'scatter her enemies and make them fall' and 'frustrate their knavish tricks.' Government is still dominated by privately educated, middle-class 'white' men, there are still exclusive London clubs which do not permit women to become members. There are even restaurants which do not show the prices on the menus, and people who go off to their country homes at weekends and break animal welfare regulations. Snobs and sexists, sadists and bigots—the unhappy reality of the septic isle."

"It's just as well we have a special relationship," Albert joked to Sally—"imagine what they'd have said otherwise!"

Saturday's *Weekly Monitor* had a landmark investigation by Wanda Lo, "the *La Pasionara* of Luton," who had shot to fame in her 20s with a devastating exposé of racism in the Glasgow Police, resulting in the resignation of 11 officers. It had been an auspicious beginning. She was no mere journalist, but an artist-campaigner and "an incipient national treasure," according to the *Examiner*. Appreciations lined the walls and mantelpieces of the Eastshire farmhouse she owned with her English husband, nicknamed "Mr. Lo" by those few who registered his presence. A few years previously, after Wanda had had an unpleasant experience with a mugger, they had quit Islington for a former farmhouse near Williamstow. She had therefore been one of the first nationally recognized writers to arrive at the scene.

She had wandered watchfully amongst the crowd, watching for seemingly insignificant remarks, fleeting facial expressions, revealing body language, things that no-one else would notice. Her antennæ were so finely tuned that sometimes it was almost painful to her to have to move amongst the less observant. There were few who could match her for observation and intuition. In this article, she had excelled even herself by finding a hitherto unsuspected type of vileness, and from an unlikely source.

"Bodies and bacon butties" was the sub-editor's headline for a piece assailing paramedics for their "sickening, disturbingly dismissive language—and what was even more astounding, eating *bacon* rolls while handling the tragic victims—many of whom were members of the Muslim faith-choice group."

> I repeatedly asked one of the senior paramedics, James Brown, whether he considered that the so-called 'professional' approach was appropriate in these sensitive circumstances. Were the tragic victims just pieces of meat to be processed? I asked him and his colleagues several times whether it was appropriate for them to be handling the remains after snacking on bacon rolls. How did they know, I asked them, that the tragic victims they were manhandling were not Muslims? What sort of message was being sent out? I received no substantive reply—but I could

> tell I had struck a nerve, because eventually Brown came up to me menacingly—he is a well-built 6'4" man who must weigh 15 stone, and I am 5' and weigh 8 stone—and told me to 'piss off with my stupid questions'. It was a blatant attempt to interfere with the freedom of the press, and I was therefore compelled to ask the local Primary Care Trust whether Brown's aggressive attitude is consistent with his position.

She had scored again. The health trust had suspended Brown while they investigated the allegations, and he had resigned immediately. The trust had also appointed a special outreach officer, and would be adopting a new code of practice and the mission slogan "Proactively to respect." Their caterers would from now on provide a full range of other meal choices, including *halal*, *kosher*, gluten-free and vegetarian options. They would provide a prayer room for Muslim employees, because although they were not lucky enough to have any at present, they were seeking actively to redress this injustice. It was "a Wanda-full result," John wrote on his blog—"how lucky we are to have so many brilliant anti-discrimination professionals!"

John also mentioned in dispatches the tireless work of Jensen Johnson, whose latest column in the *East of England Courant* also took a larger view:

> Is it so surprising that racism is ubiquitous when the political climate is set by a grubby tabloid agenda—and when the journalists themselves are from an unrepresentative clique of white, middle-class males? African stories are not covered by African journalists, nor Asian stories by Asians—this is a disgrace. We need a diverse workforce to guarantee a good understanding of the *whole* media-consuming audience. They are editing out the black experience. We cannot allow the press to keep sticking two fingers up at anti-racism. We need a greater ethnic presence at senior levels in the media.

Albert chuckled later, "A very convenient solution!" Jensen, whom he had met several times and quite liked, was always a good source of indignant incandescence—not that there was ever any shortage of outrage ore.

Fifty-one eminent sociologists courageously co-signed an open letter to the Prime Minister, saying the events grew out of the "downplaying of a hidden interracial hybrid consciousness and culture… [O]ur notions of 'race' have been constructed out of a repression of the interracial, driven by a government which seeks to make use of fear rather than facts to promote its own agenda. Racism is more than prejudice plus power; it is also partly a medical condition, caused by loss of mental faculties in the frontal lobe. We will purge it from our actions by purging it from our thinking."

That letter divided the diversity-practitioner community, but everyone agreed about the gaffe by Estonia's LuvSex—all the more unfortunate because the band had recently performed at Adenya Ukingo's 70th birthday party in Madison Square Gardens. But "Blacks on the Beach" struck all kinds of wrong notes.

> *Black their gasping mouths*
> *In their black faces*
> *Black the outlook*
> *For less-favoured races.*
> *Oh yeah.*

The *Examiner*'s "Culture Czar" was aghast: "It had all the easy charm of Atrocities Against Civilians and the social awareness of the Salò Republic…tasteless, tasteless, tasteless." Wanda Lo anguished in *Suburban Shopper*: "What *were* they thinking? How could four great guys from Europe's most happening city come up with these *Hitler*

Jugend-like lyrics? Humiliating, stigmatizing, *incredibly* offensive. 'Blacks' is bad enough, but 'less-favoured races' is straight out of the Auschwitz anthology!"

The band apologized, and dedicated all the proceeds of the download to anti-racist charities. Their next release would be in collaboration with a Malian singer and a gospel choir from London. "Blacks on the Beach" would eventually be rehabilitated, and a year later, it made number 42 on a program of *The 50 Most Significant Songs.* "It may not be politically correct to say so, but that song defined a generation," Scum would explain, in a generous tribute—all the more so because his own "Don't Diss De Dead" never made it onto the list.

Educating 4 the Future hurriedly brought forward its eagerly anticipated report, *A World of Possibilities—A Roadmap for Ethnic Education*. The nine authors made long-overdue recommendations, like prohibiting schools removing asylum-seekers' results so as to improve their league table positions, because this "perpetuated irrelevant hierarchies of 'achievement' over human dignity."

They proposed that French and German should be replaced by Mandarin and Marathi, while the "white" staff should role-play.

> What a fantastic signal would be sent out to our kids if White British teaching personnel would wear a *shalwar kameez* and a *dupatta* during Muslim festivals! During Hindu festivals, staff could be encouraged to wear *dhotis* and hold *chakra* workshops! And what better way to include Afro-Caribbean kids than to talk to them in their own lingo? A short course in 'street' could be included as part of the National Teaching Qualification. There are so many ways to put the 'fun' into functional.

But Eastshire was already leading the way, insisted the chair of the Eastshire Local Education Authority. Anti-discrimination on all curricular levels was "top priority for our kids" she said angrily. All very well, retorted Roger Swithin on behalf of the Christian Democrats, but CD-run LEAs elsewhere had introduced it much faster.

Cameras went into Crisby Primary School, where Dan had been educated (a point made in the reports), filming the teacher looking down smilingly at her charges, encouraging them to think about what it must be like to be without a home, to leave your family and friends behind, to be in a war, with all your family and friends having gone to heaven. What would it be like not to have enough to eat? What would it be like to have no home? How would it make you feel? Now draw some pictures of things you are thinking. You might want to use black to show darkness, mightn't you, or red for blood? And what about blue for the cold sea? Yes, Kylie, there might be sharks. Next week, we're going to have a special play for your parents, and we're all going to sing "A Land That's Free to Make Us Proud." Won't you all enjoy that? Yes, you will. Let's all think of our Asyl-chums!

The Jumping With Joy Frog Puppets then worked through "the issues that should make us all HOPPING mad," with the ever-popular "Frog Who Jumped (From the Frying Pan Into the Fire)." "Oh, Mr. Springy, why did I ever leave my own pond? All the frogs here are so horrible to me!" "They don't mean to be horrid, Jumpy Jim—they just don't think, they just don't think."

Not to be left behind, academia was rising obscurely but importantly to the challenge. Capital University's 1990 classic *Ethnicity and Swimming Pool Access in North-Eastern England* had been a milestone in Discrimination Studies, and since then, they had always been ahead in the game. They had coincidentally been planning a symposium on *Differentials of Racialization and Rhetoric of Descent: 'Race' and 'Nation' in Postmodern Discourse* for that weekend, and Channel One took the unusual step of clearing some of their sport schedule so the conference could be streamed live. Their gay anchorman, Mark Clark, was reprimanded for joking on children's TV that even he wouldn't mind not seeing men playing with their balls for such a great cause.

The head of the Global Refugee Agency gave the impassioned keynote address at the symposium: "What is it about your country that you should seek always to denigrate Africans? How I wish Adenya Ukingo—with whom I was privileged to shake hands last week—could be co-opted into your government for a while! He would teach you wisdom and forgiveness. We were practicing village democracy in Africa when you were still painting yourselves with woad! [Laughter.] Our people remember the 'No dogs, no blacks, no Irish' signs that used to be all over London in the 1950s, even on the very gates of your Buckingham House. I have written about it in my book, *Prejudice in my Pocket*—which you may purchase here today at a special reduced price, or visit my website.

"To this day, your news programmes always present Africa in the worst possible light, as if all African life was made up of war and famine and disease. Is this not also an example of blatant racism? We must weave a multicoloured ethnic embroidery for the ages. There is a Gobandan proverb I would like to share with you—we are all waterwheels in life's river."

John gave a coveted "Double Thumbs Up" rating on his website to the especially insightful talk by the Bishop of Blackpool, "Transphobia and Tropes of Difference."

"Nothing is more crucial now, and here, at this point in time, than to reclassify all classifications. This would be an act of truly liberal imagination against the devouring claims of national identity—Daniel in the lions' den. Some may say that reconstruction may lead to its own form of essentializing of the difference. The same people say that 'here' is more important than 'there.' But where's 'there'? In a way we are all 'here,' and we are all 'there' on a tiny ball spinning in space. We are all refugees, as Jesus was. We are all activists. There are no 'majorities' and no 'minorities,' just people. Nothing is nationally *sui generis* in the age of globalization. Racism is nothing more or less than a direct extrapolation of the linearity and 'bad infinity' of Newtonian physics and the Enlightenment ontology. Theirs is a grave but recurring error, based on a false and divisive view of 'human nature' (whatever *that* is). We need a radical transformation of social memory. We must dare to 'transgress,' as Jesus 'transgressed' against the establishment."

The conscientious Albert read even that, his head aching slightly. That such a symposium was sponsored by Sentinel Media was slightly surprising—but then Sentinel was also the majority shareholder in *Sub-Dom* and *Lady-Boys*. Albert doubted whether most *Sentinel* readers knew about this other side to their nice conservative company. It wouldn't have happened in Lord Thornley's day—something he seemed always to be saying to himself these days. He smiled wryly—he had become a caricature. That didn't matter, so long as he continued to be hated.

The phone. Damn! 5:03. Sun slanting in. Bloody jackdaws making their noise in the chimney. 5:03. Sunday. THE PHONE! An emergency! Dan ran stumblingly downstairs, tying his dressing gown as he went, almost falling over the cat halfway down, and picked up the receiver as it rung for the 12th or 13th time.

"Dan Gowt?" A cold Cockney voice.

"Speaking. Who is it, please? What's wrong?"

"You're what's wrong, Dan—totally fuckin' wrong, you racist prick. You fuckin' toe-rag—and do you know what, Dan, we're watching you and your family—every fuckin' minute of the day. We know about you and your fascist friends. One day, when you're not looking…one day soon. *Very* soon!"

He hung up laughing, leaving Dan standing with his heart pounding and his dressing gown hanging open, while the cat rubbed round his ankles, Sammy 'ruffed' quizzically from the kitchen, and worried interrogatives wound down from Hatty on the landing.

Later, there was a hastily-organized mass rally at Speakers' Corner, following a march from Parliament Square. The police had at first refused permission because of the short notice and the difficulty of getting personnel to cover it—but the up-for-election Mayor had telephoned the Commissioner personally to ensure he stretched a point.

All the big unions and groups of all sizes were there—including Workers Against Racism, Halt National Union, East London Community Front, North London Says No to Racism, Smash the System!, Kwa-Zulu Solidarity, Kurdish Christian Council, Anglican Action, Afro-Islamic League, Global Love, Local Love UK, Communist Challenge, Undocumented United, the Afro-Asian Civil Service Federation, the Muslim Alliance, the Shalom Centre for Human Rights, the Black Liberal Party, Christian Democrat Reachout, Enough is Enough, Afro-Asian Voice, Mothers Against Guns, Out of Iraq Now, No2BorderZ, and International Outrage United, with their fist-shaped banners and "IOU" slogans.

There had been unpleasantness *en route* to Hyde Park. The police had arrested a young man who had thrown a bottle through a window of one of the older St. James's clubs, and two men who had kicked each other in an argument about Israel. There was also some spray-painting of slogans on statues and cars.

Such exuberance had left a slightly sour impression on Richard Simpson, one of 20 MPs marching at the head of the column holding a banner reading "IT'S TIME! TOGETHER AGAINST RACISM!" while he pantingly explained to a panting reporter that he hated the way some exploited tragic events to further their political careers.

Some of the less radical quit the parade, but there were still several thousand by the time they reached the Park—watched by hundreds of police. Protestors and police alike stood in almost intolerable heat under a small woodland of banners—"Frontiers Are Fascism"—"No Frontiers, No Fear"—"Here for Good"—"Root Out Rural Racism"—"Battle the Homophobes" –"No to Racist Controls—Open the Borders Now!"—"No to U.S. Imperialism"—"No to Welfare Cuts"—"Support Abu Jamal." They stood and sweated and listened to MPs, trade unionists, student politicians and ethnic representatives talking through a slightly distorted PA system, while fungus-toed pigeons quested around their feet.

Richard Simpson, strawberry-visaged in a shiny suit, drenched the foam microphone cover as he bellowed a typical peroration.

"Every dye people are being depor'ed and frone into destitu'ion 'coz of their immigrition sta'us. Every dye people are pide peanuts and mide to work in life freatening conditions 'coz of their immigrition sta'us. Every dye people die trying to cross artificial borders. These are the shadow people—the yooman beings 'oo we need, and 'oo need us. IT DOESN'T 'AVE TO BE THIS WYE! So, people, let's mike this 'appen!"

He punched the air in a way he hadn't done since leaving university and stood back, to whistles, stamps and enthusiastic applause. He had set the bar very high.

The chelonian-looking Lord Chimbay had been acclaimed "Britain's leading Jamaican theorist of equality" after his influential report, *A*

Perfect Tempest? Racism in the British Theatre. He had been rubbished at the time by Albert Norman in a column entitled "Exit, pursued by jeers" and was still smarting. Now, he attacked the *Sentinel*'s "mendacity, slyness, patronising sleight of hand…. Crude, loud, prejudiced moans increasingly dominate the public space. This is the same platform that gave us apartheid, and Hitler!" The audience groaned and swayed, and someone shouted "Fuck 'em!" He then spoke of the paper's grubby agenda that led directly to death camps and concluded that the Christian Democrats were dogwhistling towards Dachau. Wild cheers, shouts of "No!" and a Mexican wave of banners.

Wayne Smith of Christian Democrat Reachout, a bad-skinned recent graduate with annoying habits of gabbling and chortling, had the bad luck to be on next. But he tried hard, denouncing national borders as an affront to free trade and saying that people trying to get here were really the most patriotic of all, because they admired Britain's friendliness to entrepreneurs. The crowd seethed and murmured. Some even began shouting "Fascists!" and there was a growing slow handclap, as the young man grew progressively more panicky, eventually retreating to jeers, rough laughter and even a few half-hearted missiles.

The man from the Guatemalan Action Group spoke a few heavily-accented words—few could make out what was being said, especially as a jet chose that moment to fly overhead. Shadow people…*los rotos*, the broken ones and the black heads…CIA…Spanish exploiters…take back what belongs to us! But he was obviously on the right side, and got a rousing cheer and a fist-bump from Rt. Hon. the Lord Chimbay of Tulse Hill.

Next was the Black Muslim firebrand, Mecca Morrow. Pentecostalist Matthew Morrow had gone into Brixton for five years and emerged as Mecca, up from drugs and rippling with muscle and Malcolm X. He made some Jewish protestors slightly uncomfortable, because they had heard of speeches he had made to different audiences. But his reception was assured by the small but focused cohort from the DA21 Massive. His sunglasses glittered as he punched the air, and his clip-on bowtie was slightly askew, a pathetic garnish for a neck with that much muscle—not that anyone would have dared to laugh at it. But Mecca was in a reassuringly reflective mood.

"Brothers, when I look at the country today I feel fear for the future. What are we sayin' to our kids? What message are we sendin' out? I see our streets filled with hopelessness and fear. I see those rich racists saying as how they don't want no more immigrants in their backyards. When I hear the words 'bogus' and 'flooding' it sends shivers down my spine. I see the police beating up on our people. I see National Union spouting their horseshit and getting elected up and down the country. The Islam-bashing in this country has reached a point that I want to puke, know wot I'm sayin'? Behind it all is the international capitalist system—the fading, failing white world—holding on to its privileges because they know that WE, brothers and sisters, WE are prevailing! Thanks to the power of Allah, and to the justice of our cause, yes, we are winning. But how many more of our people have got to die before Whitey goes off to his country club in the sky? How many little children have got to suffer? How much more terror? Brothers, I say to you, have hope! Never give up! Feel the force that's coming through us. Let's shut them down BY ANY MEANS NECESSARY!"

There was incontinent cheering and pushing in the crowd—and a few around the fringes moved uneasily away.

The speeches ended with the Bishop of Milltown, practically a permanent fixture on such occasions, as his ecclesiastical duties left him a lot of free time. There was a joke that he always brought his own microphone, and that he wouldn't need one anyway to address *his* parishioners. He served up suitable words in fluting tones.

"What we're doing here is creating citizens of the world. I'm not sure where national identity fits into this picture. Do we any longer have a national identity? Should we *have* a national identity? What is 'national'? We are bigger than nations, bigger than empires. There are changing configurations of 'otherness'—soon, there will be no 'other,' only 'we.' Soon there will be no 'us and them,' but only 'us.' We need tolerance, transcendence and truth. But remember this above all—today will be written about in the history books. I want you all to remember this moment. Remember how it feels. Think of the passion. See all the Londoners who've come together to say that ENOUGH— IS –ENOUGH!"

The cheers, foot-stamping and waving sent the pigeons momentarily skywards. The event was over, and the speakers were all leaving—but many in the crowd were in no hurry to disperse. The police shuffled slightly closer as a new, raw, rhythmic sound started to emerge from the heart of the crowd, a stamping and a clashing of sticks.

Chapter 16
Passage to England

Rotterdam

The travellers followed their guides through lines of lorries bearing the names of towns they had never heard and phone numbers with too many digits. There were very high buildings in the distance, and the sky was abuzz with hundreds of thousands of lights. All seemed quiet except for the swishing of ring-road traffic.

They came to a deserted road of old and inconvenient warehouses, some bearing faded 19th-century names. There was a CCTV camera high up on one wall, but it was pointing in the wrong direction and moved tiredly. Long before it had tracked drily towards them, they had dashed across the exposed thoroughfare into a cat-smelling alleyway, breaking up an amorous encounter between a tom and his queen, sending them spitting and scattering behind dustbins. At the far end was an expansive view of the night city across a slick ebony channel of the Nieuwe Maas, with brightly lit, humming vessels berthed in the foreground by a long, straight quay wall scored by rusty rails, with weeds growing between the cobbles.

As they were about to leave the shelter of the alley, a Dock Police van came round a corner and everyone froze—but the bored driver was groping for a CD in the glove compartment and his eyes slid carelessly over their shadows against the slightly darker background of the alley. When it turned the corner and disappeared, Kruja signalled to wait, then darted over the road and up the gangway of a battered-looking trawler several hundred metres along the quay wall. A tall figure came out of the shadows at the top of the gangway and the two disappeared below decks for several very long minutes.

Those waiting felt horribly conspicuous. But the port traffic had almost all moved downriver when the container ships had become too large to come so far upstream; these areas were given over mostly to chandlery, light repairs, and foxes scratching a living on rats and rubbish. Even the sex shop that had done so well out of ships from buttoned-up countries had long since closed. There were hectares of docks like these, used just often enough not to have been redeveloped for apartments, patrolled by acrylic-uniformed guards with hair below their collars who rarely got out of their cars, and monitored by cameras whose footage was never checked. The Dock Police's under-resourced attentions were on other sad ships and woebegone warehouses. So the quay remained electrically empty in both directions when the travellers clumped and stumbled up the steep gangway in answer to Kruja's beckoning. The trawlerman silently signed to them to descend into the hold, counting them in as their feet felt gingerly for the icy rungs of the metal ladder. Ibraham felt sick as he renewed his acquaintance with rancid fish and essence of diesel. That such a feculent vessel should be his ticket to hygienic paradise!

A fluorescent light flicked on to expose a salt-crystalled cavern running most of the vessel's length. The Albanians relieved their clients of the final installment of their fees, as agreed a continent away and what felt like years ago. The travellers had heard stories about 20 minutes of machine gun fire near a certain Serb village, and paid without demur. Kruja was not a man to annoy; besides, he had not let them down.

The *Sint Niklaus Enterprise*, launched in Vlissingen in 1963, was one of the last wooden trawlers to be built in the Netherlands. It had been already outmoded in 1981, when a deckhand had painted a naïve flag and haloed saint on the stern to commemorate the 10th anniversary of municipal status—a solitary hint of former pride in the old stager. It was crewed by two Dutch deckhands and the tall man who had received the migrants, who was both owner and skipper. Down below somewhere, there was also a faceless engineer.

Shortly afterwards, this mysterious operative switched on the boat's still powerful Eindhoven engines. There were purposeful movements above, and the businesslike voice of the *Kapitein*. The hold hatch was rolled shut; ropes thumped against the hull and were hauled dripping aboard, and the *Enterprise* edged into midstream as she had done thousands of times before.

She moved slowly downstream between banks sparkling with streets. Vehicles ran remorselessly along the coast road, headed for or from houses, factories, airports, railheads, galleries, concerts, wives, husbands, prostitutes, philosophy, fights, cannabis bars, revivalist meetings, Maasluis, Utrecht, Breda, Tilburg, Germany, Belgium, France, and further. Cranes worked or were still, men watched or were inattentive, buoys flashed in their sequences and distant lighthouse beams stroked the universal plain, signalling the congress of *Land* and *Zee*, dangers to be avoided, coasts to be conquered. It was a scene of constant movement that even now could sometimes make the *Kapitein*'s dry heart flutter in excitement.

The *Enterprise* dropped anchor quietly an hour later, a few hundred metres off a north shore village chartered in 1336, civic bearer of a Delft-blue triton emblem once borne in battle against Alva's *tercios*, but now almost overwhelmed by industrial parks and ironically incandescent dormitory suburbs. The engines were powered down, and Ibrahim and the others settled as comfortably as they could in the dripping clamminess.

A few hours afterwards, a launch buzzed businesslike across the channel, crowded with heads made black by the brightness behind, almost shipping water with the weight of scions of Sierra Leone, Somalia, Cappadocia, Kurdistan, Canton and points east and south, transported to this boat on this night at this time by a half-understood impulse and the organisational abilities of an Albanian syndicate.

Kruja exchanged muttered greetings with a bearded co-clansman in the bow of the launch, then secured the expertly thrown painter. The launch-man held the craft to the *Enterprise*'s rope-ladder with a boathook as his passengers clambered up clumsily. A young Sierra Leonean woman panicked, and refused to climb the ladder. She had to be threatened and prodded for some minutes before she finally essayed the rungs, breathing and moaning heavily all the way until eventually she plopped panting over the gunwale like a porpoise disgorged from a net. The launch then went back for more human cargo, and these last few additions to the freight were accompanied by large waterproofed packages.

There were *sotto voce* farewells, then the launch buzzed back into the darkness while below the original occupants shifted and grumbled to make room for another 25 would-be British citizens. Ibrahim sat fastidiously slightly apart with his back against a slimy bulkhead, looking with displeasure at a large and stolid black man wearing a colourful shirt and jeans. Beside him were his gaudy-robed woman and their child, all surrounded by plastic bags. They spat out semi-masticated pistachio nuts onto the deck, while talking loudly and at length in a language Ibrahim didn't recognize but tended to dislike. He felt these were not the sort of people he would have chosen as companions on this important boat.

The engineer flicked switches somewhere, there were orders on deck, and the chain clanked in the hawse-pipe as the *Enterprise* gave up her sucking purchase in the mud. She edged into the channel and chugged gamely seawards, rigidly following Traffic Separation so as not to attract attention, a crewman steering in accordance with infrequent instructions from the captain, who was standing on the wheelhouse wings drinking cognac-laced coffee against the chill (and his conscience).

The Albanians hid as the *Enterprise* passed the pilot station, where launches with powerful lights came and went at all times. But the pilots ignored them, except to acknowledge her passing by radio. Their horizon was densely populated with ships awaiting tides and guides… Liberian container ships with Chinese iPods for Dutch high streets, Japanese tankers bearing Gulf oil to keep the *Ringstad* shining up to the satellites…and they had little interest in such a regular sight as the sad old *Sint*.

The waterways were opening out. Bright embankments had become black, bird-hung reedy islands fringed by mud, and now these were getting further apart and further away. The *Enterprise* started to feel the slop of the sea. It nipped neatly between two tankers that towered over it like cliffs—and Rotterdam's port and civil authorities relinquished responsibility for the *Enterprise* with a final blazoning of buoys.

The hold hatch had been opened, but the only illumination came from a storm-lantern on the bulkhead. The noise had abated except for snores or odd murmured exchanges, but Ibraham felt again thrillingly awake. Slight nausea notwithstanding, this was too good a feeling to miss—the last stage to England. He would look back on this night when he was grey, sitting at ease in his beautiful London house!

He hoped there would be grandchildren to tell how he, an uneducated labourer, had stepped out from all he had known one spring day, with just a few things in his kitbag—how he had crossed a country in chaos, crept secretly across the face of the Middle East, passed over seas of shining creatures, through riots and over fences, by plane, truck, and on foot until making the last step over this final defensive ditch.

It was like one of the great journeys of old times—Sinbad brought up to date—and at the end there would be the realization of a life-long fantasy. He felt superior and strong—a man who had risked all and come through intact. And he was more than intact—he was tougher and wiser. He tensed the muscles of his stomach and relished their tautness; he curled and uncurled his strong fingers and toes. Every part of his body responded just as it should, in tune with his dauntless will which had carried him here through such difficulties.

He carried his soon-to-be-vastly-increased belongings toughly and wisely up the companionway. It was as pleasant on deck as he had hoped—cool breeze, colder than on the voyage from Antalya but pleasant after the old fish and new people, an indigo-purple sea with the radioactive coast carelessly letting them escape. He could see the strong reassuring silhouette of someone—the *Kapitein*—behind the wheelhouse glass—no common mariner he, but also a sort of saviour.

That tall tactician's plan was to head north then north-east towards the Dogger, to drop his cargo in 26 hours on a desolate sandy beach he had picked out from the chart weeks ago. Filip Duplessis had fished legitimately for many years, but catch restrictions and his desire for a nicer house had eventually impelled him to seek riskier income. A meeting a few months ago with a man who knew a man who knew of someone who wanted to do some discreet business in England had therefore been fortuitous. He preferred not to think about the details of that business, but sought unsuccessfully to assuage his shame by telling himself that the migrants were refugees, just wanting to get away from war. Wouldn't he have done just the same?

Such rationalizations, easy in the abstract, had been undermined by Kruja's appearance. "*Schlecht*, that one!" he had told himself, surveying the round-headed client with the scarred forehead and the little sharp brown eyes. And some of the migrants didn't look like refugees either. There was one down there now on the deck now, an Arab, wandering around—looking for something to steal, probably. He looked too well-fed, un-traumatised to be a real refugee—almost as if he was enjoying himself.

But Filip was in too deep now. He told himself that this would be the first and last time. "I'm getting too old for this kind of shit. Eh, Jan?" The man on watch smiled loyally back, his teeth seen momentarily in the glow of the binnacle.

The radar screen was pleasingly clear except for a fishing-boat sized blob satisfactorily far away. After a while Filip set the automatic pilot, left instructions with Jan and headed to his cabin. The watchman paced unceasingly across the wheelhouse with a sea-gait like the skipper's, scanning the horizon and periodically checking the autopilot and radar—a blond genius of the dog watch, listening to Europop beamed across the widening wastes from Rotterdam.

Ibrahim leaned over the stern and watched the off-white wake. How far he had come and, in fact, how easy it had been! All those lucky meetings—the coincidences and connections—the tests he had passed—the Iraqi border officials who didn't care—the guards looking the wrong way—the perfect timing of the riot at Lavrion—the weak spot in the fence and the nameless Moroccan who hopped over with him, and their smiling dazzlingly at each other, how they would have been great friends.

How amazing, really, to have done all that—and now to be so nearly in England. He could almost touch the streets of tomorrow. He hoped the police and the people would be kind. But why shouldn't they be kind? They must understand that he had not embarked on his journey lightly. He was coming to work; he would pay his way. He would be grateful; he would learn the language and make the others learn it, too; he and they would fit in. He would touch a fair girl and see her smile back in love and loyalty. It was only right. The English were a fair and tolerant people, a people defined by their willingness to welcome people of all backgrounds, as their distinguished-looking Prime Minister had once said in a TV broadcast, glimpsed years ago in a shop window one breathless Basra afteroon.

It was too chilly on deck, so he went back to the hold and curled up in his by-now-distinctly-fishy spare clothes and blankets. There was pantomime whispering between the African nut-masticators, who were all wrapped up together, exchanging echoing, hissing remarks with the big Equatorial Guinean who had sung so beautifully on the truck. But their noise did not annoy him now. In a way, it was reassuring to think of others being alert while he was helpless—and looming above all in the hold was the calm, sleepless, almost angelic watcher in the wheelhouse. Soon he slept while the whispering went on.

His cheeks were pinched with dew. He was dazzled and delighted to look straight up into an unbroken rectangle of sunny morning—an unsulliable beauty beyond the close compartment, some of whose occupants had evidently thought it too much trouble to go to the heads during the night.

He emerged onto the deck and stretched. The North Sea extended everywhere, empty and smooth. The *Kapitein* was on the bridge, pacing from side to side drinking tea, looking at the sun-soaking migrants and the Albanians smoking aft. He could not get rid of these ghastly people soon enough. This would definitely be the last time.

The day grew tedious, but it stayed warm and bright until late afternoon, as the skipper began to insinuate the *Enterprise* nearer the limits of British waters. A hump of England was off to port, on the edge of radar but still out of sight, and the *Enterprise* described a straight, slow NNW course that allowed the engineer to doze. The captain had selected his course cunningly.

The radio had promised fog, and around 4 p.m., a low grey wall rolled obediently out of the east. The man on watch roused the captain, who nodded satisfiedly and muttered "Perfect" as he surveyed the shrinking horizon. He had a lot of capital tied up in the *Enterprise*, and he did not want to take any chances. Sometimes he felt quite sentimental about the old girl.

The temperature plunged as the greyness engrossed the trawler. The migrants' dark hair was dewed with droplets, the colour leached out of their features. The *Enterprise* throbbed through silk-slick sea, under a matte coverlet that became more impenetrable as the day became evening and the evening, night. Gulls came abruptly into view, then flicked away. Ibraham chewed on chocolate, and enjoyed not feeling ill. Noises sounded louder as the skies folded in and pressed down. The captain imagined nervously that every tiny sound might be audible in England, and winced at every raised voice and even the engines. They were well inside territorial waters, and this was the most dangerous phase. Landfall would be in two hours, around midnight when the tide would be at its lowest, and he could drop the cargo hundreds of metres out, to wade through waist-deep water and across a kilometre of sand. And then home as fast he could go—home to a warm bed and re-legality.

Ordered several times to keep quiet, everyone knew they must be close. They checked and re-checked their belongings, exchanging whispers and suppressed giggles. What would be the first thing you would do, they kept asking each other. "I am going to have a hell of a good shit!" said an

Arab, and the Arab-speakers roared—and the sound made the captain jump and send Kruja forward to order them down into the hold, before pulling over the hatch to stifle further outbreaks. Expectant quietude built up tweendecks, whispering and giggling, thudding hearts and damp palms. Joshua from Equatorial Guinea was sitting near Ibraham, and sometimes they exchanged tight smiles. His massive face was full of surmise, and the good-looking girl with the glasses was clutching his hand tightly.

The skipper *knew* now. There could be no mistake. For 30 minutes, as they had been nosing in for the last approach, the radar had obstinately shown a fast approaching object. He had tried to persuade himself it was a trawler; but it was too big and too fast. He watched fascinatedly as it bled towards them, every revolution of the radar showing it slightly closer. Then the VHF crackled into life on the hailing channel, and it was the worst thing that could have happened.

"UK Fisheries patrol vessel *Hector* calling unknown vessel in position"—the signalman gave the grid reference—"UK Fisheries patrol vessel *Hector* calling unknown vessel. Please identify yourself. Over."

The *Hector* had left harbour that morning to investigate a yachtsman's report of a mysterious explosion. Finding nothing, they had eventually called off the search as a false alarm and had been sloping gradually back to base. Then the *Hector*'s young commander had spotted an unidentifiable craft on the radar, and they had come to investigate, more to give the new crew some practice than out of real concern.

"What filthy luck!" exclaimed the captain, and he and Jan looked at each other for a haggard moment. The captain consulted the chart for the thousandth time. They were still eight kilometres out—*eight!*

Hopeless. There was no way they could outrun a fisheries vessel. He leaned over the wheelhouse wing and called for Kruja. The hailing channel continued its demands, acerbity creeping into its challenge.

"UK Fisheries patrol vessel *Hector* calling unknown vessel. *Hector* calling unknown vessel. *Please identify yourself.* Over."

Kruja appeared on the bridge, a powerhouse of stocky capability. The captain seemed attenuated, almost childlike by comparison with such dynamism. Kruja guessed the problem at once and spoke in English.

"Are we discovered?"

"Yes. A fisheries vessel."

"How far are we?"

"Eight kilometres. Too far!"

"We can't outrun them?"

"No chance."

"Then we must drop them."

Kruja spoke with such clarity and conviction that the captain was momentarily pleased to have the decision taken out of his hands. Then he realized what Kruja had said.

"WHAT!?"

"We must drop them. Over the side. While the British pick them up, we get away. You can then put us ashore or—if that's too dangerous—bring us back to Rotterdam."

"You can't put those people over the side! They'll drown!"

"They will *not* drown. The British will stop for them. Radio them there are people in the water, and they'll stop to pick them up. They'll have to. It's the law. Then we can get away. It's easy. Then they get where they want to go, you keep your boat and none of us go to prison. Okay?"

This went against every principle the *Kapitein* had ever imbibed—including the code of the sea. He had always prided himself that, whatever else he had done, or would do, he had never betrayed that trust. But *now*, tonight, now that it had come down to this—faced with disgrace, a criminal record, prison, confiscation of assets, the end of the nicer house, the end of *everything*—this honour-bright code seemed less satisfactory. But even as he battled with his conscience, one half of his mind was already supplying justifications.

The awful Albanian was surely right. Of course the British would stop. They always did. They were a fair people. It was a mild night, and these were safe waters. Yes, the Albanian was right. What choice was there? And what were these people to him anyway?

And there was another thought—if he *did* refuse, the Albanians had guns and would surely force him. He would get hurt, maybe even killed, if he didn't go along with what they happened. And in any case, the Albanian *was* right. If only he hadn't agreed to this filthy job! This would *definitely* be the last time! So, after an anguished minute, he nodded shortly, hating the Albanians and himself, staring at his sea-boots as the *Hector* called again. "Identify yourself *immediately*—or we shall intercept and board you. Over."

He yanked at the engine-room telegraph to stop the ship. Kruja had already dashed along the deck and thrown back the hold hatch. "Everyone up now! Quickly! Quickly! We're there!"

The New Life! England! They hurled themselves at the ladder, trampling on the hands and faces of those behind, dropping bags and picking up the wrong ones, knocking a child against a bulkhead and cutting his face, everyone except his mother too excited to pay attention to his cries. "All out! All out! Quickly! We're there! Quickly!"

Within less than two minutes, everyone was up on the congested deck, trying to pierce the dense fog, holding onto windlasses and davits and each other to keep from falling. The *Enterprise* was rolling long and smooth now that they were no longer under way. The *Kapitein* looked down guiltily onto his former freight, then went back into the wheelhouse, shutting the door behind him, as if to disclaim responsibility, to stare fixedly at the orange image of his nearing nemesis. A deckhand closed the hatch cover over the now empty hold, and Kruja shouted in an execrable but mostly understandable hotch-potch of English and Arabic:

"Over the side! Now! We're nearly ashore! It's only waist-deep! It's safe! Jump!"

The migrants stood shocked, looking at each other, at the cold-looking water, back at the Albanians, for any hint of land, shivering with anticipation of cold and the start of fear.

"Over the side! We're nearly ashore! It's only a metre deep! Jump! It's safe!"

And Joshua from Equatorial Guinea, strong and simple, kissed the girl with glasses, removed his shoes and shoved them into his kitbag, took a tight grip of that container with one huge hand and placed the other on the rail before catapulting over in unthinking obedience, after months of unthinking obedience to similar orders from similar people all the way from home. His brave and graceful action caused one of his compatriots—and then another—to follow his example. But almost before they had hit the water with a more-than-waist-deep sound, the others had realised the trick.

Voices came up from below calling for help; limbs were flailing and kicking. Those left on deck were transfixed. Then one of the Albanians had a sawn-off shotgun, pulled from his coat in a smooth movement, and Kruja had a Yugoslav Army issue automatic pistol—his lucky gun. They know what they're doing with those, Ibraham thought as his brain sprinted and his stomach turned over. Kruja spoke in a normal tone of voice, a reasonable man seeking co-operation.

"My friends, calm yourselves! We *are* almost on the beach. It's just a few metres away over there. If it wasn't for this fog you'd see it. There's an English navy boat coming, and we're not going to wait to be arrested. But it is very close, and it *will* stop for you. We've told them you're here, and they've said they'll pick you up. The British always do. They have no choice anyway, because it's the law. While they're picking you up, we'll get away. So you get to England, we get away, we're all happy. Get over carefully and stay together, and you'll be out of there in just a few minutes. We'll throw in some lifejackets and things for you to hold onto. But do it *now*! If you don't get over the side now, you'll be caught and sent back to Holland, then back to whatever shitholes you came from! Do you want *that*? *Well*? Come on—have I let you down yet?"

Whether they really believed him, or because they had become accustomed to obeying orders, or because they were scared of the guns, more did go. Husbands and fathers lowered dependants and effects over the side and then jumped in afterwards. Ibraham marvelled at a man with a moustache who kissed his trembling wife and son, then lowered them carefully into the water whilst making reassuring noises, before he scrambled onto a stanchion and dived in headfirst after, as blithely as if he had been jumping into one of the Keralan pools of his boyhood. Many had gone over—then most—but Ibraham and a distrustful remnant stayed pinned against the rails, facing what were now unadorned threats.

"Jump, or you are dead! Jump! The water's shallow. The English will stop for you. Fuck you, GO!"

There was a ragged movement towards the Albanians, but it was halted as quickly as it had begun. There were two flashes, a small and a large explosion, and an Egyptian and a Sudanese crumpled. The others stopped in their tracks. Resistance was obviously out—and maybe England *was* just a few metres away. After all, the Albanians hadn't let them down before. They'd come across Europe without breaking their word.

Cursing, threatening and crying, more jumped until the water bulged with bodies stroking westwards, seeking for sand with shod feet, hoping to hear waves on the sought-for shore. Ibraham was left against the taffrail with a hard core of three others, facing angrily into the guns. Kruja spoke more gently:

"Come on, lads—you know you've got to go. And frankly if you don't go, we'll kill you. Over the side, you have a chance. With us, you have none. Don't make it hard for us, and don't waste our time!"

They did not—all scrambled over the side and leapt desperately for life—except Ibraham, who simply could not comprehend that there could be such an end to his adventure. Kruja's flashing brown eyes assessed him, and he said quietly: "Come. You're last. Over you go now, and happy landings!"

Ibraham opened his mouth to explain, or to plead. This filmy fog, this rusty deck, his dirty trousers, his grubby running shoes, these killers' faces—these would be the last things he would see, and his eye travelled covetously over everything to memorize it in every detail, focusing lastly on the blackest of all the black things he had ever seen, the tiny round holes of the shotgun's side-by-side barrels. And see there, deep inside! A tiny fire, an infinitesimal flash of beautiful brilliance.

When the pellets pierced his side, he felt nothing, but nonetheless felt obliged to collapse. As he fell, hard hands grasped his ankles and wrists. Then he was rocked once, and thrown—like when his father had rocked him in play before flinging him giggling onto a pile of sand. He felt peculiarly detached. Even when the waters boiled and churned over his head, he only felt a sort of ticklishness—as if he had an indestructible core that even the worst cold and pain could never reach.

He saw father, Saddam's statue, the hoopoe's nest, AK47 tracer over Iran, spangling stars over the border, Maged on the train, the flying fish, Mandoor's nose squashing as he hit it square and true, the droop of the wire as he cleared the fence at Lavrion, the singers in that fœtid lorry, Holland's receding diamantine brilliance, the *Kapitein*'s silhouette square and tall and reliable behind the wheelhouse glass, the half-Western children he would never now sire. Would Miss Karatakis ever hear how his story had ended?

What a fine adventure it had all been, what a gallant attempt, and what a pity no-one would ever hear the story. He floated easily, pleasantly, tingling in the cleanly ocean. Looking casually to one side, and then the other, he saw his hair fanned out, twisting like weed—and there were his hands and feet. Others floated past; their feet were threshing the water, and their mouths were opening and closing, but he couldn't hear them because the ocean was in his ears. There was flame somewhere, and he knew the Albanians were firing down in the water. But he didn't care, because there was nothing they could do now, and it was too late to be interested in anything. There was just the freshness of things and their coolness, and his mouth was crisped with salt. The trawler was a coast, then the coast fell away, leaving just the fog closing down and crowding out things that had once seemed interesting and important, for reasons he could no longer recall. He felt the fondling of the cloud, and it reminded him how cold his face had felt one shining morning many years ago.

He bobbed and bled, and span in the water, then drifted beyond knowledge in an immense and argent universe.

Part II

WELCOME TO ENGLAND

*...we are here as on a darkling plain
Swept with confused alarms of struggle and flight...*

—Matthew Arnold, "Dover Beach"

Chapter 17
RESPITE CARE

Elmcaster, Eastshire
Tuesday, 13th—Thursday, 29th August

Soap and polish. A dark face looking kindly down into his. Sunlight behind and around. Comfort, languor, cleanliness. The face disappeared, and there were voices—in what language? English? English!

Ibraham's throat was too dry and raw to speak, although he tried repeatedly. Dark face again, then a pale one with cool grey eyes—a very *English* face, Ibraham decided. Its mouth opened.

"Hello, and welcome to Britain! Do you speak English?"

Ibraham stared up, enjoying the crisp sound, the woman's features, the sheets' clean slipperiness. He felt deliciously helpless. Guessing rather than understanding, he shook his head. "No English! No English! Iraq!" He coughed rackingly. As it went away again, leaving him aching drily, his eyes flicked wide in remembrance.

He felt again something hitting him *there*, where he had just become conscious of dull pain and itchiness—remembered tumbling into the slick sea—saw again the dark underside of the boat against the slightly lighter background—heard again the muffled thud-thud-thud of the engines as the dark shape pulled out of sight, feeling himself sinking down, down. There was one more random memory—shocking coldness as his head popped out of the water, his mouth filled with salt as well as air, making him gag. But how long ago had that been? And how had he got here? Where were all the others? He drifted puzzled but pleased into the past.

Words heard but not understood: "...hypothermia on top of gunshot wounds, and he hasn't been living too brilliantly for some time before that. He's very weak, but I hope he may be able to start answering questions very soon now. But not too many!"

Curious faces coming in and going out of focus. Aches soothed by gently probing fingers; toes wriggling in pleasure of being clean; arms weak, but it didn't matter. It didn't matter at all.

It was evening and the sun was leaving, except for a vermilion stripe that had not quite relinquished the respond of the window to his left. So *very* beautiful, so unexpected.

His brain had repaired itself in sleep. He now knew that he had been shot, that he had been plucked miraculously out of the sea, and that this must therefore be England. E-N-G-L-A-N-D. He relished the musicality of it.

Another nurse hovered into view. The black girl must have gone home. This one was white, older, with brown hair. She smiled tiredly. "Hello. How are you feeling?" Ibraham smiled back and shook his head in courteous incomprehension. He mouthed "Hello"; it was the only word he had understood. The nurse lifted his head and put some pills into his mouth, followed by a delightful stream of water. She plumped his pillows, smiled, and went away—coming back a few minutes later, with a fat, Arabic-looking man. "*Salaam*," he said. "*Salaam*," Ibraham managed, with an effort. It was pleasant to hear the familiar word, but the idea of longer conversation made him tired.

"My name is Mustapha Sayeed. I am an interpreter. What is your name? And where have you come from? No hurry—I know you're still weak."

There were things Ibraham needed to know. Eventually—"Where is this place?"

"Elmcaster Hospital, on the east coast of England. You were found over a week ago, washed up on a beach at a place near here. I'm sorry to say you were the only survivor. You're really very fortunate."

The only one! All those people in the hold—the excited young men, laughing and singing—the big Equatorial Guinean—that Sudanese girl. He saw a cigarette butt arcing through the dank darkness and heard again whispers in the cold and fishy fug. He touched his aching side.

"And the Albanians?"

"Which Albanians?"

"The killers."

"I don't know about any Albanians. But I think you'd better leave off talking now, because the police will want to hear what you say. If you tell it all to me now, you'll have to tell it all over again to them. Now if I were you I would just have some food—it's *halal*, don't worry—and then go back to sleep, and concentrate on recruiting your strength. If you need anything, the nurse is nearby. I've taught her a few key words—so if you want to use the toilet, or want a drink of water, you ought to able to understand each other. Now, good night."

He vanished, but was soon replaced by the nurse and the smell of hot food. She helped him to sit up, and watched closely while he ate a small quantity of lamb and carrots. She picked up some crumbs and mopped up some spilled fruit juice. "Toilet?" she asked, in what sounded slightly like Arabic. Ibraham had never discussed such things with a woman and felt horribly awkward. Accustomed to male squeamishness, she retained her neutral expression. He nodded shortly, but couldn't meet her eyes. He was surprised, and ashamed, when she deftly lifted up the covers on her side of the bed and shoved in a bedpan. He couldn't believe that a Western woman was attending to his filthiest functions. He wanted desperately to defecate, but not like this, and in front of a woman. Intuiting the problem, she moved away—and soon he had done what he had to do. When she came to take it away, he stared at the wall. She left and his embarrassment receded, and dark warmth enveloped him again.

He could feel his blood moving again, thrumming through his legs and feet. The pain had become stiffness. He was eating well and was eventually allowed to make his own way to the toilet, using a walking frame—and to look out the window down over the hospital car park, and dismal suburbs festooned with satellite dishes. The vista wasn't at all what he had expected.

Over several hesitant days, he told his story to the police, while the world's media camped outside the hospital. Mustapha came in every day to show the patient some of the papers and read extracts. Ibraham was amazed by the volume of the coverage, and by the inaccuracies. The Iraqi press had at least been consistent. He heard half-comprehendingly about songs, school assemblies, programmes, concerts, demonstrations, parliamentary debates, summits, and even a riot. All these people he had never heard of, and even some he *had* heard of, and they were all seemingly talking about *him*! *Him*, a poor man from a poor city in a poor country, unimportant, and inconsequential—the subject of such concern! It frightened him to think that soon he would need to leave this place—and look this multi-eyed monster in the face. He was bound to disappoint them.

One paper had a picture of Dan, looking fat, flustered, and furtive. "That man," Mustapha explained, stabbing the picture with his index finger, "is a racist. He lives near here. He wants to send all brown people home. But he is getting some bad publicity! Serves him right, I say!" Ibraham's eyes slid carelessly over the picture. Dan wasn't an interesting-looking man, he felt. The paper fell onto the floor and was forgotten.

The public reaction puzzled and worried him. It didn't chime with the image of England he had carried all those thousands of miles. He hadn't expected the English to react in this way. He wondered if Iraqis would have behaved the same way if dead Englishmen had been washed up on the Iraqi shoreline; he was forced to conclude they probably would not, and this made him feel oddly ashamed. There seemed something noble in the English reaction.

But maybe all this putative concern was some kind of elaborate game, some ritual that had to be played out before less kindly people came. Kemali had been fond of exaggerated courtesy, long and ornate compliments paid just before his little eyes went hard and small like a jackal's. His men had always said he was at his most dangerous at those moments. Saddam, too, could be courteous, even kind immediately before, or following, an outburst of atrocious cruelty. Maybe this was something like that. He brooded long on this possibility.

One morning, his thoughts were interrupted in the most agreeable way, as Ayesha rushed into his room, shouting in joy as she threw herself exuberantly onto his seated form. The impact made him wince, but what was a little pain compared with the delight of seeing again his favourite sibling and hearing what had been happening at home? The British had flown her over specially, and they were taking care of the others. They exchanged news and embraces long into the afternoon, until eventually the nurse came and told her Ibraham needed rest.

His journey and hers had been extraordinarily different—one furtive, one free, one dangerous, one luxurious. She had heard about the disaster and said they had all felt sure he had been on the boat. It had been a terrible time, weeping and wondering until two days ago, when a very polite young British man had turned up at the door with an interpreter and an army escort, to tell her that Ibraham had been found alive and there was a first-class plane ticket at her disposal whenever she wanted to go. They had all cried with joy and the whole village had been electric with excitement. She had been nervous about the journey, but it hadn't been so bad—and, of course, at the end there was Ibi waiting! And they were putting her up in some hotel nearby—her eyes were wide with wonder as she described all the comforts and conveniences of her three-star accommodation.

But Ibraham's joy at seeing her again and hearing about home was tempered by the knowledge that soon he would have no more reason to stay in hospital. Then what? Where would he go? Would he be allowed to stay in England? He was, after all, illegal, without any skills. And his money had all gone. Mustapha tried to reassure him, by telling him there were a lot of media people who wanted to talk to him—and they would pay for the privilege. The amounts mentioned made Ibrahim's head ache.

With this hanging over him, he malingered shamelessly to stay in his lovely, safe bed, and delay the dreaded departure—although he felt bad lying to the nurses and doctors, who had been so kind. But one day, Ibrahim could see in their faces that he had run out of excuses. So he submitted apathetically to donning the clothes they had provided. They were ugly clothes—jogging bottoms, T-shirts, a hooded top, running shoes—but they were the best he had ever possessed, some bearing logos he had previously only seen in magazines. He stood in front of the mirror, stroking his beard and staring at his sophisticated alter ego.

The interview requests brought by Mustapha (who accepted an introduction fee from each applicant) worried him greatly. He had never spoken to a newspaperman in his life or appeared on any kind of program. Then Mustapha also brought the answer—a little rectangular card, heavy with a handsome crest, the nicest thing Ibrahim had ever handled. It read simply "Jakob von Grönestein, Media Mediation," with an address in London SW3.

Mustapha explained that Grönestein was an actual German lord, a kind of diplomat who dealt with newspapers and television for private clients. Ibrahim had never heard of such people, and the knowledge that they existed made him realize just how odd the new country and culture were. Why would a lord do such work? Mustapha explained that media mediation was actually one of the most important and respectable jobs one could do in the West. Every moment in the West was a defining moment. Ibrahim wouldn't even need money up front, because Grönestein would just take a percentage of whatever was earned. So he agreed, although he felt like events were slipping beyond his control. But hadn't they always been? And if this man would take some of the burden from him it would be a good investment.

The German stood smilingly before Ibraham, wearing what even Ibraham's inexpert sartorial sense told him was a very expensive suit and glasses that looked like they were rimmed with real gold. Now Ibraham believed he was a real lord—and he had a surge of giddy snobbery as he thought of having a Western lord working for him. And when he heard that Jakob—as he insisted on being called—had once represented one of Ibraham's favourite footballers, and he would only take 30 percent of Ibraham's fees, all he could do was nod in wondering acceptance.

The long-feared media were finally at hand, but at least they were controlled by Jakob, whose eyes ranged contemptuously over the overflowing suite at the hospital. Ibraham envied the German's quiet mastery. As for him, he was paralysed with fright.

Jakob had arranged for a "world-exclusive" later on with one of the tabloid newspapers, for what Ibraham felt was an extraordinary amount of money (although, had he known it, the real amount was very much larger) and had promised that the press conference would be short and businesslike. But it was still all he could do to walk into the hot and glaring room and see a fizzing crowd of curious faces turning hungrily towards him—to see the artillery fire of cameras—to hear the excitement and know that all of it was caused by his presence. Just him—nothing more—an ordinary man from an ugly street in a run-down town.

The panel gazed at by the globe consisted of Ibraham, Jakob, a senior doctor and a senior policemen—plus Mustapha, slightly to one side. The policeman and the doctor laid out the facts forensically, then the questions hurtled towards Ibraham like AK47 rounds—but soft, with filed-down tips, dum-dums of delicacy carrying payloads of empathy.

How long was your journey? How did you travel? What was your route? How many others were with you? What dangers did you face? He answered at first shyly and shortly, and rather too quietly, but gradually gathered confidence as he realised how kind everyone was being. He realized they wanted him to come across well, to be attractive to their readers, to arouse compassion and awe. What fine people they were! He felt great warmth towards them, and, as if subconsciously to thank them, his explanations became longer and more elaborate. They nodded encouragingly and smiled as he replied, and inhaled when they should—and he wanted to keep them there, just where they were, urging him on, absorbed by his story.

He remembered more and more vivid details—tired-looking American troopers at the checkpoints, distant explosions, the picture of the Jordanian king at the border crossing, the stars dashing above the desert, the greenly glowing sea and the long slow roll of the Aegean, the sweaty smell in the lorry, the puke-spotted trawler hold, and, of course, the night of the drownings—and he elaborated on some of these, while Jakob watched minutely and the globe admired and condescended.

Can you tell us a little about your background, please, Mr. Nassouf? He said he would like to, but it was not very exciting. They were politely sure it was, so polite that he felt a sincere wish to please them, to give them something that would help them. So he told them about his parents, the family house, his gardening, his work at the depot, his time in the army. But his tale lacked spice.

Just as he was thinking this came a question—"Were you involved with any anti-Saddam political activity?" He knew they would love him to have been for the sake of completeness—and so almost unstoppably he heard himself saying "Yes," and once that was out it could not be retracted.

Now he was providing details that sprang from street stories. As he spoke, there grew an intoxicating excitement in the room. Jakob was looking on in annoyance, and for a second Ibrahim regretted his rashness. But then he saw the rapt face of a journalist from Channel One—a brunette angel, as lovely as Miss Karatakis—and he felt it was too late to retract.

Yes, he told them, he'd done some leafleting—attended a few meetings, met people, made plans, become known to the secret police—and then, of course, they had taken him in for questioning. It had been *very* unpleasant questioning. Yes, you *could* call it torture. He had in his mind a picture of that Mandæan hanging by his arms in the lock-up and was about to apply it to himself—but just then, Jakob interceded with a reminder that his client was still very weak, and it would not be good for him to go into these traumatic details at this stage—grimacing fiercely at Ibrahim to be quiet. Ibrahim, brought up in shock at his hitherto unrealised capacity for fabrication, instantly subsided, grateful for having been silenced before he went too far.

The conference ebbed into inconsequentiality—How do you feel now? What do you think of England? So kind all of your people, and so beautiful a country—although, of course, you will understand I have not seen much of it yet. Sympathetic laughter. Your country is very clean, and quiet, and kind. He did not know what would happen to him now, and relied on the famous generosity of the English people and Prime Minister Smith. But he did miss his family. He was glad his sister Ayesha had already joined him, and perhaps the rest of his family could come, too, some day to your lovely kind country.

A modest man, the journalists would agree—a good man, a prisoner of circumstances, a symbol of what was good in the Iraqi people, in all people. And such a paragon had been tortured for his beliefs! He was an Everyman—and a hero. So unassuming, such a nice smile, so handsome. The desire for free markets and equal opportunities burned bright in Iraqi hearts, conservative commentators would suggest—while their social democrat counterparts preferred to stress his outraged human dignity and the plight of all the others.

"Why the fuck didn't you tell me all this stuff about the secret police? Do you know what that story's worth?" Jakob asked angrily afterwards, and resentment radiated too from Mustapha, who had thought he was a confidant. Ibrahim felt foolish but defiant—and, besides, he couldn't now admit that he had made it up. They couldn't prove he'd made it up. Only Ayesha would guess, and he would explain to her how it had been there in the glare—how his tongue had simply run away, like the tongues of the itinerant story-tellers they both remembered from youth. *She* at least would understand, and that was what mattered.

Who cares what *these* people think, and he looked at Jakob and Mustapha with something like loathing. He hadn't thought it was relevant, he told them; it had just come out; it had been years ago. "OK, OK, OK," Jakob had said, thinking rapidly, drumming on the desk. Then he asked some detailed questions, to which Ibrahim (amazed at his inventiveness) made up believable replies; Jakob outlined exactly how Ibrahim would handle the *Globe* interview.

The interview would be the *Globe*'s bestselling issue of the year. Across the front page was a fetching photograph of Ibrahim and Ayesha sitting smiling, her arm around her brother's even-skinnier-than-usual shoulders. Her headscarf framed her worried, proud face, and lent contrast and depth to Ibrahim's tired and tense physiognomy, as both smiled their way shyly into British hearts.

The *Globe* dispensed with subtleties:

MIRACLE MIGRANT'S AMAZING STORY—EXCLUSIVE

> *Torture, war, murder, poverty, a family to support, a secret journey across a closed continent—Ibrahim Nassouf's extraordinary story, only in the Globe.*

Political prisoner Ibrahim Nassouf left a country at war to take a long and dangerous journey into the West—a journey that almost ended in disaster and death. Yet against all the odds, he survived. Today, EXCLUSIVELY, we can reveal how the plucky Iraqi faced down secret police, war, murderers, and racism—to feed his starving family and build a new life in the West.

It is one of the great adventure stories of modern times. Ibrahim's incredible 4,000 mile journey began in southern Iraq, and crossed Jordan, Syria, Turkey, Greece, Bulgaria, Romania, Hungary, Slovenia, Austria, Germany, Holland, and finally the North Sea. He travelled on foot, by car, bus, train, plane, Greek army lorry, hidden inside a refrigerated truck, and then finally on a trawler, where he was the only one of 43 undocumented innocents to survive drowning and racist murder—at the very gates of the country they had travelled so far to find. For them, the promised land would not be paradise, but a tomb—the tomb of all their hopes and dreams.

Modest Ibrahim, 28, seen above with his beloved younger sister Ayesha, downplays his extraordinary heroism and resilience. He told me, 'It was nothing—nothing at all—apart from the ending, which was truly horrible and shocking. As for the rest, it was a mere adventure and experience—and in any case I had no choice. I had my sisters back home, perhaps starving, perhaps engulfed in war. My duty was to them.'

A modest and unassuming man indeed, but with an amazing story to tell, of hope and courage, resilience, and faith in the face of evil.

The modest and unassuming man, sitting in a sunny corner in the ward being read the article by Mustapha, snorted in embarrassment. But

Ayesha clasped her hands and exclaimed, "Isn't it wonderful?" Ibraham just grunted, but he was privately pleased. And the article hadn't gone on about the secret police and all that kind of stuff, because Ibraham had not responded to the *Globe*'s probing on that subject. The reporter had been disappointed, and Jacob had scowled, but Ibraham's reluctance to augment his falsehood was regarded as resilience rather than role-play.

> Ibraham would rather not discuss what happened to him in that Basra police station—the wounds are too raw. All he would say was this: 'In a way, all of Iraq has been tortured, and we all bear Saddam's scars. But perhaps we can all now rebuild our lives.' To which this paper can only say a fervent Amen.

The media ordeal was over—but only for now. And now it was time to leave—and he had nowhere to go. His journey, long and dangerous though it had already been, was not yet at an end.

Chapter 18
POLITIC POLITICS

City of London
Thursday, 29th August

Albert laughed scornfully and threw the *Examiner* right across the office, to join a crumpled pile of the day's other papers. "That's what we're up against, Sal." He was looking ruefully at the curling grey hairs showing among her relatively tasteful peroxide and enjoying the luxury of holding forth to someone who would never cavil or quibble.

"John Leyden—the Puritanical prig *par excellence,* at the apex of a slimy system of smugness, a sanctimonious conspiring against commonsense—and at the centre of it, a rather stupid, frightened farmer, whipping boy for the whole Western world. The voice of the fucking future! Awful, isn't it?"

"Yes, Albert," Sally said politely. She always ignored most of what he said, which often reminded her of a rather odd public meeting. And she never really liked all his swearing. She was trying to concentrate on his expenses, always a complicated affair because of his unwillingness to retain receipts. The amounts were always modest; Albert rarely went to good restaurants these days because he did not need to impress anyone now. Sally wasn't quite sure if he had ever impressed anyone. He was not the type of person many people would warm to. He was so cocksure, so acerbic and relentlessly negative about everyone and everything, and his columns and conversation were littered with all kinds of obscure allusions. She wondered if he was looking forward to retirement, which surely could not be long delayed, and this made her think of her own impending obsolescence. She would miss that whole routine of seeing him and hearing (if not often listening to) him—although she would not miss this poring over crumpled, stained, delayed, and incomplete invoices, or this grubby office, which she longed (but had never dared) to clean.

"Coffee? Ah, you heard *that*! Here you are—a chalice of dung-hued ambrosia…drink it while it's tepid!" He put her cup heavily on her desk, then lumbered back over to his, slopping coffee onto the floor, as it had slopped every day for years, leaving a broken and discoloured line from door to desk. He started to type. "Smugness-on-sea…" He was pleased with the title and sat there looking at it, cracking his Stilton-hued knuckles.

> In yesterday's *Examiner*, a new tactic in the War Against England was revealed. Our old chum John Leyden has left his fashionable London stamping ground, and descended into a part of the country where real people live real lives. This commitment to disinterested research is to be commended. But what he finds there appals and offends him. He discovers—*O tempora, O mores!*—that normal, decent, hardworking people do not share his views—that real, normal, decent, hardworking taxpayers would rather be Anglo-Saxons than Afro-Saxons—that many (perhaps the majority) would rather like to preserve England's present identity.

His descriptions of Crisby—and by extension all of the countryside—as an incipient Auschwitz must amaze and pain millions of people, who will recognize nothing of themselves or England in this foul caricature. Leyden's supposed fact-finding mission was just a vehicle to reinforce his prejudices about the people who choose to absent themselves from the dubious delights of inner-city London, who vote CD, who work hard at real jobs (like feeding the nation). It was Johnny Boy's projection of N1 or W11 onto the whole country—an attempt to make independent-minded country people conform to a certain stereotype.

His *ad hominen* assault on the character and beliefs, real or imagined, of Mr. Daniel Gowt is actually an assault on everyone who does not share his own views. Here we have an apparently decent farmer caught up in events beyond his comprehension, who has blurted out something in a confused moment. For this, he has been tried at the bar of 'acceptable' opinion and condemned as a symbol of evil 'racism'. This pillorying of Mr. Gowt is a gross injustice, from a writer who calls himself a liberal. Such irresponsible and hateful tactics can only serve to inflame the already superheated public mood, and to place what must be almost intolerable pressure on Mr. Gowt and his family.

Then he changed subject. There were all the other usual things to toss and gore—not that the objects of his ministrations ever really seemed to notice, or to mind if they did notice. His mind ranged as his fingers travelled restlessly over the keyboard, but often it flicked away to an image of an old house and its even more outmoded owner, far away on the breached barricade of their coast.

Ministers had been discussing how to handle this especially delicate case. Coalition opinion was generally pro-immigration. However, government strategists reported that things were far from well in some urban areas, pointing to a possible electoral surge in favour of National Union or even worse parties. The previous month, a formerly safe WP seat in Birmingham had almost been lost to NU, whose candidate had taken a worrying 31 percent of the vote. There were seats where even worse outcomes could be envisaged. They already had one MP, and everyone was predicting there would soon be more. Thankfully, Richard Simpson's Private Member's Bill to ban the party was moving swiftly up the legislative ladder, with the strong backing of most MPs. But the CDs were also making headway on immigration, although everyone except their electors knew their interest was essentially rhetorical.

The government knew that if Ibraham were allowed to remain in the UK it would be accused of being soft on immigration. Yet if he were removed, the government backbenches, CD modernizers, and the media would go on the attack. Then there were the EU, UN, and all the African governments who must not be insulted in case they boycotted next year's Commonwealth Games. The government was still smarting from the case of a Rwandan woman, a seven-times warned illegal who had eventually been removed by force, only to die from asphyxiation during what the last immigration minister had unfortunately referred to as the "struggle process."

Prime Minister Wilberforce Smith was very large and vaguely Welsh, his almost square head topped by thick wavy whitening hair that had been black—this strongly carved capital surmounting a burly body like a capital D balanced on a pair of tree-trunks. He stood bad-temperedly (and hæmorrhoid-aware) in front of a window high in the Palace of Westminster, breathing on the glass and drawing crude faces in the mist while listening to his chief political adviser. They were the only people in the office. He looked down into the deep valley between the two towers—a gloomy and dirty domain of pointy roofs, Pugin-friendly, user-unfriendly small-paned windows, scaffolding and pigeons and vans delivering stuff a hundred feet below, with a colourless stripe of Thames beyond. Lights were coming on to counter the burgeoning darkness in the dank vertiginious wells. The prospect always made him think of Gotham City.

The adviser had finished his briefing, and the PM spoke without turning round.

"Shit—why couldn't he drown, too?"

"Wilber…Prime Minister!?!"

"What you're saying is that if we kick him out, we're fucked; if we don't kick him out, we're fucked; and if we do neither, we're fucked."

"Well, I…well, that is about the size of it, I'm afraid."

James, the adviser, could never get used to how much Wilberforce had changed since they were at Oxford together. Sometimes he was almost *scared* of him—scared of this great liberal-in-waiting, the student he had known so full of ideals, with his unusual Christian name that combined resonant echoes of Reform with a surname that told of electorally desirable Ordinariness.

The PM was also thinking of the past, and he spoke ruminatively. "This time last week, I was presenting the Anti-Racist Shield at the New World Foundation dinner, sitting between a black Pentecostalist and that odious little shit Ben Klein. He always sits so *close*—makes my skin crawl, frankly. Anyway, he reminded me, with his little smirk, that my first ever speech from the backbenches, way back in 1983, was about the detention camp at Little Chipping. Remember all that? I was *Liberal Voice*'s 'Lamp-bearer for Liberalism' that year. I've probably still got their crappy little certificate.

"Well, anyway, if we kick this Iraqi bloke out, as we should—that torture stuff is bollocks, by the way—all that will be forgotten. It will be 'Government adopts racist policies'—'PM in cynical electoral ploy'—*et fucking cetera*. And the UN will be sending in more special investigators like that Indonesian twerp; Brussels will be jumping up and down; and old friends will cut me dead. So (a) which is better—to go through all that, or run the risk of meltdown next year? And (b) how long can we stall for? Obviously, we can't do anything until whatshisname is out of hospital."

"He's due out the day after tomorrow."

"Two days. Shame it couldn't be a bit longer. The polls? Remind me."

"Not so good. The CDs are eight points ahead, and NU are scoring 20s to 30s—but obviously that will change if Spitson can get his act together. One thing that might affect your timing is that McKerras is planning to announce a new tougher immigration policy on Wednesday. Here are the details. If you do propose to remove Mr. Nassouf, an announcement to that effect just beforehand...?"

"Umphh." There was more breathing and drawing on the glass, and an unusually long pause. The PM was still staring out of the window, so James couldn't see his face, but when he spoke, he sounded oddly old.

"You know something, James? I may be a bit of a charlatan—maybe even a bit of a shit. No, no, don't say anything! I know what I am, and so do you—better than anyone else, maybe. But strictly between us, *never* to go beyond this room, I feel a terrible *unease* about immigration. I think we've—all politicians, all parties—made, and are still making, a big mistake."

He stopped for about 30 seconds, gathering his thoughts. "You remember my walk-about in Peckham? It won't surprise you to learn that while I was doing my thing my mind was elsewhere—but what might surprise you is what I was thinking about.

"I was looking at that crowded street and comparing it with an old photo—1920s—I have of Peckham Rye. My grandfather was born in Peckham—did you know that? As you know, I'm a quarter English, and he was that quarter. The house he was born in is still there. He went to a local school—founded by some Elizabethan merchant-adventurer—all gone now, of course, even the old building, which I remember seeing when I was yea high.

"Anyway, he had an ironmongery shop and took photographs in his spare time—very mechnically-minded sort of a chap overall. By the time I knew him, he was already in his 80s, but even then he was always fiddling with machinery out in his shed. He left me all his pictures when he died, because I'd always been interested in them—and I've got them still. I find myself looking at them more and more. I find those old scenes not only incredibly evocative but increasingly attractive. And it's not just the nice old buildings, or the well-dressed, confident-looking people—there was something else they had that we've thrown away—and then I ask myself what the fuck have we got in return? Dishonesty and division, Balkanization and bollocks…"

He was shaking his head, and another 30 seconds elapsed before he squared his shoulders and turned back into the room. He seemed his usual brisk self. James, who had been taken aback by the remarks, which he would never have expected from such a source, was relieved. He had thought he wanted confidences, but the tenor of this particular monologue had unnerved him. He was glad no-one else had been present. If this were to get out…it didn't bear thinking about. He hoped it didn't betoken some imprudent public outburst. Wilberforce had always been so careful. He looked at him closely and was relieved to see no obvious signs of distraction.

That prudent statesman looked at his (conspicuously cheap) watch—one of his trademarks, like the off-the-peg suits and the artfully unbrushed hair—that showed he was "in touch." He had to make a decision. In 33 minutes, he had to give a lecture to some more-than-usually-repellent church group called the Icthys Brethren. "OK, Jim. I need to go and see these Fish Faces shortly. Here's what we'll do to Master McKerras." The PM sat down at the table, and the men's heads moved slightly closer while the lights outside waxed slowly brighter, but never quite brightly enough.

Two days later, the youngish, state-educated CD leader Doug McKerras was about to leave for the press conference to launch the party's new immigration policy (the third in two years), this one with the excellent title *New Deal for Nationals and Newcomers*—when his PPS texted urgently. The PM had just announced that as soon as Ibraham was discharged from hospital, he would be admitted to the Holding Centre where his asylum application would be processed. The PM had added that he "believed in a new deal for nationals and newcomers." "*Shitshitshitshit*," the Leader of HM Loyal Opposition expostulated, as he hastened along the oaken corridor, desperately trying to think up some good new phrases. He had been rhetorically gazumped, for what he expected would in any case be a difficult meeting. Immigration meetings were always difficult, no matter how many black faces there were on the top table with you.

An old story had unfortunately resurfaced. The *Examiner* had noticed that a friend of the party researcher who had sent those notorious racist e-mails was on the CDs' approved candidate list. She had been removed immediately, but it was undoubtedly a nuisance and an embarrassment. He had hoped the new policy would allow him to divert that discussion into more helpful channels.

But in the event, the *Examiner* asked merely, "What do you think of the government's determination to deport the torture victim Ibraham Nassouf?" Hardly daring to believe he had got off so easily, he answered, "It seems an inhuman and, frankly, bizarre, proceeding, and one obviously motivated by sordid political calculations. It is disgraceful to make political capital out of the dead." This made it onto the *Examiner*'s front page the following day—the first time a CD leader had ever been cited approvingly on that paper's front page. It was quite a coup for McKerras, as he told his Shadow Cabinet colleagues.

Other newspapers were equally aggrieved—"From survival joy to deportation threat"—"Unforgiveable, unthinkable and inhumane"—"PM's plan to expel Ibraham"—"PM caves into pressure from far Right"—"'Disgusting deportation plan"—"Miracle migrant faced with expulsion"—"Back to Baghdad for disaster survivor?"—"He's won our hearts. Now he's to be kicked out."

Wanda Lo told the readers of *Suburban Shopper* exactly how she felt. "I am ashamed of my country—for it is my country too, as much as any who have a so-called 'birthright.' Ibraham told a tale of unimaginable horror. The modest way he has held himself has made him more than just a martyr. We should be shocked and disgusted that in the 21st century, a WP prime minister is giving the bigoted affirmation by proxy. It can never be appropriate for a civilised, wealthy society to turn a sick man out of his hospital bed and put him on a plane to a very worrying future. A responsible government would focus on the *opportunities* of diversity, not its challenges. Democracy is a sham if it means forefronting fascist tactics against the most vulnerable members of our society. They say Third World citizens but they really mean third–class citizens. We should hate ourselves right now!"

The *Sentinel* ran a special feature on asylum and refugees, with short contributions from WP left to CD left. An unexpected and (for Albert) pleasant link with the past was a delightfully rambling quote from the present Lord Thornley, son of the paper's former proprietor. Albert had completely forgotten Thornley had had a son. That child was now in his 80s, and his amiable contribution did not exactly echo the *Zeitgeist*. "I feel awfully sorry for the people caught up in all those dreadful problems. I have very happy memories of my childhood in Kenya, and can tell you that Africans are splendid fellows in a crisis. Our servants always had an authenticity of character absent from Europeans." This all had an antebellum flavour that Albert particularly liked, and he snipped it out for his files.

PMQs—rustling order papers fanning crammed, squeaking green benches. Wilberforce looked contempuously at the CDs opposite, then changed his face to look over his shoulder at his "colleagues." There they all were—McKerras fidgeting, even puffier than usual. Looks like he needs a long piss. That lesbian Eco MP—what *was* her name?—who was always going on about "combine-culturalism." And she'd have her FPA and WP friends to back her up—the poisonous toad Luke Jones, well-meaning but stupid Bob Paine, that complete arse Evan Dafydd, all the *et fucking ceteras*. That was all only to be expected, and the worst to fear from most of them was to be bored to fucking death. He caught the eye of Home Secretary Alan Clough and winked. Clough looked hot and sticky. Maybe HS wasn't right for him. What about Claydon Peters? Bit young, maybe, but bright, and being black would have been useful in such a position on a day like today. It was pathetic really, all this ethnic grandstanding, but there was no way round it these days.

What perturbed the PM most was seeing the solitary National Union MP, sitting there with the usual *cordon sanitaire* of three inches of green leather between him and his fastidious neighbours, the Eco MPs. Trust him not to miss this! No doubt, he would be endorsing the government's approach. *That* he could do without. He tried to think of something witty to say about him, to distance himself from his unwanted endorsement. Look at his cheap suit—Poujadism in Pricenice! That wasn't bad, especially as Pricenice was a CD donor. But probably loads of WP voters wore Pricenice—so maybe that was out. And was Poujadism a little obscure? Maybe, but that would wrongfoot McKerras—who probably wouldn't know what it meant. He wasn't the sharpest knife in the drawer.

McKerras stood up across the dispatch box, cocky as a general at the head of a numerically superior army, and an inhalation of anticipation filled the chamber. CD frontbenchers prepared to jeer or laugh.

"Is it morally right…" (Predictable, the PM thought. Really, the man was a buffoon) "…that a homeless and penniless refugee who is furthermore a victim of attempted murder should be condemned to suffer the inhumane and degrading asylum process? Would my Right Honourable Friend not agree that human rights and natural justice are more important than winning by-elections?"

There was a roar of cheering and a stamping of feet, from all sides. "Order, order!" from the Speaker, new to the job but coping. The press peered down like circling kestrels. The PM's drawl cut through the dwindling din.

"The young man in question has been treated and will continue to be treated with all due dignity and courtesy. We sympathise with his terrible experiences whilst trying to enter the UK. His unorthodox arrival was nonetheless contrary to UK and EU law, and he must therefore be processed in accordance with that legislation. I would like to remind the House that my Right *Honourable* Friend's own party last year opposed our attempts to liberalise the immigration laws, to make it easier for deserving immigrants to enter this country."

His support was muted. Looking sideways, the PM could see his frontbenchers looked very uncomfortable. Bastards. He hoped the whips were counting carefully.

McKerras again: "This party has always pursued a responsible attitude to legislative reform. But this question rises above party politics and becomes a question of human decency and dignity. I will ask my question again—does my Right Honourable Friend propose to send a tortured, badly wounded man back to a war zone?"

"No, no!" "Surely not!" "Not in *our* name!"

The calls came as much from behind the PM as from across the floor. Bastards! Where'd they be without him? Shunting papers around in some council office, trying to score with the tea-lady—or running some two-bit legal-aid racket in Kentish Town. He'd sort them out later— he had been spoiling for a good barney with the Parliamentary Party. But for now there was that twerp McKerras lounging laughingly on the opposite bench, chortling with his public-school chums, with his legs splayed apart in a fair imitation of one of his immeasurably greater predecessors. Wilberforce sneered, and the sneer was real:

"I have already informed the Right *Honourable* Gentleman that the refugee in question will be treated fairly in accordance with the law that his own party helped to put onto the statute books last year. The unusual and unfortunate circumstances of the young man's entry into the UK cannot be used as an excuse to subvert the laws of this country. We are committed to ethnic equality, as I made clear last week when I launched our new Side by Side, Not Genocide campaign, with its distinctive black-and-white striped lapel ribbon. Furthermore, may I remind the House that just last week, the Right Honourable Gentleman's party was revealed to be still harbouring the worst kind of racial prejudice?"

It was a good stroke, one which McKerras had amazingly not been expecting. The PM could see the dolt spluttering and glancing at a note he had just been handed by the Shadow Home Secretary—the real brains of the party. This was too, too easy, thought the PM, almost smirking before remembering the cameras. He couldn't smirk discussing *this*.

McKerras came back, but deflated—and soon ambled off onto less dangerous subjects. He eventually gave up the podium, and the PM sat yawning as Luke Jones, Bill Paine, and several other "allies" whose names he couldn't remember placed their questions. He had no difficulty in dealing with the questions, but he needed to know how backbench feeling would stack up.

The NU man's question wasn't as bad as he had feared. "We congratulate the government on its tough approach, which has clearly been inspired by our party's policy. But is the Prime Minister aware of the many blatant abuses of the asylum system that take place every day in this country? Why is nothing being done about these?"

"This government has always pursued a robust but right policy in relation to genuine refugees—a policy the *gentleman's* party would do well to emulate, instead of its pattern of *Poujadiste* prejudice and grubby gutter racism. The world is changing. The world is on the move. The world is coming here. Its arrival is culturally desirable and economically essential. No one is listening to *your* racist litany!"

A laughing cheer went up from all sides, especially from his own backbenches. The NU man stood to respond but time was up, and the PM could not be late for the British-Nauru Chamber of Commerce. He bowed to the Speaker and exited the chamber in an aura of aides and drab power. The NU MP looked down at his shiny suit as the chamber began to empty. He often felt he wasn't up to meeting the expectations of Milltown West—let alone the country and civilization he had vaguely thought he could save almost singlehandedly, simply by virtue of being a voice in this hallowed place, which even now had resonance. But he had failed, and he knew that soon he would be expelled. Had it even been worth trying? He stood up slowly and straightened his polyester tie unnecessarily, then trailed sadly after all the others out of the emptying chamber.

Technically, the PM had prevailed. All his frontbenchers agreed on that in loyal texts. But the general conclusion was that McKerras had had the best of it—not because of his performance but because so many WP backbenchers had gone to the press afterwards to express their disagreement with their own government. Besides, it was *obvious* to everyone who mattered that Ibraham must and would stay.

It troubled John to assail the administration whose accession he had so eagerly welcomed, but he felt constrained to conclude that the PM's performance had been motivated by "a shabby calculus of electoral fright versus moral right." The *Register*, normally solidly WP, commented in its inimitably hearty way: "Beg pardon, Sir, but you're wrong on this one. Let the lad stay! He's been through hell and back!"

Downing Street had been receiving protests from lobby groups ever since the tragedy. This was ratcheted up until the Number 10 website crashed under weight of demand. The popular show *Relevant Radio with Roger Roberts* was emblematic of the public mood; amongst its highlights was a harrowing phone call from an anonymous illegal Ghanaian girl from "somewhere in the Midlands": "We are all so very afraid. If we get sent back, we will surely die—like my sister died and my mother, too. When the soldiers came…when the soldiers came… they took all our stuff…Give me back my gold, I said…and then…."

Roger Roberts replied in the nearest he could get to a tender voice: "Take your time, my dear, take your time. We realise how hard this must be for you. Bless! We'll go to a song now and come back to you. Now, folks, while our friend has a little respite, here's another "Delightful Ditty," this one chosen by Barbara from East Wickie, who wins our fantastic makeover prize from Preen Cosmetics—and she's on the line now. Are you there, Babs?"

"Hi there, Rog. That *poooor* lady! I hope she knows that we're all thinking of her, and the Iraquian gentleman. That's why I've chosen this song today. I wish we knew who she was, because she could have the makeover instead of me. She probably needs it more."

"Bless you, Babs—and what is the song you've chosen for us today?"

"It's Nigel Phibbs, singing 'Why is the World so Sad, I'd Like to Know?'"

"A wonderful choice, babe—couldn't be better. This one goes out to all the victims of war and violence. And coming up after, our special guest is Mecca Morrow from the civil-rights organization The Nation of Islam."

With thousands of others, he joined in with the lush orchestral sound and famous opening lines:

> *Why is the world so sad, I'd like to know.*
>
> *There's no reason why it should be so,*
>
> *Why can't we hope and not despair?*
>
> *Why can't we share a globe that's fair?*
>
> *God must know that we've sunk low.*
>
> *Build Paradise below,*
>
> *Build Paradise below.*

Hatty was listening, as she always did while ironing, with a set expression. An academic pointed out that racism wasn't simply injustice; the absence of minorities from the countryside amounted to "ethnic cleasning by omission." She advocated building "destination mosques," where there were presently no or too few members of the Muslim faith-choice group, to give the area a more welcoming feel and acclimatize the locals to living in a multicultural society. And maybe some place names could be changed too—all those church and saint suffixes were not very inclusive, were they? She had even heard of an Eastshire pub called the Saracen's Head; what kind of signal did this send? Sorry if this is too controversial, Roger, but it is up to we academics to speak as we find, whatever the consequences.

Roger asked, "What do *you* think out there in Listener-Land? Is this a much-needed contribution to a sensitive debate—or is it political correctness gone mad? Tell us after this song—from *The Poor Little Panda*, now back in the West End. Enjoy! Hatty didn't wait to hear "Bamboo-zled by Your Love," but clicked the off-switch and continued ironing.

There was the sound of a car, and Hatty went to the window and looked out through the warm drizzle. Clarrie's Fiat was winding up the steep drive past the poplars. When she came in, she was quiet and serious. She had been quiet and serious a lot lately.

"Hi, dear. Get everything?"

"Hmm? Oh yes. Everything."

"What's wrong? What is it, dear?" Hatty sat beside her daughter and patted her hand. "What is it, hon?"

"I met Annie Pridlow—and she just walked past me! I know it's because of what's going on with Dad. Elaine told me afterwards that Annie had been going on about it to *everyone*—how dreadful it was that anyone could think like Dad, wondering why no-one had complained about it before, and saying maybe *I* was like that, too!"

"Oh no, Clarrie—how *awful*! But she's your *friend*! Perhaps if you just talked to her, and explained…"

"Oh, mum! It's sweet of you, but you *know* that won't do any good. Besides, it's not just her. There was a lot of other stuff last week I didn't tell you about. Loads of people have been giving me funny looks—I mean it's *obvious*."

"Well, dear, all I can say is that Annie Pridlow can't be much of a friend if she goes on like that. I mean she never even asked for your side of the story! It's at times like this you find out who your real friends are. Elaine and Jemima have been fine, haven't they?"

Clarrie nodded, but she wasn't comforted. A girl who had always striven to be kind and considerate, she couldn't bear that anyone might think such terrible things of her. Clarrie loved her father dearly, but even more than she loved him, she hated being in a moral minority.

Dan always loved this kind of day—warm, light, reminiscent drizzle, and the sun slanting through, everything warm, bright and newly minted every minute. The farm looked lovely in this mellow, *old* light. He hummed as he stomped up the drive, his troubles almost erased by the sedge warblers' fidgety whistling, the peppery smell of damp grass, specks of rain on the sundial, sunlight bouncing back from rippling windows, a neat moorhen flicking along the dyke, Red Admirals on the buddleia. He had almost forgotten the awfulness.

But he was greeted by Hatty, who told him what had happened—and his stomach turned over in pity. He went and knocked on the door of Clarrie's room. Quiet music was being played inside. "Come in!"

There she was, 22, but lurking within was the so-loved little girl of 3. She sat at her desk, hurriedly closing a notebook as he entered. Funny girl. She had always had her secrets, but only for a while. Eventually, she would always look at him with her big green eyes and tell him everything. They had had a quiet conspiracy against Hatty—at least until Clarrie had reached 12 or so, after which she spent more time talking to her mother than to him. They were busy with woman things that he could not participate in; it was a part of growing up he had never resented. And there were still times when she would laugh with him against Hatty, or peck him on the cheek, or stand with her arm around his neck, and he would be transported back to when he had held her by the wrists and swung her round and round in circles out in the garden, while she screamed with the careless joy of being held by strong arms. Now she looked drawn and edgy. He had never seen her like this, and pity piled up inside him. How *dare* anyone make his little girl feel like this?

"I heard about today. I'm so sorry!"

"It's not your fault, Dad."

"But it is—of course it is. I just wish…"

"Please, Dad! It's OK! Really it is! It's just one stupid person."

"I don't know what to say, Clarrie—I really don't. Obviously, I shouldn't have said what I did, but how was I to know what would happen?"

"Of course you couldn't know, Dad. It's not your fault. It's just one of those things—no-one's fault. I'll deal with it—it's no biggie."

"No what?"

"Biggie."

"Oh. But there must be something I can do? Should I talk to Pete Pridlow?"

"No—please don't. You might make it worse—I hope you don't mind my saying that. I'll deal with it. It's sweet of you, though."

He persisted for a little longer, but she was obdurate, and now clearly wanted to be left alone. So after a while he exited uncomforted. She had already turned back to her notebook before he had softly shut the door.

Neither he nor Hatty ever saw what she was writing, but it was published as an open letter in the student-union newsletter two weeks later.

> My father is Dan Gowt, who has been in the media over the last few months. You will all have seen the hurtful headlines. I am writing this partly because people have been so horrible to him, but also because some people have been saying that I share his views—which I do not. It has been suggested to me that I should make that clear. I am happy to do so, because I value my friendships with many people of many different cultures, different abilities, and faith- and lifestyle-choices.
>
> My father's views are unacceptable, but they are held by many of his generation. They are a reflection of wider society, which has promoted such views for decades. I am sure I am not the only student whose parents hold unacceptable views. That does not excuse those views, but I hope it will put my father's comments into context. My father is not a bad man—just a mistaken one, but it is a mistake he shares with millions of others. We need to combine our loyalty to our parents with our duty to the future. It is up to our generation to reject the offensive and just plain wrong opinions of past times, and to educate, educate, educate to build a better world. Thank you for reading this.

The apologium drew a measured response from the editor (who had long concealed a crush on Clarrie):

Clarrie's letter is a brave response to a stressful situation. Very few people are entirely free of racism, and we can't help our family backgrounds. Clarrie's commitment to battle intolerance now and in the future is brilliant. We would like to get the ball rolling on this one by repeating our commitment to equality and creating a safe learning environment for ALL students. We also call on the university to invest in deeper diversity training facilitated by expert trainers, administered by an independent external agency and a rigorous complaints procedure to highlight presently unnoticed instances of racial discrimination—instances in which the victims may not even realise they are victims. This issue is more important even than the World Cup—and that means IMPORTANT. Listen up, and watch this space!

Clarrie had been given a second chance—but she had a feeling she wouldn't get a third.

Chapter 19

AWAKENINGS

London
Thursday, 29th August—Tuesday, 2nd September

The pathologist's report shuffled unobtrusively but insistently into history. The idea of local involvement in the deaths was expeditiously expunged from all except a few independent minds—like Scum, who in his final interview the following year would return to the theme, telling his sycophantic interlocutor that it had all been, like, a cover-up, the Secret State looking after its own, it's only a few mavericks who know the score, get wot I'm sayin'? When the singer was found dead a few days later in a pool of excrement and blood after a rash experiment with a heroin/emetic cocktail, some whispered that maybe he had known too much.

Quizzed on *Curt's Comfy Couch*, Dr. John St. Germains laughed at Curt's suggestion that his *Bugle* column had blamed rural racists. But his black eyes did not leave his much-modified host for a second, a look of the intensest dislike magnified through *Mitteleuropäisch* bottle-lenses: "Of course I did not, Curt, and it is, frankly, a little disingenuous of you to say that. If I may say so, I am a Temple Prize Winner and the author of three best-selling books on positive psychology. If you had read the article properly—but that might have been a bit of a strain for you—you would have seen that it was all theoretical, hypothetical—a what-if scenario—but one based on the latest scientific findings. You're trying to distort my findings and ideas. I know that's the kind of, frankly, rubbish you have on this show, but *I*—Curt—*I* am a scientist!" The audience "*Ooooooohed*," and Curt winked into the cameras.

Something else that had helped derail the theory was the news that three Dutch nationals had been arrested on suspicion of involvement in people-smuggling.

The taciturn deckhand Jan had belied his reputation. He had been expounding in a bar down by the docks—at first to the *Kapitein*. Then when the Old Man had gone, himself half-seas over, smacking Jan on the shoulder in comradeship as he left, there was a girl buying cigarettes—axe-faced, lips like a wound, but what a little body! So Jan had told her how lovely she was, asked what she was doing, told how he had some money to spend having successfully completed a little bit of business, would-you-like-a-drink-no-strings-attached-I-promise, and God you're gorgeous, I work on a trawler you know but we don't catch fish these days, we're too clever for that, there are much more interesting things in the sea these days, laugh, leer, hand on her knee and she didn't mind, on her thigh and she still didn't mind. Eventually she took him out of the warm and whirling bar and past lines of streetlights and shops full of things that wobbled and toppled around them as they went all the way back to her takeaway-pack strewn apartment, and they had kissed as soon as they got inside the door, and he had at last got his hands up her skirt, and afterwards, he had wanted to talk because he really felt a bit bad about what had happened. "I'll tell you," he said, "but this mustn't go any further. Do you swear?" Half-bored, half-amused, she had agreed. She lay naked beside him, smoking, but after a while she forgot to smoke, while her eyes widened with horror.

"And-then-there-were-all-these-shouts-and-people-thrashing-and-those-Albanians-those-bastard-Albanians-do-you-know-what-they-did-then-shot-the-poor-fuckers-I-mean-it-*SHOT*-them!-bang-bang! -poor-sods-didn't-stand-a-chance-and-then-they-told-us-they-would-do-the-same-to-us-if-we-ever-blabbed-they-paid-us-well-but-I-can-still-see-and-hear-the-people-in-the-water-poor-fuckers-I-can't-sleep-awful-pathetic-isn't-it…"

When he finally subsided into stertorousness, she got dressed quickly and crept out to phone the police.

The *East Eastshire Echo* had reported that the government was considering setting up a new Asylum Adjudication Centre in Thorpe Gilbert, on the site of the old hospice. It was a social necessity as well as a boon—and it would create new jobs. Yet complaints nonetheless streamed in. None of the complainants were racists *but*…there was insufficient infrastructure, it was too expensive, the hospice was needed even more, there would be traffic problems, it would disturb wildlife, and the refugees would be much happier amongst their own people. The ambitious young editor scowled; how could he achieve balance with correspondence like this?

His inspired answer was *Ethnic Eastshire*, a colour supplement launched at a stellar happening in Thorpe in the presence of national and local politicians, ethnic representatives, civic dignitaries, churchmen, and the nearest the county came to culturati.

Wanda Lo was there, with the weakly grinning "Mr. Lo"—and Dick Barge from *D. I. Davies*—Phebe Moody, best-selling and bosomy author of *Where Two Hearts Dare* and 36 similar books—Lord Chimbay, "Britain's leading Jamaican theorist of equality"—and Isaac

Ringrose, who had been a session drummer with all the big Sixties bands. They all dined from the Fusion Menu and sat through the Multi-FUN-Tural entertainment by local schoolchildren. There were ecumenical blessings by the Bishop of Eastshire and other faith-choice group leaders, including a moving message from the Chief Scientologist. There were speeches in Arabic, Punjabi, Urdu, Togolese, and Mandarin, a video message from none other than Wilberforce Smith, fireworks, a magician, free music by Thorpe's upcoming musicians (Isaac Ringrose joined them on stage for a condescending crescendo).

It was a memorable night, and the editor felt justly proud of his supplicatory supplement which had even managed to earn the paper some revenue from go-ahead local businesses who wore their huge hearts on shop-coat sleeves—"Smith's Tastee Grub—We welcome *ALL* to purchase our high quality meats and quality comestibles. This week's specials—minted lamb ONLY £5 per kg.— burgers ONLY £1!"

Dan sensed that strangers were staring at him. Even neighbours and his oldest friends gave Dan knowing smiles or ostentatiously talked about anything except politics. One or two weren't speaking to him at all, and an advantageous haylage deal had fallen through, with no reason given. His old enemy Charlie Davies gave him a Hitler salute when they met, before laughing nastily. Once when he was in Williamstow, a car passed by at high speed, and the unknown driver honked the horn madly while the passenger shouted "Racist!" and made two finger signs. So he took a sheaf of newspapers to Tom Spaggart in Thorpe, the family solicitor for decades—although it was a highfalutin term for a man whose services had not been required for at least 10 years.

The first floor office above the newsagent was crammed and stifling. Framed photographs and certificates vied for space on needing-a-paint walls with a baize notice-board and a calendar of local views—empty churches, rape fields in full bloom, snow-covered lanes, boxing hares, deserted beach. Cars were passing up and down the High Street, sending glittering lozenges dashing across the ceiling. Dan was surprised to notice that the Georgian windows above the prosperous-looking clothes shop opposite were rotting and covered over with cardboard, and the iron downpipes appeared to be leaking, to judge from the green smear that spread out fanlike below the junction. Blowsy starlings surveyed the scene from a guano-crusted windowsill.

Spaggart was tiny and slender, with the neatest hands and nails of any man Dan had known. He had come here in 1965 to work as a clerk and taken over the old local firm after the principals succumbed to age and Scotch. He always wore the same three-piece, made for him in Jermyn Street to commemorate passing his final exams in 1964, and which still fitted without a wrinkle. This made him dapper by local standards, although the too-many buttoned, too tight 1960s appearance of the suit might have earned him curious looks in London. Dan had met him once by chance on a day off, walking along a high road in the hills, miles from anywhere, and had been astonished to see him wearing the same suit. He was a man who appeared to make no concessions to environment or time. He seemed faintly embarrassed to see Dan, but shook his hand and asked how he was.

"Oh yes, I'm fine—thanks, Tom. That is I'm well, but I do have a bit of a problem I hope you can help me with. Have you seen these?" Dan fanned out the offending newspapers, and the other man's eyes dilated as he leafed through them, his face becoming ruddier. He inhaled and made tiny clicking noises of disapproval. "Well, some of them—some of them. Goodness, I didn't realise there was so much of it. It's all fairly horrible, isn't it? Even the *Three Es* is at it." He held up *Ethnic Eastshire* in index finger and thumb, before dropping it fastidiously back onto the desk.

"You can probably imagine what I want to know, Tom. What can be done about this legally? Can I take these people to court?"

"Now you're asking, Dan—and you're asking the wrong man. I'm just a country solicitor, and I've never gone in for libel, or politics for that matter. All I know about libel law is that it is a *very* tricky business—a double-edged sword, in fact. You need to go and see a specialist. Scales & Scales might be a good first port of call. I know Arnold Scales well; I'll give him a ring for you." He picked up the phone, while Dan sweated and watched the lozenges of the cars chase across the ceiling.

"Arnold? Hello, it's Tom Spaggart. How are things? Is Marjorie well? Ha, ha, ha! Look, I've got a potential client for you. It's someone from Crisby, a farmer whose family I've done business with for years. I think you'll be surprised to hear who…OK, I'll put you out of your misery. It's Dan Gowt…Yes!"

He smiled across at Dan and raised his eyebrows.

"Actually, I'm slightly surprised you've heard of him. I didn't know you followed politics…Eh? Ha, hmm, I suppose so. The thing is that the papers have been saying some fairly foul things about him, and he wants to know where he stands. It's much more your sort of thing than mine! Can I send him along to go and see you? He's here with me now…Sorry?"

He began to find the guttering on the building opposite interesting. Dan tried to read his profile. It was unusual for him to pay so much attention to someone's face, and he realised for the first time that Tom Spaggart was extrremely old. Just beneath that spruce, even dandyish, demeanour was a frail, fluttering, near-future phantasm, whose shrink-wrapped skin was slowly tightening over his whole body. Dan could see his veined hand trembling slightly on the phone handset, as if he might lose his grip at almost any moment. In that never-disturbed office with its shelves and cabinets overflowing with dry leaf-litter, Spaggart was like some outsize imago. His famous suit was almost like an exoskeleton. It was a faintly horrifying but also ludicrous notion, and Dan was surprised by his own imaginative faculties. Thinking of the lawyer this way made Dan feel guilty.

The lawyer was still talking. "Yes, yes, I can see that…I understand. If I'm honest, I can't say I blame you. Nasty business—very nasty…What's that?…You think so?…I'm surprised…Yes…yes… Absolutely…I'm sure he'll understand…No, no, of course, I won't. OK, well thanks anyway, and please say hello to Marjorie. I'll see you soon. Lunch, maybe? OK, thanks."

He turned back into the room, sat thinking for a few seconds and was about to speak when Dan interjected. "I got the gist of that. He's not interested."

"Well, he is *interested*, even sympathetic, but he feels there is probably no case to answer. He says the coverage he has seen has stopped just on this side of legality. It's innuendo, rather than accusations. Those boys always cover their backs—that was the way he put it. He also has quite a small practice, and he's busy—very busy, in fact…"

"And?"

"All right. There *is* an 'And.' I'll tell you as we have known each other for so long, but only on the *strict* understanding that you will not repeat this to anyone…OK? Good. He was straightforward in saying that even if he wasn't so busy, and even if there was a good case, he would prefer not to take you on. First, he hasn't got experience in this kind of political case, which is much more complicated than other types of libel. Secondly, he felt that the…um…fallout of having you as a client might be…um…professionally disadvantageous. Remember, I'm just saying what *he* said!"

Dan sat silent, looking less at Tom Spaggart than through him. He had rather expected there would be some pretext for doing nothing. The papers would surely not have left themselves open to legal action. The law's apparent impotence or unwillingness to help fitted in with much else he had learned recently.

He wasn't certain he would have gone through with legal action anyway. He had always had the countryman's slightly sour suspicion of the legal system, the taxman, the police, and doctors. Hatty had never understood his sour suspicion of all authority figures—but all he had seen and been through lately had just underlined his original conviction. The world didn't belong to people like him, but people like *them*—people who relished the hypocritical and Byzantine game for its own sake. Even people like Tom Spaggart, so much cleverer than he, were just interpreters and enforcers.

"I'm very sorry, Dan—very sorry, indeed. I'll have another go at him, or maybe I can think of any one else. You could find someone in London, but even there I think you might find it quite difficult. This whole subject is...well, *difficult!*"

Dan shook the neat, dry hand and left. He realized Spaggart was simultaneously ashamed of not helping and embarrassed by his presence. He didn't blame him really; he sensed correctly that the country lawyer was like him uncertain and out of place in this world. As he walked along Southgate, the hateful newspapers heavy under his arm, he became aware that a group of smoking teenagers on the corner were watching greedily. "It's him, OK!" he heard one whisper. Dan nodded stiffly, they nodded back, and he was past. A girl with a lopsided, bleached hairstyle giggled, and they huddled together, a conspiracy of youth against crabbed age.

John was similarly pondering on life's injustices. The first and worst was that Janet had decided two nights previously to make a scene in front of *everyone*. The editorial department was always invited *en bloc* to their boss's book launches, but it was rare for so many to turn up. With all the reshuffles going on, obviously people had thought they ought to be seen. Just his luck that so many had been there just when Janet decided *this* was the perfect time to bring up Natasha. What *right* had Janet to check *his* phone anyway? He never checked hers—although she never rang anyone interesting, anyway. John could still see the faces of his colleagues—*all* of them—smirking, obviously looking forward to telling everyone else who had missed this delicious scene. Some *friends*!

He and Janet were in the flat now, on an evening—but in different rooms with a banged shut door between them. They hadn't spoken to each other since the other evening, just done whatever they needed to do in the kitchen ostentatiously looking everywhere but at each other, retreating back to their own rooms as quickly as they could. Janet had made up a bed in the spare room. It was a rare manifestation of independence. He had thought she would have come snivelling back before now, as she had done before—and he was annoyed that he had miscalculated.

He reclined on the sofa but not at ease, drinking a beer without enjoyment to the accompaniment of jazz-funk-samba fusion at top volume. It must be annoying her (he didn't think much of it himself), and that was something. It was at times like this that he wished he'd never allowed her into his personal space. But at the time she'd been sweet and loving, and he couldn't blame her for not wanting to stay in Hackney. He, too, had disliked the walk up from the station to her old flat past the hanging youths—especially where the lights had been smashed and the place stank of piss, and every shadow could hold danger. It was a sad comment on society that the people of Hackney had had so few life-opportunities and did not have full access to public services. It was no wonder they were frustrated and forced to turn to crime.

He had thought it would be nice to have a pretty, undemanding girl like Janet to come home to—someone who wouldn't tire him intellectually, to whom he could read out his articles, who might cook and otherwise help about the place. Janet had seemed sweet, and he thought he could tolerate her presence for long periods. It was only after Janet had lived with him a few months that he had begun to notice her irritating habits. She drank too much, for one thing, but when he warned her she wouldn't listen. She had even started rows when he had poured away her bottles of spirits. Then there was occasional shocking Philistinism. On a couple of occasions, she had actually been insensitive enough to— think of it!—*fall asleep* when he was reading something out loud.

And yet—despite putting up with all of this, he had got no thanks from her. Instead, it was a suburbanality of sour suspicions and slammed doors, and TVs turned up loud to distract him. And he was alone, and bored. Alone—someone like him, so much to offer, alone on a night like this in London, with a healthy bank balance. He vaguely considered calling a few people to see if they wanted to do something, but he refrained—because he didn't want to seem needy, but also because he couldn't think of whom he should call. Ironic, really, to think that he who had devoted his life to improving society should be so solitary. But maybe it was always the same for such as he. He didn't have that much in common with other people, he had realized long ago. What was that Emerson quote he had always liked? Ah yes, "The Hero is not fed on sweets—Daily his own heart he eats." The thought soothed him.

Whenever he turned off his music to listen, he could hear that Janet was watching *Hospital of Hope*—or more probably she was pretending to watch the program while she blubbed. Yesterday, before she got back, he had found the waste-basket in there filled with damp tissues. She was pathetic. He didn't know what he'd ever seen in her. She'd always been sour, suspicious, uptight, bourgeois. They'd always had an understanding, he had thought. He wouldn't have minded if she had wanted....well, maybe he would, but the point was that she was cramping his considerable style. He pulled the tab on a third Singaporean beer (he despised all other brands on principle) and looked gloomily at the opposite roofline. This Janet thing was very, very annoying, but there had been an even worse setback.

It had been announced that very afternoon that the Dep. Edship John had wanted, and frankly expected, had gone to—of all possible choices—*Gavin Montgomery*! Gavin had been at the paper for only a few years, he didn't write as often as John, nor as well. He had always been more of an editor than a real creative—a generalist, good at spelling but few ideas and not much initiative. No threat. No thrust. No mojo. It had at first surprised John that such an insipid excuse for a man would stab him in the back—but then that was the way with sly people.

John had had big ideas, and he felt he was owed recognition for everything he brought to the table. Over months, he had jumped through all the requisite hoops—he had thought he was doing a good job with all the people who mattered. He had clearly miscalculated. Maybe—that must be it!—once again it was his outspoken nature that had sabotaged his chances. He was not the emollient politician type.

He had wasted valuable creative time working out how he could spend the extra 20K. He deserved a time-out for serious de-stressing, maybe in some tranquil Keralan ashram. He loved such places, seeing traditional communities in all their colour, with their strong traditions, their connection with their places, their harmony with nature. They were unspoilt people in unsullied places. And it would have given free rein to his spiritual side—realise the work-life balance—detox from the struggle. And he could have bought Janet out. But instead it was *Gavin* who would be thinking now of cars, chicks, and holidays. Lucky bastard—and he wouldn't even appreciate it. Gavin had always been essentially vulgar.

John had tried to be congratulatory, but finding the words proved unexpectedly difficult. In the end, he made a strangulated semi-joke of it—"I suppose you'll expect to be called Mr. Montgomery now?" Gavin had retorted with a similar half-joke in a dire approximation of Brooklyn, "Ya better watch whaddya say, Leyden, or you're outta here!" And they had grimaced, and John had returned to his old desk, which now looked even less satisfactory, while Gavin took possession of his glass-walled office, with that lovely big chair. He even had a *secretary*—an ugly one, but a secretary. John walked past a few times and could see Gavin on the phone or tapping on his new computer. What was he cooking up? Part of his new responsibilities were to "rationalize" the department...

Maybe Janet's little scene had operated against him. It certainly could not have helped his cause, to have him so obviously embroiled in potentially distracting affairs, and apparently in the habit of sending explicit text messages to indiscreet females. There was a strain of moral censoriousness at the *Examiner*—a trace element of the paper's Northern, non-conformist roots—and just possibly Nige and others had been influenced subconsciously by this when deciding to offer the job to Gavin. (Mr. Fuckin' Perfect, of course, was married with kids.)

As if all this wasn't enough for anyone to be faced with, Albert Norman had also had a go at him again. John was generally half-pleased when Norman criticized him. It was the kind of feedback he (almost) liked to get from someone like Norman. For a notorious fascist to accuse you of dangerous radicalism was a great accolade.

If a man is known for his enemies, Norman was the best of possible foes—morally unspeakable, yet clever enough to be a really considerable foe. When Albert Norman went after someone, it proved the Establishment was *really* worried. But this Broadside had needled him.

> John Leyden's *Examiner* columns on the Crisby tragedy have evinced their usual blend of eccentricity and irresponsibility, to which he has now added injustice. His unprovoked attacks on an

Eastshire farmer, and by extension all the people of that ancient county, for their conservative values have plumbed new depths.

With its lazy lumping together of thousands of individuals as hicks and psychos, its wild assumptions, and its intemperate tone, it resembles a dreadful inversion of *Der Stürmer* or Lenin's diatribes against the *kulaks*. Leyden is guilty of the grossest character assassination, on the basis of a couple of slightly unfortunate remarks made by a startled and inarticulate farmer when only half-awake.

Technically, Leyden hasn't libelled Mr. Gowt—but the inferences are clear. This is extraordinarily ungenerous for a journalist whose credo is allegedly based on fairness and decency—and terribly irresponsible because of where it could lead. Although we now know for certain that no local persons were involved in the murders at Crisby, there are a lot of crazy people out there, and this is a supercharged time. Remember Theo van Gogh and Pim Fortuyn. It is only too plausible that someone might conclude that Mr Gowt is a legitimate target for 'direct action'. Urgent message to John Leyden—for once in your smirking excuse for an existence *think* about the possible effects of what you write.

John had fizzed with indignation. He had never before been likened to the Nazis. Mummy was the only person who had ever dared to say such things, and even she'd desisted once her five year old son had developed his quick tongue and hard little fists. And he *didn't* smirk—everyone had always agreed he had a lovely smile. He examined it once more in the Venetian mirror above the fireplace. The sight soothed him, and he began to compose a devastating riposte.

It is arguably a compliment that I have been singled out, yet again, for attack by Albert Norman, the Establishment's most important mouthpiece of ultra-conservatism. My actions have spawned a neo-nativist counter-reaction. I am used to being called radical and revolutionary by such people, and from them it is a compliment. Radicalism in the defence of what is right is rightness. I am accused of traducing country people—and of having been nasty towards the literally boorish farmer who made those by-now infamous remarks.

Albert Norman has the temerity to say that my comments were like Julius Streicher's despicable *Der Stürmer*—pretty rich from a newspaper which backed Franco and Mussolini. As for my having traduced country people, I refer Mr Norman to the *Oxford Omen* student paper of 14th June 1994 (page 23), in which I wrote at length about the origins of rural racism, in which I make it clear it is not the fault of individuals, but the system of class deference which has persisted longer in the shires than in conurbations. I also wrote about this subject in my PhD thesis, *Imagining Community Harmony—A Nationwide Search for Post-National Allegiances*, especially pages 15 to 21. I have also covered this subject in my *New Horizon* articles of 13 September 2000, 15 October 2001, 1 May 2004, and 1 June 2004; my *Forwards to the Future* op-eds of February 2006 and May 2007; *Radical Prospectus*, Vol 21, issue 4; *The Gracchite*, Vol 23, issue 1, and *Views & Visions*, issues 45, 46, and 67.

All of these articles are easily available on my website—leydenlore.net—and can even be ordered as a collected download with a foreword by Professor Sam Sunday of Capital University. They have also been translated into 14 languages, so Norman could have read them in any language he chose, as English, apparently, does not come naturally to him." (He added the ISBN.)

In the light of this evidence, the allegation that I am ignorant of the plight of country people or uncaring is frankly laughable. As for being uncharitable about Dan Gowt—*he* wasn't very charitable about the dead innocents, and that his cause is being taken up so aggressively by the Establishment's most loyal attack-dog shows I'm onto something. Finally, although I hate to blow my own trumpet, I believe my record on charitable activities speaks for itself. This year alone, I have written no fewer than five articles on global poverty. Albert Norman is mistaken if he thinks that his gutter puerile journalism will deter me from saying and doing what is right. This is an act of moral piracy by a last-ditch obscurantist, a last desperate salvo against decency. The best thing to do is ignore him.

But he was aware he hadn't taken his own advice.

Chapter 20

THE COLLABORATIVE SPIRIT

City of London
Thursday, 29th August—Thursday, 25th September

The thing was *very* well done. There was a marvellous cowardly subtlety about it. Albert felt great admiration for the way the lad Dougie had handled everything. It was poisonous, but it was perfect.

"Broadside" was in its usual place, with the usual picture of a louche-looking (indeed, he *had* been louche) 21-year-old Albert, gazing knowingly at a world already gone awry so far as he was concerned. And his copy was its usual acerbic, uncompromising self, always with the sense of a huge secret joke behind it. But in this issue the old dreadnought had been outgunned and outsailed. "Tsushima!" Albert remarked out loud; Sally thought he had sneezed and replied absently "Bless you!"

Immediately above, there was always a slot called "Guest View—A VIP speaks out on the subject of the day," which over the years had been given over to peers, MPs, retired generals, and pop stars who had become progressively misanthropic as their music became progressively outmoded. This time, the VIP was Dylan Ekinutu-Jones, making his debut in the *Sentinel*, a paper he had often singled out for his severest criticism.

He had marshalled powerful forces along the columnar border with Broadside, aiming the tactical nuclear devices of racism against Albert's pop-guns of patriotism, and well-drilled divisions of offence against a few ragged regiments of commonsense. It was an unequal contest—the surging tides of history rushing into the stagnant pools of tradition to refresh and eventually replace them. Albert skim-read the article, which reminded him of many others—but he read out one phrase to the back of Sally's head.

"*Etc., etc.,* blah, blah...aha!...'certain media vested interests, which specialize in racist rhetoric and put circulation considerations over community relations...' What do you think of that, Sally? A palpable hit by our young Anglo-Nigerian friend!"

"Hmmm? Oh, yes, yes, Albert. Ha ha!"

Down the left-hand side of the spread was the usual editorial slot, the rarely-read "Sentry Box." Affectionately called "Mental Pox" by staff, it was usually penned by a bespectacled and bored Divinity graduate called Tristram, who had been expelled from the seminary for lewd behaviour with a 15-year-old (a girl, to the pleased surprise of his mother). His editorials were usually suitably reflexive and irrelevant, and often took their cue from Albert's adjoining copy. Albert had accordingly always got on well with him. But this time, the editorial was either written by Dougie or else under his close supervision. It called for "the gradual deletion of the discredited nostrums of race and nation. It is time to move on, to reject the casual racism as exemplified not just by National Union, but by the complacent, self-styled 'oracles' of the popular press. Times have changed; it is time to grow tolerance."

The "popular press," Albert smiled—a lordly touch. They had printed carefully-selected readers' letters—one supporting, the rest attacking or ignoring him. Normally they just printed the ones nearest the top of the pile, unless they were slightly too crazy.

But perhaps the nicest touch of all was the full page colour ad from Fonesco. It was on the facing page (it would osculate his column when the paper was closed)—a handsome black man and a pretty blonde staring intently into each other's faces in a flower-strewn field, with the caption, "Isn't it time you got together with someone spesh? Chattastic!" The sentiments were at perfect pitch, and the prices were competitive. It was time to change handsets (and history). Readers were already reaching for their credit cards; and Dylan was reading over his piece, his mouth proudly forming the words "circulation considerations over community relations," as he checked to make sure the racist scum hadn't cut anything.

There had been a sea-change at the *Sentinel* but a subtle one, and so far only the very clever or mostly mad had noticed. More noticed the next time Broadside was published. After years of prominence on the Views page, all of a sudden it was moved to a new slot—much less obvious, with a smaller headline, on a left hand page, and much further back in the paper—almost adjoining the Sports section—this too done as an insult to Albert, who detested all sports on principle.

Once, Albert would have been consulted about such changes; this time, he was as surprised as any of his readers. He rang Jack Cummins in Layouts, only to be told by a bored girl that Jack had retired last year. The voice did not know why there had been a change, just that she had had been instructed to redesign the pages a few days ago. Albert thanked her and hung up, feeling even more isloated than usual.

The same day, there came a memo saying that there needed to be maintenance on the air-conditioning, and they would need to move "temporarily" to a much smaller and less-convenient office. Albert was outraged. Apart from the fact that he hated any change, even for the better, they didn't even use air conditioning in his office, because he distrusted it. He used to joke that he was self-basting, preferring to stew in his own juices—and stew he sometimes did. There were times in the hottest weather when Albert became an overpowering olfactory presence across most of the floor—his bouquet even insinuating as far as the lift, making those bound for other floors grateful that they *were* bound for other floors.

He sensed these were unnecessary works, part of a plan to edge him out. He decided he would not take the hint and pretended to take the memo at face value. But still it was a wrench to take himself out of "his" space after all those years, knowing full well that he would never enter this office again, or look out of those dirty windows again at that dingy but curiously delightful view of the city and the world.

Feeling almost as if he was peeling off his own carapace, Albert and Sally started to throw things away, starting with the oldest unanswered correspondence, and ending significantly with the once-treasured Special Vintage File letters. He looked ruefully at the brimming recycling bins that had been wheeled into his office by a gum-chewing and surly youth.

Gone—the underlined and copiously annotated warnings of foreign infiltrations and subtle machinations; gone—the privately printed pamphlets; gone—the execrable cartoons and elaborate diagrams; gone—the wild allegations and scatological descriptions. The whole unique drawer-full of mostly nonsense, representing countless hours of strangers' suspicious existences, was dumped ingloriously in grey-plastic receptacles. Albert and Sally looked at it sadly; even the Obits man was sorry to see it go; he had been in on some of those long jokes. He was moving to a new permanent place down the corridor, so it was just Albert and Sally who would go leanly and meanly into the new office. They would be given new computers, chairs, and tables, but Albert regretted his comfortable, collapsing chair. It was all about as unsettling as anything could be; deliberately so, he was convinced. One of the very few physical connections was the salvaged clippings from the Wall of Sanctimony. They were one of the few proofs that there could be justice. "It is our sacred trust," he told Sally solemnly. "We owe it to our posterity that a few of our tribal icons are preserved from the creeping wave of barbarism."

They had laughed sadly as the paltry items were folded and packed into the inadequate number of crates. Albert labelled his chair and put it with the boxes to be moved, but it never made it—and a week later, he spotted it in a skip behind the building, the toppled throne of a banished potentate. He thought of the huge and hideous statue of Saddam toppled after the Americans had taken Baghdad, dragged down by ropes to the horizontal, but still attached to the plinth at the feet, the horrid brought low, the unspeakable become the scorn of the inconsiderable.

The new office was tiny, dark, looking onto a mouldy felt roof, and too far from the toilets, the lift, the canteen, the editorial offices, everyone—except the advertising sales office, from which there issued forth a constant hubbub of loud voices, phones ringing, and people in open-necked shirts or even T-shirts shouting "Half page from BigBank!" or "Yeees!"

Passing by the always open door, the salesmen and women could be seen lounging in their chairs with their feet up on the desks, periodically punching the air in greedy joy. Everyone in there, even the females (Albert didn't think of them as women) was "mate." They would hang around just outside Albert's office, talking loudly about targets, campaigns, budgets, and presentations. It was almost painful to Albert to hear public school accents using such terms—and he would rise heavily from his desk, lumber over to the door and slam it shut.

He would not have liked such talk from anyone, but from the products of England's best schools, it seemed ominous. These were people who had been exposed to what remained of the world's learning—and all so they could sell fools things no-one in their right mind would want. They were a new and pestiferous sub-species, and Albert moved unhappily amongst them, feeling both contempt and pity—emotions which he never realized were being reflected back at him, as these still healthy and hopeful men sniggered at Albert's three-piece suit, watch chain and centre-parted, grizzled grey hair. Hardly any even knew who he was—although the slot opposite his column was one of the most sought-after positions by advertisers. He was in internal exile—but then he had always been.

Albert did not respond to these provocations. In any case, there was nothing he could have done. Had he raised the subject with any of his "colleagues"—a ludicrous term for people he despised or ignored, and who despised him, if they couldn't quite ignore him—they would have said he was imagining it. But Sally at least commiserated—even as she was wondering which department she would be moved to once Albert had left. She liked him more and knew him better than anyone else in the building—he gave her a small but expensive and well-selected present every birthday—but she had to be practical.

Albert still slouched massively in his chair, talking and spilling coffee, reading his still plentiful mail, but he stopped answering mail almost completely, and forgot even to add new letters to his Special Vintage File—although the post of those days brought rare specimens, such as the man who informed Albert that he had clearly been targeted by a Judaeo-Masonic paedophile cult (adding, less than reassuringly, that he had been for many years a great admirer of Albert's work). Albert would never have overlooked a letter like that a few weeks previously; Sally sensed dimly that her larger than life co-worker of so many years was disengaging, slipping his cables one by one like a ship leaving its home port for the final time.

He continued going in two days a week, to chat to Sally and Polly, the cleaning lady from the East End who voted National Union. He used her as a kind of yardstick of public opinion, while she once told Sally she regarded him "a very odd gentleman, but a gentleman." To Albert, the three of them alone represented the old *Sentinel*, survivors of the days when Lord Thornley had run the paper as a personal principality and a platform for his idiosyncratic views. Albert just remembered the famous bust-up there had been between Lord Thornley and the then-editor—what was his name?—when the proprietor had wanted to include an editorial commending one L. Ron Hubbard. The editor had threatened to resign rather than run the piece, and eventually Lord Thornley had given in. Shortly afterwards, he had died, secure in the knowledge that his soul would spend eternity on a distant planet a little like Earth but purged of its grossness.

His son had sold the paper to a consortium, signalling the beginning of decades of constant change, and the gradual hollowing out and pastelizing of the defanged beast. Albert was the only person there now who had been there in Thornley's time (and he only just), but he pretended to himself that Sally and Polly had been there, too, and remembered; they were happy to indulge him when they bothered to listen.

So somehow from the inconvenient office, in between the shouting from the sales floor, in between strong black coffees and monologues, there continued to issue forth regular Broadsides—to the delight of readers and the chagrin of Dougie, who had hoped that he had done enough to provoke Albert into retiring. The column Albert wrote after the interview with Ibraham would years afterwards come to be regarded as a *samizdat* classic.

> Like everyone else in the country, I watched the famous TV interview with the 'Miracle Migrant', Ibraham Nassouf. Like seemingly everyone else in the country, I found his story

fascinating and felt a great deal of sympathy for his plight, and that of millions of other Iraqis for whom life is so bad that they will consider entrusting their lives to gangsters, crossing secretly into Europe in lorries and ships. But Ibraham doesn't add up.

Until he started to talk about his political activities, I was with him all the way. But when he began to talk about being picked up by the secret police, his whole manner changed. His voice became higher-pitched, he looked down at the table a lot, he fiddled nervously with a pen—and, over his shoulder, the face of the repulsive Jakob von Grönestein underwent a transformation. He was as surprised as everyone else in that room. Von Grönestein is a wide boy, a shyster, a huckster, a parasite, and a promoter of low-grade culture, but he isn't stupid. He would not get a client out there in front of the press pack without having wormed everything of value out of him first. He would not have overlooked that angle. And then in the lengthy *Globe* interview that appeared yesterday, the torture theme was curiously undeveloped. For all these reasons, I suspect young Ibraham made up that whole story about the secret police. Call it a hunch—call it narrow-minded prejudice (as I fear many will), but I for one think the 'Miracle Migrant' was having us on.

But looking into my infallible scrying-glass, I predict he will be believed, and his sufferings will be used to legitimize his continued (illegal) presence in England. And even if he isn't believed, he will still stay. His sister is already here. How long it will be before his other siblings are here, too, as part of some 'family reunification' scheme, is anyone's guess—but it won't be long. Ibraham isn't the only one who's been taken for a ride.

The *Sentinel*'s website crashed, and brought the newspaper back onto the early evening news. "HOW DARE YOU?!?!?!?" was the first message that popped into Albert's e-mail inbox, to his great delight, closely followed by hundreds more in a similar vein. He laughed out loud and rubbed his hands, then began to do a running tally of the F- and C-words. He was confident he could beat the total from last time. Sally was pleased to see him looking cheerful again, and smiled and shook her head at Polly.

Dougie was less delighted. He hadn't even had lunch; he had been too busy talking to directors, shareholders, and the editor of another paper, who had been considering running a lucrative joint promotion but who had suddenly cooled on the deal. All this was bad enough, but there had been an ominous new development.

A group called No Borders Now!—the exclamation mark was always present in their logo, like an outraged penis waved at the world—had called for a mass protest against media racism, starting with a picket of the *Sentinel* in one week's time. Large extracts of Albert's writings had been plastered all over their website with hyperlinks to sites about the Ku Klux Klan and World War II. Albert's allegation that Ibraham had been lying lit the touch-paper.

Their slogan was "Freedom from Oppression before Freedom of Expression," and they promised that hundreds of anti-fascists would congregate outside the *Sentinel*'s offices, with whistles and rattles and banners, to say "No to media racism, no to racist controls."

The police had warned Dougie that the protest might easily turn ugly. There had been rumours that National Union would hold a counter-protest, a rumour fed by a gasconade from James Fulford, in which he had said they would do "all in their power to protect the freedom of speech of that excellent journalist Albert Norman."

The idea of hundreds of militants of both sides colliding outside the office—and that NU would be on the same side of the barricades as the *Sentinel*—made Dougie blench. And what about the legal implications? Could the *Sentinel* be held responsible if there were a riot? He felt his head was going to burst, and the more he talked to the legal department, the directors and the police the more confused and afraid he became. Even the welcome news that NU hadn't planned anything after all did little to relieve his fears. There were still going to be all those awful people, shouting and screaming and maybe throwing things—and all because of some superannuated old faggot who should have had the decency to go years ago! Albert must surely see that it would be unreasonable to endanger the safety of *Sentinel* staff or passers-by—and perhaps a more moderate column tomorrow could avert the whole thing.

When the summons came, Albert cursed. He had just got himself a coffee and was looking forward to it as a counterbalance to last night's excesses. He had wanted to sit quietly that morning and turn out something only vaguely dyspeptic; now he had to go and see the ridiculous boy. He gulped down some of the coffee, scalding his tongue and spilling some onto his waistcoat, and tramped towards the lift. Within two minutes, he was sitting across from Dougie, who looked a little lost behind his expansive desk. Mickey Mouse in the guise of Mussolini, Albert thought, and smiled inwardly. Externally, he retained his expression of polite interest.

Dougie greeted him surprisingly affably and offered coffee—which Albert accepted. He always accepted things when they were free. Dougie then read out the news release from No Borders Now! When he had finished, he looked up.

"There's more, Albert. The police say a violent group calling itself Freedom from Fascism may infiltrate the protest. If they do, there could be serious trouble. The police will be there, but they can only spare a small number of officers, and there is always the possibility that it will all get out of hand. The police and I are all concerned about the safety of staff, local residents, and workers if this goes ahead. I don't think we have the right to jeopardize the safety of others."

"Well, Dougie, of course, I don't want to see innocent people hurt, but I think you and the police are exaggerating the possible danger and—as you have just said—the police will be there in any case. My view on these things—and this is not the first time there have been protests about my columns—is that you can't give in to such threats. This is just a possibility mooted by the police, and you know they always like to talk up how indispensable they are. It'll almost certainly amount to a big fat nothing. Do you remember the protest about….Oh, no, you wouldn't."

Dougie was annoyed by the imputation of inexperience, but kept up his smile. "This isn't about past protests, which I am admittedly too young to remember. It's about *this* protest, now, at a time of tension, when the public mood is rather volatile and emotions are running very high. It's about a protest by a bunch of proven thugs, with a string of convictions for violent crime. I don't want—and obviously you don't want—to see innocent passers-by or policemen potentially injured. The police are stretched at the moment. This could very easily get out of hand, and we would have a moral responsibility for whatever happens."

"I don't see that at all. If these people get upset by what I write, that's their problem. They don't *have* to read it."

Dougie felt the anger building, but he found it hard to assert mastery against the supremely relaxed-looking man, so much cleverer and more experienced and controlled, who sat looking coolly at him over the mug of coffee. Even the coffee stains on his waistcoat did not detract from Albert's impressive aura. But he tried again.

"Albert, you don't get it at all. It is not as easy as that. These days, you cannot get away with saying the things you say. You may think it's amusing to sit there every week and come out with offensive and outrageous things that hurt people's feelings, but times have changed. People have changed. Nowadays people won't tolerate the things that you say. And their feelings are perfectly understandable. We live in a multicultural, multi-ethnic society, and you need to come to terms with that. The rest of the paper—in fact, our whole media group—has, so why can't you? And—I didn't want to say this, but you are forcing me to go down this road—when it comes down to it, at the end of the day, I am the editor, and I have the final say over what gets printed in what is effectively *my* paper."

Albert replied almost before the younger man had finished. "So you're saying that in the interests of tolerance you won't tolerate what I have to say? To safeguard liberalism you will be illiberal. In short, you want me to censor myself—to dodge the truth, because a couple of spotty kids in ski-masks *might* chuck a few stones."

"You mean the truth as *you* see it."

Albert half-smiled; a boy like Dougie *would* come up with such a facile qualification.

"Now, Albert, you must agree that what is really important is that people don't get hurt, if it can be avoided. All I'm asking you to do is to tone it down a little, take the sting out. There are different ways of saying the same thing; we must not be gratuitously offensive."

"There *are* different ways of saying things, but my way is my own, my views are my own, and I fail to understand why I should conform to some ridiculous fashion, or some disgusting kind of censorship. And my style, as you will be aware, appears to agree with the majority of *Sentinel* readers."

"No-one knows better than me how popular your column is with a segment of our readership. But if we have a responsibility and a sense of loyalty towards you, you have a responsibility towards us, too."

He actually interlaced his fingers to represent co-operation. A Cliché of the Hand, Albert thought; Sally would find that amusing.

"*My* responsibility is mostly to my conscience and—though it sounds a little dated—to this country. These Beach people are being used as a political tool to attack England. You don't *really* think all these people who are making such a noise give a shit about those refugees? Do you? How could they? It's just a ridiculous cult, like Diana, or Hitler. Look, Dougie, as I've said to you before, our readers are loyal because we don't sway with every current. They like our consistency—they like to think that amongst all the other shit we print, there is some commonsense conservatism—although, of course, there isn't."

"That's all very well as a general principle, but the point is that extremists are planning a demonstration outside this building tomorrow, and innocent people might get hurt. *You* alone have the power to take some of the sting out of this, by making some gesture in tomorrow's column that shows you understand the public mood."

"Ha! The public mood! The Spirit of the Age—the Shite-geist. Who are 'the public,' and what do *they* know anyway? The public are herd animals. It's balls, and you know it as well as I do, or you wouldn't be a newspaper editor."

Dougie had never considered such questions. "Well, I… I mean…" A hot, short silence fell.

Albert was thinking about the way Britain had altered, not just over his lifetime, but in the last few years. He thought about the emotiveness that hung now always in the air like car exhaust—the crackling tension that suffused the media, even the *Sentinel* (outside his column). He remembered the chanting children he had seen on the television the other day, schoolrooms-full of spontaneous sanctimony, indignant intakes, the sadly singing Komsomol Kids. He thought of the mass public givings and the Safe Haven Telethon to come, which everyone said would be the biggest ever, the chained penitents on the Pilgrimage Against Prejudice, the ostentatious outrage, the smoothly sensitive faces of the broadcasters, the 'musicians' railing against everything he had always loved. And he had a sudden sharp view of dead people, lying wasted on a cold beach. Was it right to use these dead as a metaphor, even in the good cause of saving Britain? And was it possible to save Britain anyway? Was it worth preserving, if it were possible? Once again, he realized the futility of his resistance—one elderly and faithless writer with declining powers against all the weight of *that*.

After a minute, during which Dougie looked sideways at him and he stared into space and time, Albert dragged himself sadly back to that chair in that office in that ugly world, and spoke again, suddenly bowed down by the immovability of things.

"Look, Dougie. I've been around the block a few times, and I have seen these crazes come and go. Almost the only thing I've learned about politics is that there is a lot of collateral damage. I also resent the idea that we are giving into the threat of violence from a few children. BUT…I would not wish anyone to get harmed as a consequence of something I write, if I have the power of avoiding it, as you seem to think I have. Tomorrow's piece is written and I've already sent it down. But to please you, I'll have another think about my piece for next week, and see if I can find a way of making it less abrasive, without compromising myself. That's all I can say. Now, if that's all…"

Dougie was amazed. "I…I'm very grateful, Albert—very grateful, indeed. To be honest, I hadn't expected you to…."

"Give in?" Albert asked sardonically.

"To *agree*." Dougie said firmly. "But I'm delighted you have, delighted. And you'll find it's the right thing to do. As you know, I wouldn't normally ask such a thing of any of our writers, least of all our chief asset. But the key thing is not to contribute to tension. Thank you very much, Albert; I won't forget this."

Albert watched as the younger man gushed, and felt amused pity. Poor sod; he'd be out of his depth wherever he was. He raised a deprecating hand. "No problem at all. Now, I feel I ought to be getting back down to it."

"Of course, of course. Thanks again, Albert."

Dougie came round from behind the desk and walked ingratiatingly with him to the door, pumping his hand avidly most of the way, smiling oleaginously all the while, looking after him fondly as he left.

Albert walked along the corridor, thinking of other editors he'd known. They were men at least, but this one…humph! He threaded between advertising staff, sat down on his too rigid chair at his new, clean, awkwardly-placed desk in the too clean office, and thought hard for a few minutes. Then he logged on, and started to unfold his newly responsible thoughts to the eager machine. Meanwhile, a relieved Dougie was speaking to the chief sub—"Harold, can you please send me the copy for next week's Broadside before you send it down? We may need to make a few changes. Thanks. Cheers!"

Albert found it unusually hard to write that column. The spark, the impishness, the black humor he always felt, or at least affected—all these were disconcertingly absent. He plodded agonizingly through the required length, feeling as if he were wearing clay-heavy boots, or writing a management report. The bucket went down and came up heavily time and again, but all it bore was mud and rubbish. Periodically, he would delete huge chunks of text, and sit staring at the screen. Or he would get a coffee, and pace up and down, slopping the liquid uncaringly onto the brand-new carpet tiles. He normally had it ready by 2:30 at the latest; this time, the subs had to wait until almost 4:30 before a print-out of what he was acutely aware was the worst thing he had ever written dropped into their in-tray with a muffled *flump*.

Until that moment, Albert had not realized just how proud he was of his writing. He had always thought of it as just a job, a meretricious sort of talent, something he could do without thinking and people were fool enough to admire, even pay for. Now, for the first time, when it was already too late, he felt he had all along been doing something worthwhile, striking a chord that had to be struck. This latest piece was not *him*; it was group-think, compromised and mediocre, not only counter-intuitive, but counter-civilizational. He wished his name was not going to be associated with it. He sat on the Tube, faintly miserable, looking blankly through the random faces opposite as they looked blankly back.

Meanwhile, Dougie finished reading the copy and nodded in relief. He had never before realized what an excellent writer Albert could be. It seemed Albert had a good heart underneath his mannerisms, his starchy look, all those old-school ties, his fruity vocabulary, and obscure allusions. And he had also proved surprisingly reasonable, and flexible—bowing at last to Dougie's stronger arguments and greater articulacy.

Really, Dougie pondered, it had been an important victory—not just for his authority, but in a way for all of British culture and society. Given a few minor adjustments, next week's installment could be a landmark piece—disagreeing without being disagreeable, thoughtful without being provocative, constructive rather than negative. It could be a step-change, drawing a line under the Bad Old Days of Broadside as the last media outpost of antediluvian attitudes. Albert can't he happy in his skin, Dougie mused, with a surge of something resembling pity. All the wasted opportunities of Albert's old, uptight, judgmental ways, with his mind so closed to culture.

The object of his unwanted pity was at that moment reclining in his complaining sofa, drinking a third brandy, and grinning lopsidedly at the oddly appropriate words of the persecuted poetaster in *The Fairy Queen*—"If you will know it, I am a scurvy Poet."

Chapter 21
INQUISITIONS

Thorpe Gilbert, Eastshire
Monday, 29th September

The Corporation Hall had stood in the centre of Thorpe Gilbert since just before the Civil War, gift of and memorial to a now extinct family whose only son had been killed in 1643 charging a Parliamentary column outside the town. It made an elegant weathered coda to its sleepy shuttered street, with its gilt cockerel weathervane, tall windows, musket-ball-spotted blind arcading, and sandstone deities bearing eroded armfuls of wheat or leading wind-rounded bulls.

Today, the old building was unusually frenetic with life inquiring into death—officials and security guards, journalists and politicians, and members of the public. Today was the day when the inquest would be opened. It would not be a full inquest—it was far too early for that—but the Miracle Migrant would be seen in public for the first time. There was also to be preliminary testimony from the captain of a fishery-protection vessel that had been in the area that night.

People streamed through tall blue nail-studded pitch pine doors and up the Grand Staircase to cram themselves into the Eastshire Suite, turning round to glare at those barging from behind, under the glassy regard of dozens of cameras. Everyone was there, from the *Three Es* to *Money & Markets*. Poorly executed oils of ex-Lord Mayors peered down skew-eyed from gilt frames onto those occupying the parquet, which had so often borne the Brueghelesque burden of the Young Farmers and their wives-to-be. It was breathlessly hot for the latter half of September, even with all the windows open to admit the sound of sparrows chirping in the gutters. In the corridors and spilling out on the pavements and road, yet more photographers and journalists jostled, sweltered and swore, themselves the objects of the excited attentions of locals.

Just up from the entrance, shepherded by the police off the road into the gateway of a derelict 18th-century warehouse, was a small demonstration by Eastshire Ethnic Action.

Despite the group's name, virtually all of the demonstrators had come from outside the area, and the organization itself had only been in existence about two weeks. When their minibuses from London, Manchester, and Birmingham had disgorged their contents at the bus station an hour beforehand, passers-by had stared. Contrary to the now prevalent preconception, they were not staring because the new arrivals were black or Asian—in fact, almost none were—but rather because of the aggressively confident way the new arrivals held themselves, their cradled banners and placards, their general earringed and tongue-studded demeanour. They seemed slouchingly certain as they moved along the narrow pavements, effectively forcing locals to move out of their way. Some had hoods and scarves and bore unusual or unrecognizable flags—large letter As, hammers and sickles, clenched fists, rainbow stripes, a few Iraqi flags. They looked incredibly alien. An elderly idler nudged his neighbour and spoke for many others. "Wonder what thoase fellers do for a livin'!" and they cackled discreetly.

Some of the visitors had obviously been drinking on the bus and went straight into the Queen's Arms across from the bus station—while obvious organizers spoke sullenly to police, or texted and Tweeted as they threaded through the medieval streets towards the Hall. Shopkeepers looked up in curiosity and mild trepidation as they passed, but they appeared polite enough and were greeted politely enough in turn. But conversations were undoubtedly affected by their incursion—raised eyebrows as shopkeeper and regular telegraphed shared opinions when they thought the visitors weren't looking, too wide smiles, conversations resumed as soon as visitors had left the shop but not before they were out of earshot.

Dylan Ekinutu-Jones drifted dreamily among the tumult, with but not with the newcomers, looking round in wonder and paradoxical envy. What a time-capsule! And what faces these people had—time-locked like the buildings, some wearing tweedy or work-stained clothes, a few extravagantly whiskered, a man smoking a pipe. The only time Dylan had ever seen such faces before was when he had watched the pro-hunting demos in London. He had been part of an animal-rights counter-protest, but part of him had also wanted to join the hunters, join England, even as he had laughed at the old country's relict remnants. He remembered fondly the high thrill of their horns echoing down Whitehall like the war-trumpets of Vikings.

This town reminded him of all the books he had ever read about England; it was so old, so quaint, so half-timbered, so gently decaying, so unlike anywhere else. Butchers' shops, greengrocers, market stalls, an old department store, spires and turrets, carved bargeboards, and tall windows with rippling glass, men driving muddy pick-ups piled with straw bales and terriers. It was a place that badly needed to be reinvented, made relevant—and yet even as he had the thought he had a nonsensical instinct that perhaps it should be left exactly as it was. But it was too late for that. He looked around at his cohort of modernizers with pride intermingled with uneasiness.

With him were lots of the stalwarts of the vanguard—an acned Roedean girl called Arabella, Jim McTeague the shavenheaded anarchist with a face as block-like as a Rorke's Drift redcoat, that crazy Armenian woman who always made up misspelled placards and stank of cats— the England of now and tomorrow running down the phantom of an England that had disappeared everywhere else and would not persist here much longer. They were all singing now—"All Change"—and blowing whistles; as they sounded their war cry, it rose to challenge the screaming swifts.

The progressive phalanx proceeded towards the Hall, breaking away only to hand out leaflets or photograph each other holding up banners in front of the War Memorial, St. Blaise's, the Tudor almshouses, the Market Cross. The town and its people were a quaint Olde Backclothe against which they would act out their modern morality tale.

A lounging local named Simon Tranter had been leaning moodily against the window of the Building Society, smoking his third cigarette of the hour with intense concentration, interrupting what were obviously displeasing thoughts only to stick up two fingers at the Building Society manageress when she came out to remonstrate. He stayed there, oblivious to the scandalized staff, oblivious to almost everything but a dull sense that he had been leaning against windows like these for all of his life. He looked up in quick interest as he heard the first sounds of the advancing liberation army, and as they came round the corner, he stopped smoking to stare at them greedily. There was something about their looks he liked, so he threw down his cigarette and stomped over to meet them.

He told them he was on their side—that Thorpe Gilbert—in fact the whole fucking county—was one fucking awful place full of fucking dickheads. They were glad to meet and absorb him, this brand plucked from the burning, this symbol of how enlightenment was washing over even this place to sluice away the detritus of the past. Locals accustomed to see Simon's lanky, bleached-hair, camouflage-clad frame pushing scowlingly down Thorpe's streets, or seeing his name in the *Three Es* in connection with another appearance before magistrates, were only slightly surprised to see him with these strangers—high-fiving or handshaking, grinning in agreement with their noble ideals, handing out leaflets, holding a placard that read "Ibraham MUST Stay." He ventured out again and again from among the elect towards the undifferentiated, his arms brimming with resounding aspirations printed on recycled paper, his eyes flicking around all the time looking out for Emily-Rose. Useless tosser, was he? He'd show the bitch.

The visitors had found their voices, their whistles and loudhailers, and the *cri de coeur* of the oppressed was heard in Thorpe for the first time since the Corn Laws.

"Hands Off Human Rights!"

"NO to Nazi Laws"

"Equal Rights Not Just For Whites"

"Keep Ibraham in England!"

Simon loved being able to shout legally in the middle of town, and as he bellowed out the message of hope, his eyes turned challengingly on the passers-by, daring them to pick on him *now*.

Simon and his new best friends, hot police and officials, manic media, engaged pedestrians, bemused workers looking out from shops, the town's famous white doves on the cornices, although all in a state of constant movement were also trapped in the moment—waiting partly for the Coroner, Sir Smedley Cutting, Bart., but mostly for Ibraham, witness to hideous history, due *here* at any moment, in tiny Thorpe at the sleepy edge of England. It was a brush with history, an opportunity for coming together in revulsion against racism, opined Mark Clark as he moved amongst the people—the star condescending to make stars of ordinary people for a few shining seconds.

And there he was! A slight and shambling shape, brunet in brown jacket and blue jeans, staring scaredly from side to side; he was part-propelled, part-dragged in through the same tall blue doors and up the same stairs towards the breathless Suite with all its dignified daubs. People on the stairs pushed forward as if to touch his garments, and cameras went off like a strobe storm as he was borne in on a flood tide from glare to gloom and glare again from high windows, pummelled by a tempest of voices. That single view of the Miracle Migrant galvanized the demonstrators to redoubled efforts, and their throats were soon raw with the stress of shouting support.

Sir Smedley arrived last of all, fine-haired, thin-lipped, and small-lobed, his nose aquiline without being cruel, with grey eyes that could convey kindly approbation, polite scepticism or aristocratic contempt with equal facility. Toting a worn brown leather briefcase he had inherited from his grandfather, he filtered through the crowds and twinkled up the steps in Savile Row and Church's. With this last piece now in play, the shouting died away and the demonstrators hunkered down to wait the outcome—all the testimony transmitted to the outside world through loudspeakers.

Ibraham trembled to see the heaving room, and especially the grand inquisitor, so perfectly at home in this room, this town, this culture. But the Baronet hid kindness behind his official brusquerie. His questioning was carried out with such forensic delicacy that Ibraham scarcely noticed how penetrating it was. Sir Smedley was not there, he emphasised, to enquire into his legal status—just the facts of what had happened on the nights of so and so between the hours of such and such, in your own words and take your time, we are not here to judge you.

Ibraham found himself slowly opening up to the so-proper stranger. He told him more than he realized, more than he had ever told himself. In a barely audible voice, stopping often to let the translator catch up, he commenced.

"You see, my Lord Smedley, I have travelled such a long way through many countries to get to England—by foot, by truck, by car, by boat, train, even by plane. Such a long way, and it was hard—very hard."

Sir Smedley smiled, leaning forward like a friendly whippet. The Suite faded and all sounds seemed muffled as Ibraham recalled with growing fluency the hunger, the tiredness, the sick sister, the war, the dirt, the oppression, the aspiration, the pilgrimage. Then the last acts… scrambling up the ladder from the feculent hold, looking eagerly over the side, the wrenching realization that it was a trick, the closed faces of the killers, the spitting of their guns, him thrown and spinning, the water closing far above, the shock as he came to the surface, the ebbing of feeling, and, dimmest of dim impressions, an almost beyond-recall sense of solidity below his clutching hands, indistinct shapes moving and booming excitedly before—years and years later—full consciousness in hospital.

When he had finished at last, inexpressibly exhausted by the emotion, the room exhaled, and then there was a noble moment as applause started somewhere with someone whose eyes were pricking, whose neighbour took it up—and within a few seconds, everyone except Sir Smedley and the officials was applauding and cheering, and even they were trying hard to look professional. A young woman from the Coroner's office gave up the unequal struggle and clapped and cheered with the rest of them, scattering her papers but unwilling to be omitted from the moment. Even out on the streets there could be heard a ragged response. Ibraham even imagined there was a catch in Sir Smedley's voice as he thanked him.

Ibraham flopped back in his seat, while all the people around itched to touch him, to give a token of their esteem, a talisman of their pity and humanity. He turned to them all and smiled and shook the luckiest hands, and that smile on that face that had seen such suffering elicited deep emotions from some women reporters.

For the rest of that day there was irregular choppy movement in the audience, like waves in a harbour sheltered from but connected to a gale beyond the bar. That resounding room heard from Neil Parrish, who had first seen the bodies, and from the police and medical staff. The only new information was given by the young captain of the *Hector*. He informed the hushed Suite that his vessel had challenged an unidentified trawler-sized vessel on the night the deaths had occurred. He had not persisted with the investigation… although had he known then what he knew now!….because they had been running low on fuel, the vessel had not made landfall and, in any case, had been heading away from the UK at a moderate speed. It was admittedly unusual, but not unheard of, for there to have been no response to radio challenges. He had assumed it was a damaged VHF set. No, there had never been any reason to suspect people-smuggling on that part of the coast, as it was so far from the European mainland and the hinterland behind was so remote from any major conurbation or even road. His vessel, after all, was primarily concerned with fisheries protection. Nevertheless—and he looked over at Ibraham—I bitterly regret that we failed you and your fellow-travellers. If only we had known…in his honest eyes there was moisture. The Suite sighed.

Voices lifted and fell, lifted and fell, lifted and fell—which had a Morphean effect in that heat. Ibraham found himself jerking awake more than once and missing large chunks of testimony, despite the translator's unflagging efforts. But eventually Sir Smedley—who almost alone had stayed Englishly alert—summed up. His crisp verdict of unlawful killing of an estimated 42 unidentified persons by unknown assailants, the circumstances to be detailed at a further inquest, surprised nobody, yet it was still sobering—and more than one in the room shivered slightly awake, as if they had been splashed in the face with seawater.

As everyone began to shift and search for cases and bags, a lightheaded Ibraham found himself being practically lifted up and borne away from the room of high windows and peculiar paintings, back downstairs through thinner crowds, past the shouting and clapping demo, into the new-smelling car, and off, sliding smoothly out of the town and through lambent countryside, back to Long Shore Camp.

He was living in the moment, loving the luxury of just sitting and looking out as lush long vistas unfolded themselves one after another— swelling fields of brimming green rolling tumidly to round horizons and distant steeples, handsome houses, high-circling buzzards, fat livestock dreaming knee-deep in dock-leaves, trees saluting with drooping foliage, everything stroked by the sun. This was ENGLAND, and it was much too beautiful to be real. He cried quietly for a while, and the interpreter pretended not to notice.

Back in the exhaling town, everyone had crowded out much less excitedly than they had crowded in, leaving the littered Suite empty except for men collecting chairs, staff peering vaguely out of irrelevant offices or making a start on vacuuming the stairs, even as the final few interlopers headed past. Outside, the streets were emptier and people were thinking of locking up their shops.

A notable exception to the new quietude was the milling hard-core of protestors and their ally Simon—who felt reluctant to quit this new world of high politics to return to his boring terrace house and his shouting mother. She would be doubly angry today, because he had taken £60 from her purse that morning. He accordingly offered himself to his new friends as an adviser on pubs and places to eat. He was also determined to stick close to Arabella, whose mellifluous Southern voice he found enthralling. When it was dark, her skin wouldn't look so bad. Emily-Rose wasn't such a big deal, anyway—common, really, by comparison with this bit of skirt. He was very pleased when she invited him to come with them for something to eat. He started to tell them about the burger place, but had the wit to see that several of them looked pained—so steered them instead towards the Constitution Arms, which did what he thought of privately as "veggie crap," and from which, fortuitously, he had not been barred.

Someone bought him a beer, and he sat in a corner with Arabella (he got occasional glimpses down her blouse) and several others—that black bloke Dylan, the skinhead, and some man who lectured in a university. He was delighted to see people he knew over the far side of the grubby bar and nodded to them in a lordly way.

Someone bought him another beer—then a third appeared. As the lagers vanished, he leaned ever closer to Arabella, but she was talking mostly to Dylan. Simon wasn't up to what seemed a deeply intellectual conversation, so he began to talk instead to the skinhead, like him a man of action rather than a talker. He soon became less sulky. What a nice bloke he was—they had a lot in common—football, music, and girls. They pledged each other in beers—and they talked louder and louder, more and more coarsely, until Arabella made a tactical withdrawal, slipping off to her organic B&B to pamper herself after her well-expended day. Simon didn't even notice her disappearance, because by then he and his new friend, Jim, were leaning tipsily into each other, often laughing incontinently. When he did notice she had gone, this led to yet further confidences, this time on the perfidy of women.

By closing time, they and a semi-detached Dylan, who was not quite ready to go to his B&B, were the only demonstrators left, the others having melted away at intervals. The oddly assorted men exited into what seemed to Dylan ill-lit streets, lined with cars and comfortable houses. It was a vista Simon knew better than he liked. He had seen these streets from every possible angle, at every time of the day and night, and from the age of eight onwards, had often wandered through them late at night, while his mother snored stoned in front of the television or entertained assorted "uncles" in her room. "What a dump—what a fuckin' dump!" he exclaimed, as he looked up and down at the villas and bungalows—Eastholme, Baobab, The Laurels, Darjeeling, Simla, Luxor. Jim was silent—but, wait, what was he doing?

The other two watched in excitement as the Liverpudlian progressed expertly along the road, his left arm outstretched lazily towards the assembled cars, and as he went there was a thin scraping noise, as his keys parted the paint all the way along. Simon was in awe at the wantonness of the action, this perfectly-pitched protest against unfairness; Jim was clearly a man of style and resources. He looked around; no-one was looking out of windows yet but any moment they would be. He grabbed at Dylan's arm and they hurried up behind Jim; all three turned the corner and were safe. No-one answered the door at Emily-Rose's, though they rang and banged on it for about 10 minutes. Eventually, Simon invited the others to his house for beers.

Dylan was in two minds whether to accept; he felt he had virtually nothing in common with these inarticulate yobs, but something about their casual decisiveness appealed. And to think—they were doing this for people like him! Those unpolished exteriors clearly hid noble hearts. The vandalism to the cars was horrifying—but it had also been thrilling, the perfect mute protest about Everything. Jim had literally made his mark, in a more profound way than all of Dylan's blogs and media appearances. It was an unsubtle stroke, which put them on the wrong side of the law—but it was a socially significant *sgraffito* and memento of the day tomorrow came to town. He felt there could be yet bigger events in the offing.

That was how three very different men thrown together by events much greater than themselves were sitting in front of a huge television (his mother's TV was on in her room, where she had gone with an "uncle"). They were smoking skunk to the sound of Atrocities Against Civilians—more shared tastes between Simon and Jim, although Dylan liked his music more melodic. They were young and bored, and Simon asked Jim whether Arabella was "up for it." Jim shrugged and advised him that her boyfriends were all people who had, "you know, done political stuff—proved themselves."

It was at that moment Simon was struck by his big idea, and he told it to the others in a few pungent phrases. Jim laughed carelessly and said he was definitely on for it if Simon was. Dylan took a little more convincing, but the skunk had made him feel gloriously reckless, as if he were 18 again, about to embark on some ill-advised but irresistibly delicious affair of the heart, where all the senses would be indulged and even falling would be fine.

They shook hands in token of solidarity, smoked more pot, and Simon got some things out of the garden shed. They would have to leave it for a couple of hours. Their music thumped through the thin walls to the infuriation of neighbours.

Dan was wondering sleepily why Sammy was making uncertain *woofs*. Badger, maybe—or maybe a fox. Owls? Or maybe Sammy was just having a dream of puppyhood, his grizzled old legs kicking as his dream self dashed after dream rabbits in fields that had vanished, down after them into dream dykes…

Then the windows went in downstaits, the *woofs* became enraged barking, and harsh voices were shouting from an outré universe— "RACIST SCUM! RACIST SCUM! FUCKIN' RACIST SCUM! FUCKIN' RACIST SCUM!"

More breaking glass, something falling over. The clock! The living room! The house! *Oh no!* Hatty was screaming, and Clarrie, too, and Sammy yowled and jumped at the door downstairs while Dan half-fell, half-leapt out of bed, grabbing for his trousers. Already he could hear heavy feet retreating rapidy through the kitchen garden. He yanked open the curtains to see in the moonlight the back of a man dashing around the bend, while a car engine came to life down the lane and someone shouted "COME ON! COME ON, FOR FUCK'S SAKE, JIM! DYLAN!"

Shouting "RING THE POLICE!" Dan tore-stumbled downstairs and into the kitchen, opening the back door for Sammy, who raced out as Dan scrabbled in a drawer for the gun cabinet keys. There! He scrabbled in the cabinet for cartridges, grimly alert to the sound of the car engine revving up and more shouts, his enemies escaping, while Hatty and Clarrie hyperventilated upstairs. Why could you never find what you wanted…!

At last tooled up but with his shoes still unlaced, Dan got out into the cool silvery night and dashed down towards the lane and the noise of the car as fast as his years would permit. Somewhere ahead, he could hear Sammy yelp in pain (the bastards had *kicked* him!) and then start barking again, even over the fierce revving of the car, now moving quickly down the lane. If he cut across the angle of Home Field he might be able to get a shot at the bastards as they rounded Fisher's Corner.

But he could not run as he had once been able to run, and he was only halfway across the field when he saw the lights of the car reach the corner and pass on towards the coast road. Just then, he tripped over one of his laces and went sprawling, hurting his knee and hand and dropping the gun, which discharged harmlessly into the air. He lay there breathless and cursing, while the car raced to the road and safety. He tried to rise, but his knee was twisted, and already swelling.

He was still lying undignified and gasping, when Sammy limped back up the lane, and over to where his master lay. Sitting up painfully, Dan patted him and scratched his ears. Sammy was not used to Dan fussing him in a field in the middle of the night. But he appreciated it, pushing his head against Dan's hands and licking them, his stern swishing, groaning in pleasure. Dan stood with an effort, noticing a sharp pain in his knee, and went back towards the house. There waited the worst shock of all.

In large, ragged, white letters painted right across the front of the house in between the broken drawing room windows and across the sundial, was painted "RACIST SCUM LIVES HERE" and "KILL RACISM." He stared in horror and disbelief. It was like seeing a scar on the face of a family member. There were lights on all over the house, and Hatty and Clarrie were talking rapidly and breathlessly in the drawing room. "Oh my God, look what they've done!" "Oh no!"

He moved slowly and sadly over grass, glass and gravel to the windows and leaned in, careful to avoid the jagged edges, and saw their wide-eyed faces staring back. The carpet was covered in glass and stones, and the longcase clock lay face down on the floor in a puddle of glass and bricks. A brick must have hit it near the bottom and toppled it onto the uncompromising tiles of the hearth, ruining its two century old face. The phone was ringing and ringing.

"Dan! Are you all right? Did you see them? What happened?"

"I'm fine—but the bastards have gone. I couldn't get near 'em. Sammy tried, too, like a good 'un. They *kicked* him! But they had a car. They went off towards Thorpe. Have you rung the police?"

"They said they'd be here straight away. But how are they going to catch them? It's 10 miles."

"They'll never get them. That must be the police calling back. Clarrie?"

Clarrie picked up the phone and spoke in a high but controlled voice, while Dan led Hatty out onto the lawn by the hand and showed her the graffiti. She stood there equally appalled, looking at the filthy letters, then at him, her eyes filled with tears. "Oh, Dan!" was all she could say, and he put his arm around her to give them both comfort.

He was shaking slightly—thinking of what could have happened. In a way, they'd been lucky. What if they had set the house on fire—or broken in to attack them? *Christ*. It didn't bear thinking about. The realisation that it could have been even worse than this…desecration… filled him with a shocking sense of his inability to defend his people and his property. It was something he had never considered before—had never needed to consider before. Through his crass stupidity, he had endangered them all, and now he was almost powerless to protect them.

He told Hatty and Clarrie not to touch anything, to leave it for the police. They dressed, and Hatty was making breakfast, shaking slightly as she poured tea. Dan went down to the yard to check on everything. All seemed in order, except…what was that movement down on the road? He groaned as he realised the bullocks' gate must have been opened. He went back to the house for the car keys, told Hatty and bumped down the dewy track in the Land Rover, scattering the first rooks.

The gate was swinging loose, blocking one side of the road. Thankfully, the road had been quiet and the animals must have been down the far end of the field, as only a few had left the field, and they were all bunched together in the lane, so there was no harm done. But what if the road had been busy? Whoever had done this had known what would most distress a farmer.

He parked the Landrover to block the lane, and had no difficulty herding the animals back into the field. He was about to close the gate, when it occurred to him that it might have fingerprints, so he used his sleeve to pull it to and clip the latch back into place. Just as he'd finished, a police car came up the lane and stopped. Dan didn't recognize either officer; they kept rotating them these days.

"Are you Mr. Gowt? We're going to the house now. But before we do that, do your sheep have a green and yellow mark?" Dan admitted they had. They had seen about 40 sheep with this marking wandering along the main road, and had reported them to control. Dan asked permission to get them rounded up, then rang and got Ted Fisher out of bed, arranging to meet him at the cross-roads.

It didn't take him long to locate the animals, which were picking their way curiously along the verges, sampling the sorrel and rosebay willow herb. He couldn't do much until Ted got there, so he just put on the hazard lights and did his best to keep the sheep into the side. Thankfully, only one car came along, and the driver was considerate, creeping past while Dan contained the animals. But surely there was an animal missing?

After a few minutes, he found what had been a fine ewe lying by the side of the road. It looked as if she had died instantaneously when the car had hit her; her head was smashed almost to pieces. Dan felt sick. Unconcerned about rearing animals for the table, or eating them, he could still be sentimental. He also had a hatred of waste and, strongest of all, felt deep resentment that some bloody bastard had made him look like a bloody fool.

Ted turned up, and Dan was more grateful than he could tell for his unquestioning support—and for the sympathetic slap on the shoulder Ted gave him after they'd got the animals back in the field. He still had some friends, it seemed—some standing and dignity.

He bumped back along the track, feeling old and cold. The defaced farm, with the police car parked in front, looked oddly foreign and the encompassing acres accordingly impersonal, as though his title to it, his place in it, were weaker than he had always imagined.

The policemen were drinking tea and taking statements. They seemed unexpectedly unsympathetic, almost bored. This made Dan aggrieved and even sarcastic, which made the atmosphere deteriorate further. The tall, dark policman kept asking him about timings, and what he had intended to do with the gun. They asked to see his licence, although it had been issued by their station. They even told him that he had been wrong to have left his gun lying around in the kitchen, after he had gone to check on the animals. The tall one then said, "You know, in these circumstances it might actually be counter-productive to have a weapon in the house. There is always the temptation to use it, and then matters could escalate. Someone could have been hurt this morning."

"Ha—yes, *someone* might, and it would have served the bastards right. If they ever come back, or I can catch up with them, I'll make sure they never…"

The policeman lifted a long, pale hand.

"I'm going to stop you there, Mr Gowt. I must caution you not to threaten individuals with actual bodily harm. It is an offence, and had you fired your gun at the assailants when they were outside your house, and not threatening you or your family members directly, then we would be arresting you now, rather than helping you."

"Do you call *this* helping? Why aren't you out trying to find those scum rather than bothering us? *We're* the ones who have been attacked—not them! And all you can do is sit like a couple of…of…I don't know whats, while a passel of dangerous thugs have probably got as far as Thorpe by now. It's not on…but then that's you all over, sitting on your arses in speed traps while real criminals do what they like. What do we pay our taxes *for?*"

The tall, dark one said there was no need to take that attitude and explained in an aggravating, condescending way that as the assailants were probably from outside the area, it would not be easy to find them. He also explained that unfortunately they were unable able to offer full police protection at the moment, although there would be a 24-hour link to the part-time police station in Williamstow. (Dan said "Huh!") Then the policeman said something extraordinary.

"You know, Mr. Gowt, none of this would have happened if you hadn't made those provocative comments in the first place. I have to tell you that you are lucky your comments have not been made the subject of a formal investigation—*yet* at any rate. We take these kinds of comments very seriously. The police service is committed to equality of access to all."

Dan almost choked on a mouthful of Hatty's strongest tea. He opened and shut his mouth again as the enormity sank in, while the policeman looked on in lugubrious satisfaction, believing what he had said had suddenly struck home. Dan had scarcely recovered when the quiet policemen actually suggested that maybe they should consider selling up and moving away—as if Home Farm was just a house. *Here*, which Gowts had built and where they had always been—where men like him had endured since who knew when, telling the time by the same sundial, doing similar things to the same soil, seeing the same sunshine, smelling the same sea-tang, hearing the owls calling in winter as they had always done—to swap all *this*, for some anonymous new house, some mean horror on some suburban estate!

Dan realised intuitively that it would be pointless trying to explain himself—to *these*. They probably lived in that kind of house; they looked as though they did. He smouldered for the last few minutes of the unprofitable interview. Veins were standing proud along his arms and on the backs of his square hands; his heart was beating in his head—so loudly that it drowned out his words, their words, his world, their world, the reality of being in that compromised house on that violated morning.

Eventually, assurances ostentatiously unmade, the policemen drove away and Dan exhaled. He had always felt that the police were on his side, and the side of all decent people, but this disastrous interview showed how wrong he was, had always been. It was terrifying to realize just how officially friendless he was.

Hatty yielded into Dan when he put a strong but useless arm around her shoulders, and she cried shudderingly into yesterday's shirt. He would have had the other arm for Clarrie—except that she preferred to lean against the worktop and drink black coffee, looking over at her parents without really registering them, shifting her feet incessantly, her painted fingernails tapping tensely on the hot mug. Their taut faces cut at his inadequacy. "I'm *so* sorry" was all he could think of saying.

Chapter 22

TODAY IN PARLIAMENT

Westminster
Tuesday, 30th September

It would be a landmark day for yooman rights. Richard Simpson was to propose and the House to debate his eagerly awaited motion to exclude the National Unionists from this and all future Parliaments. Of course, it would pass. But it would be a febrile day nonetheless.

The debate would coincide with a large cross-party rally in Trafalgar Square—addressed by, among others, Dylan, whose excitement was tempered with tiredness, because he had just got back that morning from the foray to Thorpe Gilbert. And not only tiredness but also flatness and worry. Last night's raid had been so wonderfully exciting, and he had been so stoned and drunk (he still was, slightly), that for a time, he had not given any serious thought to what he had been doing, and the possible consequences.

As they had driven away at frantic speed from Crisby immediately after the raid, with the stoned Simon driving surprisingly masterfully along those narrow and dangerous little marsh roads with the dykes on either side, the atmosphere in the car had been dynamic and joyous. It was like being a teenager again, steaming through the bus in Peckham with the brothers—an electric empathy, an awareness of outlawry—a delicious feeling he had deliberately spurned when he had turned his back on all that, to build a meaningful life, to contribute rather than take.

He had never previously realized how much he had missed that uncomplicated emotion—the delight of having no doubts. These two were brothers, too, of an abstracter kind—and he loved them in that instant as much as he had ever loved anyone. Jim had opened another beer and passed the glass bottle around, and even its jarring him on his front teeth as the car turned a corner in fifth gear did not matter in the slightest.

They had done it! The Three Musketeers had struck a blow at The Man—and got away with it! They had descended quietly, cleverly, into the dangerous place where the fascist laid his fat and foolish head, and left a noble calling card in the form of those crimson letters right across the complacent conservative façade. They crowed and whooped in pagan triumph, and Simon turned up the heavy metal CD full blast, making early morning animals clear the road in alarm even before the car had charged into view, and waking dozens of annoyed local residents near the train station where they had dropped off Dylan just in time to catch the first train.

It was only when Dylan had collapsed into his seat on the train that the magnitude of what had just happened sank in, and he was dumbfounded by his carelessness. "SHIT!" he exclaimed aloud—and looked around hurriedly, only to discover that he had the whole carriage to himself. He stared out at the luridly lit fields and reed-fringed rivers and at his own reflection in the window. The flashing sun hurt his eyes, and he shaded them with his hand.

What was *that* about? *What* was I doing? Here I am, 31, a public intellectual, a cultural critic, a columnist, a community organizer, a chat show guest, a friend of MPs, a police adviser, a mortgagee, a careful sports-car owner—and inside all these husks I'm still just a 14-year-old punk kid raising Cain, living in each crammed-full second, despising the present and with nothing to hope for or guard against from the future—and reinforcing all the stereotypes…I was drunk, yes, and stoned, but *why, why* was I drunk and stoned? I hadn't been drunk or stoned for years. I was drunk, Your Honour. I regret to say I had been taking recreational drugs, Your Honour. No, I can't explain it, Your Honour. I am normally abstemious. This was totally out of character, and I feel a deep remose for my actions. All I can offer in mitigation is my natural anxiety to improve the world, which made me slightly over-zealous…the high emotion of the day, the justness of the cause….I regret if I have brought the cause into disrepute, or disappointed all the people who have such high opinions of me, who look to me. I hope I can leave this court and resume my column-writing and bridge-bulding activities. It won't happen again, Your Honour… But why, Mr. Ekinutu-Jones, had it happened at all? Your aims may be laudable, but your means were wholly unacceptable. I have no option but to…It just needed one person to have seen him being dropped off at the station…he was a public figure, and even up here someone might have recognized him.

He alternately fretted and fought off sleep all the way down to London.

The smaller than expected crowd was peppered with placards—"Hands Off Our Human Rights!"—"NO to Nazi Laws"—"Immigration = Human Dignity"—"Keep Ibraham in England!" An embarrassing notice reading "Feck the Fascist Sistem" was annoyingly prominent, hoisted bravely aloft by a scruffy Irish-looking man who unfortunately always turned out for these events. Dylan saw a grinning Channel

One cameraman zooming in on it. There were trade union banners, hammers and sickles, and the sable vexillography of the anarchists, while the sound of their cries and whistles sometimes even penetrated the Central Lobby, where the MPs clustered and cleared again excitedly.

Around the edges of the rally, there were scuffles as tense police wrested biting, spitting students to the ground under the televisual *tsk-tsks* of demonstrators' cameras. Then a few drunken rugby fans laughed at the "Feck the Fascist Sistem" placard. The man holding it used it to hit one of them, a policeman grabbed him, they both fell over, and a ski-masked young man shouted, "The filth are fucking our people!" Within seconds, there were several dozen in a scrum with the policeman and Irishman on the bottom, and panic lashed through the crowd, briefly distracting its attention from Dylan's sub-par peroration, before the mêlée was broken up by the knocking unconscious of the Irishman. A shocked gasp went up; all the cameras whirred.

Inside the Commons, for probably the last time in his life, the cynosure of all this controversy sat perspiring on Pugin's handiwork. He had thought he had an impermeable epidermis after three years of contumely and contempt in this place, and he maintained a semblance of scornful bravado. But inside, he felt dried up, *tired* of the endless struggle against everyone and everything. Even the Palace police, normally so blandly professional, had seemed offhand over the last few days, as if they knew he would not be troubling them much longer. This would almost certainly be the last debate he would sit in on in the Mother of Parliaments.

"*Debate!*" he snorted. That was a good word! He had not even been given a slot to speak in his own defence—and that was paradoxically his strongest weapon, because the blatant injustice of this ruling worried quite a lot of MPs, even some from the WP. One of these, an elderly ex-Trotskyite, had actually said as much to him when they had met fortuitously in the lavatories earlier that day—and the unexpectedly considerate words had touched him more than he would have expected.

The two men had been washing their hands at adjacent marble sinks and looking furtively at each other in the long mirror. The WP man flashed his eyes fearfully in the mirror to check they were alone then spoke out unexpectedly, making the other man almost jump. He was amazed to hear the WP MP using his first name.

"You know, um, Dave, it bothers me the way they're handling this debate. It bothers me a *lot*. Apart from the fact that they're not allowing you to speak, it's all too fast, and it's being carried out in an atmosphere of panic. You can smell a sort of fear behind the grandstanding. If it hadn't been for the dead migrants, I believe this would have been postponed, and they would have extended you the common courtesies. It wouldn't have done you a damn bit of good, of course—but at least it would have been handled decently. There are ways of doing these things. I'm bound to tell you that I'll still be voting against you, but not with any degree of pleasure. As I see it, this is a dirty job, but it's a job that's got to be done."

He paused for a moment, and looked thoughtful while they dried their hands on the white towels.

"I'm not being precious about this. I know that views like yours are surprisingly common. I can think of people in my own family who actually vote for your lot and, although I probably shouldn't admit it, one of my cousins is one of your councillors. Nice man, too. I see him at family get-togethers and we get along fine. My mother's views on our coloured friends would have been right at home with your lot. But the fact remains that not only are your views at least a century out of date, but they always lead to terrible things. Have you ever heard Ben Klein's family history? I have, and all I can say is that I don't blame him one little bit for his little crusade."

"Nor do I—but he's got it all wrong. We're not like that."

"*You* may not be—I don't know—but lots of people in your party *are* like that, and if it ever gets anywhere it will lead to filthy events like those which torture poor Ben Klein. I don't blame him for being a monomaniac. And that is why, Dave, that tonight you will be treated extremely badly by this place"—he waved his hand around to signify the whole complex—"and why I and some others will be slightly ashamed, but in the end, we will make the right choice. You're part of the past, mate, and the sooner you realize it, the better for all concerned. It's nothing personal, but at the risk of sounding pompous, tonight we're doing history's business. Good luck to you!"

He threw the towel into the big wicker basket and left. Not for the first time in his Parliamentary career, the NU man thought of several excellent things he could have said, when it was just too late.

He was thinking of that conversation, and gazing over towards his late interlocutor, who was avoiding eye contact. He gave up and looked up at the Public Gallery. The only real allies he had in this whole building were all seated in the Public Gallery—his wife, party leader James Fulford, and a few other NU officials, including Daniel Williams, respected, at least in party circles, for his recent cameo on *The Capital Today*.

Not everyone in the Gallery was a supporter—sitting within 30 feet of the NU leader was (what a coincidence) none other than Ben Klein, grinning as broadly as it was possible for his unaccustomed face to do.

All his politician contacts had guaranteed support—in the cases of two CD MPs, against their instincts, but they knew that Ben knew interesting things about their adolescent political activities. Besides, the result was a foregone conclusion, and they preferred to start as well as end up on the right social side. There was no party whip on the motion, because none of the main party leaders wished to be seen supporting the motion just a week before the capital hosted the International Congress on Free Expression. Neither would be available to vote. But both nevertheless had made it clear they wanted their MPs to support the motion. Ben was enjoying the knowledge that his presence there was disconcerting the NU leader, and once he waved sarcastically at him, daring him to do or say something that would get him ejected.

The lupine features of John Leyden could also be discerned among the audience. He had come to listen to the debate before going on to a dinner party, and was accordingly in full black-tie, looking (he was pleasurably aware) like one of the languid aristocrats he was helping to displace. He nodded over at Ben before registering the puffy face of James Fulford sitting among his ill-dressed henchmen. He gave his little superior smile, which girls found so maddeningly attractive, and studied the far-Right leader's saggy profile and saggier clothes. "Poujade in Primark," he thought, and jotted the phrase in his notebook.

As the NU MP listened to the declamations, he felt pathetically grateful to those MPs, mostly from the Fair Play Alliance, who defended his rights while deploring his despicable agenda—and apathetically angry towards the CD MPs, many of whom were reputed to hold views like his in private, and some of whom had allegedly even been NU members. He glanced up towards Ben Klein—bet *he* knew which ones! He looked around at the crammed Chamber, trying to fix each feature in his memory, and wondered if he would be expected to get up and leave as soon as the vote was taken. Presumably. And he mapped out the route for what the papers would no doubt call "the walk of shame" or some such. The prospect was not a pleasant one; all he could hope was that he would do it like a man, and not give the bastards the pleasure of knowing that they'd cut him.

Richard Simpson stood with his legs apart as if braced for foul weather, a pugnacious finger jabbing the air, small gobbets of saliva sailing forth into the large leathery world. He was enjoying himself, conscious of the cameras and unconscious of the sniggers of some fellow legislators. It was a bravura performance, now sarcastic, now outraged, tipping metaphorical garbage over the head of the NU MP—whom Simpson would never mention by name. "…racis', sexis', Islamophobic and 'omophobic hagenda, inconsistent wiv Ar'icle 2 of the Dignity Act, and wiv the UN Charter of Fundamental Yooman Righ's. To these intellectual harguments I add one more—that the presence of this hunspeakable horganisation in This Place is a source of hintimidation for visible hethnic minori'y staff. It is for these reasons, Mr. Speaker, that I move the expulsion of the member for Milltown West, and the proscription of 'is party from these premises which are consecra'ed to the fundamental dignities and inalienable righ's of the yooman bein.'"

Evan Dafydd was next on the order paper, blond and clean, quietly sure, an administrator administering abstractions, eminently reasonably espousing an eminently forgettable philosophy.

"Mr. Speaker, no-one in this room deplores the foul and obnoxious politics of National Union more than our party. Nothing can excuse their abhorrent policies, or gutter tactics of dividing and ruling. However, the fact remains that he has been elected in a fair and free election, for a legal political party, and he has—unfortunately—therefore got an absolute right to be here in this Chamber, representing his electors, and saying what he wants to say consistent with the rule of law. The Honourable Member opposite makes a most eloquent case for expulsion, based on rightful abhorrence of the party's divisive agenda. I will not try the House's patience by reminding them of Martin Niemöller's famous aphorism 'First they came for the Communists…' The parallel is inexact, but tolerance of even the most hateful views is the very essence of our democratic system, forged in adversity over centuries…"

Stanley Symons was as bored as he could ever remember to have been. In a 31-year career characterized by excruciating debates, to some of which he had contributed, he decided this must be classed as one of the worst. And they were only having this bloody vote because of all those blackies who drowned up on the east coast. It all seemed a bit of a fuss about nothing, if you asked him—although no-one ever had, or if they had, he had given such an evasive answer that they had forgotten it even before he had finished speaking.

He extended pinstriped legs out straight in front of him (pink socks just visible, hinting at an inner flamboyance) and tilted his large-lobed head back to look at the barrel-vaulted ceiling, dislodging a small shower of scurf onto his suit. That Pugin feller had known a thing or two. After this charade (not long now), they could all bugger off home.

Later, Dan was filling in an insurance claim form laboriously with the radio on quietly. He stopped writing to listen.

"Tonight, the House of Commons passed a motion to expel the solitary MP from the far-Right National Union, and to ban the party from contesting future general elections. The Bill's sponsor, Richard Simpson MP, spoke to Channel One afterwards—'I'm deligh'ed the 'ouse 'as tiken this view—it's a grite dye for yooman righ's. And now goin' forward we can see clearly a better dye for all our citizens.'

As the announcement was made, there were scuffles and cries of "Judases!," "Traitors!," and "What price democracy?" in the Public Gallery, which had to be cleared by officials. One man was arrested and another was taken to hospital with minor injuries. NU leader James Fulford, who had been in the gallery, was later cautioned by police."

The story disturbed Dan. Obviously he had nothing in common with such extremists—but a democracy was surely a democracy. And if a parliament was not the place to express unpopular views, where was? He exhaled perplexedly; these things were so deep.

Ben had punched the air and cried "*Yeeees!*" when it was announced that the Ayes had it. Thanks to the perversity of the FPA, the margin was narrower than he had hoped, but all the CD MPs present had voted in favour, and that had made the difference.

He looked along gloatingly at James Fulford and saw he was ashen even by his unhealthy-looking standard, while a sidekick—he recognized Daniel Williams of the Romford branch, who had made such a fool of himself on *The Capital Today*—had a look of deep shock. There was also a football shirt-wearing man whom Ben did not recognize, probably a bodyguard with a face and build like that. This man's face was contorted in anger, bellowing "Traitors!" as officials started to converge. He then looked around, conscious of impending manhandling, and unluckily caught Ben's eye as that stalwart raised two middle fingers at the NU delegation and shouted "Fuck you!" It was the work of just a few seconds for Football Shirt to traverse the intervening space, oblivious to Fulford's shouted "NO!" and, dodging the arms of an usher, to land a terrace-experienced *thwaaack* square in Ben's still smiling face, making him describe a partial somersault over the back of the seat and his head connect with the bench behind with considerable force.

The MPs looked up, Stanley Symons grinning at the delightfully outré turn of events—and John Leyden, close but safely out of the action, could not believe his luck. Quick-witted Richard Simpson was already on his feet, triumphantly vindicated by Football Shirt's actions "Members can now see for themselves exactly why we were righ' to tike the vote we took. The hextremist hagenda is lide bare by wot 'as jus' 'appened in the Public Gall'ry…"   Ushers moved in efficiently.

Carole Hassan heard the same bulletin, and the news gave her a brief fillip. It was a hint that her daughter's future would be more certain, where such people would not be able to make the laws.

Her daughter was in bed, and she had taken off her *hijab* to reveal flattened and greasy fair hair and an oval of ivory skin surrounding her slightly more tanned face. She looked at herself ruefully in the cheap mirror about the false fireplace. Once, she would have been ashamed to have seen herself so bedraggled. But now it didn't seem to matter because there was no-one there to see or talk to—let alone *touch* her.

She was smoking, a habit she had given up because of her husband's disapproval, but which she had now taken up again out of sheer boredom. Worse, she had drunk a few tins of lager. She always argued with herself on these nights, which were becoming more frequent, that sometimes she just needed it, OK? It wasn't as if she didn't do enough for Islam during the day. Allah would empathise; she didn't remember smoking being mentioned in the Koran. OK, she definitely shouldn't be drinking—but her husband had drunk sometimes. It had been after one such bout that he had come home and hit her so hard across the face that he had broken two of her teeth—and that night she had packed a few things, picked up her daughter, and left him to go the women's refuge. She had never gone back to him, despite all his threats, and she had stayed in the refuge until she heard that he had gone back, humiliated, to Pakistan. That was now almost two years ago, and there had been no man since.

It was much too quiet at nights, when activism was over and all there was was the dreary house in the dreary Close, 40 identically badly built houses with mold in the kitchens, and outside, faintly menacing shifting shadows. It was mostly at nights that she reproached herself for her choices and when she felt a passionate longing for the people and things of her girlhood, to be able to go out into the world again and do what other women of her age were doing—to use this still desirable body and her spirit before it was too late. She imagined what it would be like to talk to a man again, and see desire rather than discomfort in his eyes—a man, perhaps, like that handsome Miracle Migrant, about whom the media were saying such horrible Islamophobic things.

Jim Moore was at "his lovely home" (*Society Style*) in one of those parts of Hertfordshire that are separated from London by a few scrappy fields and shreds of snobbery. *Society Style* had *adored* his *hacienda*-style house on a new and un-Hispanic cul-de-sac looking onto an award-winning golf course—and he was proud of it, too, and of himself, for having conjured it into being solely through the magic of his vocal cords. It was filled with new furniture in the Sheraton style, and the white walls between full height windows were decorated with platinum discs and pictures of Jim with everyone from the Queen and the Prime Minister to Atrocities Against Civilians.

He had lilac carpets, coffee tables staged with beautiful, unreadable books on *Tuscan Style* or *Wonders of the Universe*, and in pride of place on the 30-foot-long glass table, a trilby under a glass dome that had once belonged to Frank Sinatra—for which he had paid an amount that even now made him feel slightly dizzy. But was he not the much-acclaimed, much-purchased "Sinatra of the suburbs"? If Frankie was looking down, Jim knew he would have approved.

Everything in the room was wired so he could control ventilation, temperature, sound, satellite TV, security gates, garage doors, CCTV, external lights, swimming pool controls, servant buzzers, and even the rarely-used ovens from any room or anywhere in the immaculate

Italianate garden. His wife was out there at the moment, somewhere out of sight, showing his new young producer the gardens. They'd been gone ages; what *were* they doing?

He sometimes wondered…no, he mustn't think along *those* lines. It was bad for his heart. Anyway, she had never given him the least grounds to suspect her of anything—and yet she was so pretty, and he…well! He stomped up and down, muttering, the tension pains in his chest very bad tonight.

He turned up the radio very loud using the Techno-Wand, enjoying the ease with which the task was done (should be easy, at that price!) and listened interestedly to the news.

So they've banned that lot—hardly surprising, really. Funny, really—he knew people who had voted for them. Mum, for one. His neighbour still voted for them. They all thought it would save the country or something. But the world moves on…He winced at the bubbling stress in his chest.

Dylan looked exhaustedly out of his window towards the great black blank of Hackney Marshes, hiding who knew what horrors, what prejudices, what feral boys waiting to make jiggy with middle-class joggers. But then he had been something of a feral boy himself the previous night, with that mad escapade against the Gowt place, which exploit had even made a sketchy appearance on the TV news.

But he was paying for it now—physically, because he hadn't been to sleep in almost 36 hours, and mentally, because he was sick with worry, half expecting the police to come calling.

He was also angry to learn that he was not as much in control of his passions as he had hoped. He was, after all, a serious person, engaged in serious business. Last night was the first time he had done anything like that—and it would be the last time, ever. As befitted a serious person, he listened to the news with a thin smile. NU banned! Another milestone attained, another logical step taken, the law catching up with the street, as so often before.

But there were still many steps on this ladder with no topmost rung. There would be new injustices, new challenges. He had heard about a CD MP who had said a few *interesting* things... Then there were all these stories about the Anglo-Saxon Alliance, a new militant organisation. The report he had just read about them was full of alarming imagery— "40 motorcycle gang members conducted a PAGAN ceremony to summon OCCULT powers...they sat around venting HATE." Tonight's news was excellent, but there was still a vast hooded country out there beyond the lights of reason—a country that would always be in need of cleansing.

John had made it to his dinner party and had at first been annoyed to find himself sitting beside, of all people, Gavin Montgomery. But the discomfort had passed; Gavin had been his usual inarticulate self, so John had steamed in to steal the show, as so often before at other parties. And tonight he had an extra advantage—everyone had adored, even as they abhorred, his story of the assault on poor Ben Klein.

But now it was very late, and most guests had gone home or sloped off to find places where they could sleep off the assorted intoxicants. Most had found beds or sofas, but a few lay where they had been overcome. A girl from an art gallery had passed out in a chair across the room and was unknowingly displaying an enticing expanse of thigh. John found this very distracting, as he thought of pleasantries to impart to his new boss. The cannabis was helping greatly. They were at the stage when everything made them laugh—even the very fact that their bow-ties had been untied, and their legs could not presently support their weight. Their hostess had gone to bed, accompanied by a stockbroker on the rebound from his third failed marriage.

John and Gavin had examined the prints on the walls, in such bad taste that they were really in ironic good taste. John had told Gavin, in considerable detail, all about the artists. But for John, always sensitive to interior decoration and what it signified about society, the sensibility which found such pictures wryly amusing seemed itself out of date. The New Earnestness Movment was very well timed, he advised Gavin. I know old thingie who runs it—good friend of mine, great bloke. If you like, I'll profile him for the Arts section.

Gavin had nodded goodnaturedly and his easy acquiescence made John laugh all over again. What a clown! He could run rings around someone like Gavin. They talked about the party, and who'd been there earlier—the *Meteor* columnist, that stockbroker now abed with *über*-slag Louise, and that big African who had looked so miserable that just remembering his face set them laughing again. All evening the big man had sat quietly, out of his depth, unaware of who was showing what in whose gallery, who was shagging who, what bands were hot and which decidedly not. He had never even heard of New Earnestness. All he would talk about was politics and his family, who were still out in Zaire, or Zambia or Zanzibar or wherever it was—no-one could quite remember. Began with Z, anyway. People had got bored when his conversation kept reverting to the war. John didn't know much about the local situation, so he drove the talk swiftly into other channels.

Only once had the African's conversation aroused any interest, when he had referred to a prominent interior designer as a "faggot"—and that had been the wrong sort of interest. Forks froze in mid-air, there was a raised eyebrow or two, sidelong glances, someone cleared their throat—and then the conversation flowed freezingly on. He had disappeared hours before, and he had been a Grade A *bore*, John averred loudly. The African had been so fucking earnest that John had started to dislike him.

Encouraged by Gavin's apparent agreement, now the recklessly stoned John did something totally out of character—something he would never have done had he not inhaled so much good stuff. Pulling himself up to his full height, looking as portentous as he could, making his voice rich and resonant, he half-mimicked, half-exaggerated the African's voice.

"In my country today, dere is a major crisis of legitimacy, and dere is much unrest. How I worry about my family in Matuba Province!"

His impersonation was very close to the mark, but even if it had not been, he and Gavin would have laughed just as much. In some remote cerebral chamber, he did wonder vaguely whether such a caricature might be racist. But then, he explained to Gavin, *of course*, he wasn't. He was just treating the black bloke as a human being—looking beyond the skin to the individual, do you hear what I'm saying, mate? It's like, you know, overcoming stereotypes through subverting them. It's post-racial realism. And besides, everyone knows *my* views! So he continued the mimicry, and they continued to laugh. The accent was contagious, and John outdid himself by saying famous lines from films in the same rumbling African accent.

John had just said "De name's Bond, James Bond," when he noticed a disembodied, round dark shape in the middle of the wall. He tried fuzzily to work out how it had got there, all by itself in the middle of that vertical plane, and then realised that there was a mirror, and the mirror faced the doorway behind him. He swivelled around, his lips forming naturally into his winning smile.

The Zambian stared expressionlessly, and even through the narcotic curtain, John felt nervous. He was a big bloke, after all. He wanted to say something that would defuse the situation, but could think of nothing.

"Oh, hi, er… I thought you'd gone ages ago?"

That rich voice came—really very like John's impersonation: "I just wanted to let you know that I'm heading off now. Everyone else seems to have gone, or they're stoned. Natasha's in the kitchen—out cold on the floor. I would have put her into a chair, but they're all occupied. She's fine now, but can you check her occasionally? I wouldn't want her to come to any harm. She's a nice girl."

"Yeh, mate, no problemo. Are you going then?"

The man nodded and was about to withdraw, when John spoke quickly. Drugged-up he may have been, but there was a need to explain.

"I think I know what you were thinking. You were thinking I was doing impersonations of you. But you're wrong; I wasn't. So if that's what you were thinking, you were wrong to think it…DAMN!"

The last word was because through the druggy dream had shone a forensic ray of light which lit up his babblings all too clearly. The African said nothing, just stood there looking blandly from John to Gavin.

"I'm afraid I didn't get your name, er…?" Still no sign.

"The thing is, mate, I'm John Leyden. Maybe you haven't heard of me in—wherever it is you're from—but I'm very well known in this country. I write articles and shit, and I just wanted to say that being racist to someone like you would be the *last* thing I would *ever* do. You'd better believe it—the last thing I would ever do!"

He banged the table (it hurt his fingers, because it was much closer than he had expected) to emphasise his passion. His heart swelled with swift love for all Africans—like this one, standing there so patient, polite, taking the long view, authentic.

"I don't doubt that, Mr.—er—Layburn. Now if there's nothing else…"

"LEYDEN! L-E-Y-D-E-N. John Leyden. No, not a thing, mate. I just wanted to explain myself! But now I shall bid you *adieu*."

John's final flourish—his hands waved mock-dismissively as if shooing away an insect—was intended to be humorous. The disconcerting head vanished and with it its mirrored alter ego. A few seconds later, John and Gavin heard the front door thump shut—and they looked at each other again, and laughed and laughed, enjoying the sudden absence of reserve. Standing below the open window, the African shook his head in sadness and disgust, before heading off into the dawn.

Albert often found it difficult to sleep, and then he would stay up all night listening to music, reading or watching old films. As the Zambian was walking away from the party, Albert drained a glass of port and shifted his raw silk dressing gowned bulk on the Knole sofa. He had the almost too richly furnished, too traditional room to himself. He was aware that it was too richly furnished and too English to be quite English, but he enjoyed the delicate hint of exotica and foreignness the scheme conveyed. It brought him into distant comforting contact with his ancestors, who had also lived sumptuously, in but not always *of* their countries, and whose most strenuous efforts to fit in to wherever they were had so often made them merely the objects of suspicion from those who felt no need to prove themselves.

Anthony had gone to bed hours ago, leaving Albert to air-conduct Purcell. He was always glad to be alone, without being looked to all the time for witty remarks, which even Anthony seemed to expect—because tonight's news had made him even more than usually despondent.

It had been on the cards ever since it was first mooted the previous year by that ghastly Simpson—but Albert had dared to hope against his whole life's experience that *somewhere* in *some* MPs' innermost aortas there persisted some modicum of moral courage. But if so, it had not persisted in enough of them, and so the thing was done. The last legal political expression of the national character that Albert had simultaneously deprecated and defended since he could remember had been edited out of political life.

Those last, un-Hansarded shouts from the Public Gallery—those anguished "Judases" and "Traitors"—those had been perhaps the last shouts of Englishmen speaking *as Englishmen* in their own Parliament. And all those obtuse, ahistorical timeservers, those Simpsons, Smiths and McKerras—almost all of the media—almost all of the late-night listeners to this bulletin—these would be unheeding, unknowing, uncaring that earlier that evening they had executed England.

Some of the stupidest and nastiest people in Parliament would be congratulating themselves even now in some filthy club, getting pissed on lager or alcopops, handshaking, backsmacking, and osculating, telling themselves over and over in adenoidal tones that they had struck a stupendous blow on behalf of the soon-to-be-reshaped-universe. He toyed with his oldest and darkest daydream of them all, of standing tasteful and tall beside an ever lengthening line of bound traitors, about to give the order to mow them down in swathes and leave them lying disregarded, the-murderers-of-England-themselves-murdered.

The spasm passed, as so often before, and once again he was rueful and reflective, his lip curled in a cynical semi-smile at the lovely ludicrous image. He used the remote control to navigate between tracks until he found the valediction he had been seeking—an unutterably sad declining ground on baroque guitar and theorbo, a thrillingly clear female voice, and the plaint of Dido bidding farewell to Aeneas:

> *When I am laid in earth –*
>
> *Remember me, remember me,*
>
> *But oh, forget my fate…*
>
> *Remember me, remember me,*
>
> *But oooooh, forget my fate.*

Carthage had been a great power, too.

Chapter 23

THE USES OF LITERATURE

City of London
Thursday, 2nd October

It was *Der Tag*—the unveiling of the long-anticipated "collaborative" Broadside. The grand old behemoth was back in its original location and given its usual prominence—and reading it while drinking his first skinny decaf of the day, Dougie felt real pride. It was the best thing he had ever done—or co-done. A little courage, a little leadership was all that had been required, and he had prevailed over his formidable adversary. He hoped Albert would come to see that he had been right; he toyed with the fantasy that the old curmudgeon might even ring to thank him. He could almost hear the break in the old guy's voice as he rumbled gratefully down the line.

But in fact its author—or co-author—was reading the copy with very different feelings—almost physical pain. The youth had even changed the title from "The stormtroopers of love" to "Progressives call into question 'free speech.'" Albert hated the inverted commas around "free speech"—and that there were none around "Progressives." It was throwing the argument before it had even begun. But what infuriated him was the management-speak—"This newspaper has always espoused equality of opportunity and of outcome, but this does not mean there are not legitimate questions that can be asked about the methodologies utilized to achieve key aspirations." Dougie's copy-editor had even replaced "Muslim" and "black" with "visible-minority communities," because Dougie had thought this less confrontational. Albert did not much mind being thought vile, but he hated being thought responsible for such crimes against the language.

Sentinel loyalists read the column with faint dissatisfaction, feeling (not that most could articulate the emotion) they had been given water when they had expected ale. The half-hoped-for, half-feared cannonade had become—a popgun. It was Albert, yet not him—as if he were sick and light-headed. Broadside had once leapt bristlingly off the page, awful but alive, but this installment plopped stillborn to the floor. A few over-complicatedly thought it was some kind of a joke—one they didn't get.

But the only thing that annoyed Dougie was that the emollient tone and equivocations of this column had apparently made no difference to the planned demonstration.

The No Borders Now! Chair (it was Arabella from the Thorpe Gilbert demo) was interviewed on the morning news, and Albert was sorrier than ever that he had agreed to censor his column. He was reminded again that he had real power—a strange enchantment that could yank seemingly rational strangers out of their condom-strewn bedrooms early in the morning to stand about and shout all day on behalf of people they had never known, and probably would not like. His gorge rose as he watched the TV in the bedroom; he gave a running commentary down the phone to Anthony, who was in the gallery, half-listening while trying to write a business letter.

"Look at 'em—oh, I forgot there's no telly there. A load of stupid well-educated children, trustafarians all, dolts acquiescing in their dispossession, shouting about their niceness the way a beggar shows his sores to the punters! They're a kind of skin disease, except serious…no, it's not gross…I'm being strictly factual. As you know, I am wedded to scientific objectivity…And you should hear what they're saying. A bit of Mao, a bit of management-training manual, and trace elements of Methody parson. Not a bad looking girl, either, if only she'd keep her mouth shut. At least if the lights were low, in the right kind of clothes and if her hair was done—but above all, if she was quiet! Some people never know when to stop talking, do they? Ha, ha. Very fucking funny, but at least I don't make a damn fool of myself every time I open my big mouth. At least, not all the time! All right, all right, I'll let you go and fleece some of the Great Wen's gullibles."

He hung up and gave his full attention to the TV. Arabella was still speaking, in her poorly disguised upper-middle-class tones.

"The shareholders of the *Sentinel* should be constantly aware of how their work contributes to race equality and promoting good race relations. They should seriously consider whether having such a vociferous xenophobe in such a prominent role is compatible with the ethics of their company, their obligations under race-relations legislation, and the human rights of their BME employees. I seriously doubt that it is, and these outrageous columns should lead to his position being immediately reviewed. We also invite the paper to reconsider its editorial line and join the 21st century. It is irresponsible to appeal to people's fears rather than their hopes. Even if Mr. Norman's columns do not overtly refer to race, they are clearly creating an opportunity for those who are inclined to come to those conclusions. Free speech simply cannot override issues of human rights and morality."

"Reviewed"! "Invite"! She had nice, Home Counties style—charming smiles and beatific bromides, backed up by merciless stiletto thrusts.

"We believe immigration controls are inherently racist, and inexcusable by any standard. Immigration controls lead only to suffering, deaths, and human-rights abuses...They are a cruel aberration everyone finds offensive."

Albert couldn't help admiring her skill. She was pressing all the fluffy futurological buttons, while sweetly implying violence if their "suggestions" were not met. She was an emblematic opponent, and he was sorry that the morning's column was not a worthy weapon to aim at her and her chuckle-headed kind. Her best moment was when she was asked about the possibility of infiltration by violent groups.

"Of course, we don't condone violence, but sometimes the completely understandable frustration of anti-racists and community activists will spill over into unlawful activities—especially when the laws are illegitimate. Racist views are themselves acts of violence, and a blow at human dignity. Our mass rally is open to any members of the public who feel strongly about these issues, and of course we cannot control who might turn up in a democratic society. The policing of our legitimate protest is a matter for the police, and we cannot take any responsibility for their shortcomings."

It was a perfect touch—simultaneously assailing the system and hiding behind the police in case any nasty rough boys turned up. Again Albert rued his self-censorship. How he would have liked to face down these so-sure-of-themselves people, without apology, without demur, without compromise! It would have been a check to these cocksure cherubim to have their old bear opponent come out growling and at a run, showing yellow but still serviceable fangs and still with a kind of decayed massive strength—able still to inflict some damage, pull down some of the tormenting dogs and mark others, before the inevitable denouement, the last blood-flecked struggle before the younger animals rose in Pyrrhic pride, clasping his decapitated head by its grizzled locks.

The only thing that comforted him was thinking that Dougie would by now know that his gambit had failed. Albert hoped it would be a *really* big protest, and daydreamed pleasantly about Dougie being manhandled by the mob he had wished to mollify—a postmodern Philippe d'Egalité, *mais sans le panache*.

At about 11:30, the organizers arrived and were shepherded into a railed-off area across the road from the *Sentinel* offices, watched warily by 12 policemen. They had placards and whistles, and Arabella had a loudhailer. Her distorted voice made itself heard as high as Albert's 15th-floor office—but what the protestors did not know was that he was never in the office on Thursdays.

"Albert Norman, racist scum—We will shut him down; no racists in our town—Racist scum, we will fight, we know where you sleep at night!"

Watching at home, Albert had winced at the metre, and joked to Anthony that he would have to go and lie down for a while to recover. And he did switch it off at last and picked a book at random from the shelves. It was *The Fairie Queene*, a book which always appealed to his macabre personality, because of its contrast between its even then archaic romanticism and the author's day job of slaughtering the Irish rebels on behalf of Tudor modernity. It fell open at Canto XI, where he was amused to see a relevant verse:

> *Slaunderous reproches, and fowle infamies,*
>
> *Leasings, backbytings, and vaine-glorious crakes,*
>
> *Bad counsels, praises, and false flatteries.*

That to him had always been the chief use of literature, to make one remember that however awful things and people were, they had all been seen before, and they would always be seen until the end of time, if time ever ended. He lost himself in the story as often before.

An hour later the mass rally had attracted only 34 participants, and the words came less frequently and with less conviction, starting to tail off altogether. A few peeled away "to the shops"—which everyone knew really meant home. The relieved police commander exhaled and moved most of the officers onto other duties. The increasingly piccolo picket became a small street entertainment, watched with mild interest by passing local office workers, most of whom had no idea what it was about. By 2 o'clock, there were only two officers left on duty, standing bored but comfortable in the sun, when a group of five men with masks and iron bars ran quickly and silently along the road.

They came up behind an elderly journalist who was returning for what he had planned as a pleasingly uneventful afternoon on the Autos Features newsdesk. He knew there was some kind of demonstration, but being utterly uninterested in politics had paid it no attention. He knew nothing of Albert Norman except the name.

Something else he did not know was that he bore a passing resemblance to that ogre—similar age, similar physique, grizzled graying hair, a jacket and tie, old school, old attitudes.

He was thinking about Volvos and how the sun glittered on the dragon weathervane of the church he had never once explored in 36 years of working next door to it. One-and-a-half seconds after these sapient reflections, an iron bar descended pulverisingly onto his cranium, and he felt himself falling, apparently from a very great height. Then his face was pressed sideways onto the warm stone pavement, which he registered for a mica-flecked second before steel-toed boots kicked his glasses into his eyes. There was just time for him to register a confused and ferocious tumult, screams from a glimpsed girl in a blue trouser suit, a segment of sky and scared pigeons, a red flood, and then a sort of signing-out while his left-behind body jerked and shuddered with incessant impacts.

The policemen dashed the few hundred yards to help, and at exactly that moment, another small group of masked men came from the opposite direction and ploughed in through the doors of Sentinel House, in a shining shower of glass. The receptionist screamed and ran into the toilet—which was just as well, as crowbars cracked crushingly on her desk, smashing her phone, a plant and the 19th-century *Sentinel* sign that had been salvaged from the old building and re-erected in the lobby by a 1980s owner as a deceitful symbol of continuity.

The Antiguan security guard made bravely for one of the young men, but was pushed to the ground where he lay wriggling in amongst the remains of the yucca and shattered glass. A crowbar caught him in his solar plexus, and he lay there seeking desperately for breath, as other bars caught him across the throat and agonizingly on his shins. One attacker threw red paint all around the foyer, before they all re-emerged as one, bowling over the policeman who had run back in response, easily outpacing him and the lame security guard, amazingly up on his feet despite what was later proved to have been a broken ankle.

The cleverly planned attack had only taken around a minute and a half, and the assailants just as swiftly melted back into the horrified onlookers, haring off, shoving bars, gloves, jumpers, and masks into holdalls, splitting up and slowing into walking as they turned several corners and heard the pursuit fade, making their way on foot eventually to remote Tube stations where the CCTV cameras would not be able to make connections, their hearts filled with eldritch joy at their exploits. Back at Sentinel House, there was a carpet of glass, and a ruckus of police and everyone talking at once, except for atypically speechless Arabella, who sat on the curb hiding her acne behind shaking hands.

London Cable News showed the events within a few minutes, courtesy of a quick-witted tourist who had recorded it on his phone. Ben Klein watched it in bed, with a huge white bandage over his nose, which he found very distracting.

The Yahoo's fist had collapsed the cartilage of his nose in on itself, and the whole appendage was twisted out of shape, and throbbing so much that he couldn't sleep, even with the painkillers. The back of his head was also throbbing where he had hit it as he had fallen. He felt slightly dizzy with concussion. But through these discomforts, he felt satisfaction.

The thug would, of course, go to prison, and NU had been banned, as Ben had advocated—and the incident had demonstrated that he had been right all along about the nature of the party and the constant danger of fascism. Even the *Sentinel* had taken that view; it had suddenly become a much pleasanter paper.

That had been an unfortunate incident outside the *Sentinel* that morning, which would elicit awkward questions. The people who had done it would presumably argue that in a war, there is no such thing as a non-combatant, and that even a motoring correspondent for a rag like the *Sentinel* bore a modicum of moral responsibility for the views of their editorialists. Ben had met people like that—he could even guess at the identity of some of the perpetrators—and had sympathy for their view. No doubt some of the munitions workers incendiarized in the firebombings of the Ruhr had been agreeable enough in their private lives.

But try as he might—and he did try—Ben couldn't hate all of the people he had dedicated himself to eradicating from public life. Once in a while he even came across one he felt he might have liked, had he met him in some other context. He had occasionally been talking to someone in an attempt to gather information and had found himself briefly forgetting why he was there—just relaxing into the company, enjoying the moment, finding the joke genuinely funny, the observation genuinely insightful. The boundaries would sometime break down, and he and they would meet in their minds just for a moment, before spinning away again.

Once in a weak while, he would feel remorse for someone he had exposed—like that Croatian Cistercian, who had died a few weeks after he had been expelled from his monastery. He had deserved it, and he was old and going to die anyway…*but*…the man had once been very young, perhaps misled, and, after all, living in the worst war of them all. He often regretted the impulse that had made him scrawl "Yes!" across the man's picture on his wall. He had considered taking it down—but he had always told himself it must stay, as a reflection of his mood at that time. It was therefore part of history—and ideally history should never be curtailed, any more than people's lives. Wherever history led, one needed to be honest to it, and to oneself.

He wondered what Albert Norman was feeling about the events of this morning—whether he would be honest enough to assume the moral responsibility. Because it *was* his. Ben hoped he would be man enough to own up to it, and not to turn it into one of his inexplicable jokes. Because it was not a joke, could never be a joke. Albert's time was all too obviously up; it was time for him to recant and rejoin his people.

Had he ever seen it, Ben would have found Albert's almost orientally splendid bedroom with its carefully placed paintings and ceramics profoundly disturbing, because of its implied lack of interest in the world's problems. But at that moment, the world's problems were very much on Albert's mind.

Alerted by Sally, Albert watched aghast the events on TV—the wobbly and fuzzy journalist being beaten down by big-shouldered masked men yelling venomous things, a dizzying turning blur of buildings and open mouths, a crooked clip of the backs of the second group as they raced away while a policeman and limping guard spilled out in a quickly-abandoned attempt at pursuit.

He kept running over and over in his head what Sally had said—"They mistook that *poor* man for *you!*" Her voice had been full of compassion—and something Albert had never registered in her voice before, something rather like disgust. Disgust for *him*—the so-clever man who must have known what he was playing with.

Albert had not known the victim, had never even heard his name. He never read any of the supplements as a matter of principle; he shared the professional journalist's disdain for advertorials, and besides didn't believe in pandering to public frivolity. In any case, all modern cars looked the same.

But this awful thing shocked him more deeply than anything else he could remember. This had happened solely because of something *he* had written. He may as well have wielded those iron bars himself. He had always known that the swollen ranks of his opponents included a minority of stupid and violent children in adult bodies, emotional axolotls, full of testosterone and theology, always-on-the-edge-of-angry. He had always slightly relished the idea that he was baiting such people by writing what he wrote, by being who and what he was. But it had always been abstract. He had never thought he would ever really be attacked—although he hoped he would have been consistent enough not to have whined too much had it ever happened. The assailants were after all prisoners of their own emotional incontinence and could no more have helped hitting him than a mosquito could decline to bite.

But this determined and perhaps lethal assault on someone so utterly innocent of evil thoughts, or any thoughts—this presumably respectable taxpayer, of the sort Albert had always professed to love and serve—was inexpressibly awful.

Albert imagined a wife, children and grandchildren, neighbours receiving the news in their semi-detached home in Uxbridge or somewhere from a kind policewoman—or even worse seeing the footage by chance and recognizing their husband, father, brother, friend in the falling figure. The man might die—*die*—and if he did, Albert and Albert alone would be to blame. No opinion was worth *that*. No witticisms were worth an elderly infant's crushed cranium.

After he had watched the clip three times, he sat still and silent for almost an hour. In the background, the phone rang repeatedly, and the sun stalked across the antique kilim, bringing to tasteful life its muted oxbloods and cobalts. He could hear tinny, urgent voices leaving messages, but he didn't care who they were or what they were saying. He could guess. His journalistic life was passing before him, a review of things that had once seemed impressive and important, but now just appeared ridiculous.

Almost from the outset of his "career," when he had filed his first article at the age of 20 (one of the few really thrilling moments in his life had been the first time he saw his name in print), he had been out of touch, out of sympathy. Such notions had always delighted him. As he watched the world worsen, the cosmos coarsen, he hugged to himself the knowledge that *he* at least was not to blame. He had *told* his countrymen, he at least had tried to strip away the trumpery and reveal the skeleton beneath the rotten flesh. As time depleted his stock of things to say and brought its payloads of disappointments and damaged goods, he was perversely proud that he was becoming a caricature of a caricature, an interesting irrelevancy—but someone who was also *right*, and would one day be remembered for having been right when everyone else was wrong.

There was always the faint hope that in some recesses of some minds his endless iteration of eternal verities was having an effect—that maybe *this* parliament would bring something more than the semblance of change. Maybe *this* year would be published *the* book he had wanted to write—the comprehensive apologium, the elegant explication that would hold the line against all the madness, shock the stupid into silence, and allow the essential English to wake from their unquiet dreams. *Ach*, what a fool he had been, to think of such things even semi-seriously, even for a second. That hope was dead, had died decades ago, had never lived.

When it came to it, now, today, in this revelatory moment, Albert finally knew that it had all been a total waste of time. It had been an exercise in sheer vanity. He had wasted his life and misled thousands, even millions, of readers of his half-believed columns—offering a nugatory hope, holding up a signet ring to be kissed, a flag to be saluted, while all the time he himself stood humorously aloof—almost *wanting* to fail, because to a mind like his, failure was sweeter than even the most stunning success could ever have been.

There had never been any real humour in the equation, and Broadside had really been what so many had averred—the dyspeptic last rites of an old order declining to go gracefully. And he *was* old, hideously so, his physical age and ill-health exacerbated by his serio-comic ultra-views on every question. After this awful thing, there was no longer any savour in his lifelong game.

Shaking his head slowly as if dispelling delusion, he picked up the phone and asked to speak to Dougie. He had gone to see the journalist in hospital—editor-like, Albert thought approvingly—but the secretary said, "He does *particularly* want to speak to you, Mr. Norman."

Albert found out the hospital, promised the secretary he wouldn't speak to the press and would be available for a phone call at 4. Then he ordered six bottles of his favourite single malt to be delivered to the injured man's bedside. He dictated a card too: "I'm *so* sorry. It's all my fault. It should have been me. Is there anything I can do? Just ask. I'll come and see you. Good luck and get well—Albert Norman." He put his phone number at the end.

It should have been me. It should have been *me*. The phrase reverberated. There would have been a justice in it, a certain panache. It would have been a compliment to him to have been struck down by equality's angels, like the Romanovs in the cellar.

The small hand on the 18th-century porcelain mantle clock ticked thinly towards the IV, as precisely as if it was still clicking into some brittle Tuileries *salon*—and the langorous shepherd and shepherdess reclining above the dial seemed to loom larger. Albert found himself staring at the shepherdess's slender bare foot.

It was a beautiful piece of modelling—a delicate classical conceit wrought from clay, animal bone, and ash in a Paris of poverty, disease, and Encyclopedists. That was what he liked about the clock—the refashioning of ordure into order, ugliness into beauty, the triumph of elegant inconsequentiality over boring function. But it was only ever a temporary triumph. The clock had somehow survived the centuries unbroken, but the spirit that had called it into being had gone extinct. No-one believed in anything now, except vile things; ugliness and beauty had changed places, charm had become *kitsch*, commitment was camp, and earnestness irony.

The clock was ticking louder in the irrelevant room, and its face was glowing larger—until Albert wondered if anyone from outside was hearing this same extraordinary noise that was in his head. Then clock and phone both came to life—and he extended a suddenly certain hand towards the receiver.

It had been hurtful—although career-advancing—to John early in his career when Albert had made him the butt of his raillery, including no fewer than seven "Broken Record Awards." He had never quite forgiven him for this, although he tried to pity him. But even leaving aside this personal interest, Albert's departure was worthy of a valedictory column, and he had written this with a mildly carefree feeling, as if hearing that human rights workers had reached the scene of some distant disaster.

> With the sudden resignation of Albert Norman from the *Sentinel*, a new and more hopeful era has begun for British society. For almost 50 years, twice a week, Norman's Broadside column served up patriotic pabulum for a defiantly lower-middle-class audience. It was a column marked occasionally by mordant wit, which sometimes hit upon a truth by accident, but underneath roiled a malignant matrix of acrid prejudices, of the kind that many of us have dedicated our lives to eradicating. It looks as if our criticisms finally turned the scale.
>
> For Albert Norman, all the wasms were still isms—and the jingoism, nationalism, racism, sexism, Islamophobia, homophobia, and disablism that have been eradicated across the rest of the British media festered and throve under his satrapy. His column was peripheral to political policy, but it was indisputably *there*, a canker on the green leaves of Hope and Progress. How a seemingly well-educated man could have held onto such antediluvian views through decades of relentless change—how he could not have seen the damage he was doing, not only to society but to himself—will probably always be a puzzle.

Another presently unanswerable question is what exactly his readers will do now for racist 'inspiration'. But we can be sure that their bile will find other outlets, and no doubt Christian Democrat strategists are already attempting to shore up what is for them a key demographic. So three cheers for Norman's too-long-delayed departure—for which I hope this column may take some small part of the credit—but even as we are celebrating, we should turn our thoughts to the emerging battlefields on freedom's front line.

Chapter 24
TRUTH TO POWER

London
Thursday, 9th October—Thursday, 6th November

It was unusual for Wilberforce Smith to feel warmly towards *News From The Inside*. The Channel One documentary strand had often explored episodes he would rather have been left in kindly obscurity. But he snorted good-naturedly as he watched from the overflowing kitchen table at Number 10, while tadpoles of rain rushed down the window outside. He was eating spaghetti bolognese from a microwave dish, and a trickle of orange sauce was trickling unnoticed down his chin and onto official papers.

A man wearing a flak-jacket and a pained expression was standing in a radiant street, eyes narrowed against the dust and glare.

"We came to Basra with the best intentions—to explore the human story of a man we had taken to our hearts. We found a hoax that fooled a nation."

"Ibraham Nassouf, the so-called 'Miracle Migrant,' was never involved in anti-Saddam activism and was never tortured by Saddam's secret police. Not only that, but for years, he was a bodyguard and enforcer for one of Iraq's most notorious gangland bosses. Tonight, we reveal the incredible story of The Refugee Who Never Was."

The PM had never believed in Ibraham's torture story, but even he was surprised by some of the program's revelations. He seemed to have been instrumental in all sorts of unpleasant activity in the detention center in Greece—sexual harassment of a female human-rights lawyer (the PM sniggered at this), making an unprovoked attack on some Sudanese man called Mandoor, and even starting a riot, during which he had contrived to escape. A resourceful sort of a feller, it seemed. These revelations presumably meant he could be expelled nice and quickly, which would offset some of the recent bad polling on immigration. The PM whistled tunelessly as he pushed aside the smeary plate and got to work on his red box, leaving carmine fingerprints on the top sheet of a confidential defence review.

Of course, it had been old Albert Norman who had broken the story the previous month—not long before he had resigned after that incident when the other hack had been nearly killed. He wondered how many people would remember that—very few, probably. In a strange way, he felt he would miss Albert's acerbic take on life, which was so very different from all the other papers. It reflected some perverse aspect of English identity, a kind of dour, ultra-individualist, small-c conservatism, which persisted despite decades of official disapproval from the likes of—well, himself!

He had been annoyed by Albert's tongue-in-cheek "endorsement" of a few years ago, which some of the more literal-minded WP MPs had taken at face value—and by a few of the disobliging things the old fossil had come out with since then. But in the end, it hadn't hindered his getting the premiership, and Albert had been just as hard, in fact often harder, on the CDs. That was a kind of family squabble, and they were often the worst. And he could be hilarious—and just once in a while, as with the "Miracle Migrant," the old man had put his fat finger on something everyone else had chosen not to see. It would be a duller mediaverse without him. However, his disappearance had removed one of the last remaining obstacles to a *Sentinel* endorsement. The young editor down there must be one of the right sort. He made a note in his sauce-stained notepad to phone him.

There was one more piece of good news that night. That combed-over creep Jim Moore had dropped dead that afternoon of a too-long-deferred heart attack. The only possible drawback, mused the PM, was that his publishers would almost certainly rush out a "Best of…" collection. An amused tic flickered in his left eye; he had always had a highly developed musical sensibility.

Ibraham had been in an agony of impatience all that day. For the last fortnight, ever since those journalists had started to direct increasingly awkward questions via Mr. Basser he had withdrawn into himself—refusing to meet them or answer their questions in writing, refusing to explain himself even to Basser, whom he suspected shrewdly of being in the journalists' pay. Basser had looked on with amused contempt as he squirmed and demurred—and Ibraham knew that even if the program was never shown, his story would get out into the public domain. Again and again, he cursed himself for having got so carried away at the press conference. He had hated even the positive press coverage; he began to realize what it might be like to be the focus of less fulsome attentions.

It was not just that the exposure of his fabrications would undermine—probably fatally—his asylum application. It was also the thought that he would be portrayed to millions of people as a fraud—and a fool. This was an appalling thought. For it to be on British TV meant everyone would believe it was all true. After all, as he had been told in classes at the holding centre, Britain prided itself on its precious traditions of free speech, open media, and fairness.

He saw a thousand phantoms—his street, central Basra, Kemali laughing with Saddam, jets dashing overhead, the beach at Crisby, the ill-starred press conference—and Lavrion. Most of what the programme was alleging was mostly true, but he was astounded by just how wrong they'd got the section on Lavrion. He was angered to see Mandoor, being filmed in what looked like a restaurant and looking well-fed and prosperous, saying in all seriousness that Ibraham and two Egyptian had set upon him and robbed him—and then there were the other false allegations, about Miss Karatakis and starting the riot. He began to think maybe he should have spoken to the journalists after all. He tried to explain about all these things to Basser and the interpreter nodded, but Ibraham had an idea he was being humoured.

His only comfort was a vague superstition that maybe all these tribulations had been "sent." His mother had always insisted there was A Plan, to which he had always smiled sadly, seeing it as just part of her incapacity, her means of dealing with all the tragedies and disappointments of her life. But during the dangers and difficulties of his journey, he had reevaluated all kinds of things and found himself relying more and more on this psychological prop. As he had moved physically, he had also been travelling extensively inside himself. Just maybe, he thought, he had been foreordained not only to leave, but also to return. Maybe he would emerge on the far side cleansed—able to start again somewhere no one knew him, in some small but useful way. The troubles at home couldn't go on for ever; they'd be needing men like him to help rebuild. He was still relatively young and could help shape a new reality in what was, after all, his home.

Basser took pity and tried to rally him. So what if you embellished the truth? So have others. Who can really blame you? Anyone would have done the same. And you can't be sent back to a war zone. Don't forget, you still have a whole arsenal of defences. If I were you, I wouldn't worry too much. You'll see. But Ibraham refused to cling to this delusion. He resigned himself to the inevitability that in a day or two, officials must inevitably come with his name on some papers and take him straight to the airport—stripped of his freedom, yes, but also any further necessity of lying. Some small part of him was gladdened by the end of the pretence.

It was disgraceful, the *Bugle* suggested, that this government could permit such blatant abuses, which could only cause resentment. It was typical of this grossly irresponsible government that they should have taken the word of a thug as gospel. It was political correctness gone mad. Was it any wonder that there was extremism? Ibraham Nassouf must go. The minister should go…or else every Tom, Dick, and Ibraham would be able to drive a coach and horses through this government's immigration policy. The *Bugle*'s sentiments were echoed by other papers, and government strategists feared meltdown at the local elections. But the minister did not go—and no-one came for Ibraham.

Not only that, but soon a counter-counter-mood was emerging, led, as so often, by John Leyden. He pointed out that the fact that one applicant's details had proven partly factually incorrect did not invalidate the wider point that immigration was a social good and should continue, in tandem with an ethical foreign policy; furthermore, there was no room for racism in Britain. There was a wider social truth, and right-wing hysteria must not be allowed to obscure that salient fact—for we are all guilty in a very real sense.

Then the *Register* ran a long interview with Ibraham—a brilliant *coup-de-main* in its circulation war with the *Bugle*. Jakob von Grönestein, reading it beside his pool in Dubai, actually burst out laughing.

Ibraham is sitting huddled in his tiny cell, his only companions, a traumatized Syrian, a silent TV set, and a few pathetic possessions on the table beside the bed: a notebook, a half-eaten sandwich, some cigarettes, some sweets—and, of course, the translator, without whom Ibraham would be marooned on a cultural desert island. His thin, sensitive face looks tired, and he looks shamefacedly down at his hands for most of our snatched hour. I ask him the question that is on every Briton's lips—'Ibraham, we took you to our hearts. We knew you had suffered, and we wanted to believe what you told us. What made you dream up these stories?'

With a heartfelt sigh, Ibraham replies brokenly through his translator. His teeth are pearly white, his deep brown eyes filled with a secret sadness—'It's not actual reality, but it was my reality...It was my way of coping... I seek forgiveness from those who feel betrayed, but I implore them to put themselves in my position; I had lost everything, I had to survive... I feel a fool, and now you all hate me... I have received racist letters, and yet I feel I cannot blame the senders. It is all my fault.'

And as I sit there listening, I try to put myself into Ibraham's battered old shoes—those shoes which have done so much running. I am compelled to ask myself one simple question— would *I*, would *any* of us, have behaved very differently?

The *Register*'s editorial answered its own correspondent, with the generosity of spirit on which it so frequently prided itself:

Ibraham, you needn't have lied. This is a great nation, and a big-hearted one, with a tradition of fair play and refuge for all who really need it. And even leaving aside your background of poverty, hunger, totalitarianism and war, your experiences at the hand of the human traffickers alone would have qualified you for sanctuary. So despite what's happened in the past, we say let bygones be bygones—and urge the government to let Ibraham stay. He's said he's sorry.

Ibraham started to think Basser had been correct. He looked on in silent thankfulness as he faded back out of the headlines; he was inexpressibly glad to become just a part of the process, on the same terms as everyone else. As that year's perfect autumn burst around, seen but not felt through the plate glass of the complex, there were meetings with caseworkers, presentations, medical examinations, psychological examinations, hearings about hearings, hearings, adjournments to hearings, deferred decisions, a verdict (heart-stoppingly negative), notice of appeal, submissions and evidence-gathering, appeal, adjournment of decision on appeal…

He was intrigued one day to be told by a winking warder that he had a woman visitor. He went wonderingly along to the interview room, where he found Carole Hassan waiting. She stood and introduced herself through the staff interpreter. He was puzzled that she was a white woman, and not an Albanian. He had never thought of there being English converts—especially ones that smelt strongly of cigarettes. She spoke shyly; she met very few fellow Muslims, and rarely spoke to men of her age.

"I am here on behalf of the whole Muslim commuity to show our solidarity, and make sure that you are being treated well. Do you have any complaints about the way you are being treated here in this awful place?" She looked around at the bright and cheery room, and shuddered.

"*All* Muslims?" Ibraham, who had seen Sunni and Shia interacting at home, was gratified to learn of this unexpected solidarity.

"In a way, yes. I represent our interests as a group, because if we do not organize ourselves in this way, we would be badly treated by the state. There is a lot of Islamophobia in England and in America. That is why London, Washington, and Israel launched their war against us. I have money given to me by the state to ensure our people are protected."

The translator appeared to be rolling his eyes humorously, but Ibraham ignored him, trying to digest this seemingly contradictory news. Why would the state give money to a group that was opposed to them? And why would an English girl be interested in Iraq anyway?

"Our view is that the present outcry against you is part of this Islamophobia. If you were a Christian or a Hindu or a…a Scientologist… they wouldn't be making these allegations against you—you know, all these stories that you are lying. We know what The Book says about lying."

Ibraham didn't, but didn't care to admit it, so sat looking sapient as she went on, speaking rapidly, nervously, as if expecting him to correct her.

She was reading from a scrap of paper.

"*Sura* 42 explains why the Christians lie—it says, 'They like to listen to falsehood, to devour anything forbidden'. *Sura* 96 says, 'We would certainly smite his forehead, A lying, sinful forehead." And of course *Sura* 104 says, 'Woe to every slanderer, defamer.'"

She paused and sat silently for a few second, with her head slightly inclined in ritual obeisance. Ibraham didn't know what to say, so said very slowly, "Oh, yes, of course…" The translator winked at him, and then Carole came to his rescue. She smiled, but cast down her eyes as she spoke.

"May I call you Ibrahim? I must tell you that I used to be a Christian, but one lucky day, I realized that I had been wrong—that my parents had been wrong, and everyone else in my family going back hundreds of years. I learned to be brave enough to reject my mistaken religion and culture—but also to bless Allah (to whom all blessings) that He had allowed me wisdom to see The Way. And since then I have devoted my life to reading His Book and helping all those, like you, who are victimized because you, too, have seen The Light. So I am here as a kind of friendly spirit to offer my help to you, as a friend and fellow searcher after truth. That is why I have come."

She looked up at him, her blue eyes beseeching. He was amazed to see that her hands were trembling and felt a curious mix of emotions—a wish to protect her and slight sexual arousal, plus puzzlement and repulsion. He could detect that she wanted him as much as what he represented.

He was deterred by the smell of cigarettes, but also a feeling that by becoming a Muslim, she had become too obvious, too attainable. She was too similar to all the girls he had known back home. He had come here partly to escape what she was apparently seeking. He had wanted an English girl and would have been willing to accept even one who looked like this—but he wanted one who had something of the coolness and poise he had ingested from all those magazines years ago. He had always fantasized about being with one of those lovely long-legged, light-haired models in one of those lovely luxurious interiors, content just to be in her presence and adore her lovely strangeness, her advanced and exotic assumptions. He had thought he had found something approaching this in Miss Karatakis…but he didn't want to think about that.

How to explain these private thoughts to a stranger, and furthermore a slightly sluttish facsimile of a woman from home? He couldn't articulate them even to himself—and besides he had no wish to hurt her feelings. He spoke gently, dreadfully conscious of the translator's ironic presence.

"Please, you are very kind to come all the way here and offer your help. But I think you may not understand everything. The truth is that I *did* lie in the hope that I would be allowed to stay here. I don't think that you can really help me to get around that!

"And as for the rest, for me Islam is just what I was born into, and I don't think about it much. I am not a well-educated person, like you—just a man who wants the best for his family."

"Oh—you have family?" Her disappointment was pitifully plain. He stroked his moustache complacently, flattered.

"I have three sisters. I have no wife, though. I was too poor to marry. And then there was the war; there seemed to be always war. And when there wasn't war, there were people killing each other. Sunni killing Shia, Shia killing Sunni, both killing others—that is why I am pleased to learn that all Muslims are friends here."

The interpreter made a noise that sounded like a snigger. Carole flushed as Ibraham continued, speaking quickly now:

"Miss, these are the facts. I am here as an illegal immigrant. I lied to get here, and I have been found out. Soon I will be deported. And it will be my fault—and my fate. I don't blame anybody, and even if I did, I do not think you would be able to help me. No, I will go home, my sister will return with me and—who knows?—maybe it will be for the best? Maybe the bombs will stop, maybe there will be a peace, and I can be made richer by this experience and be happy."

She was marvelling at Ibraham's acceptance and composure, qualities she knew she lacked—qualities she associated with his having been born into Islam. She felt she would never be able to attain to such an elevated state without help from someone as wise and calm as he was. She wanted to ask him where she should go on her spiritual path, but her appointment was almost over and she had not been able to offer him anything he was willing to accept. But she didn't want to lost touch with this kind, wise (and handsome) man. She took out one of her professional cards and, amazed by her forwardness, wrote her home address and number on the back. She gave it to him, and as their hands almost touched, she shivered almost ecstatically.

"I must go. But please take this—these are my contact details. If you need any help in your battle—information, advice, contacts, money, spiritual consolation—call or e-mail me. And don't give up! You may yet be allowed to stay. And even if you are not, you may need a place to stay for a while. Remember—you have at least one true friend!"

She stood up red-faced and almost ran out of the room, leaving an open-mouthed Ibrahim sitting at the little table. She had vanished by the time the by-now broadly leering interpreter had finished rendering her last sentence.

Ibrahim dreamed of her that night and woke up overheated. The fluorescent light in the twin-bedded room was still on, and his silent Syrian roommate was lying looking at the blank ceiling, as he did most nights. He always gave Ibrahim the creeps. What *did* he see up there? It was like the evil eye! It was said that he'd been shot at by troops in Damascus and had seen his family die—but that was just speculation, because he rarely said anything. When he heard Ibrahim groan, he turned his head on the pillow and stared expressionlessly at him for a few seconds before resuming his examination of the ceiling. Ibrahim shuddered slightly, then turned away from the light to face the wall. There was a long silence—and then there was a brandishment of dawn striping the blinds, cheerful whistling and the squeak of a trolley's wheels along waxed floors as a new day came calling.

John had frowned when he had first heard the news about Ibraham's subterfuge. It was a bit embarrassing for him and would furthermore be used to attack all immigrants, all immigration. But on reflection, he felt less concerned, reasoning that at least it demonstrated that he had a big heart. And at least the *Sentinel* had been neutralized. It was such a great benefit for society not to have that open sewer spilling its offensive contents out onto the clean sands. The new regime there seemed to be anxious to make amends for its past. They might even accept articles from him again—in the meantime, he had taken a professional pride in turning the mood around with his article.

He had also been excited by a request from Capital University for him to lead a module in their new course, *Radical Voices—Writing the Revolution*. He loved the idea of having his name attached to one of the country's top universities. He particularly relished what the Administrator had written—"As one of the most articulate radical voices of our generation, we hope you might consider lending your keen insight to our proposed module." He had forwarded the e-mail to Gavin and a few other senior editorial staff, ostensibly to ask if the paper would have any objections, but really so that they could see the e-mail. It was good policy to remind others how well-regarded you were, especially now that your former friend had become your boss, and was probably intriguing against you.

And Janet had gone, and *quietly*, without making any more embarrassing scenes. When he came in from the Chinese one night, he had found a note folded over on the dining-room table and noticed there was no booming TV beyond the door. It was on her usual lilac-coloured paper with the faint smell of peppermint—she had insisted on using that paper, despite his often-expressed disdain.

> John, I can't see any way of fixing things between us, although I have thought hard—VERY hard. It was probably wrong of me to be so horrible to you, but I couldn't help it. So although it

cuts me up (sappy, eh?), I think it's probably best if I go. I'll be staying at Tammy's for a few days, after that I might go home—in case you need to contact me for ANY reason. I've taken most of my stuff, and I'll get the rest out of your way as soon as I can. Sorry—and take care. All my love, J.

P.S. Here's my mobile number for emergencies.

P.P.S. There's some bacon in the back of the fridge, which needs to be eaten before Tuesday.

P.P.S. Don't forget—ANY reason!

He folded the note carefully before putting it into a drawer in the old bureau. By now, he had quite a collection of love notes, going all the way back to the age of 17, and found it quite diverting sometimes to read back over them. Once he had brought some of them along to a dinner party and read them aloud, which had been hilarious. He locked the bureau again, then took a few pages of a magazine and scrunched them into a small ball. He tossed it up towards the high ceiling and leapt exultantly to meet it on its descent, nodding it perfectly into the back of the fireplace. Then he did a victory lap of the room acknowledging the cheers of the Wembley crowd.

The journalist who had been beaten in error was doing well—even if one eye would never be as strong again, and although he did find it more difficult to concentrate on writing about Volvos. He still had no real idea what it had all been about—even though Albert had been to see him often and explained it each time. Dougie had visited a few times, too, but had now stopped coming. He had too much on his plate with a sudden steep decline in sales.

Getting rid of Albert Norman had been The Right Thing To Do, Dougie knew, whatever the board said. *He* at least had not been afraid to confront the old dinosaur, and one day the board would thank him for his foresight. They had certainly been wrongfooted when he had told them that the Prime Minister had rung him personally, to arrange an exclusive briefing at Number 10. It was the first time the paper had been so honoured since the 1930s.

But there was still work to be done, to drag the paper kicking and screaming into the 21st century—seemingly against the board's and the readers' wishes. Yet it could and would be done—*must* be done. He roamed ceaselessly throughout the building, looking at things without seeing them, nodding at staff without having any idea who they were, lost in abstractions, thinking of his necessary work—a figure of both fear and fun.

Albert had felt briefly vindicated by Ibraham's exposure—even though only a few *Sentinel* readers would remember that it had been he who had first raised doubts. Once he would have had hundreds writing in to say how thankful they were that someone of his calibre and courage… *etc.*, and maybe even some grudging acknowledgement from another columnist…but now there was ungrateful silence and dreary days emptying endlessly into each other like enfiladed doors opening to reveal yet more dust-sheeted rooms.

Now that he was at one remove from deadlines and headlines, he paradoxically found himself taking more of an interest in external events—sometimes even getting annoyed by some act or statement. He had never got annoyed by things before—but that was when he had it within his power to strike back. One afternoon, he even found himself feeling infuriated by a photo of the Prime Minister, who had been caught asleep whilst attending the Royal Opera House. He felt he would like to reach into the picture and shake the insensate brute by his cheap shirtfront until his yellowing teeth fell out of his receding gums and the shambling jackanapes opened his eyes and *listened* for the first time in his life…and stopped, surprised yet faintly pleased that he could still summon up such reserves of feeling.

But what was the point of still being able to feel, and to describe what he felt, if he had no means of transmitting it to the patriotic public he was sure still existed? He thought more and more that his decision to resign had been premature.

The government were buffeted but not defeated in local elections at the end of the month, thanks to Doug McKerras's astonishing incompetence, and a surprise *Sentinel* endorsement of the government. McKerras had resigned after the vote, but had been replaced by someone who appeared to have even less substance or style.

The rest of the repellent crew remained precisely where they had been—Wilberforce Smith, Richard Simpson, Dylan Ekinutu-Jones and all the rest of the dittoheads. Naturally, John Leyden was still at the *Examiner*, still writing his highly literate, highly-regarded rubbish, while he seemed to crop up on almost every radio or TV panel show Albert had hoped to enjoy. Albert had even seen John once in the flesh—from across the hall at the Barbican after a concert, a sleek and smiling demi-god with a doting demi-goddess on his arm, with other demi-goddesses looking at her in envy. John had eventually become aware of the elderly and obese man looking at him so thoughtfully, but had clearly failed to recognize in him the once-famous Albert Norman. After a slow and contemptuous look, he had turned up the collar of an elegant coat against the weather outside, and he and the svelte demi-goddess had dematerialized into the night, leaving the concert hall feeling all the emptier for their having once been there. "What a waste!" Albert had muttered, and a passing couple stared at this ancient oversized eccentric in the Continental-cut coat.

And these were only some of the most egregious members of the barbarian brigade—behind them stood thousands more automata waiting to be wound up and set in pointless play. It was always the same, probably would always be the same—the ordinary people outmanouevred, the good causes subverted, the deserving and undeserving alike never getting what they really deserved.

Part III
AFTERMATH

What has happened is a decisive and perhaps terminal defeat for an older Europe, a place of tribal hatreds, double-headed eagles, flaming swords and obscure martyrs. A better world order survives…

—1990s *Observer* editorial

Chapter 25
PASSING STRANGERS

London
April

On a damp and drizzly afternoon in London, Mr. Justice Perkins was adjudicating on a case. It was one, he reminded the almost empty court, that would have been a matter of great public interest had it come up before him some months previously, but that had now mercifully fallen from view and could be viewed somewhat more objectively. He regretted that this particularly sensitive case had been abused for political and commercial ends and hoped such would not recur—but such was the volume of similar cases that he feared his hopes would not be realized. But that was a matter for the legislature.

His considered judgment was that deportation would not be in the public interest—because it would be quite wrong to raise the temperature in the wake of the recent unrest. He further ruled that the applicant was entitled to apply for family reunification, as was his right under the European Convention on Human Rights as expressed in the 1998 Human Rights Act. And now we shall adjourn for the lunch recess…

(Far to the east, a Turkish trawler captain was standing on a sun-speckled quay, picking tobacco off his lip and looking calculatingly at a rangy-looking black man carrying a kit-bag.)

In the rec room of a jail outside The Hague, three former sailors passed the tedious time by talking about the way the low coast had looked sometimes as they were heading home with a full hold, pleasantly tired and anticipating home—or even better, in the very early morning, when they were heading out from Sint Niklaus on a promise of good fishing, and the lifting sun would capture the *Enterprise*'s shadow and carry it far out in front, as if showing where to search and helping to bear the trawler bowling along with its bodyguard of shining birds. Great days, sighed the *Kapitein*, but all gone, never to return...and the landlocked prisoners would fancy for a moment that they had breathed that same air and been touched by something vast and free.

The width of the continent away, Liberation War hero Lekë Kruja would soon be confirmed as a minister for a small new country, destined to spend the next few years exchanging public assurances with American congressmen and private backslaps with Islamists—after which he would be implicated in a financial scandal that would bring down an administration and bring the region once more to the edge of war.

Richard Simpson would shortly take his seat in The Other Place as Baron Simpson of Newton-Juxta-Water—which people joked was a highly appropriate territorial designation.

The Prime Minister, who had recently been singled out by Adenya Ukingo for exemplary anti-racist statesmanship, explained that Richard's unexpected elevation was due largely to his political courage in driving forward the bill banning NU and being an actor and significant stakeholder for change. He added that he was looking forward to the new baron's "Ciceronian contributions" in the Upper House.

Evan Dafydd had come to terms with his conscience over the proscription of political parties and began to concern himself more with prescriptions—accepting the Health portfolio in an otherwise underwhelming reshuffle. He was already enjoying being criticised for his flagship policy of compulsory chlamydia tests for 10-year-olds.

His trajectory was going in the right direction, unlike that of Stanley Symons who, after what he later ruefully described as "a very good lunch," had fallen into conversation with a female Channel 1 reporter with a hidden camera and recorder. Sir Stanley had been unwise enough to describe the Leader of Her Majesty's Loyal Opposition as "frankly, my dear, a total moron." Afterwards, he had expounded upon the subjects of homosexuality and immigration at considerable length and in detail, finishing by putting a large wedding-ringed hand on his interlocutor's knee. His magnified carmine features looked fleshily out from the front pages of all the newspapers for a day, after which he vanished forever from public consciousness.

John was busier than he had ever been, with his columns, his weekly slot on a satirical radio quiz show hosted by Wanda Lo and his forthcoming book, *Towards a Better Tomorrow—Today!*

He was so busy, he told *Work-Life Balance*, that his personal life had to take a back seat. But he reassured readers that he would always find time to attend events of epochal significance—like the West End premiere of the multiple award-nominated play *The Undocumented*, which he attended in the company of the beauteous Samantha Simmons, in the frame to play the refugee's upper-class girlfriend in the film of the play. Her pulchritudinous cornflower-blue eyes were darting with delight at her brilliant beau who was, she confided to a gossip columnist, "*sooo* sensitive—but don't tell him I said so. He'll get *such* a big head!" John disclosed to *Work-Life Balance* that he *adored* being busy and hoped that he was making a difference, contributing to the sea-change he could sense all around in society. He was, *Work-Life* concluded, "That rare thing—a modest man, a truly fulfilled human being"—and that was the caption they used below the full page, beautifully lit photo of a smiling John in blue, open-neck shirt and cream chinos.

Looking at that photograph the following day, Albert found it darkly desolate. For such handsomeness, energy and intelligence to be used for such ends…

He had never been able to understand what could cause such grim self-gnawing in such as John, who had it all and stood to lose it all—and who wanted others to lose it all, too. There must be something buried in his background that drove him so rapidly and recklessly onwards, to the detriment of an old and proud country—something unutterably appalling. He suddenly felt an unaccountable pity for his old adversary, as if he had suddenly glimpsed the skull beneath the still perfect skin. Was there a phantom in the picture? Could that be *doubt* in those far-seeing eyes? The reminder that John was doomed like them all was not the comfort it would once have been. Perhaps it was his over-active imagination, perhaps Albert was only seeing what he wanted to see—but to his quizzical and briefly compassionate gaze, John Leyden looked somehow hunted.

It was raining (had it *ever* been sunny?) in London N9, and Ibraham was in a repellent room frowning at a huge television, where a black-clad band was making the oddest sounds. Scum was duetting with his new girlfriend, "Goddess of Grunge" Fee Culmatter, in front of an audience of children, many of whom were dressed like the performers and shaking their heads like them, lost in a precocious facsimile of gloomy introspection. Ibraham switched swiftly to a cartoon channel and smiled as he watched the duck and the wolf trying to murder each other.

He had become incredibly bored with television and with just sitting around, eating the most horrible food he could have imagined—plastic trays taken straight from the freezer and put into a microwave. The novelty of having these two extravagant electrical items had worn off swiftly, especially as he had to share them with everyone else in the house, not all of whom were as hygienic in their habits. He thought from time to time of the meals he'd had at home (*home!*) —lamb cooked slowly over a fragrant fire until it was slightly blackened, dipped into mint and eaten with crispy *falafel*. To think he had thought such food boring!

He had been out for several hours that day, looking again for a job, squelching kilometres to save the bus fare—down to the same sad shops to see if any of them needed any staff yet. But it was always the same story, the same shaking of the head, hints of acerbity from proprietors asked for a third or fourth time. And so he had squelched back, chilled to his bones, subterranean-spirited, to the stained brick terrace with all the dustbins outside, the mouse-and-beetle-haunted kitchen, his frigid bedroom, which smelt of the filthy adjacent toilet, the plywood doors with holes where drunks had kicked or fallen against them, the rising damp and outside, the despondent square of long grass, which concealed brick rubble, food waste, car tires, and rats.

Islam-compatible though the house was supposed to be, some of the lads staying here behaved like animals. Ibraham was shocked by the way they comported themselves—all low-slung jeans and baseball caps, drinking and cursing, listening to loud rap or watching salacious late-night TV. Ibraham would complain, but he would also stay in the room while these shows were on—both because he was sex-starved and because he hoped these shows might give him some insight into this new culture. Meanwhile, the others would snigger at him as he sat red-faced, embarrassed for himself, embarrassed for them, embarrassed on behalf of the women and all of England.

He never met any English people, and if he had, would not have had enough English to hold a simple conversation. But then the more he saw of England, the less he understood it, and the less interested he became in mastering the keys to this culture.

He had tried with all his heart. He had even felt fleetingly thrilled to see for the first time the Houses of Parliament and Westminster Abbey, the backdrop to so many romantic fancies, from dramatic politics to fabulous weddings. He had entered the Abbey with a feeling of something like awe—and it had therefore been a massive disappointment to find he was expected to drop money into a box and join a moiling mass of casually dressed loafers, wandering boredly around looking at everything through their cameras and chattering on phones. He had been shocked to see women in there in short skirts, and men wearing T-shirts. To think this place was the centre of English religion and history! Why did they have so little respect? Why were they suffered to be there? He would have preferred to see it echoing and empty.

When he had come eventually out of the Abbey, he had needed to sit for a while, puzzled and perturbed, looking back at the huge hulk of the Abbey. He realized then that London was vast and indifferent and pointless—and the weight of all its assembled emptiness was so overwhelming that he almost wept.

He saw a girl in the crowd, almost the only person he had seen that day who approximated to his ideal of Englishness, and wondered if he dared speak to her. Just as he was trying to decide, she caught his anxious eyes and reddened and pulled her handbag closer before walking swiftly away. Ibrahim was mortified to realize that she had been *afraid*—that she had thought him a thief or maybe something even worse. But then everyone in London looked like she had—hard, over-experienced, wary, rushed. It had been a moment when he had realized that he did not know where to go, or what to do, either for the next few minutes or for the rest of his life.

After that disconcerting experience, he no longer wanted to go into town. Even if he had wanted to go, he never had any money. And even if he had had money, he couldn't think of anything he would want to buy.

His sisters and aunt would be here soon, and that would help counteract his aching *ennui*. But they would all probably be living in a house rather like this one, scarcely better than their shack at home, with the houses on each side populated not by watching-out-for-each-other neighbours but by suspicious transients—which was the way *they* would appear. At least the house at home had been theirs—and they had been members of a *community*. He remembered countless casual, inconsequential encounters in Basra—serendipitous street meetings, everyday conversations, shared jokes and complaints—thousands of tiny previously unnoticed nothings that in retrospect had amounted to something as undefinable as it was unmistakeable. He suspected that when the others arrived, he would then be even less likely to venture into the cold city.

He was already spending as much time as he could with the Iraqi community group—older and polite people, who spoke wistfully of going home and argued about Iraqi politics, while they played dominoes and drank Iraqi coffee. The rest of the week was at his disposal, so long as he signed on at the Job Centre every Wednesday. So it was invariably back to the house, hoping the others were all out and he had the place to himself.

Sometimes, he actually hated this ill-favoured place and resented the inexorable events which had driven him here from home under what he knew now had always been false pretences. Had this miserable room, those television shows, that shit-smeared toilet, really been worth that expense, the labour, the danger, the loneliness, the lying and cheating?

He had travelled storybook distances to reach the auspicious shore and fulfilled the deepest desires of his heart. Yet now that he had done everything he had set out to achieve, he was bitterly aware that he still hadn't arrived.

Spring had come soggily to Thorpe. It was raining and had been doing so for days, the little hills above the town funnelling the flood from miles around until the Thor ran high, brown and foaming, tugging threateningly at the keystone of the old Georgian bridge.

Below the town, out in the marsh, the river had burst its banks in several different places, as if seeking to unite itself with the countless other dykes and drains similarly breaching their bounds. Fungal cultures bloomed on walls, and failing gutters dashed their gurgling payloads down onto the darting shoppers. It had been the wettest spring since records began.

Dan hurried with the rest, one once more with all the others, united against the wet, the outside world rising against their little town. He recognized several people, they nodded and he nodded back. But he didn't recognize the rotund man standing sheltering in a doorway, wearing an expensive if slightly shabby coat and even a trilby over his grizzled hair.

Albert had left London very early on an increasingly rare whim, fed up suddenly with the place, annoyed by the news and bored by the rain. He hadn't been out of the city for many months. Although he had always recommended that people should not travel, his advice had always been meant chiefly for other people. So he had lumbered downstairs as it was getting light, thrown his pigskin case into the back of the immaculate BMW and nosed out of the cobbled mews before deciding where he should point the car's elegant nose. And then his destination flared up in imagination before him as if on a notice board…of course! In fact, where else?

Ever since the significant summer, he had often tried to imagine what Eastshire was like. Friends who had flashed through on their way to some more fashionable demsesne laughed and said "cabbages," "miles of nothing," and "terrible roads" before changing to some more scandalous subject. The sheer unknown-ness of the place had sparked Albert's interest—and he also wanted to believe his own frequent asseverations that such backwaters harboured some quasi-mystical essence of England, long since driven to the fens and fringes, like Hereward the Wake seeking refuge from the Normans. And he felt he had unfinished business with poor old Dan Gowt, the nation's erstwhile kicking boy. "Come, come, come, let us leave the Town," he sang along to *King Arthur*, as he barreled northwards and eastwards as John had done the previous year.

But to Albert, high spirits were always an abberation, and soon he relapsed into his customary cool detachment. The weather refused obstinately to improve, so he saw everything through a cold curtain of moisture. The hot fields John had grudgingly admired in August were scraped and soggy, in places waterlogged, with single herons standing miserably in wastes of reddish-brown clay. Even the church towers, which would normally have enlivened his journey, were obscured by suspended rain, and the whole country looked inconsolable. He had to drive slowly, and got a headache with the strain of concentration. He was much too old for such chivalric expeditions—much too old and much too fat.

By the time he got to Thorpe Gilbert, he was about as tired as he ever remembered being. He followed the "Historic Market Town" signs (surely *everywhere* in Europe was Historic) and parked, like John, behind the Perseverance. He was pleased to see the famous spire of St. Blaise's, and got an agreeable impression, even through the weather, of the town's architecture. If there really was an incipient peasant army in Eastshire—the proverbial "people of England who have not spoken yet"—a place like this would be their Lilliputian capital, and weather like this would predominate.

And it was as he was standing thinking this in a doorway that he realized the scruffy old man pushing along the puddled pavement with his head down as if charging at the world was none other than Dan Gowt. He had only a few seconds warning, so he stepped slightly forward with his silver-mounted umbrella in his left hand so he could shake hands with the right. He extended his hand and opened his mouth and... said nothing, as Dan pushed irritatedly past this utterly out-of-place obstacle. With a restraint that might have helped him before, Albert realized that there was nothing he could say that would have been either helpful or appropriate. He watched as Dan disappeared around a corner, and shook his head in wry amusement as a cold rivulet of rain ran down the back of his collar.

Dan didn't understand what had happened, or how or why—and he was left with an unfocused sort of resentment that too often translated into testiness. He paid closer attention to the news now—but it still never really added up to anything. It was just a lot of things that happened, which, although unconnected, somehow always added up to unpleasantness. He listened for names he had come to know and when he heard them, sometimes got angry all over again.

He could always be temporarily soothed by the familiar vistas—fields, pumping station and sea, the castellated churches—and by the circular tasks of each season. He mended and fenced to make the world more manageable; he traded real things for real things with real people. As his plough ripped open his fields for the following gulls, he would sink with a sigh into routine and rightness, preoccupied with just keeping the lines straight—looking always over his shoulder, lost in a reverie of patterns and permanence.

But whenever he got back home he would see again the semi-erased graffiti on the house, still visible from certain angles, like the Civil War bullet-holes in the Corporation Hall. This would never disappear completely, at least not for many more years of the interplay of sun and sea-wind. And Hatty sometimes jumped when the phone rang, or came unaccountably awake in the deep night to listen—although there was never anything to hear, only the owls and the muffled metronome of the clock coming up from drowsy downstairs.

They hadn't seen much of Clarrie in recent months. It seemed she was working hard at last on her degree—but they also saw she was less happy to be at home than she had been before. When Dan had once haltingly raised the subject, she had laughed and kissed him and told him not to be silly. But he knew that the odds of her taking over the farm had not been improved. Crisby was simply too small for the likes of her, and England, just a place like any other.

The only thing that was certain was that Crisby had changed, the world had changed, and everything would always now be changing. For him and others it was too late to adapt. Clarrie had time, though, and she would do the right thing—yet what a pity it would be if all the restless young were simply to walk away from their inheritance, and leave all these old, outdated places to the old and outdated.

It would even be a species of betrayal, betrayal not only of their parents, their parents' parents, and so on all the way back—but also of themselves and their children. It would always be deeply disappointing for him to think that never now would grown-up grandchildren of his face and name stand where he had so often stood in summer, on the highest point of *his* land, gazing east over spreading fields and beyond the uncertain edge of England to that omnipresent azure immensity that had once so delicately and disastrously cast up the future. The boundaries of his lands, so long established and clearly defined, were overshadowed, and after he had gone, they would be redrawn. He was the last of his kind, and when he went, how long would he be remembered?

Going home from Thorpe under lowering rain, descending towards home with the turbulent Thor on his left and the level grey sea dead ahead, Dan saw through a closing soaking curtain a country that was both intimately familiar and deeply strange.

Derek Turner

Derek Turner was born in Dublin in 1964 and has lived in England since 1988, first in London and now in Lincolnshire. He is the former editor of the conservative magazine *Right Now*, and currently edits the *Quarterly Review*, a 2007 revival of the celebrated journal founded by Sir Walter Scott in 1809. He has contributed articles on current affairs, literature, history, and travel to many publications, including the *Times, Sunday Telegraph, Literary Review, Country Life, Chronicles, University Bookman, Salisbury Review, New English Review*, AlternativeRight.com, and Takimag.com, as well as many in continental Europe. *Sea Changes* is his first book.

Visit Washington Summit Publishers online at
www.WashSummit.com